PRAISE FOR

"Coleman's unique vision of Wonderland brings many of our beloved characters to life in vibrant new ways. A joy to read!"
—Marissa Meyer, NYT Bestselling author of The Lunar Chronicles

"Daniel Coleman is an utter delight! I was very pleased with Coleman's efforts to provide some fascinating glimpses into the probable motivations of some of these characters, tease out their back stories, and all in service to his own plot. Absolutely wonderful!"
—Lawrence M. Schoen, Hugo-nominated author of *Buffalito Contingency*

"*Hatter* is another great book for young adults to read if they want a taste of a fantastical realm with real depth and imagery. Daniel Coleman paints a picture of human nature within each character that is spot on."
—E.A. Younker, *The Crimson Pact*

"*Hatter* takes you to a world of intrigue, fantasy, and action. The characterization, dialogue, and setting are so good my oldest two sons and I have read the book together and on our own. Highly recommended."
—Cami Checketts, author of the Billionaire Bride Pact Romances

"Daniel Coleman, you are the next Gregory Maguire. My recommendations: Run, don't walk, saunter, sashay or shimmy your way over to Amazon and buy this book. Then read it, nonstop. I can't wait to read anything else Coleman comes out with. Bring it on Mr. Firefighter who can write, bring it on. This book gets infinity stars from me!"

—Amy Denim, *The Coffee Break Guide to Self-Publishing*

"I loved the use of color and colorful language in this story. It became a five-star book for me when I got to the ending."

—Christine Haggerty, *Grimm Chronicles*

"*Hatter* is wonderfully written and creative without taking away the magic that is Wonderland. *Hatter* is one of those rare gems that needs exploring again and again."

—R P Blotzer, Top Goodreads Reviewer

"Once again Coleman shows a mastery of the characters in the world of Lewis Carroll. I actually have never been a huge fan of the original stuff, but I will personally read whatever I can that Coleman writes."

—Scott, Indie Book Blog

"From the nail-biting opening to the satisfying conclusion, *Hatter* is impossible to put down. Inventive storytelling combined with engaging characters makes this book a family favorite we've read over and over again."

—Elizabeth Dorathy, *Scripture Power!*

"Best book I've read in a long time. Wow. From page one I was hooked. I was so enthralled with the story line I finished the book in a day!"

—Bri-Mel Pubs, Editor of *Absolute Surrender*

"Entertaining and thought-provoking. I loved it!"

—Karlene Browning, LibrisPro.com

"Hats off to Daniel Coleman. *Hatter* runs the emotional gamut with a richness that makes reading it thoroughly enjoyable without becoming traumatic or emotionally waterlogged. This is definitely recommended to everyone, whether you love Carroll's characters or not. If Lewis Carroll hasn't sold you on Wonderland, Daniel Coleman will!"

—Jennifer Schultz, *Shadowcaster*

A NOVEL

DANIEL COLEMAN

WITH ILLUSTRATIONS BY E. K. STEWART-COOK

HATTER
Second Edition 2016

Copyright © 2014 by Daniel Coleman
Second Edition Copyright © 2016 by Daniel Coleman
www.dcolemanbooks.com

Published by Vorpal Words
PO Box 246
Wellsville, UT 84339

ISBN-13: 978-1463523930
ISBN-10: 1463523939

Interior Illustrations by E.K. Stewart-Cook
estewartcook@gmail.com

Cover Art by Antonio José Manzanedo Luis
dibuja2@gmail.com

Cover Design by Stefan Mark
Stefan@silkdesignco.com

Cover Design © by Daniel Coleman

Edited by Daniel Friend and Nancy Felt

Formatted by KristiRae Alldredge
bookformat@gmail.com

All rights reserved. No part of this book may be reproduced or transmitted in any form or by any means without written permission of the author.

This is a work of fiction. Any resemblance to persons living or dead is entirely coincidental.

Dedicated to Timothy Barrett
Who is, to pilfer some of his lyrics:
Magic mixed with wisdom . . .
A spirit strong and independent . . .
Branded like an iron from the fire . . .
Who flies bravely into battle but with the
children gently plays . . .

A self-made rogue

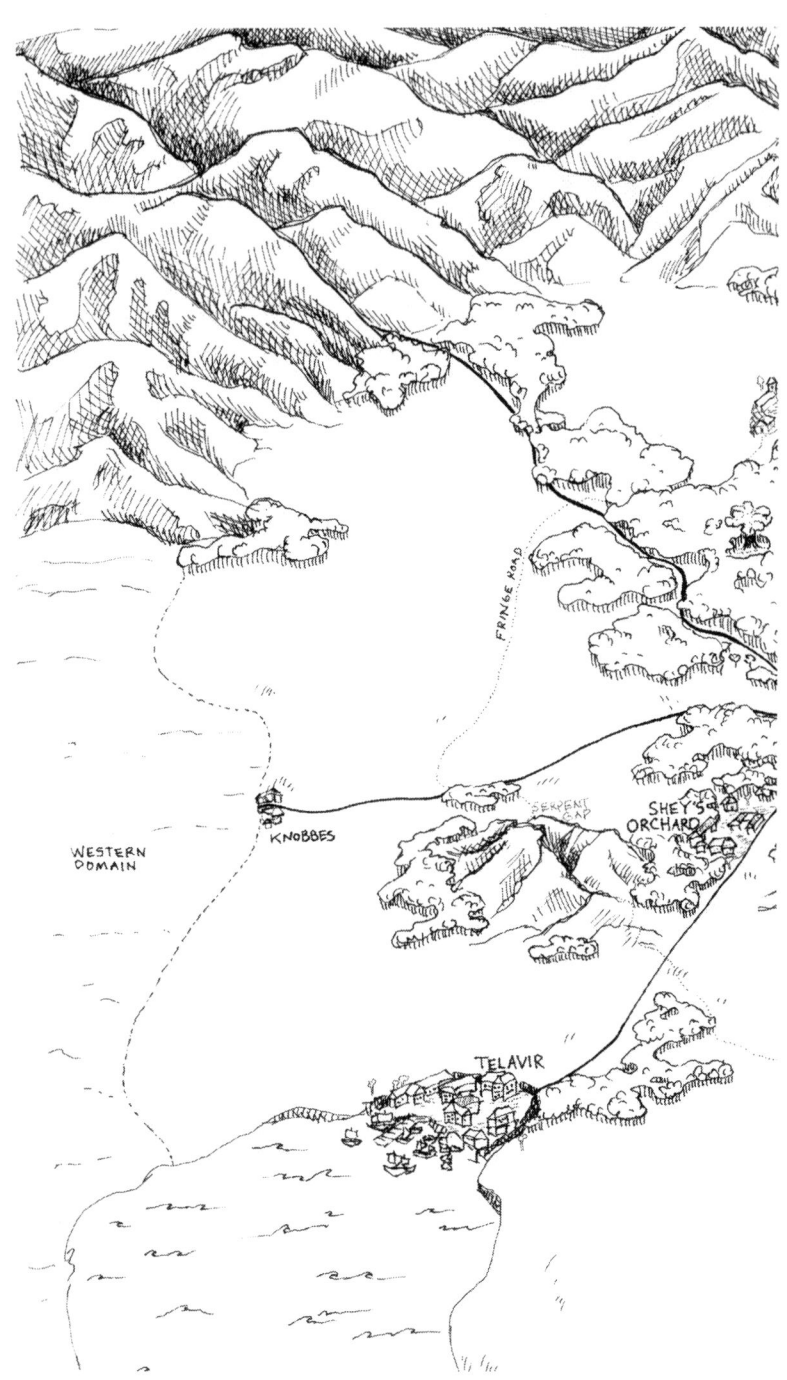

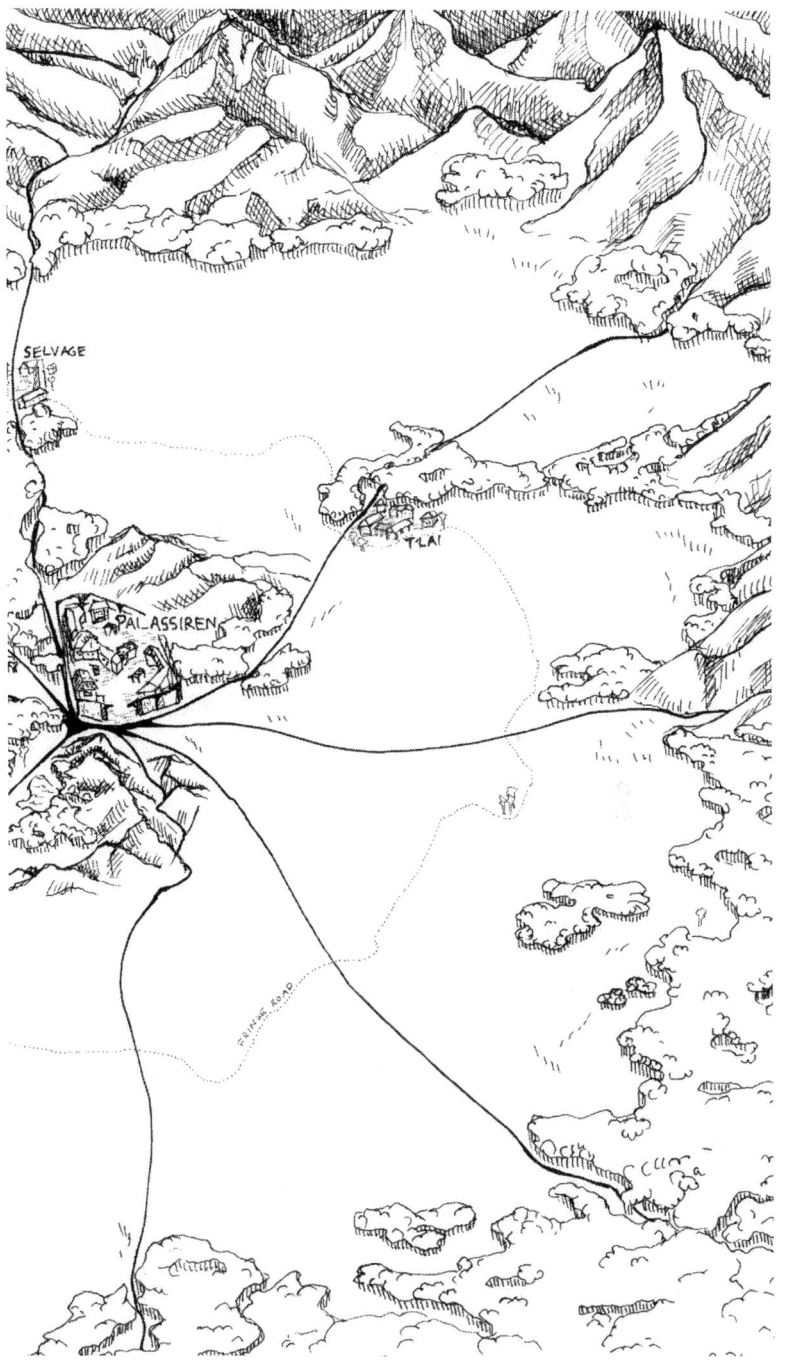

CHAPTER 1

'13'

The dark morning painted the landscape in shapes and textures only. For Chism it was no different than any other time of day. While some colorblind people lacked only certain colors, to Chism everything was black and white, but he saw them more clearly than anyone.

He dropped his tunic on the ground as he walked. The cold morning pushed on him from all sides. Just three weeks earlier he had earned his treasured Elite uniform, but it lay folded carefully in camp. He walked toward the estate, palms open and arms outstretched, counting his steps to soothe his nerves. The men holding the duke for ransom wouldn't be threatened by an unarmed fifteen-year-old. Especially one who could pass for a boy five years younger. They had no way of knowing they were about to take prisoner one of the most dangerous people in the kingdom.

One thousand steps. Halfway to his goal. A stone tower rose alongside Duke Enniel's wooden estate home, three times taller than the other buildings. The asymmetry of the structure irritated Chism, but he pushed it from his mind when he saw the duke's twelve-year-old daughter sitting on a plank at the top of the tower. In the event of a rescue attempt, her captors would release the plank, sending the girl to the cobblestones twenty-five yards below. It was a cruel technique often used by Domainers to prevent rescue attempts.

Chism clenched his jaw. He'd have to get much closer before sentries would see him. Not everyone had near-perfect night vision like he did.

When Chism entered the outer edges of the torch light, an archer yelled, "Halt!" through an arrow slit. A hard man with graying hair stepped up to the edge of the tower. The bushy hair and beard gave him the appearance of an old bear.

"I'm alone," yelled Chism.

"But I see yee've not brang the ransom!" Gray-bear yelled. "Walk away if yee've no desire to see girl's brains dashed on dirt!"

Chism swallowed his anger and lied. "I've come to surrender. I'm Duke Enniel's nephew and I'm here to offer comfort to my relatives."

Gray-bear stepped back from the wall. The girl didn't fall. Another man must have been manning the far end of the plank.

A cold wind bit Chism's naked back as he waited in front of an ornate door. The wind seemed to nip the ragged *13* carved into his lower back, even though he knew the scar had no feeling. "Chism the Chicken," Father had loved to call him. Chism preferred Chism the Challenger.

More like Chism the Chilled, he thought, as a shiver ran through his skin, raising goose bumps along both arms.

Gray-bear finally came back. "If this be any type of trick, yee'll be filled with arrows and this family will die. Yee'll be granted quarter to enter, but yee'll not leave until ransom is paid."

A wooden door opened and a pair of bearded men in animal skins pulled Chism inside the keep. One yanked him by the hair and the other gripped his arm harder than necessary.

The hands on his skin burned like a bad run of itch oak. It had been years since he'd allowed anyone to touch him. Chism concentrated on deep breaths and on the girl up on the plank. If he couldn't resist the urge to fight, the mission would be ruined and people would die.

Well, people were going to die. But if the plan worked, only the right people would die.

"Look, boy is *13*," said one of the men, laughing.

"Thirteen? Why is thirteen funny?" asked the other.

"Vaylee's beard!" said the first. "You know nothing about Provinces. Thirteen means he is runt. Useless."

"That I could tell ye without seeing scars," the other man chortled.

The scar labeling him a thirteen was a lie, but underestimation was crucial in the mission. As Lieutenant Fahrr had predicted, they didn't even search him.

The corridor emptied into the receiving room of the estate home. The Maner on Chism's right let go of his arm; Chism rubbed at where the hand had been. The other man kept his fist knotted in Chism's hair. Skin to hair contact wasn't pleasant, but it was tolerable.

Duke Enniel sat in a plain throne with his wife, Lady Tanet, at his side. They were shackled hand and foot. Both of the duke's eyes were bruised, one was swollen. His forehead and chin had small gashes. Lady Tanet only had one black eye, dark and swollen so badly that Chism couldn't see her eyeball. A cut above one eyebrow looked like it needed stitches days earlier but wasn't seen to. Her neck and arms were spotted with bruises. Some were dark and fresh. Others light enough to be taken for a light dirt smudge if Chism didn't know better. He could see the fingers of a painful grip in one bruise, the sharp blow from a switch in another. A bruise across her forearm still bore the shape of links from a chain.

Chism forced his eyes away and studied the other people in the room. The Maners on either side of him had medium length beards with three small discs woven into them. Chits, they were called. Symbols of manliness or something in the Western Domain.

A Maner with a longer beard stood near the duke, holding a half spear to his heart. His full attention was on Duke Enniel; he didn't even glance at Chism.

The only other person in the room was a black-haired Maner with a beard longer than any of the others, marking him as their leader. He was shorter than the other men but had as many chits in his beard as the other three combined.

The duke's son was not in the room. Chism cursed inwardly. That changed everything.

Longbeard approached him, manacles in hand. He stood a head taller than Chism.

"How nice of ye to join us. It appears ransom has increased." He secured one shackle to Chism's right wrist with a greedy grin. "If it is not paid within one week, yee'll come to Domain and visit famous Pit of Indomitables."

Chism froze in indecision. If he acted without the duke's son present, he risked the boy's life. But if he allowed himself to be shackled, he might never be able to overcome his captors.

Others might not agree, but to Chism the boy and his sister were more important than any of the rest of them. Chism had to protect the boy, even if it put everyone else at risk.

He offered his left wrist. As Longbeard reached for it, the man with the spear shifted his stance and Chism glimpsed the duke's son, Odion, behind the thrones. He was larger than Chism even though they were close to the same age. His back was straight, but his features were innocent and boyish. His eyes, framed by bruises, cuts, and peeling skin from his time on the plank, were as wide as Longbeard's smile. The boy's arms were shackled, but his legs were free; Domainers never respected anyone who couldn't grow a beard.

Chism felt sudden freedom; the whole family was accounted for. The relief didn't last long. Anger at the mistreatment of the boy and his mother surfaced and he had only moments to act.

The second manacle gaped wide to encircle Chism's wrist. It never touched him.

Chism dipped and spun vigorously away from his captors. Pain like fire spread across his scalp where a clump of hair was yanked out, but he ignored it.

He swung the shackle in an arc like a ball and chain. Longbeard took it on the top of the head and crumpled, still in the motion of reaching for Chism's wrist.

In the same movement, Chism withdrew two knives hidden at the back of his thighs. The boy, Odion, pulled against the shackles around his wrists and reached out a leg to kick the spear away from his father's heart as Chism threw one knife at the same Maner. It landed in the side of the man's neck.

The spear clacked across the stone floor.

Two men down, two more to deal with. Both within striking distance. The knife in Chism's hand was already moving toward the man at his right, sheathing itself in the barbarian's chest at the same moment the man's sword cleared his scabbard.

The last guard stood gawking at the clump of curly black hair he'd ripped from Chism's head. The clump seemed disproportionately small for the amount of pain it caused. The Maner and Chism looked away from the hair and into each other's eyes at the same time.

Chism was quicker. The Maner joined his companions on the floor.

None of the Maners had lived long enough to raise the alarm, but Chism wasn't done. A few more dead barbarians and a rescued girl would satisfy him

He knelt, removed a small key ring from Longbeard's belt, wiped his knife, then tossed the keys to Odion. Chism saluted the boy by bringing a fist up to his own heart. He hadn't needed the help, but the boy's pluck impressed him.

"We have to save Saya," said Odion as his shackles fell. He started to free his mother.

"Don't worry," said Chism. "She'll be fine as feathers in no time."

"Four of my sentries survived," said Duke Enniel. "They're bound in my quarters. They can help you rescue her."

Chism shook his head. "They'll get in my way."

The duke opened his mouth to argue, but then his gaze shifted to the carnage. He nodded without a word.

"I've been to the tower," said Odion. "You need a password to get through the door at the top. Knock twice and say 'fortune, fortune'."

"How many are there?" asked Chism.

"Two on the stairs and two with Saya."

Perfect. Even numbers always made Chism happy.

Blood from the patch of missing hair trickled in front of Chism's ear and dripped down his bare chest. It felt like his entire scalp had been ripped off.

"Let me help you rescue her," said Odion.

Chism looked the boy in the eye. "I need you to help your parents."

Chism gave a few instructions, then picked up the short spear and crept back into the hallway. The throbbing of his injured head sounded like a drum. As he climbed the stairs, the only other sound was a man breathing as he kept watch through the arrow slit. Chism cut his throat before the man knew he was there. Amazing how most sentries watched only one direction.

Chism braced the body so it wouldn't clatter down the stairs. The second bowman was dispatched just as easily.

A heavy wooden door blocked the exit at the top of the stairs. Chism was angry enough to kick through it, but he restrained himself. With the short spear in hand, he knocked twice.

Someone asked, "Who are ye?"

Hoping his voice wouldn't crack, Chism uttered, "Fortune, fortune."

The grubby Maner who opened the door was greeted by Chism's spear point. He groaned and grabbed the spear weakly as he fell to the ground. Chism stepped casually over the body and out onto the tower top. The sun hadn't quite appeared yet.

The stone landing was circular, surrounded by a parapet wall. A plank extended between two of the crenellations. Gray-bear, the only Maner left, stood on the near end of the wide board. His weight was the only thing keeping Saya from falling. She was scared, peeling even worse than her brother, and shivering in the cold morning air.

Chism couldn't stop the suffering of every child, but he could do something about this one.

"If ye move, she falls!" Gray-bear was yelling, though a whisper could have been heard in a morning so quiet. He held a curved axe toward Chism.

Saya noticed something below her and looked down at the drop of more than twenty-five paces. Luckily, all of Gray-bear's attention was on Chism.

Don't give it away too soon, silly girl, thought Chism.

Chism planted the spear tip on the floor and started whittling the other end with his knife. "It's a shame I had to leave my uniform in camp, or you'd see by the Circle and the Sword that I represent King Antion. Unfortunately, negotiation isn't my specialty."

His knife made a scraping sound on the hard wood of the spear handle.

Swihp, swihp, swihp.

"I'll free girl if ye promise safe passage to Domain."

Chism shook his head. "How about this: the girl goes free and you die on this spear."

"If I die, she dies! And what will yeer Elite Captain say when ye tell him girl could not be saved?"

This was why Chism hated negotiating. It never led anywhere.

Swihp, swihp, swihp.

The girl continued to peek at the ground, but Gray-bear had forgotten about her. If she moved carefully, she could inch back to the tower and dive to safety. But the ordeal held her frozen in place.

Not much longer, child.

The child was only three years younger than him.

Gray-bear stared. Once in a while he raised his axe.

Chism focused on carving. He had to pass the time somehow, and there wasn't enough room to pace without coming close to the Maner. Blood continued to ooze from his scalp. It dripped down his cheek and bifurcated at his shoulder, meandering down his chest and back.

Around the time a rough likeness of the Circle and the Sword emerged from the grain of the wood, the curved edge of the sun appeared over the far hills. The first ray of the morning passed between two stone crenellations and hit Chism in the face and chest. Out of the three people atop the tower and everyone else indoors at the Duke's estate, he was the sole recipient of the first rays of sunshine.

If that wasn't a sign of good luck, he didn't know what was.

"You call yourselves the Indomitable," said Chism, taking a ready grip on his spear. "Let's see if you deserve that name."

He walked toward Gray-bear, who stepped off the plank. Saya dropped out of sight in an instant. The girl's shriek was joined by a woman's horrified squeal from below.

Gray-bear attacked. Chism blocked two sloppy strokes then ran him through. He held onto the end of the spear and felt his anger bleed out along with Gray-bear's lifeblood.

Released from his rage, Chism peered over the parapet wall. Saya and her parents clung to each other at the top of a large pile of straw and quilts. The duke and duchess and Odion had built an impressive mattress in a short time.

Careful of the people below, Chism broke the rough-carved Circle and Sword off the end of the spear and dropped it over the parapet. The boy chased it down then saluted Chism formally with both fists crossed over his chest.

Chism saluted back with one fist. A rare smile softened his face.

CHAPTER 2

Purpleful

Hatta walked into the town of Shey's Orchard at that time of morning when it's impossible to tell the difference between what the eyes see and what the mind perceives. For him, it was little different than any other time of day.

Change was uncomfortable—agonizing sometimes—but he couldn't stay in Frenala. And he couldn't go back to T'lai after running off as he had.

He let the rhythmic sound of gravel distract him from whatever might lay ahead in the new town.

Crunch. Crunch. Crunch. Crunch.

A merchant startled him with a casual "Good morning."

Hatta smiled genially, nodded, and pulled the brim of his traveling hat down. By the time it returned to its normal position, he was past the store.

The inn was easy to find. In between the words that ran along the top and bottom of the sign was a bed and dinner bowl that even an illiterate could recognize.

A stocky man was dusting an oak shelf in the front room

and whistling when Hatta slipped in. The tune was "Dipping Dipping Caterwauler," and Hatta sang along softly. The man didn't notice until Hatta began to whistle in harmony.

"Well hello, then. I didn't hear you come in."

"And thanks be for that," said Hatta, "or you may have stopped the whistle sooner."

"I'm Tellef."

"Hatta, Sir, and pleased to be meeting you." He smiled briefly. "I'll be in need of a room and some boarding, please."

"You won't find finer lodging anywhere in Shey's Orchard." The stocky man chuckled and smiled warmly. "Of course, this being the only inn, you're unlikely to find poorer lodging either."

What a delightful first friend in this new town!

A young man entered carrying firewood under both arms. *Eighteen?* wondered Hatta. *Nineteen?* Close to Hatta's age in any case. A strong underbite gave him a surly look, like a bulldog. A bulldog looking for a fight.

"Brune, make sure the first room upstairs is ready for our guest."

Brune nodded, then *oomphed* as he dropped the wood into a rack. He sneered as he looked at Hatta's colorful hat, coat, and pants.

"How do?" Hatta asked. He started to extend his hand but drew it back. Brune's unfriendly scrutiny made Hatta's feet want to squirm, and he stared at them so they'd remain still.

His purple boots always made him smile. What could be more wonderful than purple leather? The color complemented his blue, double-thick cotton pants. Not many people wore blue clothes—or purple, for that matter. It usually put people in an easy mood and he was always dressed well enough for any occasion he found himself in.

Once in a while it drew attention that wasn't what he would describe as positive. Hatta had no idea how to charm people who despised him from the first glance. Luckily, when he looked up from his boots, the boor was gone.

"How long will you be staying?" asked the innkeep, Tellef— or was it Teelif?

"Longer than I've already been here and shorter than the rest of my life." Hatta's smile came more naturally now that it was just him and his friend. From a pocket inside his maroon coat, he took out approximately half his coins. "Will this cover until I find a more permanent domicile?" The coins were mostly silver pennies, but there were a few copper cuppies as well.

"With coin to spare. I'll see that what's left over is returned when you leave."

"And perchance would you know of work to be had? I'm an assiduous worker. It means I work hard." Another smile so the innkeep didn't think him supercilious.

"If that's the case, you've arrived at a fortunate time. Aker's daughter is to be married tomorrow, and he'll need someone to replace her in the mirror shop. It's not far up the market street."

"I'm obliged for the advice. By your leave, I'll get settled, then."

Before returning to his dusting, Tellef said, "It's a pleasure having such a fine young man in Shey's Orchard. I'm at your order."

When Hatta reached the top of the stairs, Brune was closing the door to the first room.

"So are you supposed to be some kind of minstrel or traveling jester?" Brune sneered at his clothes again.

"No," answered Hatta, feeling tense. If there was an introduction he could give that might befriend Brune, Hatta didn't know it.

Brune continued to stare, so Hatta added, "I care for colors quite a bit."

Hatta stepped aside as Brune stalked past muttering, "This tweedle has coin to travel the kingdom while I'm stuck here . . ."

Finally in his room, Hatta was able to relax. The innkeep's confrontational helper would make his stay uncomfortable, but there weren't any other options in Shey's Orchard. He situated his bag at the foot of the mattress, then sat down on the floor with his legs crossed.

> *"My fancy gave her eyes of blue,*
> *A curly, auburn head;*
> *I came to find the blue a green,*
> *The auburn turned to red."*

The verse cleared his road weariness and buoyed his spirits. After reciting a few more rhymes, Hatta sprang to his feet and retrieved his green-checkered town hat. As opposed to his traveling hat with the purple turtle shell pattern, the town hat was more stable—more suited to spending time in a single place. Setting it just right, Hatta ventured into the awakening town.

As with other small towns, people greeted him warmly enough. Most either raised an eyebrow or stared openly after he passed. No one was aggressive or demeaning, and the street seemed a little brighter in his wake. On the second street, he found a group of children playing kickaround. Hatta joined in and helped each team score points before seeking out Master Aker. Once he had some sort of income, he could once again focus on creating.

It was the middle of the morning, but the mirror shop's doors were closed. The adjacent home, however, was bustling. A woman carrying dark blue flowers passed without acknowledging him. Hatta didn't want to interrupt, so he followed her into the house.

The dining table had been moved against one wall. In its place was a young lady in a white dress who seemed to be the center of the home's activity. The lack of color wasn't very appealing, but her face was as radiant as any person he'd ever seen, and more radiant than many sunrises. She wore a bright red ribbon in her hair that contrasted starkly with a faded red ribbon around her wrist. He'd never seen one girl wear two ribbons. Women surrounded her, trying various flowers in her hair and around her neck. A man in the far corner noticed him and approached.

Before the man could speak, Hatta said, "That's the only exquisite shade of white I've ever seen. I prefer bright colors, but the person who made that fabric is quite an artist. What would it be?"

"I think I heard someone say it's called sateen. Like satin, but made from cotton. Are you a tailor?" The man inspected Hatta's attire without openly staring.

"No, but I care for artistry in any form."

"Yes, I see that. I don't recognize you; are you here to help with the preparations for the wedding?"

For a moment Hatta forgot why he was in the man's house.

While Hatta thought, the man asked, "Friend of Tjaden?"

"No, I—I just arrived into town. I'm pleased to introduce myself. Hatta." He smiled and made a half bow.

The man appeared perplexed, which set Hatta at ease. *At least I'm not the only one.*

"My name's Aker, I'm the—"

"Yes of course! Master Aker, mirror maker. Rhyming helps me remember, but it doesn't always work."

An almost imperceptible smile twitched on Master Aker's face.

"I'm a very hard worker, and I learn quickly," said Hatta. "I have seventeen skills, but mirror making isn't one of them."

"If you're asking for work, that's an odd way to do it."

Hatta was sure he'd already mentioned employment. "Yes, I am. Asking for employment, that is. Not odd. The innkeep with the wooden shelf mentioned your daughter's wedding and so forth and so forth. Telf, or Tellef. Yes, that was his name."

Master Aker's smile widened. With a nervous glance at the women, he whispered, "I've sworn to not even talk about the shop for the next two days, but come by after that. I'll give you work for a couple days to see what you can do."

"I'll be very appreciative and you'll be undisappointed. Or delighted, I should say."

He extended his hand and was relieved when Master Aker accepted his grasp.

Hatta spent the rest of the daylight getting to know the town. He introduced himself to the most approachable people and smiled and tipped his town hat to the rest. The bakers, Coles and Hettie—*rolls* and *bready* to remember them—provided a warm lunch and more information than he could ever remember. If he tried to repeat half of what they told him, it would just come out jumbled.

When Hatta mentioned the trouble with Brune, Hettie said, "Tarts. That's the way to make friends with Brune. I can barely make them fast enough."

Coles nodded. "I think the only reason he works is to feed his tart habit."

Hatta had them wrap a pair of tarts to take with him.

Other than the bakers' names, Hatta tried to absorb three things: Someone named Tjaden jousted the Jabberwock, Talex's tools are only for fools, and stay far away from bandersnatches; two had been seen near town over the last year or so. He shouldn't need a trick to remember *that* one.

By the time Hatta returned to the inn, the sun had set and the air had turned chilly. He could see his breath in the air and stood outside, studying it. The ability to produce mist with something as simple as breath had always fascinated him. When he breathed on his fingers, he half expected them to freeze in the frosty breath, but his mist was surprisingly warm. He picked up a twig and tried freezing it, but the wood remained supple. Another puzzle to figure out.

As he reached for the door, a bout of laughter erupted inside the inn.

It must be a popular place on these nippy evenings.

It wasn't just busy; it was overflowing. Hatta barely had room to squeeze in. The handful of tables were overfull, and twice as many men stood as sat. The room was warm even though no fire was lit. In front of the empty fireplace stood two young men, a couple years younger than Hatta.

The shorter one had an arm around his stout, blushing friend and a bow over his shoulder with the string across his chest. He seemed not to notice the weapon. The story he was telling about his companion's soldier training had the attention of the whole room.

It didn't have Hatta's. Soldiery things were worse than boring, so he paid no attention as he pulled the brim of his hat down and quietly excused himself through the room. The tarts and Brune could wait until morning.

Why was it that he never had trouble remembering names following a confrontation? Just as he was about to reach the stairs, innkeep with the shelf—Tellef, that was it—put an arm around him.

He had been so close to safety.

"Won't you join us, Hatta? Tjaden's the lad I said was to be married, and we could use more help celebrating." Tellef leaned closer and said, "He's the Vorpal Knight. One doesn't get many chances to rub elbows with Knights."

Hatta could only hope. "I'm obliged for the invitation, but if it's no trouble, I'll just go up to my room."

"Nonsense! I insist." He forced a tankard into Hatta's hand.

Offending the kind innkeep seemed worse than escaping the raucous crowd, so Hatta didn't resist.

"Perchance would you have a less spirituous beverage? Tea?" He showed the innkeep a smile. "Liquors tend to affect me overstrongly."

"Aye," said Tellef, and waved to Brune. "Liquor does not agree with our new guest. Would you get him some tea?" Tellef walked off.

Before Brune could go to the kitchen, Hatta handed him the tarts and smiled his crooked grin. He never seemed to notice his crooked smile except when he faced unfriendly people.

"What're these?" Brune unwrapped the bundle halfway, then looked at Hatta suspiciously.

"Those would be tarts."

Brune licked his lips and rewrapped the tarts. "I'll be right back." He walked toward the swinging doors of the kitchen. Hatta followed so Brune wouldn't have to navigate the crowd again and found himself at the back of the room. The evening would be easier to bear in this inconspicuous spot next to the kitchen doors.

When Brune came out of the kitchen with a teacup, Hatta tapped him from behind. Brune handed him the cup and said, "This is a local tea. What do you think of it?"

Hatta didn't mention the crumbs at the corner of Brune's mouth. He blew on the tea to test the heat and managed a sip. It was mint with a strong orange taste, not pleasing at all, with a kick he hadn't tasted in other teas. Brune waited expectantly.

"I find it . . . unique," said Hatta, forcing a smile.

"I'm glad you like it. I'll prepare another cup when I have a chance." He smiled for the first time Hatta could remember and returned to his duties. The tea was unsavory, and it burned his throat even after it cooled. But along with the tarts, it somehow helped smooth whatever problem Brune had had with him earlier, so he sipped it every time Brune caught his eye.

Just when he had finally conquered the first cup, Brune

appeared with another. Hatta tried to act appreciative. He didn't dare refuse and risk offending Brune just as they were starting to get along.

The fellow with the bow finished talking and more men followed, both praising and embarrassing the taller one, who must have been Tjaden. The Jabberwock was mentioned repeatedly. That was a creature Hatta longed to find out more about, but all they ever talked about was killing it.

Brune, who stood near Hatta, asked, "Would you like to know some of the traditions here in Shey's Orchard? It's the least I can do to repay you for the tarts."

Hatta's head was spinning from the distance traveled, the busy day meeting new people, and the large gathering in the inn. He was glad for some guidance and nodded anxiously. Minor conflicts sometimes arose due to ignorance of local customs.

"It's customary for the men in town to offer a gift to the betrothed on the night before the wedding. It starts with the person who is least familiar with the man of honor and continues through the group until his closest friends and family present him with their gifts. Since you just arrived today, everyone is probably waiting for you so they can start." He looked at the teacup and Hatta forced down the last of the tea.

"I've come unprepared. What sort of gift would be customary?" Hatta was definitely in a muddle and glad to have Brune to guide him.

"Articles of clothing are perfect. Tjaden's a soldier, so I know he likes blue." Someone motioned for more ale and Brune excused himself.

Blue, thought Hatta. *He cares for blue.*

He set down his empty teacup and looked himself over slowly. His head was spinning, and he had to concentrate. Of all his clothes, only the pants were blue.

How fortunate there are no ladies present.

Hatta knelt and unlaced his boots. He emptied his pants pockets, placing a marigold, a spool of saffron thread, some purple yarn, six buttons, and an assortment of colored pebbles in various pockets of his coat. Using the shoulders of the men to steady himself, he pushed through the crowd to the front of the room.

A man who looked like a much older version of Tjaden, perchance his father, was speaking. He stopped when Hatta approached, and the room watched Hatta, waiting.

They must be anxious to start their gift-giving.

"I congratulate your impending wedding, Jabberslayer."

Did his speech sound slurred? The jumble in his head was thicker than usual. Everyone watched curiously, probably wondering what he would offer as a gift. He fumbled at the laces of his trousers, managed to remove them without falling over, and offered them to Tjaden. The young man took them but apparently didn't know what to say.

Having fulfilled his responsibility, Hatta, in his striped socks and red unders, walked toward the stairs. The crowd began sniggering, and it grew into open laughing by the time Hatta reached the foot of the stairs.

Brune stood there, nodding approvingly.

"I thank you, Brune. Your advice surely saved me from looking the fool." He meant to say it quietly, but it came out loud to bounce off the walls.

Before Hatta stepped onto the first stair, the innkeep—what was his name again? Something to do with a ledge or bookshelf—said, "Wait!"

He tramped toward Hatta and Brune, face as red as a . . . a . . .

Something was definitely wrong in Hatta's head. The innkeep's enraged face made his stomach knot and he felt like vomiting. The angry man stormed up to Brune and demanded in a quiet but terrible voice, "Did *you* put him up to this?"

Brune shrunk and looked around for someone to rescue him. But he stood alone.

"I was just trying to liven up the party. Have a little fun."

The innkeep swore, forcing Hatta to lean against the wall and Brune to cringe.

"I didn't think he'd be idiot enough to take off his pants." Brune's words shot across the silent room. The smile had left his face, replaced by the surly underbite.

The innkeep stormed to the kitchen door and picked up Hatta's cup. He sniffed it and swore twice. Each curse struck Hatta like a blow.

"And you put orange liqueur in his tea!" He slammed his fist into the table, rattling tankards. "Get out! Get out! I tried to help you because your father's worthless, and this is how you repay me?"

He was moving toward Brune, but the young man didn't wait to be tossed.

Before Brune reached the door Hatta spoke up. "No."

Brune froze then turned his eyes to join all the others in the room on Hatta.

"Please, not on my account," Hatta said to the innkeep. "Most likely it was all in fun. Please."

Brune's eyebrows went up like a puppy trying to avoid being sent out into the cold.

All eyes were on the innkeep. Only a muffled belch broke the silence. The innkeep's face returned to a normal color as he looked between Brune and Hatta.

After a dozen or more breaths he shook his head and said, "No. I can't forgive this. On your way, Brune." He pointed at the door but didn't watch the departing young man.

Hatta would never forget the sound of the slamming doors. Tears came to his eyes, and he held his stomach in hopes of keeping inside the things that belonged there.

"I'm sorry, Jabberslayer." He swallowed back the sick. "I'm sorry, townsmen. It was the last thing I wanted." Any more words would pave way for the vomit.

As he turned to climb the stairs, he heard. "No, it's alright. I'll see to him."

In another step the innkeep was under one arm, providing a steady shoulder on the difficult stairs.

"Master Hatta, I hope you'll accept my apologies. You never should have been subjected to that."

The last thing Hatta cared about was himself.

"And Brune? Does he have where to go? What about the Jabberslayer and his ruined celebration?" He couldn't control the hot tears that ran down his face.

"Don't worry about Tjaden. He's been through worse." Somehow there was a smile in the innkeep's voice, but it faded in the next sentence. "And as for Brune, he has a history of cruelty. I've given him too many chances, and it's time he learned a lesson. Anyone in town would agree with me."

Not me. But Hatta wasn't about to make another enemy by arguing. This night was already the worst he could remember.

The innkeep helped him into bed. "I'll get your trousers and leave them outside your door. You're not Brune's first victim. Tomorrow will be a new day."

Hatta just nodded. As soon as Tellef was gone, he staggered to the chamber pot and threw up. The tea burned as badly coming back up, but his gut felt cleaner.

The best thing would be sleep, but Hatta was too tense. Even the alcohol wasn't enough to soothe him. He tried reciting verses, but the words scrambled in his head. He spent an hour rocking on the edge of his bed. The room had a small window, and eventually he stood and watched the men file out, many clinging to each other for support.

At least the entire celebration wasn't ruined.

He cringed as he recognized some of the men who had witnessed the confrontation. Rolls, no, Coles the baker. Master Aker mirror maker. And eventually Tjaden the Jabberslayer and his bow-carrying companion. Tjaden practically had to drag his friend down the road.

The road cleared and the lamps went out, but Hatta remained at the window, staring into the grey street. Some time later, hours perhaps, a silhouette appeared in the shadows. Hatta straightened when he realized it was Brune. He had a bag slung over his shoulder. For some reason he was keeping to the dark edges of the streets. Directly across from the inn, Brune stopped. After looking up and down the street, he studied the inn.

Hatta leaned back into his own shadows. The look on Brune's face was not one that Hatta wanted to fall on him. From his bulky bag, Brune took out a handful of something that looked like grass. He slunk across the street toward the inn and disappeared into the area under Hatta's window.

Only moonlight moved outside. That and clouds. Maybe Brune had come inside. Maybe he'd accidentally taken something and had decided to return it.

Brune appeared suddenly in the road, watching the inn over his shoulder. There was no more skulking; Brune was practically running. His shoes made a slapping sound on the dirt of the road. The soles of both shoes were loose.

Without hesitation, Hatta ran to his door and yanked it open. Purple boots and blue trousers were waiting there. He put the pants on as fast as possible, tying them hurriedly, and picked up his fine leather boots, then ran down the stairs and through the front doors of the inn.

A flash of fire and sparks sprayed into the street ahead of him as he pushed the doors. Some careless person had left a fire burning in front of the door. Hatta looked around for water or sand buckets but was too nightblind from the sparks to see anything. Clouds were blocking part of the moon. Even the flames, which were responsible for his blindness, had stopped burning. Only embers remained, spread across the dirt of the street.

As Brune ran away, Hatta stood in the street torn between following and staying to put the fire out. If only the fire was still burning, he could use the light to find something to put it out.

"Bother and bustle," he said, and ran in the direction Brune had been heading. The fire would still be there after he took care of the important things.

Even at his quick pace, his besocked feet made almost no sound. Just after passing the last building in town he heard the *pa-fwap, pa-fwap, pa-fwap* of Brune's worn-out shoes. Hatta slowed to an unhurried jog, silently following the sound.

When Brune's outline came into view, Hatta stopped and set his purple boots in the middle of the road. He reached into his coat and took out two pennies and two cuppies. He placed one of each in each boot. That didn't seem right, so he pulled them out. The pennies he placed in the right; the cuppies in the left.

Yes, he thought. *Much better.*

He retreated a ways toward the town and took cover in the mesquite trees that lined the road.

Once he was situated, he shouted, "Brune!"

The faint shoe sound stopped and Hatta yelled again, quieter. "Who's there?"

Hatta remained silent and the slap slapping resumed, more slowly but growing closer.

"Who is it?"

Pa-fwap, pa-fwap, pa-fwap.

Brune came tentatively into view. The bulky bag was slung over one shoulder, and he carried a walking stick in the other. He approached the boots, and after studying them, he prodded one boot as if expecting a snake to emerge.

"Where are you?"

Silence.

When Brune picked up the boots, the muted jingle of coins rolled through the dark morning and into Hatta's ears. Brune reached into the boots and pulled out the coins. Hatta couldn't make out the expression on his face, so he imagined a genuine smile. And maybe a slight nod of appreciation.

After rubbing the purple leather with road dirt, Brune unlaced his worn out shoes, removed them, and put the boots on. With sideways glimpses, he cleared his throat and said quietly, "You think this makes things even between us."

Properly shod, Brune walked into the darkness and said, "Thanks for nothing."

Hatta smiled. Things were even between him and Brune. The purple boots had done it! No, *purple* wasn't a potent enough description.

"Purpleful," whispered Hatta. "Yes, the purpleful boots have done it."

Hatta tried counting fifty breaths but got sidetracked by the feel of his heartbeat all the way up in his neck, so he focused on the faint mists of his breath for a while. Confident he was alone, he stood and walked in the opposite direction with a whistle on his lips.

Hatta had nothing but good feelings for his fellow men, and they for him. The dark night held a bright yellow tinge of hope.

In front of the inn he found nothing but ash and unburnt tinder, as if the fire had been kind enough to extinguish itself while Hatta took care of the more pressing matter.

All was right in the world.

CHAPTER 3

Orphans

When Hatta awoke, he laid in bed, trying to remember where he was. The sun was well up, and he eventually recognized the room of the inn. Shey's Orchard. Before rising, he took a moment to practice the names from the previous day. Using memory tricks, he came up with Tellef, Tjaden, Master Aker, Coles, and Hettie. And Brune. The events of the evening came to mind, and he rose with a mind to offer Tjaden a more formal apology.

The sight of his blue pants brought on a wave of nausea and a headache. Whether aftereffects of the alcohol or the conflict, he couldn't tell. How long until he felt comfortable wearing the blue pants he was so fond of? The apricot pants would have to do in the meantime. A lavender shirt, maroon jacket, and the town hat completed the outfit. His red-and-brown striped socks were stained with ash and dirt, but they were the only ones he owned. The good feelings brought by the fate of the boots outweighed the bad ones.

Some soldiers waited for breakfast in the dayroom. They

all wore dark blue, and half of their uniforms bore the Circle and Sword emblem. Elites and Fellows. Though he'd never had trouble with soldiers, they brought painful thoughts to Hatta's mind, especially those wearing the Circle and the Sword. Hatta ducked into the kitchen and found Tellef scrambling to assist a woman who was preparing porridge and bacon.

Without taking his attention from his duties, Tellef greeted him. "How did you sleep, Hatta?"

"Like a bear in winter, thank you. Where might a cobbler be found?" He smiled uneasily. Tellef and Brune were not friends, and Hatta didn't want to explain his shoelessness to Tellef.

"He's not the best in the kingdom, but Cobbler Whit should be able to mend any problems you've got. You'll find him right up this street, a hundred paces toward the wabe." Tellef didn't notice Hatta's socks.

"I thank you and wish you a pleasant morning."

Hatta started to hurry out, but heard, "Oh, Hatta?"

He poked his head back into the kitchen but kept his feet carefully concealed, showing Tellef a crooked smile.

"Have a seat out there. Breakfast will be ready in no time."

"The offer is kind, but I've matters to attend to that don't want to wait."

"Suit yourself." Tellef looked up for the first time. "I really am sorry about last night. I hope you don't hold a grudge."

"No, grudges don't agree with me."

"I wish I could say the same for Brune," said Tellef, his face turning into a scowl. "Someone tried to light my inn on fire last night. I suspect it was him."

Suspecting Brune of something like that hadn't even crossed Hatta's mind.

The innkeep continued, "Either he lost his nerve and put it out or some hero came by and extinguished it after he left. No one can find Brune this morning. I doubt any of us will ever see him again."

Hatta thought back to the embers from the night before. If the fire had continued to burn, it could have done a great deal of damage to the door of the inn. Perhaps it would have spread to the dayroom and if it wasn't extinguished at that point it could have—

The direction Hatta's thoughts were headed kept getting darker so he cut them off. Brune was gone. What did any of it matter now?

"Well, then. What's past is forgotten and forgone." Hatta smiled again and let the door swing closed. He needed to cover his guilty socks as soon as possible. Pulling his hat as low as it would sit, he made his way past the soldiers and into the street.

Whit's selection of boots was disappointing. Only two pairs of boots fit, and both were an unremarkable tan. They'd do in the short term, but Hatta would have to fix that. He thanked the cobbler, paid him five pennies, and went in search of Tjaden.

He was directed to a home on the outskirts of town. It was surrounded by groves of orange, lemon, and heartfruit trees. Some rows of trees were bare, but ripe fruit hung on others. When he called at the door, the man he assumed to be Tjaden's father emerged and looked at him curiously. The gaze made Hatta forget why he'd come. The only thing he could remember was humiliation.

"Did you get your pants back?" The man was stoic.

Hatta didn't know how to take him, so he forced a smile. "Yes, thanks. My name's Hatta."

"Mikel. What can I do for you?"

"It's a pleasure to meet your acquaintance, Sir. Would these be your trees? The colors are splendid. I especially care for the deep greens and orange."

"Thank you, Hatta. With the wedding today I need to—"

"A wedding! Yes, of course. You wouldn't be Tjaden's father?"

"I would. I mean, I am."

"Ah, yes. Where might he be found?"

Mikel chuckled. "Tjaden's the only one not helping with preparations. He went with Ollie to their little archery range, just on the other side of those lemons."

"I thank you." After a quick smile at Mikel, Hatta turned toward the lemon trees.

"Hatta."

The sick feeling in his stomach returned. Before he had a chance to apologize for the previous night, Mikel said, "You'll be at the wedding, won't you?"

"I'm sorry," Hatta blurted, not registering what Mikel had said.

"I said we'd be glad to have you at the wedding. It's in the wabe at brillig time."

"Oh, I don't think so. What if I did something inappropriate? Or forgot to do something appropriate? Or did something appropriate at an inappropriate time?" Considering the possibilities, it was a miracle that anything ever turned out right.

"Don't worry about last night. I heard Brune left town. Far as I'm concerned, we're better off."

Hatta didn't see it that way, but at least Mikel held no hard feelings. He didn't know how to express it, so he grinned and turned back toward the grove. The man meant him well, so Hatta tried to sow Mikel's name in his mind as he passed between lemon trees. *Mikel. My-cull. Cull oranges. My-cull.* It might work.

Before he was out of the grove, he was startled by the *swang* of a bow and *thunk* of an arrow. He followed the sound and came upon the short friend of Tjaden's, who appeared Tjadenless at the moment.

Swang! Thunk. The weapon seemed to shout profanities at Hatta. One arrow was lodged in a bullseye forty paces away with two more arrows just outside of it.

"You're almost an excellent bowman," Hatta said, startling the shooter, who was a couple years younger than him.

"What do you mean 'almost'? You won't find a better archer in fifty miles. Maybe a hundred."

"Why don't you get them all in the bullseye?"

"Give me perfectly fletched arrows and a windless day and I'll give you all the bullseyes you want."

"I know a fletcher who makes perfect arrows. He's the best there is. The king's advisor requested arrows for the soldiers, but the fletcher was disinclined. He refused Captain Mark—, Mark—" *Markum? Markellin?*

"Markin," said the archer.

"Yes, Markin. The fletcher only makes arrows for sharpshooters. He might make them for you; he's the best there is."

"Yeah, you said that. Who is he?"

Hatta thought for a moment. "Either I can't recall his name or he never told me. Perhaps it's Fletcher."

"You mean he *is* a fletcher? He makes arrows?"

"Yes, yes, and yes."

"Where does he live?"

"In Frenala. That would be north of here. Were you in the company of Tjaden when he was in the company of the Jabberwock?"

"What? No, I wasn't." The young man paused for a bit. "You're a bit odd. What's your name?"

Hatta's heart sank. His efforts to put on a normal front weren't working.

"Hatta."

"I'm Ollie."

"Ollie. Ollie. Hmm, that might be tricky. Would you know why he fought the Jabberwock?"

"Isn't it obvious? It terrorized the kingdom. Would you rather have it still killing humans?"

"I don't mean to say he *shouldn't* have killed it. But it seems the kind of thing one would have a reason for doing. What's that medal for?" He pointed at one of the medals on Ollie's chest. It was white and gold and featured a wicked claw.

"I helped Tjaden kill the Jabberwock."

"I was told you weren't there when he did that."

"Yeah. I'm the one who told you that. I punctured its wing with an arrow a week before Tjaden found it. The injury helped him kill it."

"I'm saddened I never got to meet it. What would a creature like that tell you?"

Hatta didn't expect an answer, but Ollie said, "No one ever asks that. It actually told Tjaden and Elora a lot." Ollie nocked another arrow and continued before Hatta could inquire. "You'll have to ask them about it, though."

Swang! The jarring bowstring made Hatta flinch like a bird. *Thunk.* Another near bullseye.

"If you had better arrows you might hit the bullseye every time. Do you always wear your uniform?"

"No. Tjaden's getting married today, and I'm his groomsman."

Swang! Flinch. *Thunk.*

Hatta took a small step back and asked, "Weren't you telling me about the Jabberwock?"

"I only got close enough to shoot some arrows at it the day King Barash was killed."

"Why did it kill the king?"

"Why would a watermelon wear waders?"

"Ooh, a riddle! I don't know. Why *would* a watermelon wear waders?"

"No, I was just saying that I had no idea."

"I heard the new king is very young."

"I've met him," Ollie said.

"Would he be smaller in stature than you?"

"Of course. He's only nine years old." Ollie looked offended.

"You're short, but you're not a small person. I can tell these things sometimes."

Ollie's playful smile returned. Hatta smiled back, felt the familiar calm come over him, and hoped his smile affected Ollie the same way. If nothing else, it hid the cloud inside his head from outsiders. Better they think he's happy rather than mad. More and more Hatta wondered if the reverse was true.

The silence discomfited him. "Have you shot many people?"

Ollie shook his head. "Never. But someday I'll have to, and I'll be ready. Tjaden's an Elite, the Vorpal Knight actually. I'm his Fellow. Do you know about the Elites?"

Hatta knew more than he wanted to. He looked at the plain brown boots. Maybe orange peels could brighten them up a little.

Ollie mistook the distraction for ignorance. "Elites are the best of the best. There are no better soldiers in the world. Every Elite has a Fellow, kind of like a partner, but more in the background. Tjaden and I just graduated from the Academy less than a month ago. Soon we'll start going on missions in Grimblade Squadron."

No matter how hard he tried to escape, the Elites . . . . No sense in thinking about that. Hatta blinked and gulped to clear the traces of tears.

"Where?"

"I don't know," said Ollie. "People are saying the Western Domain is getting ready to invade again."

"Will you have to . . . kill people?" Hatta hoped no one he loved was ever Ollie's target.

"That's what we do when it's necessary. We're soldiers."

"Is there any other way? Maybe build peace instead of making war?"

"It's much more complicated than that. It would take days to explain . . ."

Swang! Flinch. *Thunk.*

". . . but right now I need to find Tjaden. The wedding's in a couple hours."

"Yes, that would be it! Tjaden's why I came. Where would he be?"

"He went to his brother's house to get dressed."

He smiled at Ollie. "Well, might we descry him?"

"Tjaden might be a bit distracted today. He's full of nerves and needles."

"I don't mind," said Hatta. "Perchance a discussion will help ease his nerves."

"Suit yourself," Ollie said as he headed to retrieve his arrows. He walked with a limp in one leg. It looked like he was incorporating part of a dance into each step. It made Hatta like him even more.

Ollie returned with a full quiver. Walking toward the town, he said, "It looks like you're already dressed for the wedding. You'll be there, right?"

Hatta had no excuses. Though he was sure he'd do something to ruin another occasion, he agreed to go.

"Why did you leave Frenala?" asked Ollie, slowing to allow Hatta to meet his stride.

"I . . . had to."

"Why?"

"Because I had to."

"That's not a reason," said Ollie.

People usually didn't ask so many questions. It was usually a simple matter to dismiss or disrupt a line of questions without even trying, but Hatta's mind was unfogged. Some days his fate seemed cloudy, but today his destiny shone as clear as a twinkling star.

"I'm actually a very important individual," he admitted humbly. It wasn't something he bragged about, but he had accepted his fate. "It wasn't safe for the kingdom if I stayed there any longer."

"Are you a noble or something?"

Hatta shook his head. After looking over his shoulders he whispered, "Someday I'll save the entire kingdom."

Ollie looked dubious. That wasn't an uncommon reaction. On the few occasions Hatta had revealed the truth about his destiny, he'd seen it more often than credulity.

"If memory serves," said Hatta, "your Tjaden did just that. Why not me too?" Stated that way it did seem a little mad, but that didn't change the truth of it one iota.

"I can't argue with that," admitted Ollie. "But the types of threats Maravilla faces need soldiers, not," he looked over Hatta's clothes, "whatever you are."

Hatta wasn't sure how to respond. The deep green leaves of the orange trees they passed changed to the richer red-tinged leaves of heartfruit trees. Hatta stopped to examine the trunks, curious if the trunks were reddish like the leaves and center of the fruit.

Ollie called to him from the road. "What about your family? Do they still live in Frenala?"

"Frenala? They never were in Frenala." *What a strange question,* Hatta thought as he brushed past the leaves to the road.

Ollie's eyebrows rose. "Are you an orphan?"

"Orphan. That depends on how you mean."

"What I mean is someone whose parents are dead."

"Yes, well in that case you mean me."

"Me too," said Ollie without joy. "Since I was four." He waited, but Hatta had said enough.

Ollie continued. "My parents died of an ague, along with half a dozen other townspeople that winter. What about yours?"

The tread of their footfalls on the gravel was the only sound.

"Shall I tell you what I can't make sense of?" asked Hatta. "Insanity. A curious word indeed. After all, it means the opposite of *in sanity*. Perhaps *outsanity* would be more accurate. Do you think it might catch on?"

Ollie stopped and waited for Hatta to turn and face him. "Hatta, what happened to your mother and father? What did they die of?"

"If you put it that way, Mother died of Father and Father died of Brother." Hatta stared at the peppery brown gravel, feeling alone. "Hatta, he just ran. He loved his brother too much to stay."

CHAPTER 4

Shoeless

The smell of campfire drifted by Chism as he sat on the ground in front of his tent. He felt an urge to inspect his horse again to make sure the hobbles were applied correctly and the tether was tight, but he'd already checked them twice. His throwing knives had been cleaned and oiled and now lay just inside his tent. Thirsty, his sword, was at his hip.

Still, Chism couldn't relax. He removed a palm-sized piece of leather from the pouch at his waist and began stroking it with his right thumb. After one hundred rubs, he passed it to his left hand. One hundred strokes with the left, then back to the right. It was working already.

The previous three days of travel had kept Chism busy, and he hadn't used the leather since the night before the rescue of Duke Enniel and his family. His calloused thumbs barely felt the smooth leather, but the repetitive motion soothed him. The squadron had camped early today near a stream, giving Chism more time than he wanted.

Voices from the nearby fire rose in pitch. Chism was on his feet and moving toward the flickering light before he realized it.

"If Lady Cuora had her way, the entire army of Maravilla would cross the border and kill every man in the Western Domain." Chism recognized Dugar's voice as he entered the clearing.

Caroon, Dugar's Fellow, said, "Why would she do that? She doesn't care about what happens in the Provinces. She's safe in the center of the kingdom."

Dugar responded, "Lady Cuora cares because anyone who breaks the law or defies Maravilla deserves to die. There's no middle ground with her."

Chism moved into the circle of the conversation but didn't speak. Four soldiers sat in the fire's glow. Two were seated side by side on a log and the other two stood upwind of the smoke, making it impossible for Chism to fit into a symmetrical pattern. Five wasn't a good number anyway, and he shifted uncomfortably as the discussion continued.

Poking at the fire with a stick, Banivar sighed and said, "Do you Provincials ever talk about anything besides how much you hate Lady Cuora? She's strong and just. I don't know why that bothers you so much."

"She's one member of the Council, but she acts like she's queen," said Caroon. "If Lady Palida wasn't there to temper her rulings, half of the population of Palassiren would have a death sentence. We'll be better off when King Antion is old enough to hold court."

Ulrik, a seasoned Elite from one of the Eastern Provinces, spoke up. "We'd be better off with Lady Palida as queen. This nonsense of a nine-year-old king with so many advisors is ridiculous. It's no wonder nothing's being done about the Western Domain."

Chism took a small step toward the older soldier. He forced his voice to remain subdued as he said, "Watch your tongue,

Ulrik. You talk about one of the Council subjecting the others, you talk treason."

"Get on," said Ulrik. "I'm loyal as a pup, and you're as young as one. Stay out of discussions that don't concern you."

"Sedition concerns me." Chism took a step closer.

"Sedition my right foot," said Ulrik, scowling into the fire. "We're just talking."

But there was no more talking. The fire popped and crackled in the silence. One by one the men wandered to their tents. The unburnt ends of a few small logs protruded from the fire ring. Chism arranged the nubs in the center of the fire and stayed until the flames died.

He was awake before sunrise, repeating forms with Thirsty. His brother, of all people, had named the sword, saying that once it tasted blood it would ever be thirsty. The thought of his brother made Chism stumble during thrust forty-four, so he started over at one.

After breakfast, the soldiers broke camp and continued on the road. Chism and his Fellow, Ander, rode at the back of the neatly arranged column.

They were a few hours away from Brito, a city in the northwest Riza Province. The outlying portions of Maravilla were organized into twelve Provinces that surrounded the interior of the kingdom. The king's soldiers worked with Provincial militias to keep the peace. Recently, incursions from the Western Domain had strained the kingdom's resources, causing tension between the Provinces and the interior. Local nobles felt the King's Council didn't take sufficient measures to protect the Provinces. After all, the Provinces served as a protective buffer for the capital, Palassiren, and the rest of the interior.

The clatter of a rickety wagon caught Chism's attention, and he leaned sideways to see a farmer and mule approaching. A dirty boy, eleven or twelve years old, walked barefoot alongside the empty wagon and shouted, "Hurrah! Soldiers!" Random

HATTER

scars dotted his face and arms, as well as some recent cuts and bruises. Part of one ear was missing. He was walking shoeless even though there was plenty of room for him on the wagon. And somehow still smiling.

Lieutenant Fahrr brought the column to a halt to question the dumpy man, who looked like a toad in a tunic, about happenings in the Province. The Elites and their Fellows maintained two straight columns. Even at the back of the troop, Chism was within hearing distance.

"How far are you going?" asked Lieutenant Fahrr.

"Far enough," answered the toad. He had only stopped because Lieutenant Fahrr's horse blocked his way.

Shoeless pointed at a side road. "Our farm's up that road there. We sold that whole wagonfull of beets in Brito."

"Boy!" said the toad. He slid down from his seat in the wagon and hit the boy upside the head.

Shoeless cringed and moved out of striking range. Even as he rubbed his temple he kept smiling up at Lieutenant Fahrr.

"Any sign of Maners?" asked Lieutenant Fahrr.

Before the toad could answer, the boy said, "Papa says if Domainers ever come to our farm, he'll chop them up and feed them to the pigs."

The toad struck the boy with his mule lash. Shoeless cried out, and a spot of blood formed on the back of his course shirt.

Chism dismounted and walked swiftly toward the father and son. Ander, his Fellow, followed. "Snails and snot, Chism, what are you planning?" he whispered just loudly enough for Chism to hear.

Chism reached the farmer before Ander could stop him. A punch to the center of the chest made the man drop the whip. Chism caught it before it hit the ground and wrapped it around the toad's bulging jowls.

"That's a boy, not a mule," growled Chism.

Ander grabbed him around the waist, and the other Elites tried to break his grip with their hands. They were more suffocating than pythons.

Chism released the whip and tensed everything else. "Don't touch me." He spoke with too much control in his voice for the situation. He was frozen, worried that if he fought back, Elites and Fellows would be seriously hurt.

"I got him," Ander told the other Elites.

The others tentatively released him but stood alertly between him and the toad. Ander held him by the back of his tunic. The portly man rubbed his neck, cursing.

I could get past the Elites and put a knife in his chest before anyone stops me. But it wasn't worth hurting Elites.

The toad didn't wait for another assault. He climbed into the wagon and used the mule lash for what it was intended. The boy saluted Chism and walked alongside the wagon.

Father and son veered off down a narrow dirt road, and the toad glanced nervously over his shoulder.

Chism shouted, "If I ever see you again, you're as dead as desert!"

Lieutenant Fahrr stepped in between Chism and the wagon, grim as a gravestone.

Ulrik was by his side. "I tell you, he's dangerous. He has no control and looks for a fight wherever he goes. He doesn't belong around people."

What did Ulrik know about Chism's self-control? No one had more discipline, but when someone offended the Circle and Sword, Chism wasn't afraid to act. He ignored Ulrik and said to the lieutenant, "You're just going to let that toad go home and beat the boy some more?"

"What am I supposed to do after you overreact like that? People already look at us askance in the Provinces, and incidents like that could put the whole squadron in jeopardy." He considered for a short moment and said, "Double sentry duty for Elite Chism for one month. It will give you some time to think about consequences. Mount up."

That was perfect. More time to think about that smiling boy and his miserable life.

CHAPTER 5

Vorpal Knight

Hatta followed Ollie across the grassy wabe at the center of Shey's Orchard. It was larger than most, and even though winter wasn't far off, it was uncompromisingly green. The sundial at the center, standard to all towns, was obscured by a small pavilion decorated with blue and white flowers.

Without announcing themselves, Ollie and Hatta entered a small, red-brick home that faced the wabe. Tjaden sat in the front room at the dining table, wringing his hands. He was dressed in a blue uniform like his Fellow's, but Tjaden's had the Circle and the Sword embroidered on the chest.

"You gonna make it?" Ollie asked, slapping Tjaden's back.

He nodded. "I've waited this long. What's a couple more hours?"

He noticed Hatta and stood, extending his hand. Hatta grasped it and said proudly, "Tjaden."

"I'm . . . yes, I'm Tjaden. And you are?"

"I'm Hatta. I'm glad I've found you. I've meant to tell you something."

Tjaden waited, but Hatta couldn't remember. *Tjaden jousted Jabberwock.* It was as good a place as any to start.

"Why did you kill the Jabberwock?"

Tjaden looked puzzled. "That's what you wanted to say?" He sat back down. "I had to. He kidnapped Elora, my wife-to-be."

"And how did you find him?"

"Lord Captain Darieus told me where his lair was."

How could he put it in different words? "What I mean is, how *was* he?"

"The Jabberwock? Manxome. Dangerous. Intimidating."

"That's still not what I meant to ask."

Tjaden looked at Ollie. Ollie shrugged. Tjaden looked back at Hatta and raised an eyebrow.

"*How* was he? As in 'How are you?' or 'How do?' I heard you talked to him."

Tjaden glared at his friend. "Who could have told him that, Ollie?"

Ollie shrugged again and sat, leaning his bow against the side of the table. Compared to Tjaden, he looked undersized in his uniform. *Ollie smallie.* Hatta repeated it five times in his head.

"What did the Jabberwock say?" Hatta always knew what animals were thinking, but hadn't ever heard one talk.

Tjaden still looked skeptical, but said, "I felt his words through my whole body. They were powerful."

"What was good in the creature?"

"Why do you ask that?" Tjaden studied Hatta.

"Everyone—every animal, tree, insect, and stone—must be at least part way good." Without thinking he added, "Even Brune."

"After what he did to you last night, you still feel—"

"That's it! Yes, that's what I came for to tell. I regret ruining your celebration."

"Don't mention it. It wasn't your fault, and Brune got what he deserved."

The turn in the conversation made Hatta nervous. He shifted on his feet, then asked, "Do you talk to any other animals?"

"You change topics more often than the Cheshire Cat."

"The who?"

"Never mind; I shouldn't have mentioned him."

"Did you say 'Cheshire Cat'?" Hatta didn't think he'd ever heard of such a creature. "Wildcat, bobcat, pussycat, copycat, caterpillar, cattails. Yes, I think I've never heard of a Cheshire Cat."

Tjaden sighed. "The two of you would get along perfectly."

"We would?" Hatta was intrigued. "When can you introduce me? Us? And exactly what kind of cat is a Cheshire?"

"He's not a cat at all; at least that's what he says. He talks in riddles and never gives a straight answer. I don't think he's right in the head."

Hatta had to meet him. "Is he near?"

Tjaden shook his head. "I met him on the road to the Tumtum tree. I came to a fork in the road a day and a half out of Palassiren. He was perched in a tree there."

Hatta turned toward the door, prepared to seek the Cheshire Cat, but he was almost sure it would be considered a mad thing to do. The invisible social expectations were worse than shackles. Hatta forced himself to stay where he was.

A man entered, and Hatta greeted him. "How do? I'm Hatta."

"Hannon. I'm Tjaden's brother. I remember you from last night."

Hatta forced a smile. "Tjaden has assured me all is fine as feathers. I do believe we've struck up a friendship." He turned to Tjaden. "I had already met your betrothed earlier that selfsame day."

"You did?" Tjaden's face came alive. "I haven't seen her since the day before that. I can still hardly believe today is actually here. The last fourteen months—"

Ollie interrupted with a groan. "Now you've done it. He'll spend the next four hours talking about how he's the luckiest man in the kingdom and how wonderful Elora is. Trust me, it'll be unbearable."

"Someday you'll understand, my friend," said Tjaden, still smiling. "It's too bad you can't marry that bow of yours."

"You're one to talk about inanimate objects, *Vorpal* Knight," replied Ollie. "You were named after your sword."

Their banter gave Hatta the opportunity to slip out. He walked the short distance to the wabe, trying to figure out how Tjaden could be such a violent person—an Elite soldier—and yet love so strongly. It was as if he switched love and hate at will, caring deeply for his betrothed one day and the next day hating someone enough to kill.

Hatta felt empathy for the soldier groom. Two people in one body and mind. For Hatta it was the constant battle between sanity and happiness that he could never reconcile. Maybe someday Tjaden could come to terms with who he really was and not have to try to be two things.

Maybe someday Hatta could.

Without realizing it, Hatta had reclined on the lush grass of the wabe. A curious tove approached. Its spindly nose, more like a feeler, reached out to examine Hatta.

"And how is this fine day treating you?" Hatta asked.

The tove, which resembled a scaly-skinned badger, grunted and pawed the grass lightly. *Not happy about being kicked out of home.*

Hatta glanced at the sundial behind the pavilion. The toves must have been evicted from the sundial when the pavillion was set up.

"Don't worry. A few more hours and you'll have your happy abode back." Hatta smiled at the tove and reached out to feel its snaky skin. He found it smoother than it appeared.

Hungry.

The tove waddled off on short, scaly legs, leaving Hatta to wonder if a snake and a badger had mated to produce such a curious type of animal. He spent the hour considering and conversing with the animals in the wabe—cardinals, borogoves, a mouse, and more wandering toves. When guests arrived for the wedding, he listened but didn't talk to the animals any more.

From the time people started to gather until the happy couple stood in front of Tellef—Hatta hardly had to use the shelf memory trick any more—very little time passed. Hatta remained at the back of the congregation and concentrated on not doing anything unordinary.

He grew restless during the ceremony and turned his attention to a pair of raths that rooted in the grass nearby. The green, piglike animals moved irritably, huffing to themselves.

As Tellef neared the end of his discourse, Hatta watched the raths, hoping they would come closer. His hoping must have worked, because one of the petulant animals roamed to within touching distance.

Under the guise of adjusting the laces of his boot, Hatta bent and whispered, "Why so uffish?"

As the animal turned to face him, Hatta heard Tellef ask, "Do you, Tjaden and Elora, accept one another as husband and wife?"

But Hatta never heard the lovers' answer, for just at that moment the rath outgrabe loudly—a bellowing whistle combined with a strident sneeze. Hatta turned bright red and looked around, but to his pleasure, no one stared or pointed at him. They chuckled at the timing of the rath and clapped for the newly married couple, but no one realized that Hatta had instigated the disruption.

Why do I subject myself to these situations? he wondered.

The blush faded from his face, and Hatta snuck away from the wabe before being compelled to attend any more festivities.

CHAPTER 6

Treasures

*L*iquid metal rolled silently across Hatta's palm. It flattened momentarily after rolling off and landing on his other hand, then tightened into a bead. It was much heavier than water, so much so that he could feel the weight of the droplet on his palm. Passing it back and forth a few more times, he wondered how metal could be liquid.

The small vat of molten tin to his right was metal, but it had been heated. Mercury was liquid in his hand. It looked like metal and acted like metal when mixed in a compound, but Hatta was unconvinced. He lifted the droplet to his nose but it had no odor. Curiosity got the best of him and he popped the bead of mercury into his mouth.

The weight of the metal spread over his tongue and settled underneath it into two tiny pools on either side of the little tongue divider Hatta couldn't name. The mercury tasted cold, weak, and flavorless. Nothing like he'd predicted.

Hatta swallowed the mercury and its weight dissipated as it slid down his throat. Nothing like other metals he knew of. Real

HATTER

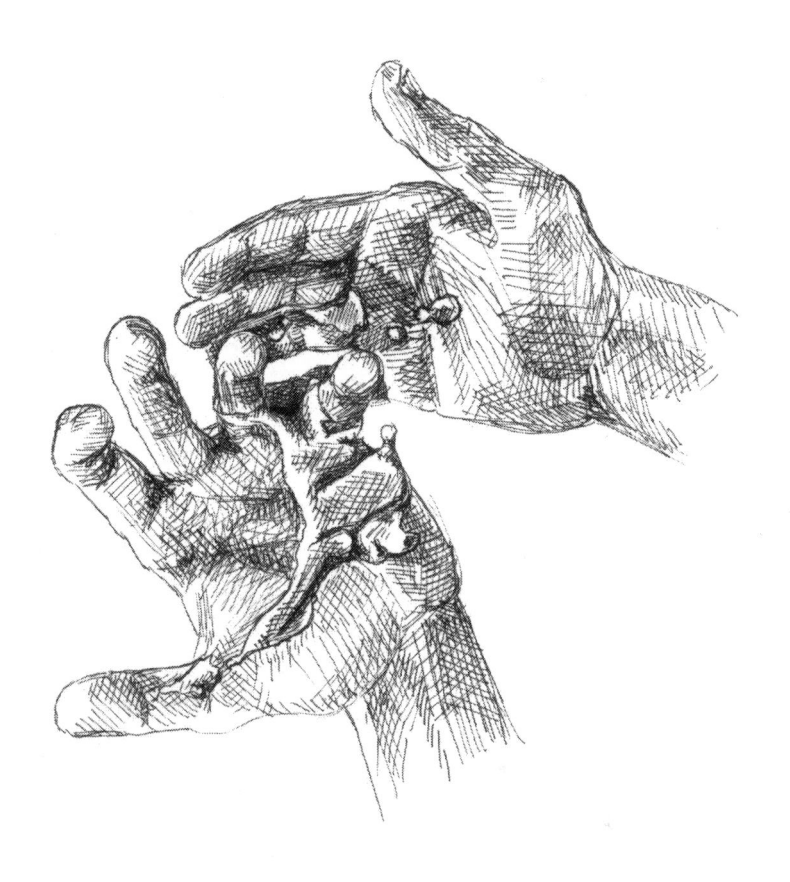

metal would hold its shape and go down in a chunk. Somehow mercury was putting on a front, acting one way while trying to hide what it really was.

When Hatta woke up that morning, he had known he would never save the kingdom—definitely a blue day. Not bright blue like bluebells or vibrant like a sparkling lake, but steely blue like a cloudy winter morning. It was difficult to make it through such days, but there was one glimmer of hope. If things went according to plan, he would soon create again.

A particularly loud bubble from the molten tin caught Hatta's attention.

One part mercury, four parts tin, Hatta reminded himself. He poured the vial of mercury into the smelted tin and stirred. Using a measuring ladle, he scooped the mixture onto glass in flat molds. The polished liquid spread to fill every nook and corner. He wanted to touch the reflective surface as he had done with the mercury, but knew he would burn himself and risk marring the perfect lining.

Master Aker entered the workshop and examined Hatta's work. The mercury mirrors were the clearest mirror they made, a significant improvement over plain tin mirrors. In other parts of the kingdom, silver mirrors were available, but they were much too expensive for a town like Shey's Orchard.

"You've learned quickly, Hatta. I have to admit I was skeptical at first."

Hatta smiled. In one week he'd become proficient at the basics of mirror making and already felt unfulfilled. Every mirror Master Aker made was plain—either rectangular or oval with very simple frames. Hatta longed to make something special, something unique.

"I thank you, Master Aker." Hatta forced a smile.

"You can call me Aker. You realize that, right?"

"Yes." He shrugged and added, "Habit." Without the memory trick, he could still forget Master Aker's name, embarrassing both of them.

"I'm fortunate you showed up in town just when I needed help. You're a hard worker and always cheerful."

"That was quite serendipitous," said Hatta. At least he was seen as happy, no matter the truth. He didn't want the turmoil in his head to show, and the cheerful persona came easiest. Whatever madness he felt had to be veiled. Mad people caused problems. Conflict. And Hatta couldn't abide conflict.

As Master Aker inspected the final mirror, he said, "No one's as happy about you being here as Lily, though. Lora didn't mind so much, but Lily actually hates this kind of work."

"How wonderful," said Hatta. If the daughter was happy, Adella, the goodwife, was most likely happy. If Adella was happy, Master Aker was surely happy. It was a good time to ask.

"Master Aker, a favor?"

"Sure, Hatta. What is it?"

"I'd like to make some mirrors."

Master Aker glanced at Hatta's work with a confused look.

Hatta said, "No, I'd like to make some mirrors of my own making. I have . . . ideas."

"If you buy your own supplies, I have no problem with you using the shop in the evenings."

Hatta was thrilled. "Oh perfect! And I can sell them in your shop? You can keep the money, of course."

"If you sell any mirrors, you'll keep most of the money. But I have to warn you, people in Shey's Orchard are very conservative. Even the merchants that come from the Provinces are only interested in simple designs. I traveled to Palassiren last year and saw some fine work, much of it finely styled. But folks in the city are different than here."

Hatta barely heard the warning. He was already planning his designs. All the reservations about the day were gone. After all, his mirrors just might be the key to saving the kingdom. He liked the sound of it.

My mirrors.

That night he poured over his sketches under the flicker of lamplight. Filled with inspiration, he created new and wonderful designs no one had ever imagined. The sun had set hours before, but Hatta was energized. When his ideas for designs began to dry up, he started constructing a new frame. This one would be neither rectangular nor oval. It would be new. It would be his.

As he worked on the multi-curved frame, the workshop grew brighter. His inspiration filled the workshop with radiance, and he felt someday his influence would reach every corner of the world.

His exhilaration was disturbed by the sound of the door opening.

Who would come into the workshop in the middle of the night? he wondered.

"Have you been at this all night?" asked Master Aker.

Hatta didn't know what he meant. Why was Master Aker out of bed when he should be sleeping? In the brilliant jumble of mirror ideas, he couldn't find an answer.

"Hatta? Have you slept at all?"

He shook his head. "Why would I..." Hatta couldn't tell if the light in the workshop was a result of his superlative creativity or if the sun had risen.

Master Aker groaned. "If you're going to do your own projects, you've got to be ready to work in the morning. You're no good to me falling asleep all day."

"Yes, I..." Reality was fading, a worse reality trying to take its place. They collided, and Hatta couldn't tell exactly what was real. Eyes downcast, he said, "I had no idea."

With a sigh, Master Aker muttered, "Just when I think..." but he didn't finish the sentence. "Get a couple hours sleep, Hatta. Tonin's in town today. I'll wake you when he makes it over here."

Hatta felt like he would never need sleep again, but in no way would he argue with Master Aker so he retired to his small quarters at the back of the workshop. In his bed the image of his yet-to-be first mirror filled his mind, and joy made sleep elusive. He must have dozed eventually because Master Aker's knock woke him at some point.

Tonin waited in the shop, inspecting the mirrors he had purchased. The burly merchant traveled from Hannil Province to towns throughout the southern half of the kingdom, selling supplies to craftsmen and carrying their wares to other towns.

Hatta wrapped a dozen mirrors in the sheepskins Tonin provided, secured them with twine, and then carried each one to the wagon. In the meantime, Master Aker and Tonin bartered for the supplies. Hatta was thrilled to see two large vials of mercury among the goods; a portion of it would be used in *his* mirrors.

While Master Aker and Tonin finished their business, Hatta climbed into the trader's wagon and rummaged through the piles of commodities. Tools, brushes, hoops, dyes, cups, dishes, and a thousand other things. Just when he'd given up on finding anything unique, he pulled a pouch of some silvery blue soil from the bottom of a barrel. It wasn't powder; it was too coarse and earthy, liked crushed ore, but unlike any he had seen.

Outside the wagon, it gave off a silvery blue sheen in the sunlight. He'd only seen that kind of color in fish scales. Master Aker and the trader were in the middle of a conversation, so Hatta said, "Pardon my interruption. What could this be?"

"If the man who sold it to me can be trusted, it's cobalt ore. Similar to iron, says he. I've been carrying it for over a year and have yet to find an artisan with a use for it."

Hatta ran his fingers through the pulverized ore. The color did not cling to his fingers as dye would. It was exactly the zest his mirrors needed. "You've found an artisan with a use for it!" In his high spirits, referring to himself as an artisan was thrilling.

"Give me half a penny, and I'll be glad to lighten my load."

Hatta pulled his eyes away from the curious ore just long enough to count out ten cuppies.

"Would you be interested in any other colors? I've got a few more shades somewheres."

That was enough to rip Hatta's attention from his discovery, and he nodded enthusiastically.

Tonin disappeared into the dim interior of the enclosed wagon. Though his girth filled the wagon from one side to the other, he somehow found room to rustle around. Hatta waited anxiously, listening to clinks, bangs, thuds, and creaks until he finally heard, "Aha!"

When Tonin squeezed out of the wagon's narrow doorway, half a dozen pouches filled his arms.

A treasure, each one.

The trader opened the pouches to reveal contents similar to the bluish ore but in a rainbow of colors: magenta, saffron, aquamarine, lime, lilac, and plum. Hatta couldn't remember ever feeling happier. The trader gladly accepted more than half of Hatta's meager savings, oblivious to the fact that his unique ores might someday be pivotal in saving the kingdom.

CHAPTER 7

Swine

The rough wood in one hand and familiar knife handle in the other helped Chism channel his anxiety. He wandered the cold streets of Knobbes, whittling to kill time. It was better than sitting in his room counting the wooden planks in the wall or rubbing leather strips until his thumbs bled.

Knobbes, the capital of Far West Province, was the biggest city he'd ever seen besides Palassiren itself. The captain of the garrison at the city walls claimed there were no rooms for the Elite squadron, so they found and inn in the city. Lieutenant Fahrr was furious, claiming it was a sign of the growing tension between the Provinces and the interior of the kingdom, but he had no authority to press the issue.

Most of the squadron was thrilled to board at an inn. They hadn't seen a decent city in the two months since lodging in Brito and they couldn't reach the tavern of the Borderhaven Inn fast enough. Chism, on the other hand, abhorred alehouses of any type. He didn't care about the judgmental glares of the tavern owners or spending a few cuppies—but giving up his self-control to a mug was beyond his understanding. Drink had only ever been a destructive influence in his life.

He snaked through the city, his attention divided between his carving and his surroundings. Thirsty hung at his hip, his closest friend and perfect companion to wander through dark streets with. In certain areas of the city, strong odors of garbage and human waste dominated. In others, cookpots slung over hearthfires filled the air with enticing aromas.

In a more populated part of the city, dozens of people exited a theater. Chism stopped thirty paces down the well-lit street to observe. Everyone wore rich fabrics and jewels. Some were accompanied by personal guards. Chism continued to carve away his small block of wood as he stood in the shadows.

The sixty-fourth and last person to leave the theater was a portly man with pale hair and an air of self-importance. He was accompanied by a fancy Lady and three armed men dressed in the dark uniforms of Far West Province, complete with the Flame and Stars crest. The woman took tiny steps, resting one gloved hand lightly on the portly man's forearm. She had pursed lips and raised eyebrows and was careful not to touch anyone or anything as they made their way toward a waiting carriage.

Having three guards struck Chism as odd. It seemed like a peculiar number. Two or four would have been much more comfortable. They didn't even surround their employer evenly—two walked to the left of the couple, and the other strolled casually to his right. Their hands hung lazily at their sides.

Suddenly, a short, dirty woman dressed in a rough smock detached herself from the shadows of a nearby doorway and knelt in front of the nobleman. She had sharp features and dark, bristly hair that reminded Chism of the peccaries from Lord Captain Darieus's museum. The peccary-woman gripped the noble's robe in her hands before the guards intervened. Chism left his observation point and quietly approached.

The woman spoke loudly enough for Chism to overhear. "My Lord, my sow was robbed away."

The finely dressed Lady looked on the stocky, kneeling woman as if *she* were the sow. As the guards surrounded her, the nobleman kicked her hands away from him. With their noses turned away so they wouldn't have to smell her, he led his Lady around the figure on the ground and said, "Take it up with the earl. I am a duke; I don't judge *pig* disputes." He said the word "pig" as if it made his mouth dirty.

I should have recognized Duke Jaryn, thought Chism.

Peccary continued her plea. "But m'Lord, the earl is him that sent his men to make off with her. He won't see me, and I've no man of my own to take up the matter."

With his back to her, the duke responded, "Most likely it was claimed as a rightful tax on your miserable farm."

"I pays my taxes. I even offered a hog instead. A healthy yearling at that. But they took the sow and now I've no means of meat to feed my family."

When the duke ignored her pleading, the kneeling woman added, "Please, my Lord."

Duke Jaryn stopped but continued to face the road ahead of him. Chism was close enough to hear an exasperated sigh.

"I told you, I do not deal with swine, you filthy woman. I have borders to guard and thousands upon thousands of citizens to protect. Appeal to the earl and leave me alone. Unless you'd like to try to feed your piglets from a prison cell?"

Before she could respond, Chism spoke up. "She said she's already appealed to the earl. My Lord." He stood close enough to be heard without raising his voice. The three soldiers grasped the hilts of their swords.

Duke Jaryn finally showed some interest. He turned slowly, sneering as he examined Chism's uniform. "I see the Elites are recruiting children now. This is none of your business, boy. Run back to your mother's skirts and let adults see to matters of the Province." He waved Chism away with a flaccid wrist.

"It's my business if you allow nobles to rob honest people."

The duke stepped toward Chism, his guards looming around him protectively. He spoke carefully, pronouncing every syllable.

"I am Duke Jaryn. Do you expect me to intervene in the matter of one worm-infested, teat-dragging sow and her pig problems?"

Ironic how much you look like a pig, Chism thought. Out loud, he said, "You solve it, or I will." Chism deliberately laid his hand on Thirsty's hilt.

Duke Jaryn's face flushed. "You dare threaten me?" he spat. "I am a duke, and you are nothing more than a pup who's discovered his bark. Your lieutenant will hear of this before morning." He turned toward the awaiting carriage but said to his guards, "Teach the mongrel a lesson, then find his lieutenant and bring him to me. Tonight."

The guards drew their blades and closed in on Chism. By the way they held their swords, Chism could tell that the guards were mediocre at best, no match for him. One hid behind his sword as he advanced, the others had them raised like sickles in the hands of farmers ready to cut wheat.

Chism felt like a blur as he stepped into the fray—a very meticulous blur. He disarmed two men and sliced the leg of the third. Chism placed the cut carefully; it would take time to heal, but the man was not ruined forever. One of the unarmed guards rushed him while the other clambered along the cobblestones after his sword. A quick sidestep and a blow to the side of the head with Thirsty's hilt dropped the first. Just as the other guard reached his sword, Chism met him and felled him with a knee to the temple. He lay as still as his companion.

Peccary huddled in a shadow. Chism switched Thirsty to his left hand and held his right out to her in a soothing gesture.

Duke Jaryn glanced over his shoulder at the commotion and was obviously surprised to see his men down and Chism advancing. He at least had the decency to send his Lady hurrying toward the carriage before turning to face Chism. Even by torchlight, the flush in his face was clearly visible. The duke's mouth opened and closed as he searched for words. The fool actually walked toward Chism.

When he finally formed coherent thoughts, his words were loud enough to summon the City Watch, but Chism didn't care. "You have no authority here! I am the ruler of this Province, you insignificant, meddling spawn of a rat!"

The duke reached Chism and stared down at him. Chism returned his gaze unflinching.

"This Sword," Chism pointed with his free hand at the Sword in the center of the emblem on his chest, "says I have the right to defend citizens of the kingdom from anyone who would break the Circle. And *this* sword," he raised Thirsty's tip to the notch at the base of Duke Jaryn's neck, "is how I defend the Circle, even from greedy and indifferent rulers."

"This is outrageous! I'll have you banished for this. You'll find out what the barbarians think about your precious Circle and Sword." Spittle flew from Duke Jaryn's mouth with each word. He swatted Thirsty away from his throat with a wildly flung arm, but Chism just spun behind the duke and kicked the back of his knees, forcing the shocked noble to the ground.

Standing behind the duke, he laid Thirsty's edge across Duke Jaryn's soft throat. Just a little more pressure would be enough to draw blood. The duke was frozen, each nervous swallow adding to the pressure of the blade on his neck.

Chism leaned close and said quietly, "It appears you need further education on the order of things. The Circle I wear represents a lawful bond between every man, woman, and child in the kingdom, from the humblest swineherd to the most arrogant noble, to King Antion himself. The Circle is sustained by the Sword. When injustice or threats appear, it becomes necessary to take the Sword in defense of the Circle."

The duke didn't budge.

Chism continued, still talking lowly in his ear. "I represent Captain Markin and the King's Council, and I represent the people of Maravilla. I care for you no more or less than I care for a crippled child in its mother's arms. What I do care for is justice. You will swear that the woman's sow will be repaid with two sows of equal value. You will swear that no vengeance will be exacted upon her or her kin. And you will swear to treat your subjects like humans, not animals."

"I'll swear no such thing," muttered the Duke, careful not to move against the blade.

"Then I'll spill your blood on the street, and your heir will have a chance to be more just than you."

"You wouldn't dare."

"I've already drawn the sword. How much worse could it be for me if I use it?"

The scuffle had attracted a small crowd. Some of the duke's fellow theater-goers and some other random citizens. Chism only paid enough mind to keep track of their number. Sixteen fancy folk, not the kind who would interfere with an Elite. Nine plainly dressed people.

Duke Jaryn didn't speak, so Chism pulled the sword even more tightly again his neck, causing the duke's breath to rasp. A quick glance revealed a slow trickle of blood along Thirsty's edge. Chism could practically feel the blade's pleasure.

"As you wish," choked the duke. Chism let up the pressure to allow him to speak. "But don't think for a moment that I am through with you, boy."

"Do what you wish to me. Just give your people the care they deserve. Now swear it so all can hear."

"Let me stand first. I'll not swear anything on my knees like a peasant."

"I just told you that you're no better than them. Now swear."

The duke made to stand, but Chism stepped on the back of his calf, forcing him to remain kneeling. Thirsty still waited at his throat, begging Chism to allow him just one deep slice. Chism was dangerously close to obliging.

After a groan of pain, the duke spoke clearly. "I swear that two healthy sows will be given to this *woman*. And no retribution or reprisal shall be meted to her or her kinfolk."

"And?" whispered Chism.

Duke Jaryn cleared his throat. "And I shall endeavor to treat all subjects with dignity."

"Fail to keep your vow and I'll kill you without a second thought." Chism shoved Duke Jaryn sideways, sprawling the fat man onto the cobbled street.

As he walked away, Duke Jaryn shouted, "Lady Palida and King Antion will hear of this! And Lady Cuora, curse her!"

Chism didn't spare a glance for the humiliated noble. The onlookers, now twenty-eight in number, parted without speaking, none of them bold enough to risk a confrontation. Even the four men who wore the armbands of the Knobbes City Watch melted away from Chism's determined march. He barely reached the shoulders of many of the men, but they cringed as though he were a giant.

Though he had left his anger behind, Chism's heart pounded in his chest as he counted the steps back to the inn, silently marking every other footfall: *two, four, six, eight, ten, twelve*. At step seven hundred and forty he rounded a corner, bringing the Borderhaven into view. In order to avoid the other Elites, he decided to use the back door. Step eight hundred and eighty brought him to the stone landing of the inn, and a handful of forced shortened steps left the number of paces since leaving Duke Jaryn lying in the street to an even eight hundred and eighty-eight. The outing had been a total success.

Chism knew there would be a cost for the night's actions, but the improvement in the lives of the people of the Far West Province would, he hoped, far surpass whatever recriminations lay ahead for him. Within minutes, a commotion arose in the tavern downstairs.

The words were too vague to make out. They came from numerous pitched voices. If a fight broke out, Chism could be downstairs almost immediately. Eventually the inn quieted. Footsteps approached and someone tried the door but it was locked.

Chism half expected Ulrik to be the one to fetch him, but instead he heard his Fellow's voice.

"Chism, open the door."

Still dressed in his Elite uniform, Chism calmly opened the door.

Ander's nearly white hair hung loose to his shoulders. "Maggots and mice, Chism! What'd you do?" It didn't sound like a question.

"Where's Lieutenant Fahrr?"

"He's looking for someone really important to pick a fight with. Oh wait, you've already assaulted the biggest man in the twelve Provinces and saved him the hassle." Ander rubbed his hands through his hair and muttered something under his breath.

The lieutenant would probably be in his quarters so Chism walked toward the stairs.

Ander fell into step behind him. "I really hope you're not stripped of the Sword and Circle after this one. I thought you were in our quarters until a full brigade of the Watch showed up, swords drawn and crying for your head. You're lucky we were downstairs or they would have been in your room!"

No, they're *lucky.* Defending a single doorway against a crowd of so-called soldiers would have been a simple task. Only one man at a time could fit through, while the others, trying to force their way in, would cause that one to be off balance. One or two dead bodies would hinder any further attempts to enter as the others scrambled over their fallen companions to get at him. Chism could defend his room indefinitely.

Ander continued. "Even so, we barely stopped them. You have no idea how close to a pitched battle we came, right there in the dayroom. Against soldiers from one of our own Provinces! Everyone had weapons drawn, and the citizens couldn't get out fast enough. It was like a tinder pile just waiting for a spark. The whole squadron is standing guard in front of the door, but I don't know if that will stop the Watch from trying something. Things were tense before, but this might well be what it takes to split the kingdom."

Chism said nothing as they reached the second floor. Lieutenant Fahrr's Fellow, Idam, stood at the end of the hallway in front of double doors. Chism approached and saluted, but the Fellow just sneered back at him. After a few uncomfortable moments, Idam turned and went into Lieutenant Fahrr's room, leaving Chism and Ander waiting outside.

"A duke," Ander muttered. "You don't do anything by halves, may your fingernails curl."

The doors flew open, revealing Lieutenant Fahrr. Though he didn't speak, his unkempt hair and puffing cheeks said enough. He looked ready to lay hands on Chism.

Lieutenant Fahrr pointed into the room; Chism hurried inside. Antagonizing his lieutenant further would accomplish nothing. He stood at attention in the center of the upscale room and heard Ander take his place behind him and to the right.

The doors slammed, and the lieutenant huffed back and forth in front of them. When he finally gained a semblance of control, he faced Chism and barked, "Do you have a mote of sense in that hot head of yours? What possessed you to attack the duke?"

Chism was not sure if the question was rhetorical, so he stared straight ahead. Despite the hornets' nest he had stirred, he still hadn't found any regrets.

"Answer me!"

"Duke Jaryn is a threat to the Circle, Sir. He fails to protect his citizens from other nobles when it's within his power and his explicit duty." Just as Chism's brother had failed to protect Chism.

"So you tried to cut off his head? Ulrik is right about you; you're out of control. You make me regret requesting you for my squad."

The comment stung. Chism's whole life was being a worthy Elite and defending the Circle and Sword. He had been slated to join Bandersnatch Squadron. As a brand-new lieutenant, Fahrr wanted to make an impression, so he'd taken a chance on young Chism. He made no secret about his intent to lead them to a top ten squadron.

Surely Lieutenant Fahrr understood Chism's reasons on some level. The intentions behind what he had done. But his eyes showed no understanding.

The shame of Lieutenant Fahrr's comment weighed on Chism; he had to try to deflect it.

"Sir, if I had tried to cut off his head, Far West Province would be looking for a new ruler right now."

It wasn't a lie, but apparently it wasn't what Lieutenant Fahrr wanted to hear because he threw his hands up and turned away. When he looked back, there was hurt on his face. "This is way above me, Son. My only option is to take you back to Palassiren to stand before Captain Markin and, most likely, the entire Council. We both know this can't end well for you, but I need to know right now: Are you going to give me trouble if I try to take you back to the capital?"

The question reflected the immense respect Chism had for his lieutenant. People often thought Chism was as unpredictable as a wounded badger, but he would always deal straightly with the only man who'd treated him like a son.

Just when he was about to promise compliance and seal his fate, Ander spoke up. "Sir, permission to speak to Chism alone."

The lieutenant stared at the Fellow with curiosity. "Make it quick." He waved them out.

Back in the hallway, Ander spoke in hushed tones. "He's right, Chism. There's no way this ends well for you if you go back to Palassiren. Lady Palida will side with the Provinces, Lady Cuora will call for your head before you even walk in the room, and when it comes to politics, Captain Markin has as much spine as an earthworm. He'll never stand up to them to defend you."

As usual, Ander's argument was solid, but Chism saw no other option. "What choice do I have? I won't fight Elites. We all make choices, Ander, and I've made mine."

"There are other options. Ask Lieutenant Fahrr to exile you instead. Beg forgiveness from Duke Jaryn, may ticks discover his nethers." Ander's eyes were pleading. Sad and serious. "Slip away and disappear. The squadron is at the front door watching the Watch—may they never enjoy offspring—but the back door is unguarded."

The idea of staying alive appealed to Chism; he could do no good for anyone if his head ended up separated from his body. But all of Ander's suggestions meant losing the Circle and the Sword. He wasn't willing to give them up, even in exchange for his life, if the slightest chance of retaining both existed.

Without giving Ander an answer, Chism opened the lieutenant's door and said, "There will be no trouble, Sir. I placed the sword and I'll follow it through."

For the briefest moment, Chism thought he saw a sheen in his lieutenant's eyes, but the older man turned away too quickly to be sure. After clearing his throat, he said, "Make ready. We ride in one hour. Idam, give Sub-lieu Oply the order. The men can pack in turns to keep the guard up. Have the ostler and porter prepare the Elite horses, then return to their rooms. They can follow us with the cook and groom in a few days; they're in no danger. If Jaryn wants us out of his Province, we'll oblige him."

Lieutenant Fahrr didn't turn back, and Chism knew he was dismissed. He led Ander back up the stairs.

Once their things were packed, Chism and Ander went to the inn's dayroom. Some chairs and tables were wedged against the door as a barricade. Chism settled into a chair to wait. Repeated calls to turn the boy over to the Watch filtered through the front doors.

Elites passed in pairs, returning to their rooms to make preparations. None of them could know Chism's reasons for assaulting the duke yet. Most ignored him, but some gave him disgusted looks as they passed.

Only Ulrik spoke. "It's about time we lost the deadweight. I always knew you were nothing but a thirteen."

Chism's chair clattered to its back as he shot to his feet. Ander stood between them, but that wasn't what held Chism back. Only his promise to Lieutenant Fahrr kept him from attacking Ulrik. Leaving the chair where it lay, he paced until the lieutenant entered the dayroom.

Lieutenant Fahrr spoke to the squadron. "Is any man unwilling to fight for a brother?"

Chism expected everyone in the squadron to speak up. No one did.

"Even a brother who has made poor choices and placed us in jeopardy?" Still no answer. Chism couldn't believe it. "Good. The Watch outnumbers us three to one, and they want blood. But an attack on one wearing the Circle and the Sword is an attack on the king and kingdom. We are one body, and we'll fight to defend each and every member."

Spear butts pounded on the floor and swords rapped on shields in agreement. The first twinge of guilt bit at Chism. His own life and limbs he'd been willing to risk, not the whole squadron's.

The barrage on the doors grew louder and the tables shook under the impact. "Out the back to the stables," said Lieutenant Fahrr. "We'll proceed in double riding order, Chism and Ander in third position instead of last. Elites draw steel, Fellows carry the packs."

Two members of the Watch waited at the back door, but fled when they saw the full squadron, weapons drawn, emptying into the alley. By the time the Watch arrived in force, the Elites and Fellows had barricaded themselves into the large stables. Heavy wooden doors resisted the pounding of the men outside, but they wouldn't hold for long. Fortunately, the horses were prepared, and within moments the soldiers were ready.

Lieutenant Fahrr took the lead, and Chism and Ander lined up behind Hile and his Fellow. Elites formed the outside of the four-wide column with their Fellows next to them in the center—the best place for their spears, throwing knives, arrows and darts. If it came to that. Chism and Ander were the only exception. Ander brandished Thirsty while Chism carried Ander's spear and the packs.

No sooner were they seated in their saddles with sacks secured than Lieutenant Fahrr lifted the beam that barred the doors. The dark-clad procession of Elites rode into the cobbled street.

Dozens of men wearing the armbands of the Knobbes City Watch crowded on them, torches raised, eyes searching for Chism. From his position at the center of the formation, Chism caught occasional glimpses of the scene but remained mostly hidden. Three to one might be an understatement of the Watch's advantage, and they weren't the only threat. Scores of citizens—he couldn't get an accurate count due to the blocked view—stood in positions of safety but still yelled for the blood of the boy who had threatened their ruler. From what Chism knew of Far West Province, it was more proof of the rejection of the interior, than it was affection for Duke Jaryn.

Though the Watch attempted to bar the way, Lieutenant Fahrr maintained a steady pace toward the city gates. The well-trained horses of the Elites remained calm amidst the mounting hostility.

Cries of "Surrender the traitor!" "Death to the Elites!" and "Down with Lady Cuora!" rose from all around, but the convoy did not slow. More citizens appeared around each corner, adding numbers to the mob.

Frustrated by their inability to slow the soldiers, a large group surged forward with staffs.

"Deflect weapons but do not attack!" Lieutenant Fahrr ordered. The command was passed down the line to soldiers in the rear.

From his position at the center of the formation, Chism couldn't do anything. Hiding like a frightened rabbit was not in his nature. He itched to grab Thirsty from Ander's hand and cut a path through the dark Watch armbands and anyone else who prevented their escape. Lieutenant Fahrr had been wise to bind him with his word.

A fist-sized rock flew over the first rows of soldiers, striking Ulrik's Fellow square in the chest. He didn't have time to dwell on the injury because the stone was followed by an increasing barrage of rocks, bricks, roof slates. Anything within reach.

The squadron had only covered two blocks. Soon the mob and Watch would find their way to upstairs windows, and the painful stones would become fatal arrows and crossbow bolts. Lieutenant Fahrr forced the horses to a trot.

The mob still pressed them, Watch and city folk mingled into a single enraged mass. A body passed under Chism's horse's hooves, then another. He couldn't tell if it was Watchman or citizen, man or woman. A brick caught Chism on the shoulder, and he grabbed his pommel to steady himself as the barrage of projectiles continued.

The squadron didn't slow, and Chism's horse trampled yet another body that had been ridden down by the leaders of the pack. Each step left a trail of blood on the grey cobbles, blood of the people of Knobbes mingling with the blood of the King's Elite.

Chism swore inwardly. *I was trying to protect you, you fools!*

The horses' pace increased, as did the number of bodies who fell under the horses. The trot became a canter, then a full gallop, leaving the people to hurl acrimonious curses at their backs as the Elites gained some distance. Some damage was done, and while they all still held their saddles, many of the Elites bled. At least the carnage was over.

Relief only lasted until they reached the twenty-foot walls of the city. Eighteen torches lined the parapet wall on either side of the gates. The Elites slowed to a walk a hundred paces from the gatehouse. The massive wooden doors stood open, and the first portcullis was raised, inviting them to ride into the tunnel-like sally port of the gatehouse. But in the shadows on the far side, Chism saw the grill of another heavy portcullis. The gaps in the metal lattice allowed enough room for a spear or an arm, but not even a scrawny boy could squeeze through the gaps in the gate. The Watch's plan was as painfully obvious as it was deadly. If the Elites rode into the sally port, the inner portcullis would drop, trapping the Elites and leaving them at the mercy of the arrows, spears, stones, and boiling oil of the Watch. The gatehouse was designed to repel attackers from without, but it also served as an efficient means of preventing escape.

As soon as they were within shouting distance, the Elites pulled up in their square column. Twenty-six Watch members, holding bows and spears, lined the superior fighting position of the walls. Chism's view of those on the ground was still limited, but he counted at least thirty, all with swords drawn. More trickled toward the gate from side streets to reinforce the guard that held it. It was only a matter of time until the mob caught up from behind. The men of the Watch would restrain themselves until given orders to attack, but an angry mob of citizens that had just seen friends trampled by the Elites' horses would not demonstrate such self-control.

A large group of well-mounted men came into view from the street that led west along the base of the wall. They wore the Flame and Stars of Far West and surrounded a portly, blond-haired man. Duke Jaryn had arrived.

CHAPTER 8

Escape

*D*uke Jaryn led his horse deliberately past his guards and sneered at the Elites. His horse looked strong enough to kick a hole through the city's stone walls. It would have to be that strong, considered Chism, to carry the large duke all day. The torches, mostly behind and above him on the walls, painted his face in shadow, giving him a demonic appearance. He stayed far enough away from the Elites to allow the bowmen on the wall to cover him. Despite the bandage around his neck, flippant delight showed on his face.

"Leaving so soon, Lieutenant? Did the hospitality of our city not meet your expectations?"

"You dare detain us?" demanded Lieutenant Fahrr with honest surprise in his voice. "An attack on soldiers of the king will not go without retribution."

Chism scanned the wall and gates for any chance of escape or advantage. Nothing in any direction offered hope. They were stuck deeper than a pig in a well.

Jaryn knew exactly how strong his position was. "Attack?"

He acted shocked. "You are free to leave at any time, and your men with you."

"Open the portcullis and we'll be on our way." Most men obeyed Lieutenant Fahrr without question, but Jaryn's sneer just deepened.

"Nothing would give me greater pleasure than to see your horses' backsides as you run from my Province. I'll gladly give the order as soon as you hand over the boy."

"He'll be escorted to Palassiren to stand before the King and Council. They'll decide his fate, not you."

With a mock pained expression, Duke Jaryn said, "I'm afraid I can't allow that. King Antion and his Council have shown they are unconcerned with our problems here in Far West. The boy king has proven as neglectful as his father and twice as incompetent. Besides, the crime occurred in Far West. My Province, my jurisdiction. You will turn over the impudent brat and leave. You and your ilk are no longer welcome."

"Would you permanently reject the protection of the king over a matter as simple as where my man faces justice?"

"Your *man*?" The duke chortled, which set his jowls quivering around the bandage. "Your thirteen, you mean." In a voice he obviously used for giving speeches, Duke Jaryn continued. "The time is far past that the Provinces should have cast off the derelict interior. If the taxes we sent to the capital were spent on our own militias, we could secure our border for good."

"You don't need a war with the interior to go with the other problems facing this Province."

Duke Jaryn barked a laugh. "Do not presume to offer me advice on ruling my Province. Hand over the runt and be off."

A clatter from behind caught Chism's attention. The mob, as angry as before but emboldened by the night and the Elites' trapped position, was within sight. He had to act if no one else would.

The wall was impenetrable and too well-guarded. The city had other gates, but they would be defended with portcullises and guards of their own. The only way out was through the narrow gatehouse. He studied the portcullis in the flickering light. Based on the city defense training he had received as an Elite, the metal gate appeared to be a standard portcullis. The mechanism was most likely a typical counterweight with a wheel and chains.

Glancing back, he saw the mob closing the gap fast. Lieutenant Fahrr would never willingly abandon him, even to save the rest of the squadron. If Chism didn't act immediately, the squadron would be killed, along with scores of citizens and Watchmen.

Thirsty called to Chism from Ander's grasp, and it chafed Chism that the sword couldn't solve the impasse. Forcing Ander's spear into the Fellow's hand, he whispered, "Lean this just inside the gatehouse as you leave the city."

Surprised, Ander replied, "Lean it yourself. I'm not leaving without you."

There was no time for argument. "If *you* don't leave, *I* will die. It's your choice." Chism urged his horse forward. He heard Ander curse, something about incurable flatulence, then slam the butt of the spear against the stony street.

By the time Chism pushed through the Elites to Lieutenant Fahrr's side, the mob was only five hundred paces away.

"Sir, I told you there would be no trouble. I have a plan, but you'll have to trust me enough to leave me behind."

Lieutenant Fahrr stared at him, searching for answers on Chism's face.

"Trust me, Sir. I won't surrender."

Chism heard indistinct shouts and threats from the mob. Precious little time remained, and Lieutenant Fahrr was wasting it deliberating. Anger like flames burned inside Chism, but he forced calmness. He hadn't been this furious since the day he'd killed his father. That wasn't an option in this case; the man responsible for the situation was too well defended.

A nod from Lieutenant Fahrr was all Chism needed. With his arms spread wide, Chism advanced his horse into the breach between the two forces. A victorious grin spread across Duke Jaryn's face.

Chism spoke to the duke. "I will surrender as soon as my squadron is safely outside the city walls. As you can see, I'm unarmed."

Duke Jaryn was ecstatic. "Your bravery has bought the life of these men, but will count little when you face my justice." He waved one arm toward the gate house. "Open the portcullis!" As an afterthought, he called to his archers, "If the runt attempts to run, shoot him!"

Two members of the Watch disengaged from their position to raise the gate. Chism stole a glance up the street. Three hundred paces.

Cursing the mob, the Watch, and the Elites, Chism thought, *Hurry, you fools! The timing has to be perfect.*

Lieutenant Fahrr led his men forward but kept an inquisitive eye on Chism. Though concern showed on his face, Chism also saw a fury that mirrored his own. Appropriate—a large part of it was directed at him for surrendering. Surprise and confusion registered on the faces of Elites and Fellows as they reluctantly followed their leader toward the gatehouse. All except Ander. Ander's look held exasperation and anger. His lips moved, but Chism couldn't make out the words over the clatter of hooves on stone and the cries of the mob.

Chism could imagine the Elites' internal conflict—torn between abandoning a brother and refusing to follow orders. The Elites were a brotherhood, and the worst crime one could commit was to betray a brother of the Circle and Sword. Yet Chism gave them no clear choice. If they ever forgave him for the assault on the duke, they would never forgive this. Especially Ander. A Fellow could be stripped of his rank and whipped for abandoning his Elite.

Unless by some miracle his plan worked.

Chism waited, showing open palms as his squadron entered the gatehouse. Ander casually leaned the spear against the stone wall just inside, and it blended into shadows. The men who had raised the portcullis on the other side of the gatehouse returned to their position inside the city walls, away from the levers that would allow the heavy gates to fall. But there was still a chance that a hidden switch could trip both portcullises, slamming them shut and trapping the entire group inside the gatehouse at the mercy of the Watch.

Lieutenant Fahrr passed the outer portcullis, free from the city. Chism breathed a sigh of relief and nudged his horse forward at a slow walk. Not toward the open gate, but toward the Duke.

The mob was only a hundred paces behind.

"Stop and dismount if you want protection from them," ordered Duke Jaryn, motioning to the mob. They were close enough for Chism to hear the anger in their curses.

Half of the Elites were past the gatehouse. Chism continued forward. For the first time since the standoff began, Duke Jaryn's face showed concern. He was a mere fifteen paces from Chism.

"Stop where you are!" he shouted.

Chism paid no mind. From fifty paces, the mob sounded like it numbered in the hundreds. Chism fought the urge to turn and count them.

Duke Jaryn pulled on his reins, trying to distance himself from Chism, and yelled, "Bowmen, take aim and fire if he does not stop in three—"

Thirty paces.

"—two—"

Twenty paces.

"—one!" With a face empty of everything but fear, the Duke raised a hand, even though Chism could never reach him in time. The mob would close within moments.

The last of the Elites cleared the portcullis as the front of the mob reached Chism. Clubs beat his legs, arms scrabbled to dismount him, and stones struck his back.

With reluctance, Chism put the slightest amount of faith in the Duke. *He won't open fire while I'm surrounded by citizens.*

A tight grip on the reins, a sharp kick to his horse's flank, and a tug to the left sent Chism careening toward the gatehouse. Both he and the horse ignored the grabbing men that tried to block the way.

"Don't shoot!" ordered Duke Jaryn. "Close the portcullis! Close the portcullis! Drop the gate!" His voice rose in pitch with each command. The last view Chism caught of Duke Jaryn, and the image that would remain in his memory, was the duke shouting spittle from atop his horse, jowls quaking and pudgy arms waving wildly in the air.

The two men who had opened the portcullis raced to carry out the Duke's orders. They entered the gatehouse well before Chism, who was now clear of the mob. Archers fired from the wall, but the steep angle made it a difficult shot.

The first man reached one of the heavy levers when Chism was two strides away from the first portcullis. He yanked the bar and the heavy gate plunged downward. Chism ducked under the falling points at the bottom of the portcullis and seized Ander's spear. Pain shot into Chism's right thigh. Chism hesitated, confused. The portcullis had missed him. He was inside the gatehouse with a heavy iron gate separating him from the Watch and mob in the city.

But there was no time for pain. The second lever was only two paces past the first, and the other man pulled it before Chism had a chance to drop him with the spear.

It was impossible for his horse to cover the fifteen paces before the outer gate fell. Already it creaked downward, the sound of a solid chain passing around pulley wheels clanging through the gatehouse tunnel. Man and horse continued at a full gallop, and Chism let the spear fly toward the mechanism. It lodged with a grinding *CLANGK* in the turning wheel, arresting the gate in midair.

Chism tried to lean to his left so he and the horse could duck under the motionless portcullis, but something pulled at his right thigh. His leg was stuck to the saddle, and tremors of pain shot through him when he tried to move it.

He pulled his horse up with just enough time to avoid the gate. In the dim light of the gatehouse he saw a thick wooden shaft adorned with feathers protruding a few inches above his knee. An arrow. All the way through his leg and buried in his saddle. It prevented him from leaning over. The gate was high enough for a riderless horse to exit, but there was no way to get low enough without separating himself from the saddle.

One guard moved toward Chism with a drawn sword while the other began working the mechanism of the inner portcullis to raise it. The mob, eager for his blood, pressed angrily at the rising gate. One man lay on his belly, trying to wriggle under. None of them had bows or crossbows. Yet.

Chism considered subduing the two guards, then raising the outer portcullis, but then he remembered that he was bound to his saddle and weaponless. He couldn't do anything until he freed his leg.

Grasping the arrow with both hands, Chism snapped the shaft, trying unsuccessfully to keep the lower portion stationary. Working so close to something sticking all the way through his leg was sickening. He threw the fletched end of the arrow at the approaching guard, but it barely made him flinch. The guard was only a few paces away and would soon be joined by the crowd at the gate. Already the crawling man was half way through, and others were bending to duck under.

Chism placed both hands under his knee and, with a gut-deep bellow, heaved upward. The splintered shaft scraped the inside of his leg like a thousand claws and for a moment the pain was so intense he thought he saw colors. But he was free. He swung his injured leg over the horse and crouched in the left stirrup. Urging his horse forward, he left the Watch and mob behind.

The outer portcullis passed overhead. If Chism could just avoid the arrows from the city wall, he'd truly be free. Well, free to face the headman's block in Palassiren.

Staying low, he swung his leg up, placing it crooked in the saddle next to the broken arrow. He started to lead his galloping horse into a meandering pattern when a magnificent sight distracted him. Still on horseback, six Fellows were lined up, facing the walls of Knobbes. With speed only possible for the best bowmen in the kingdom, they loosed arrow after arrow toward the parapets, forcing the Watch's archers to keep their heads down. Only sporadic, inaccurate shots made their way from the wall.

Chism's rash actions had endangered the entire squadron, and now they were risking their lives to protect his retreat. More proof that friendship was irrelevant where brotherhood existed.

The six Fellows pinned down at least two dozen of the Watch in an elevated position. Chism smiled. Even numbers. Always better than odd ones.

As he passed, Chism heard one more round of arrows fly, then half a dozen horses following him. Cold air that smelled like fresh dirt poured over his sweaty face. They left the road and spread out, using the fallow winter fields to escape. Dark uniforms and a nearly moonless night would offer perfect cover from searching eyes and arrows.

Every step of the horse pounded pain into Chism's leg. He looked down and saw blood seeping from his thigh. The saddle covered the wound on the back of his leg, and he tried to staunch the bleeding from the front with one hand.

Once out of bow range, Chism angled toward the road. The other Elites stood out perfectly to Chism, but they had to use bird calls as signals to locate each other and regroup. A headcount revealed none lost, the worst injury being the hole through Chism's leg. Ander examined the wound and reported that the bleeding was steady but not profuse. Chism would live. They didn't have time to sew up the wounds, so Ander bandaged the leg tightly.

Since none of the other Elites or Fellows had life-threatening wounds, Lieutenant Fahrr led the squadron a mile further away from Knobbes before stopping to allow the men to attend to their injuries. A few torches were lit, and Chism had to cover his eyes against the blaring light. The Fellows began stitching and bandaging wounds.

"Innards and entrails!" Ander swore as he dug through his pack for sewing supplies. The man could make anything sound like a curse, and Chism had to endure a barrage of them as his Fellow cleaned and stitched the wounds on the front and back of his leg. If Ander had his way, Chism's hair would migrate from his head to his back, foul breath would prevent him from ever kissing a girl, and he would never ride a mile without swallowing a dozen gnats. Though he'd never seen Ander so angry, the curses let him know that eventually things would return to normal between them.

Once the Elites were tended to, the Fellows turned their mending skills on one another. Lieutenant Fahrr began speaking as they efficiently and quietly rendered care.

"Tonight we faced our first real test as a squadron. We are the newest squadron in the kingdom: a recently promoted

Lieutenant, a sub-lieu with no leadership experience, three Elites who have never seen battle, and the youngest soldier anywhere in the King's service. So new we don't even have a name."

The man molded human emotion like a sculptor with clay. He slowly circled the group and after the perfect pause, he said, "Tonight, we earned a name. Tonight each of you proved that you would risk your life for any other who bears the Circle and Sword. Tonight you had to trust your leader enough to walk away and allow an Elite to stand alone. I know your hearts were near to being ripped from your chest. If any of us had faltered or hesitated, we would all be dead, along with many of Knobbes's citizens. Any Elite can fight, or he would never be chosen for training. But I would rather lead a squadron that can keep its head and survive in any situation.

"This squadron will someday be a top ten squadron. It is strong as metal. Fluid as water. If we are forced to divide, we come together and meld into a single element. When we return to the capital, I will petition for the name Quicksilver Squadron. It refers to the metal mercury—our symbol of unity, flexibility, and strength."

From where he stood near his horse, Sub-lieu Oply shouted, "Hurrah for Quicksilver Squadron!"

The squadron answered, "Hurrah!"

The shout and answer were repeated twice more as Lieutenant Fahrr climbed into his saddle, followed by the rest of the men.

Chism's days as an Elite were numbered, there was no doubt. But every day he spent as a member of Quicksilver would be an honor. He glanced over his shoulder, taking one last look at the Province he had offered his life for, and realized he might be lucky just to make it back to Palassiren.

Hundreds of torches poured out of the city gates. A stream of liquid fire. Duke Jaryn hadn't given up the pursuit. The executioner's block ahead or a violent lynching behind. Ander was right. Chism never did anything half way.

CHAPTER 9

Grey

*H*atta had given up on Shey's Orchard. The days were almost all ash-blue, and the people faded steadily toward brown. The only bright colors in his life were his mirrors. Some days he stared at them for hours. After discovering the colored ores two months before, it didn't take him long to develop his style—mirrors like no one had ever seen before.

A mule and rickety cart awaited him in the night outside Aker's shop. More than twenty mirrors—wrapped in burlap, sheepskin, and even Hatta's spare clothes—filled the cart. After one last glance around the shop, Hatta turned away forever. He lifted a knapsack with food and two water skins into the cart, and he was ready for the road.

He had purchased the mule earlier in the evening from a sour young man named Steffen on an outlying farm. The cart he bought from Mikel, the citruser. The food came from three different sources. There would be no uncomfortable goodbyes, and no one would have a chance to beg him to stay. Before anyone realized it, he'd be gone.

At least the journey to Palassiren would be more enjoyable than his previous travels. He now had a companion.

Stepping up next to her, Hatta asked quietly, "Shall we be off, girl?"

A shrill bray answered him and reverberated through the quiet streets of Shey's Orchard. Apparently she felt that night was no time for travel.

"Hush," whispered Hatta. "You'll wake Master Aker." He took a step forward and tugged on the reins. The crabby animal brayed again, even louder and didn't take a step. Pulling was getting him nowhere, so Hatta moved to the back and pushed against the mule's rump.

The animal let out another irritated holler, and Master Aker burst out of his house in his nightshirt to investigate.

"What's all this, Hatta?"

This was exactly what he'd wanted to avoid.

He doffed his turtle-shell print traveling hat and said, "No disrespect taken, I hope. I'm bound for the capital, for to sell my mirrors."

"Why didn't you give us a chance to say goodbye?"

"There's a note," Hatta offered, looking into the gray dirt of the street. "I left a note. Hettie scribed it. It says, 'Thank you, Master Aker.'"

"Did we do something wrong?"

"Not to my knowledge." Hatta didn't look up.

"Is there any way to make you stay?"

This was the part Hatta couldn't take. He didn't know how to bid farewell without creating hard feelings. Why couldn't people just let relationships stay positive? Before, the road ahead had been such a promising chartreuse, a path of color leading through the grey. As he stood quarreling, he could see the color seeping out of the path. It dissipated into the night, lost forever.

Master Aker said, "You don't want to travel at night. There's wild animals about. Twice in the last year people have seen bandersnatches. One of them would've killed Lora if Tjaden hadn't found her in time."

The lecture wasn't helping. Hatta had done everything possible to avoid the situation, but here he was again. Tight-lipped and eyes down, he simply shook his head.

With a sigh, Master Aker said, "I'm sorry, Hatta. I won't ask you to change your mind. But will you wait long enough for Adella and Lily to write notes to Lora? She's probably lonely, all alone in Palassiren, what with Tjaden out doing missions . . ." The mirror maker turned his head to the side and gulped. His lips smacked, and his voice was tenuous. ". . . And we do miss her so."

Hatta nodded in the moonlight, and Master Aker hurried inside. The urge to sneak off nagged while he waited, but that would most likely create even more hard feelings. Not to mention deprive Elora of love-filled letters.

Hatta petted the mule behind her ear and said, "Kind words should never be held back or held up, only held out and handed out freely."

Over the next short while, he did his best to win her over, but the mule had none of it. Without taking a single step, she turned her head as far away from Hatta's hand as possible.

When Master Aker returned, he handed the notes to Hatta along with a small rucksack.

"It shouldn't be hard to find her; just ask for Lady Elora. There's some food and a few coins. Life's expensive in the city; I hope it helps."

Hatta thanked him and set the sack into a gap in one of the corners of the cart. Still unsure what to say, he gave Master Aker a smile and tip of his hat. He tugged on the mule's lead, but it still wouldn't budge.

"Isn't that Titus's boy's mule?" asked Master Aker. "The

trick with this one is the first step. Give her a good scritch right here," he reached down to the side of the belly. "She'll pick up that leg, and you're on your way." Sure enough, one foot came forward, and the others followed.

Hatta didn't pause, worried the animal would dig its paw in again.

No, that wasn't the right word. Master Aker said something as Hatta walked away but he was concentrating too hard to reply. Hooves. The paws of donkeys were hooves.

Hatta waved but didn't look back. He told himself everything was fine between them, and the dingy feelings started to fade. The small pouch of coins clinking at his waist was the only fanfare as they walked out of Shey's Orchard.

By the time they reached the Telavir Spoke, it was clear that the mule was going to continue to be a dismal conversationalist. She mostly ignored Hatta, but that didn't surprise him. Her personality was colorless, after all. Hatta, on the other hand, was feeling quite orange—and what color could possibly be better for starting a journey?

After the third night of travel, Hatta came across fellow travelers for the first time. He traveled at night to avoid such encounters, preferring the meetings with nocturnal animals—owls, coyotes, scalidinks, and bats. Bats were his favorite, a little scatterbrained and easily distracted.

Just after sunrise, he caught up with the slow-moving young couple. When they heard him approach, they stopped and waited for him. The man gingerly helped his wife to a seated position at the side of the road. He was hooded, but golden hair flowed out of the cloak.

"How do?" asked Hatta, tugging at the brim of his traveling hat.

"Not well, Sir," said the man. "Traveling has been arduous for my . . . wife, and the journey to Palassiren has been more treacherous than we planned. We've consumed all of our provisions."

Hatta smiled at the stranger and fetched his rations from the cart. The bag had grown quite light, and looking inside Hatta saw only a small biscuit and a strip of beef. Barely enough for a single meal. He handed the vittles to the man, but retained the sack to use as additional padding for his mirrors.

"Is this the last of your rations?"

Hatta nodded. "I regret having not more food to offer."

"But what will you eat?"

Reluctant to say that the animals would help him find food, Hatta remembered something. "Master Aker's food, of course." *The rucksack!*

Hatta hurried to the cart and dug for the forgotten sack. It sat undisturbed in the cart's corner and was heavy with enough food for at least a few days.

"There are coins as well. You could buy food from travelers or towns perchance."

"Do you have any food for yourself?"

Hatta shook his head. The man dug into the sack and produced a fist-sized block of cheese and a round of flatbread and handed them to Hatta. "If we ever have the opportunity to repay you, I pledge to do anything in my power. I'm Raouf, from Hannil Province. And you?"

"No, I'm not." A curious expression showed on Raouf's face. "Oh, Hatta. Yes, I would be Hatta." Hatta gave another smile to the stranger, then walked to where the mule waited and gave her a tickle in front of her back leg. "From T'lai," Hatta called over his shoulder, pleased with the lack of an awkward farewell.

The weather had grown colder each day, and snow spotted the shady parts of hillsides. After rearranging the packing around his mirrors, Hatta had plenty of clothes to keep him warm. No rain or snow fell on him, or on the mule for that matter, but by the animal's disposition, one would have thought Hatta was forcing her through blizzards.

The cheese and flatbread lasted one day, after which Hatta had to forage for food. The taciturn mule was useless, but a variety of other animals helped him. After chittering idly for a while, a squirrel led him to a store of nuts in the fork of an oak tree. Hatta thought the squirrel revealed the stash by mistake, but animals were so easy to read that the hidden supply was obvious. He only took a handful of the squirrel's stored nuts. If he hadn't been so hungry, he wouldn't have taken any.

When he asked a friendly doe where he might find food, she signaled a faint path that led to an enormous berry thicket. Not only did he eat his fill, he left with half a hatful. Back at the cart, he transferred them into a sack. Tubers, mushrooms, and some shriveled wild figs rounded out his diet.

On the sixth night, if Hatta counted correctly, he loaded his bedroll into the cart and began hitching the mule. She twitched her ears and angled her body in a way that told Hatta someone else was near. Soft footsteps approached from just outside of the clearing where they'd slept through the day.

He whispered to the mule, "Stay quiet and perchance they'll pass us up."

Miraculously, the cantankerous mule obeyed. Yet despite their silence, the sound of crunching leaves drew closer. Hatta looked for men and horses but only saw a greenish shadow pass through the brush toward the clearing. It crept cautiously and at times disappeared completely. The night was clear, and half a moon hung in the sky.

When the figure entered the clearing, Hatta immediately knew that it wasn't a man, but in the silvery light he had a hard time seeing exactly what it was. The creature walked upright like a man but had hoofed feet like a goat. It wore no clothes and had pale green skin, leathery like where a cow rubs a patch of hair away. Its head was bald, and dull red eyes absorbed the moonlight, the color of a dark crab or a cherry chocolate. Leading with menacing claws, it leaned forward as it stalked toward Hatta and his mule, as if ready to pounce at any moment.

Delighted, Hatta said, "You must be a bandersnatch!" Meeting new animals was probably his favorite thing ever.

The creature paused and inspected him, head bobbing slowly to get different perspectives. Unnerved by the creature's scrutiny, the mule, not yet tethered to the cart, bolted through the brush, braying and crashing as she ran.

"How do?" asked Hatta. He wasn't sure if he should extend his hand or tip his hat. Something tugged at the back of his mind, something Hettie had said about bandersnatches, but the novelty of meeting the unique animal overshadowed it.

"I greatly appreciate you not eating myself. Or the mule's self," he added, smiling. "Even though she is a disappointing traveling companion."

The bandersnatch was still, not responding in any way. Animals never spoke to Hatta with words, but their body language and actions were easy enough to interpret. Barks, chitters, tweets, neighs, and brays all had their own quality and tone that said just as much as words could.

The bandersnatch circled to one side, still wary of Hatta. *But you look like food, and you're alone.*

Unfazed, Hatta shook his head. "I can assure you assuredly that I am not food."

As it continued to approach him in a circling pattern, Hatta noticed its sharp fangs. Fangs that would cause most men to tremble. But Hatta never had trouble with any animal; this one would be no different.

I hunger. You are vulnerable.

Hatta ignored the posture. "How long have you lived? Where do you sleep? Do you ever have gatherings with many bandersnatches?"

The bandersnatch paused. *You are not running or fighting. Food runs or fights.* It showed its fangs and snarled. *Run or fight!*

With an outstretched hand, Hatta took a slow step toward the bandersnatch, causing the creature to crouch. It looked like someone loading a spring.

"Is your skin smooth or rough?" Hatta took another step. He was nearly close enough to touch it! "I predict it feels foresty."

The bandersnatch looked around the clearing and over its shoulders. The pale green skin took on a vivid red undertone, and the eyes were now the color of bright cherries. Though the creature crouched, it seemed to swell in size.

A trap. I will not be trapped.

One more step. Hatta reached out and touched the bandersnatch's forearm. It was leathery and hot and verdant.

"Frabjous," muttered Hatta.

Unfortunately he didn't have much of a chance to examine it before the creature spun and sprang out of the clearing. It disappeared so quickly that for a moment Hatta wasn't sure if it had been there or not. The mule-less cart in the clearing told him *something* had been there, and the lobster-red eyes were vivid in his memory.

Yet as much as he loved colors, they often deceived him. That was the worst part about his mad thoughts—they came to his mind in exactly the same way the most vibrant colors did. It went beyond mere sensory perception; it was accompanied by joy and feelings of certainty. Exactly like the experience with the bandersnatch before it ran.

The best experiences in Hatta's life were indistinguishable from many of the thoughts that led him to act unstably. Colors were his greatest joys, but they often led him headlong into turmoil. They just weren't trustworthy.

There was nothing to it but to go look for the mule. He could ask her about the bandersnatch. The ornery thing probably wouldn't talk to him, but it wouldn't hurt to try. And he could usually tell when animals were lying.

With a smile in his eyes and a whistle on his lips, Hatta went into the brush.

CHAPTER 10

Stripped

For a day, Quicksilver Squadron pushed the horses as hard as Chism ever had. Most of the squadron's supplies and coins were still with the cook and groom back in the city, limiting Quicksilver Squadron to the small rations and the few coins each man carried. Just enough to make it out of Far West Province if there were no delays. And no money to buy or trade horses in the small towns they passed through. If they made it out of the Province and into the interior of the kingdom, the towns would sell food and supplies on credit. They just had to make it past Portal City, which lay at the far end of Serpent Gap, four days away.

Duke Jaryn, along with the Far West Militia and many of the Knobbes City Watch, were still only a few hours behind them. They had the advantage of more resources, but they also had the disadvantage of a moving a much larger group. It wouldn't do any good for one or two soldiers to catch up with a squadron of Elites.

As soon as the sun fell, the temperature dropped quickly.

The Elites kept riding, trying to maintain their lead over the pursuers. In the darkness, Chism saw Lieutenant Fahrr slow his horse and wait as the rest of the squadron passed. He fell in next to Chism.

"I've been thinking about this all day. There's no way around it. Your standing with the squadron needs to be decided. Ultimately it's my decision, but after the way they acted, I've decided to leave it up to your fellow Elites. They will decide whether you go back as a prisoner, or Elite or something else altogether."

"Do what you have to." Chism had known some sort of squadron justice was coming. "I told you I'd give you no trouble."

The sound of running water brought Lieutenant Fahrr's head up. He turned back to Chism and said, "I wish you would have decided yesterday to not make trouble." He raised his voice. "Camp here. Fellows see to the horses. Elites get a fire and lay the bedrolls out in a circle."

Chism followed the rest of the squadron into the nearby clearing. He dismounted gingerly and handed the reins of his horse to Ander. After a quick stretch to get some of the soreness of the day's ride out, he limped into the trees to gather firewood. Most of the other Elites had begun gathering already and Chism forced himself to keep up with their pace even though every movement was pain. Especially bending for sticks or logs.

The pain was a good place to dump the apprehension of the upcoming judgment by the squadron. His excellent night vision gave him an advantage over the Elites who relied on moonlight and the ones who carried small torches in one hand and gathered with the other. When the wood pile was big enough to last through the night, Elites and Fellows began congregating around the fire. Chism felt comfortable he hadn't let the injury keep him from contributing his share.

"It's late," said Lieutenant Fahrr in a voice just loud enough for everyone to hear. "We're only going to be here long enough for the horses to get some food and rest. First, there's the issue of squadron justice for Chism. I won't restate the details. Chism, would you like to speak to defend yourself?" He sounded hopeful and his eyes widened, pleading with Chism to take advantage of the opportunity.

Punishment could be anything from a firm tongue lashing to actual lashing from a whip followed by imprisonment or being bound during the upcoming flight from Far West. They could throw him out of the squadron. Stripped and whipped didn't happen often, but the phrase wasn't unheard of.

If he had to choose between the two, he'd choose being whipped without a second thought. Without the Circle and Sword he would have nothing.

Chism nodded at Lieutenant Fahrr and turned to face the Elites and Fellows.

"You all risked your life for me. I'll never forget that. I didn't mean to endanger anyone but myself. Definitely never expected all this." He looked at the faces, saw a hundred years of experience looking back at him. How could he expect to explain his reasons, explain the Circle and Sword, to them? They should understand the sanctity of the Circle without the youngest of them giving a lecture.

If only he had Lieutenant Fahrr's talent for speeches.

Chism held out his arms, making the emblem on his chest prominent. In a slow, even voice, he said, "The Circle—it represents a sacred connection between every person in the kingdom. From the lowest farmer to the highest noble. A farmer raises a chicken and sells it to a trader. The trader carries it to a city and sells it to a cook who feeds an earl, a duke, or king. To complete the Circle, the king offers protection, stability, and the rule of law."

Chism motioned to the Sword in the center of the emblem, which touched the bottom and top of the inside of the Circle.

"The purpose of the Sword is to defend the Circle, to ensure abuses are not committed by those who feel it's their right to be in power. To defend against foreign threats. And to punish criminals who would endanger a peaceful way of life. Without the Sword, the Circle collapses." He was pacing and his words were clear and sharp.

"When I . . ." He caught himself before sharing details about his own life. "Sometimes the people who are supposed to protect . . . If it wasn't for Lieu—" He cut off suddenly. How could he say what he wanted to without sharing details from his own past? The passion behind the words pouring out just made it harder to think. He closed his eyes and took deep breaths through his nose.

"We don't need a lecture on the Circle and Sword," said Ulrik.

"Shut yourself," snapped Ander. "Let him finish." Ander was often the center of frivolous conversations, but never spoke during serious squadron discussions. It caught Chism by surprise.

Ander nodded at Chism in support.

"You shouldn't need a lecture," said Chism. "Every one of us has taken the Sword in defense of the Circle. It's our duty to protect its integrity. Every cruelty, neglect, crime, or exploitation by a noble, parent, villain, or soldier is an offense against the Circle that connects us all." He continued, forcing each word through clenched teeth. "*And I will* never *stand idly by.*"

He wanted to shout at his squadron, make them understand. He wanted to shake or strike them.

Lieutenant Fahrr asked, "Is that your whole defense?"

Chism considered. It all came down to the Circle and Sword. How could he add to that? He nodded.

Ulrik spoke up. "You have some nerve to lecture *us.*"

A couple Elites muttered agreement. Dugar leaned forward and said, "There are recourses, Chism. You're one soldier. The youngest Elite in the kingdom. Mayors, nobles, and magistrates are there to hear and decide disputes. Not you."

"The magistrates can rot with the nobles." Chism spat in the dirt. "They only care about themselves and their friends."

Ulrik said, "But it's *their* job and *their* duty to pass judgment. And it's yours to follow orders."

"And what happens when they think the law isn't for them or they won't punish a family member?"

"They all have superiors that can be turned to," said Ulrik. "They don't need some boy getting in the middle of every argument."

Chism looked around at the rest of the faces. Some were nodding agreement with Ulrik. None of them showed any comprehension of Chism's point. He hated to share details from his past, but he didn't know any other way to make them understand.

"That's not good enough. A woman in a small town with a son and a bottle-loving husband can't leave because she fears for the life of her boy if she tries to run. Despite daily thrashings, the town's magistrate does nothing because the drunk is his brother. The woman is with child again, but that doesn't stop the beatings. One day he beats her into laboring on her deathbed. Somehow the early baby survives, but he's severely undersized, and . . . damaged." Chism's voice had an edge that stung him with every word.

"Does the man take responsibility for his son's flaws? Not a chance. He blames the boy for the mother's death, and one drunken night he brands his one-year-old son with a *13*. Undersized, underfed, and unloved, the boy grows up hearing he's a runt. Not worth the slop he eats. The proof is right there on the boy's back." Chism's voice was getting louder but he didn't care. "The beatings continue and everyone turns a blind eye. The older brother learned to hide and I learned to fight because no one else was going to protect me."

The tears in his eyes infuriated him. He thought he was past crying, and doing it in front of the Elites, even by torchlight, made it worse. But the story needed to be told. He threw his cloak in the dirt, and in one motion, pulled off his tunic, tossed it to Ander, and turned his back to the soldiers. Scars he had tried to keep hidden since joining the squadron were displayed in ragged numbers covering the lower half of his back. *13*.

After a few moments to compose himself, his voice was controlled and emotionless. He faced the Elites.

"Years passed, and I practiced with every weapon I could get my hands on. I lived for the local competitions in javelin, archery, staffs, and daggers. And one day I stood up to my father."

Chism pushed aside the image of his brother's bleeding face along with the emotions that came with the memory. He didn't feel anything at all when he said, "I've never felt a single regret for killing him."

He had their attention. The fire crackled behind like the rage inside. The heat against his bare back felt like the heat in his voice.

"Suddenly the magistrate cared. A father beating and starving his sons was acceptable but he couldn't have boys killing their fathers. Not in his town.

"Two days before they were going to hang me, a squadron of Elites happened to pass through. The lieutenant was willing to defer to so-called local justice, but one outspoken sub-lieu demanded that I be taken before a district council. My life was spared by one rotting vote, and only because Fahrr was willing to disobey orders.

"Your magistrates, nobles, and councils can burn. The Circle is more vulnerable than any of you realize, and I'll defend it with my last breath."

With a touch of softness in his voice, Dugar said, "You can't deal with your own issues by assaulting every authority figure you meet."

"This isn't about me!" Try as he might, Chism couldn't believe his own words.

"You think you're the only one with scars?" asked Ulrik. "Sit out of a fight for once in your life. Your past doesn't give you permission to stick your nose in every conflict you see. Walk by and mind your own business."

"Spoken like a mamby-pamby milksop sissy," said Ander. "Well done."

Ulrik shot to his feet, but luckily for Ander, Lieutenant Fahrr said, "Enough." The tension seeped from the area. "Chism, you are dismissed. Your Fellow will stay as your advocate while we debate, if he can keep a civil tongue."

"As civil as a strawberry," said Ander.

Chism had nothing to say, so he walked away from the fire without looking back. The discussion had to take place in his absence to prevent hard feelings or retribution, no matter what the outcome. After all, in many cases, Elites had to fight side by side after squadron punishment had been meted. Better to prevent enemies within squadrons.

Without realizing it, Chism's hand had gone to Thirsty. He drew the sword and put both hands on the hilt. There hadn't been time that morning for his routine, and the squadron would be gone before sunrise the next day, so he decided to get it done while he had the chance. Holding Thirsty in front of him with both hands, Chism breathed until calmness pushed away fear. The cold air nipped his bare chest. He ignored it and started moving, also ignoring the pain in his thigh.

Three forms later, he was twenty-four repetitions into a complex defensive form when he heard Ander's voice.

"Like some owl warrior, swinging his sword in the dark. They're ready for you."

"How bad is it?" asked Chism when he caught up with Ander.

"Fahrr should be the one to tell you the details, but they

decided to hit you where it's hurts. And I'm not talking about between the legs."

Chism swore under his breath.

Lieutenant Fahrr waited at the edge of firelight. He was holding a blue tunic. The Elites and Fellows were climbing into bedrolls. Chism stood in front of him and waited.

"You're being stripped, Chism." The lieutenant's voice sounded resigned to something he had no control over. "You will remain a member of Quicksilver Squadron until we reach Palassiren, but you are no longer an Elite." He held out the tunic. Plain and dark. No Circle and Sword.

Chism didn't take it. They'd given him the ultimate punishment, torn the soul from his chest. His brothers. They kind of wanted him to be a brother, but not really or else they wouldn't have taken nearly everything it meant to be part of the family.

Lieutenant Fahrr laid the tunic on Chism's shoulder.

"Get some sleep. Maybe in the morning you'll find some hope. Or at least acceptance." He turned and walked toward his own bedroll. Fourteen other men to worry about. No time to baby Chism and the gaping wound he'd just received.

"That's Firan's tunic. Only one small enough to fit you," said Ander. Chism went through the motions. Ander continued. "I know it feels like they took your whole life and every blessed thing in, but you'll still be alive in the morning. Maybe you can start looking for something to live for then."

"Tell Lieutenant Fahrr I'll take first watch tonight," said Chism. He knew he wouldn't be able to sleep and some time alone with Thirsty might help him make sense of his new life. He pulled his friend from the scabbard and walked into the shadows of the night.

For four days the Elites pushed. Riding always with one eye behind on the steady gap between them and Duke Jaryn's men and the other eye ahead, waiting for an ambush. The duke's men couldn't circle in front of them, but pigeons could travel faster than horses. Sleeping little, just long enough for the horses to rest. The Elite horses were sturdy, used to long days on the road. As durable as the men who rode them. During day time breaks, the men stretched muscles and stretched out on the ground. Chism used the time for his morning routine. Wearing the plain tunic, no Circle and Sword.

Duke Jaryn and his hundreds did close the space between them, but only slightly. A matter of hours, even after days of pursuit. There was no way so many men could cover that much ground so quickly without leaving a trail of dead horses behind them and forcing any town near their path to surrender food, horses, and men to the hunt.

It only confirmed to Chism that Duke Jaryn cared nothing for the Circle. He only cared for himself and his cursed pride. Thirsty was forged for men like him.

A light dusting of snow drifted through the cloud-filled sky when Serpent Gap came into view. It was the only pass between two steep mountain ranges—the Wasteland Mountains to the south and the Antidiniss Mountains to the north. The gap started wide but shrank into a trail no more than ten paces across in some parts at the bottom of the valley. The four-mile pass wound blindly like a snake, offering countless sites for an ambush.

Ten squadrons of men could easily hide in the pass. Unfortunately, the only way to find out whether word of the skirmish in Knobbes had reached Portal City was to spring the trap. The Elites and Fellows had their hoods drawn, but not because of cold weather. If they marched into an ambush, the enemy would not be able to identify Chism among them.

With Lieutenant Fahrr in the lead, fifteen Elites entered the gap. From where he sat, Chism felt nervous sweat drip down the insides of his arms.

Pale sandstone cliffs hedged the squadron in on the right, black granite crags on their left. If an ambush did occur in the Gap, there would not be time to retreat. Duke Jaryn's men would reach the western end of the trail before Quicksilver could escape.

The first mile passed uneventfully and Chism breathed easier, starting to think the squadron might make it through the remaining three miles without incident. By the time he noticed the ambush, there was no time to give warning.

Within a matter of a dozen heartbeats, men appeared on the trail in front and on the cliffs to each side. A local militia. At least a hundred men, all armed with bows or stones. Chism couldn't get an accurate count because not all the men were visible from where he sat.

Lieutenant Fahrr called a stop. In a fight, the Elites were accustomed to ten-to-one losses, but the ten were usually on the other side. Chism looked from one end of the gap to the other as far as he could see. The squadron had very few options. Fleeing the way they had come would only expose their backs to the militia's arrows. If they succeeded in avoiding the arrows, Duke Jaryn's men would surely block the entrance to the Gap before Quicksilver could escape.

Words passed between Lieutenant Fahrr and the leader of the militia, but Chism was too far away to hear them. It didn't take long for Lieutenant Fahrr to order the Elites to drop their weapons. Fifteen swords, spears, and bows fell to the rocky trail—Quicksilver Squadron was in the power of the militia.

Four men were dispatched from the militia's front line. With all the confidence their stratagem afforded them, they approached each Elite and Fellow, roughly removing hoods, searching for a boy soldier. As they neared the end of the formation, Chism hoped fighting wouldn't break out.

After unsuccessfully searching the entire squadron, the soldiers returned to their leader.

Chism smiled wryly from his concealed location half a mile up the mountain. The militia wouldn't find what they were looking for.

Though no horsemen had passed Quicksilver with news of the events in Knobbes, messenger birds must have reached Portal City days before the squadron entered the Gap. Lieutenant Fahrr had been unwilling to risk Chism's life on the slight possibility of Duke Jaryn not dispatching birds, and his decision had proven accurate. Without Chism, they hoped the militia had no reason to detain the squadron.

The night before Quicksilver reached Serpent Gap, Lieutenant Fahrr gave Chism instructions to hide in the mountains. The Elites and Fellows pitched in whatever food they could spare to give Chism a chance to escape. Even Ulrik shared some rations.

Then they parted. A full squadron could never escape undetected, but a lone boy might slip through. Chism's plan was to double back into the Province, sweep around one of the mountain ranges, and cross into the interior from there.

He spent the night climbing, searching for a point that gave him the best view of the gap. It wasn't possible to travel between the mountain ranges without entering the Gap itself, but Chism made it far enough to gain an acceptable outlook.

Below him in the gap, a second group of militiamen examined the Elites. But even someone who had never seen Chism could tell immediately that he wasn't among them. None were near his age for one thing. Also, a few of the Elites had dark hair, but none as dark as a moonless midnight with eyes to match. And while Chism never needed a razor, every other member of the squadron had significant stubble after five days with limited supplies.

Once it was clear that his squadron was in no danger, the scene amused Chism. A third, and eventually a fourth, contingent of the militia proceeded to inspect their prisoners. One zealous soldier even looked in saddlebags and under cloaks. Satisfied that the boy was not among Quicksilver Squadron, the dark-cloaked militia led their prisoners back down the Gap toward Duke Jaryn's men.

Chism hoped Jaryn didn't take it any further than just words for Lieutenant Fahrr. The story they had worked out was that Chism had deserted. What could Lieutenant Fahrr do if Chism wasn't in his custody?

As Quicksilver was escorted down the Gap, the remaining militiamen, seventy-eight of them, looked for Chism. They searched every crag and crack along the trail but nowhere near the height where Chism was hiding.

The rocky terrain would never give Chism up. It would take the best tracker in the kingdom to find the path he'd taken, and he doubted Portal City had anyone like that.

As soon as Quicksilver was out of view, Chism saw Duke Jaryn's soldiers enter the Gap and meet up with the militiamen. Even at his distance, the Duke's flailing arms and stomping feet made him look like he was trying to dance and failing.

Smiling, Chism settled into his craggy hiding place. Eventually, his uniform would be a beacon as he tried to slip out of Far West Province, but for the next couple of days it would blend perfectly with the dark granite. That's was Lieutenant Fahrr's opinion, anyway. While Chism excelled at detecting camouflage, he was the worst in his Academy class at constructing it.

Chism settled back into a crag to wait for night, which was still hours away. Wind couldn't reach into the small space where he hid, but the chill from air and stone seeped through his clothes. Without being able to move, the cold deepened the longer he sat. He wanted to sleep, but with Jaryn's men searching right below him, it was a bad idea. He pulled the leather strip from his pocket and began rubbing it between his finger and thumb. Right hand, then left hand, then right again.

Chism peeked slowly into the gap and saw Quicksilver riding northeast, toward the interior. The plan had worked so far; Chism just needed to find a way to sneak there himself. He sat back and stroked the leather strip until the sun finally dropped below the horizon.

After giving the light a little more time to fade, Chism came out of the crack just enough to see into Serpent Gap. Other than the six militiamen guarding the lower entry, the pass was empty. He used the remaining light to plan his escape route. Serpent Gap was not an option. It would be too closely guarded so he'd circle southeast to reach the interior. The dark Antidiniss Mountains offered good cover, but he didn't want to risk moving during the day. The night would be his camouflage.

He ate while waiting for night to fall in full. If he stretched his rations, they would probably last a week. Living off the land was not an option—he had no skill at foraging and carried only Thirsty and his throwing knives. The leg injury would make fast travel impossible, and he didn't have enough food to travel slowly. At most he had seven days to find another resource.

No. Eight days. I'm sure I can make it eight.

One thing was certain—Duke Jaryn wouldn't give up the hunt. He had to know Chism was somewhere in the Province, and he'd proven that he would spare no resource in pursuit. Within days, Chism would be the most infamous fifteen-year-old in Far West history.

Chism slowly emerged from the nook where he'd rested. With his superior night vision, Chism would see before he was seen, but he wanted to avoid killing any hapless soldiers. The duke would not fare as well if they ever met again, but Chism had no desire to kill men who were just following orders.

The barren landscape was perfectly still. Occasional murmurs from the men that guarded the pass carried through the chasm. A single rolling rock would be as good as an alarm bell.

A half moon hid behind the clouds, but enough light filtered through for Chism.

Hour after painstaking hour, Chism worked his way west. His legs burned—the right from his injury and the left from compensating—as he set a ponderous, controlled pace. Somehow he sweated despite his chilled extremities, and his clothes dampened with sweat, which only made the cold more bitter.

The ground flattened out eventually, but it took almost the entire night to reach the foothills. He found another crevice to shield him during the day. Some erratic snowfall had been insufficient to whiten the ground, and Chism hoped it would stay sparse. He could deal with the cold, but all of his clothes were dark, and he knew of no way to hide footprints in snow.

Dawn was still an hour away and he was too energized to sleep, so he ate a bit of food. Whittling would be too noisy, even if he could find wood. He took his leather strip from the pouch at his waist and stroked it with his right thumb one hundred times, then passed it to his left hand. One hundred times and back again. The leather was the only thing that kept him sane.

Beneath the heavy cloud cover, there were no lucky rays to start the day. He'd have to make due without. He'd switched hands with the leather thirty-two times. His thumbs were both raw, but not bloody. Yet. He finally felt calm enough to sleep.

It was hard to get comfortable in the narrow crevice, but Chism slept as long as possible. It was better than rubbing his thumbs raw, and he didn't dare venture out until night had fallen. Luckily, winter gave him hours of traveling time he wouldn't have had in the summer.

When full dark arrived, Chism emerged from his self-imprisonment. The clouds still hid the stars and half moon; there was no way he would be seen tonight. In less than a quarter mile, Chism reached flat ground and increased his speed. He wanted to jog, but it would be impossible to hear anything if he did, so he contented himself with a quick, lopsided walk.

After a mile, Chism turned south. Less than a mile later, he crossed the road that led to Serpent Gap. After waiting to ensure no eyes were on the road, Chism crossed it slowly. On the other side of the road, he walked backwards, hoping it might throw off trackers.

He was less than a dozen paces from the road, still walking backward when he noticed a cold moth fluttering around him in the still, shadowy night. Then another. Suddenly, they were all around him. In horror, he realized they weren't moths or any other kind of insect. Fat snowflakes were coming down. They were already gathering on the ground.

It couldn't have happened at a worse time, so close to the road. Abandoning his walking backward strategy, Chism turned and fled at a full run, ignoring the tearing pain in his leg. He had to get as far from the road as possible before the snow was thick enough to hold tracks. He tucked his pack under one arm while the other held Thirsty's scabbard so he didn't trip. The snow at his back would hide his tracks at first, but in snow more than a few inches deep, the depressions of his footfalls would be seen for hundreds of paces.

The stitches in his leg pulled with every step. Warm moisture began trickling down his leg. If his footsteps didn't give him away, a trail of blood certainly would. Chism cursed the feathery snow and ran into the winter night.

CHAPTER 11

Swylin

The capital city seethed like a thousand swarms of bees competing for the same hive. The mule and cart seemed as unwieldy as a full team and wagon. Everywhere Hatta turned, crowds of people pushed and chided and cursed. Every rebuke drove him deeper into his traveling hat which was already low on his brow. No amount of wishing he could be invisible made it happen.

The few people he dared talk to pointed him in the direction of the craftsman's market, but it was impossible to find. Every time he coaxed the mule into the street, someone yelled at him to move faster or decide where he was going or get out of the way. Hatta tried to do as he was told, but conflicting commands sent him onto the wrong streets.

Enough of cities and crowds and enough of surly traveling companions. Hatta was ready for some time alone with his mirrors.

By the time he reached the craftsman's section of the huge market, he was almost ready to find a quiet corner and curl into a ball. He spied a narrow street with very little traffic and directed the mule toward it. Small shops lined the street—a woodcarver, a candlestick maker, two painters, and a shop that sold wall mounts and torches.

Continuing down the alley, Hatta discovered a dead end to the left. The only merchant open for business was a tailor. Next door stood a locked shop that had a sign with a goblet and a platter. The sign hung lopsided from one hinge. A small breeze set it swinging, and Hatta stood for a few moments watching it swing and creak like a pendulum. It was soothing after the commotion he'd endured to find the alley. He wanted to stand and watch it all day. A rustle joined the swish of the hinge. Leaves and dirt circled in the breeze, where they had collected in the doorway.

"Those are remarkable vestments, young man."

"What?" Hatta turned away from the small symphony. The tailor, an old man with dark brown eyes that somehow seemed bright, had approached him. "Oh, I thank you." He glanced down at his outfit and silently agreed with the old man—the maroon coat and apricot pants made an extraordinary pair.

"I especially admire your hat. What an exceptional pattern."

"And craftsmanship," said Hatta. "The hatter in Frenala is the best I've met."

"He must be a master indeed. I myself have never had skill with hats."

"I do," said Hatta. "Not skill per se, but knowledge at least. The hatter in Frenala, he taught me."

"So you're Frenalan then?"

Hatta shook his head.

"Might I ask from where you come?"

"If you did ask, I'd say T'lai and Frenala and Shey's Orchard. I'm a mirror maker, most recently."

"And you've brought your wares to Palassiren to secure your fortune," said the old man, with a twinkle in his eye.

"No, I've just come to sell my mirrors."

The old man had such an inviting air that Hatta wanted to tell him about his destiny, but he wasn't sure it was a good idea.

The tailor was a warm yellow, and yellow people were often garrulous. He might tell someone that shouldn't know the truth about him and his mirrors. But he already cared for the old man a great deal and wanted to stay near him.

An idea struck him. "Would that shop be rented?" He motioned to the closed-up store.

"It's available, but it's no place for a young craftsman such as yourself."

Hatta couldn't disagree more. What could be more fitting than a quiet street and an agreeable neighbor?

As if he knew Hatta's thoughts, the old man said, "There's scant foot traffic in this back alley."

"How do *you* find who to sell to? If it's not a rude question."

The old man chuckled, and his eyes smiled even more widely. "I've been here as long as the city itself, and this wasn't always a dead end. My customers know where to find me, and my needs are small."

Hatta was undaunted. "Where might the landlord be found?"

"I see you've decided already, but I still advise against it."

He seemed to be waiting for Hatta to reconsider, but the more Hatta thought about the location, the more perfect it became.

Hatta offered a crooked smile.

The old man shrugged and said, "If that's how it is to be. The landlord is in the habit of calling on Friday afternoons."

Hatta furrowed his brow. "I don't keep days; when would Friday be?"

"Why, today is Friday."

"Wonderful!" The evening wasn't far off. "And what shall we discuss in the meantime?"

"I need to attend to a stew I put on." The man turned to enter his store. "You're welcome to join me."

"Stew would be a fine dinner after the day that has had me." Hatta tied the mule to a post and followed the tailor into his shop. True to his word, the old man had an aromatic stew bubbling over a pile of coals.

The tailor's prediction regarding the visit of the landlord also proved accurate. A couple hours after their meal, he arrived. A tall man who filled his coat, the landlord appeared strong but soft, as if he could work and work but avoided it whenever possible.

Most likely a shade of green. Olive, Hatta decided.

Despite his quick smile and offered hand, the landlord was intimidating. But the allure of the secluded shop gave Hatta the courage to inquire.

"How much rent can I buy in that shop with this?" He offered his coin pouch to the man.

"Anxious, aren't you?" As he greedily counted the money, Hatta saw the man deepen in color to asparagus.

"A penny and nine cuppies. Almost enough for two months."

"And the mule and cart?" asked Hatta.

The landlord looked behind him at the animal and small cart. "What about them?"

"Are they worth two months?" Hatta smiled hopefully.

"For them plus the coins I'll give you three months."

Hatta nodded anxiously. "Yes, I'll buy three months." They struck hands, and Hatta breathed a sigh of relief. He wouldn't have to venture back into the market in search of an open shop, and he wouldn't have to walk another step with the mule. And for three months he wouldn't have to talk to anyone except the old tailor and people who wanted to buy his mirrors.

The landlord glanced over his shoulder at the cart. "Is that refuse? For a pair of cuppies, I'll haul it away for you."

Hatta was stunned. He shoved past and stood protectively with his back to the mirrors.

"Your pardon, landlord, but what you thought was refuse is my wares. If you would unlock the shop," *my shop*, he thought, "I'll fain unload them."

The landlord produced a key ring from inside his coat. "I'll let you have the honor." He removed a steel key from the ring and placed it in Hatta's trembling hand.

Feeling more grown up than he ever had before, Hatta strolled to the door of his shop. With a click and a clack, the key smoothly turned the mechanism. The door opened, revealing a plain room with unfinished pine walls. It was only a few paces across and a half-dozen paces deep, but there was enough wall space for his twenty-some mirrors.

The landlord relaxed with the tailor while Hatta carried his creations, one by one, into his shop. The last mirror, his masterpiece, was double wrapped. He carried it to the small room in the back of the shop, which held only a small cot.

As soon as the cart was empty, the landlord came to collect it. Hatta showed him how to charm the mule, then bid farewell to her with a light scratch behind the ear. She twitched the ear and turned her head as if to say, *Good riddance.*

Hatta hated to part under such circumstances, but he had done as well as he could and that was as well as he could do. After watching the cart and the mule follow the landlord down the alley, Hatta joined the old tailor in his shop.

"Swylin is shrewd, but you made it effortless for him today."

The old man still had a friendly expression and pleasant eyes, but the criticism was distressing. Hatta fingered his hat, examining the shades of purple.

Still waiting for objection or explanation, the old tailor continued. "You could have gotten six months if you'd pressed him."

"I . . ." Hatta was flustered. "I need to visit, that is, there's a, uh . . ." Hatta didn't want to lie, but at that moment couldn't tell the old tailor where he was going. "I'll be leaving this city now. For a few days anyway. Might I pay you for the meal?" He reached for his purse and found it missing.

Flushing, he told the old tailor, "I might, but I've parted from my purse. I . . ."

"Consider it a gift. A token of welcome for my new neighbor." The old man's smile was genuine, but Hatta still had to get out.

"I thank you." He placed his traveling hat, tipped it, then strode quickly out of the tailor's shop and toward the gates of the city.

Navigating the streets was easier without the ill-mannered mule, but the clamor of Palassiren still rattled Hatta. The plaza in front of the gate was especially busy, so he put his head down as he scuffed toward the open gate. The grey stone street leading to the gate was a dull mirror, reflecting the dreary mood of the evening. Hatta kept his eyes just high enough to avoid running into anyone, and after some time, the crowd thinned.

Hatta watched the stone change into a multi-hued grey gravel, which in turn gave way to the dark cinnamon clay of a road. He was finally out of the city. Daring to glance up from under the brim of his hat, Hatta realized he was some distance from the gate. In fact, the Hub was only a few dozen paces away.

The eight major highways of Maravilla, the Spokes, converged at the Hub. Hatta couldn't read the signs, but it mattered little. If Tjaden had mentioned the name of a road, it was no longer in his head. There was nothing to do except try them all. He put his hand in his pocket as he turned to study the eight roads and felt the key there. Had he remembered to lock up? Or close the door?

No matter. If the door was open the tailor might close it, and if the door was unlocked, it wasn't worth facing the city streets again to go back.

The key, his key, gave him confidence that success was imminent. He ruled out the Spokes that led to Shey's Orchard and Frenala, then started walking down one at random.

HATTER

Hatta fit his lips around the air of a whistle, and finally feeling like the day might turn out for the good, he set out to find the Cheshire Cat.

CHAPTER 12

Friend

*H*unger, cold, and worry deepened as Chism ran through the night. His boots and uniform provided excellent protection from the elements, but the night was long, and unnumbered miles stretched out behind him. Seventeen thousand, four hundred and fifty steps, but with his limping gait it was impossible to know how many miles that translated into. A bandage circled his thigh, and the leg of his pants was tucked into his boot in an attempt to trap the trickling blood, but he still left an incriminating streak as a beacon for Jaryn's men.

The sunlight framing the mountains to the east was a welcome sight as he ran through ankle-deep snow across the flat grasslands. A new day, and he was the only one around to catch the first lucky rays. But when sunlight lit the blanket of snow, his optimism disappeared. Stretching miles and miles back to the base of the mountains was a slim vein in an otherwise undisturbed mantle of white, pointing straight at him. Chism's hopelessness deepened when he noticed a thin column of smoke less than two miles to the east, most likely from militia scouts. They'd spot his trail within minutes.

There was no point in running faster. Limping faster, actually. He was miles away from cover. Plodding on, Chism waited for the inevitable pursuit.

It didn't take long. A quarter hour after Chism noticed the camp smoke, four provincial militiamen on horseback gave chase. Their pace was steady but not reckless. They knew the landscape offered no escape.

Duke Jaryn doesn't know me well enough if he thinks patrols of four will take me easily. Five or seven might be too many, but four was manageable, just as long as they didn't all carry bows.

Slowing to conserve his fading energy, Chism began to meander in his path. When the men were a hundred paces off, he stumbled repeatedly, allowing himself to fall into the snow twice. It wasn't much of an act. His endurance was starting to fade.

By the time the group was close enough to yell an order to halt, Chism lay curled up in the snow, sobbing. He cursed silently when he saw four arrows pointed at him.

One of the men came close while the other three spread out, keeping their bows up. "*This* is the boy the duke wants?" asked the closest man in a raspy voice. "Calling him a thirteen was giving him too much credit." The other three soldiers chuckled.

Chism rose to a lazy seated position but kept moaning. He hoped the melting snow on his face would pass for tears. In a faint voice, he muttered, "I don't want to be here. I want to go home." He hated the pathetic pretense, but already the soldiers were relaxing visibly. They'd pay for making him act weak.

"Put a rope around him and drag him back to camp," said a soldier.

"He's just a little guy," answered the leader in his hoarse voice. The man had huge lips that angled downward at the corners and a long body as narrow as a pike fish. "I'll tie his wrists so he can walk back. I bet the duke gives me a bonus for bringing him in healthy." Pikey quivered his arrow, hung his bow, and dismounted a few paces in front of Chism. "Drop your sword, boy."

After feigning two failed attempts, Chism drew Thirsty and let it slip out of his grip. As planned, it landed tip first in the snow.

"Now step away from it," said Pikey, holding up his own sword.

Chism glanced down at Thirsty. His impromptu plan definitely didn't include separating himself from Thirsty. The temptation to act immediately became very attractive. One arrow had been eliminated, but there was still one too many. Chism took a backward step, stumbled, and caught himself. He was only two steps from Thirsty, but Pikey motioned him back two more steps.

After retrieving a length of cord from his pack, Pikey approached. With a heavy nudge to Chism's side, he ordered, "Give me your wrists, boy."

Whimpering, Chism lifted his arms unevenly, then let them fall as if from exhaustion.

Pikey turned to one of his companions. "Get down here and hold his wrists so I can tie them."

After putting his bow away, the man obeyed. Two soldiers stood in front of him, while two archers sat on horseback fifteen paces to each side. The leader, Pikey, stuck his sword in the ground behind him to free his hands while the second man reached for Chism's wrists. The instant before the soldier touched him, Chism sprang.

Jumping at an angle, he put himself between the soldiers and one of the bowmen and drew a knife. An arrow landed in the snow where he had knelt, a reflex shot by the bowman on his right. Chism threw the knife, striking the archer in the shoulder. The man screamed, and his bow fell to the ground.

Pikey's sword was already in Chism's hand, and he struck the back of the second soldier's head with the hilt. He fell like an empty uniform. Pikey reached to his scabbard before realizing Chism held his sword. It was the fool's own fault for underestimating him. Raising the tip to the leader's neck, Chism kept hidden from the other bowman.

"Drop the bow," Chism said, no louder than necessary.

Nobody moved. Only the horses seemed to be living, breathing out clouds of steam.

"You can both die or neither of you can die."

Again, stillness followed. "Your choice, not mine," said Chism.

After drawing his second knife with his left hand, Chism brought the sword back to strike Pikey. The motion was enough to prompt the bowman into action. He threw both bow and arrow to the ground and raised his hands high.

With a sword at their leader's throat, it was a simple matter to get them dismounted and unarmed. After separating them from their arrows, he ordered them to break the bows. Without ranged weapons, they weren't a true threat. In one last effort to discourage pursuit, he took their cloaks and tunics. They wouldn't die, but the shirtless walk back to their camp would hopefully take away whatever fight was left in them.

With fresh horses and extra cloaks, Chism rode south at a gallop, leading the spare animals by the reigns. After half a mile, he slowed to a pace the horses could maintain. As he rode, he tried to come up with a plan to escape Far West Province on horseback. He failed. He would be too conspicuous, especially mounted on the fine horse of a soldier. The cloaks were useless. Without a company of men, no border guard would believe Chism was a militiaman.

Now that Chism was on his own, outrunning his pursuers seemed much less likely to work than trying to sneak out of Far West.

Exhaustion was setting in, but if Chism stopped to rest he'd be overtaken. Pikey and his men would report to other provincials as soon as possible. There had been no way to avoid that without killing them, but if Chism meant what he said about the Circle and the Sword, he had to protect everyone he could. Even if it meant more risk to himself.

Hours later there was still no sign of pursuit, but it was inevitable. Sleep was not an option. Fitful naps as the horses plodded on had to suffice.

The snow on the ground thinned as Chism traveled southeast, and a change appeared in the landscape. A fuzzy line of low trees in the distance cut a path through the endless pasture land. He longed to race the horses for the trees, but kept them at a steady walk. At last, a plan was beginning to form.

As Chism hoped, the trees bordered a creek, barely a trickle at its winter low. The horses didn't need to be urged toward the water. Each found a small pool among the boulders and drank.

Chism wrapped his blood-crusted boot with one of the militiamen's tunics then leapt off his horse, careful to step only on large, lichen-free boulders. Avoiding the silt and sand, Chism located a pool of his own and drank deeply. The frigid water invigorated him. After filling his waterskin, Chism allowed the horses to drink their fill, then approached them and drew Thirsty. With a sharp yell, he slapped the nearest horse's rump with Thirsty's flat side, startling the four southward.

The animals were reluctant to leave without encouragement, so he urged them on with a few stones. A hundred paces away they slowed to a walk, but it was the best he could do to create a false trail.

Enough large boulders filled the creek bed to travel without straining his injured leg with any long leaps. If it started bleeding again, a child would be able to track him. He continued to move carefully upstream.

Out of nowhere dizziness swallowed Chism and he had to

flail his arms to keep from falling sideways into a pool. Water alone would be a bad enough sign of his passage on the boulders, but if his injured leg got wet, the trail from moistened blood would ruin his chance of escape. He looked down at his leg. The wound was closed and his boot was still covered. Everything was dry. Maybe he was out of blood to bleed. That, plus dozens of sleepless hours and dozens of miles traveled explained his lightheadedness and lack of strength. If he was out of blood, death couldn't be far off.

Chism took a few deep breaths and looked upstream. There was no end to his path, no goal he could reach then quit. The border to the interior was probably a hundred miles away. An impossible distance in his condition.

I can probably take one step, he told himself, and took it. *One more.*

Step by agonizing step. There were no Academy instructors driving him. No squadron lieutenants inspecting every boulder for signs that someone had passed. Just Chism's resolve, which he'd always considered unbreakable. It felt as fragile as a dry leaf. One step he refused to take could crumble fifteen years of willpower. But there was nothing left inside to draw on.

Doubt made its way in and Chism stopped, muttered, "I'm just a kid. Who do I think I am?"

Maybe his father and Jaryn and Ulrik and everyone else were right about him.

Chism stepped carefully to the next boulder. It was a step none of those people ever would have believed he could take after what he'd been through. He took one more.

"*This* is who I am," said Chism quietly. He took another step. "Not who I believe I am or who anyone else believes." Another step. "I am what I do."

Every inch forward proved his grit more thoroughly than anything he'd ever done. It was an opportunity to be who he'd always thought he was.

No one would ever know what it took to keep from falling unconscious in the stream. No one could possibly understand how alluring the patches of soft grass and sand were. Chism didn't care; *he* knew. And once he proved he was as hard as he'd always suspected, at least as hard as the boulders under his feet, nothing would ever stop him. Not Duke Jaryn, not the Far West Militia, not the combined armies of Maravilla.

Pain, exhaustion, and doubt waged their war. Every boulder Chism conquered expanded his dominion and encroached on theirs. They continued to defend each new battleground. Chism had never traveled so slowly, but he'd also never gained so much ground. Ahead of him at some unknown location was the man he thought he was. Step by step he moved toward the self he wanted to be.

When dark arrived an hour later, it was infinitely more welcome than light had been that morning. Chism nestled himself under the protective hooded roots of an old hollowed river tree.

Chism didn't fall asleep. He crashed into unconsciousness.

The smell of smoke startled Chism.

I'm being smoked out!

But there was no heat. Just bone-deep cold. And the smoke came from all around, a faint haze that hung under a grey sky. Chism inched out of cover, watching for soldiers. The streambed was clear. He put on the militia tunics which he'd used as pillows then snuck out to inspect the area. No blood trail anywhere and no signs that anyone else had passed. The smoke looked thicker upstream, so Chism continued his careful course that direction. After fifty paces he spotted a small house, but no people. He crept closer.

The nearest building to the stream was a smokehouse.

Tiny specks of flame showed in one corner through gaps in the log walls. The fire must have been lit recently because very little smoke escaped the smokehouse, but it poured from the chimney of the farmhouse. Between the two buildings was a drying frame full of clothes.

He pulled his tunics off, barely thinking about the Fellow's uniform under the militia tunics. Removing it was nothing like taking off the Circle and the Sword of his Elite's uniform. And no matter what he wore, he was still a member of Quicksilver Squadron. He folded the uniforms precisely and concealed them far under the lip of a large boulder. If he was discovered by the family that lived in the farmhouse, it would be easier to explain nakedness than uniforms.

The yard was still empty so Chism bolted, sword in hand, to the drying frame wearing nothing but his unders and boots. He smelled pipe smoke as he leaned Thirsty against the frame and held up the clothes.

"You know there's a '*13*' on your back, lad?"

Chism spun and raised Thirsty. An ancient man, wrinkly as a targus, sat smoking a pipe in front of the smokehouse.

"You don't look like a runt, but I guess that depends on your age. Under fourteen—not a runt. Fourteen or over—runt."

The old man's hair was wispy and thin, reminding Chism of a shaggy cactus he saw once in a covered garden in Palassiren.

Cactus was quick to continue speaking. "But I'll give you one year for the sword and up to two more depending on your pluck. You got spunk, boy?"

Chism liked the old man. For some reason he couldn't explain, he liked him a lot.

"I got spunk, Oldster." He lowered Thirsty. "More than you've ever seen."

"Come out of nowhere, next to naked in the winter? I guess you gotta have spunk. Not many smarts, though."

"I'll take spunk over smarts any day," Chism said with a proud grin. He considered putting some clothes on but didn't want to risk the old man's assessment of his toughness.

Shaking his head, Cactus said, "What thirteen-year-old wouldn't? Now who's after you?"

The direct question caught Chism off guard. A dog barked in front of the house as he decided whether to tell the truth or lie. Secrecy was best.

"Some men."

Cactus took two shallow puffs of his pipe and said, "Listen, I'm a hundred and four. I might be in the ground by the time you spit it out. Course, it won't be long 'til '*some men*' get here to answer my question. Tracker's already greeting them."

The barking rose in pitch. The old man was Chism's only hope.

"The Far West Militia. I threatened Duke Jaryn and he wants me dead."

After considering for a moment, Cactus asked, "Did you have a good reason?"

"The reason was good," answered Chism. "The results weren't."

"Well, maybe there's hope for you. Let's get you hid." Placing one hand on a cane and the other on his chair, he rose with tremendous effort. Chism went to his side to assist, but the old man swatted his hands away.

Over the dog's barking, Chism heard indistinct voices. "Hurry," he said.

Only halfway out of the chair, Cactus said, "You should see me when I'm not hurrying. Grass grows faster than I move."

The voices got louder. It sounded like a dozen men or more. Chism raised Thirsty, ready to defend himself against the soldiers who would come around the house at any time.

Unflustered, the ancient man said, "Why, last summer I started walking back here to smoke a pig, but by the time I got here, it was winter."

Chism was not amused, but Cactus went on. "Spring came before I made it back inside." He was finally out of his chair, shuffling toward the smokehouse door. Stooped as he was, he stood even in height with Chism. When he opened the door, smoke flowed under the lintel like an inverted waterfall.

"Your mind's more addled than I thought. I'll cook if I go in there," said Chism.

"Some spunk you have. Suit yourself, but there's plenty of good air down low." He bent slowly to pick up some burlap sacks from the grass.

Chism looked between the dark smokehouse and the side of the house. Trusting the old man wasn't easy, but it beat his other options, so he dove to the ground inside the door. The hard packed dirt was warm and soothing after so much time in the cold. Wet burlap landed on top of him, a freezing contrast to the comfortable warmth of the dirt.

"Cover up," ordered the old man.

Burlap in tow, Chism crawled toward a bench along the wall but stopped and looked back at the closing door.

"Fifteen," Chism said.

With a mere sliver of light remaining, the door stopped.

"That old, are you? Well, it's a good thing you got spunk. Find some smarts if you want to see sixteen."

The door closed, and while Cactus hobbled away, Chism slid under the bench. The warmth was no longer comfortable, and every breath felt hotter in his throat. There was plenty of burlap to cover himself, which immediately provided relief. Air leaked in through chinks in the logs, cooling his face as the fire sucked it in. A sliver of the yard outside was visible.

Cactus's legs shuffled past his chair and rounded the corner of the smokehouse toward the creek. The old man was singing to himself, followed shortly by sounds of a large group approaching.

"You there, old man." Chism recognized Pikey's raspy voice and silently cursed. It wouldn't take much pressing to get the old man to confess.

"Don't interrupt me, boy. My water just started flowing, and if I stop now, I'll suffer all day."

His shuffling just wiped out my tracks in the grass, and now he's making water all over the rocks I came in from. Maybe the soldiers wouldn't find the hidden uniform.

Pikey dispatched men to search while he waited for Cactus to return. Chism could tell by the steady shuffle that Cactus was moving at top speed, but the militiaman didn't wait.

"Have you seen anyone this morning, old fellow?"

"I see you. I'm not blind," snapped Cactus. "And I saw my granddaughter, and those soldiers there, and—"

Pikey cut him off. "Have you seen anyone besides us?"

"There was a deer right over there when I came out. And a rabbit too. A white one."

Chism could only see boots from where he lay, but the old man's voice sounded cheerful and innocent. Even with the blocked view, Chism could tell there were at least a dozen men with Pikey. He thought about creeping to the door to peek out for a count, but the old man had shown him kindness, and exposing himself would be no way to repay that.

He didn't know how much longer he could last in the smoke-filled shed, though. The heat was building fast. Without the gaps between logs, Chism's lungs would have already been singed beyond usefulness.

"What are you smoking this morning?" asked Pikey.

"Hogs," answered the old man.

"Search it," said Pikey, and boots moved toward the smokehouse door.

"Stay away from there!" shouted Cactus. "I spent all morning building that smoke and heat. You'll let it escape with all your openings."

The door creaked open despite the old man's protests, and within seconds, the blanket of heat relented. Chism lay as still as a dead pig under his burlap. He was confident he had covered himself completely; any exposed skin would have burned long since.

Cactus continued his protestations and curses. A few of the soldiers chuckled, and Chism heard the old man's cane slapping arms.

Inside the smokehouse, Chism heard a dull *fwhick*. A sword piercing cloth and flesh. They were probing the covered slabs with swords! The arrow injury would feel like a splinter compared to a sword wound. He considered rolling quickly and raising Thirsty, but his position was all wrong.

A woman spoke near the door. "Please stop upsetting him. He gets in a temper sometimes, and it takes days to calm him. I beg you. He's been here since sunup; no one could have come without him seeing."

Another *fwhick*, closer than the first as the commotion outside continued. A soldier's boot scuffed against Chism's back, but he didn't react. He braced for the piercing blow, vowing to himself that he would not cry out or move.

"Harvig, enough," said Pikey from the door.

Just as Chism relaxed, he felt a blunt blow to his flank. The sword should have felt sharp. Harvig's boots stomped across the small smokehouse and the door closed. As the oppressive smoke and heat began to weigh down again, Chism reached his hand around, but to his relief, he felt only pain, no wound.

I've felt blows like that before. That was no sword; it was a boot. He'd never felt so happy to be kicked.

"Pigs," said a man outside, probably Harvig.

"You think I don't know animals?" demanded Cactus. "Over a hundred years I've been farming here, and you come telling me I don't know it's hogs in my own smokehouse."

"Our apologies. The boy we seek is extremely dangerous. He tried to murder the Duke himself."

Tried? thought Chism. *If I tried to kill him, Far West would be in mourning right now.*

"Be warned," continued Pikey. "He looks harmless, but he won't hesitate to smile at your face while he slits your throat."

More boots approached and a new voice said, "The house is clear, sir."

"Very well. You men, search the stream. You, with me." The soldiers departed.

"Give me a hand, Leis," said Cactus when the soldiers were gone. After standing, he told her, "You go on inside. I'll be along soon."

After some time, the smokehouse door opened a crack, giving Chism blessed relief. He rolled and watched as Cactus, coughing and sputtering, shambled through the smoke to where the fire burned. With a grunt, he upended a container, and the fire dimmed with a great hiss.

"Was any of the blood on that spear yours, boy?"

"No."

"Lucky that. Sharing blood with dead pigs'll cause infection every time. Best you stay here for the morning."

Before Cactus could make it to the door, Chism asked, "Why'd you help me?"

The old man paused in the doorway, grasping the jamb for support. Through his coughing, he said, "I may be half-blind, but I can see you need a friend. You act like you never had one, and the way I see it, a man can never have enough."

The words struck Chism. He couldn't remember ever wanting a friend. Brothers, sure. Even brothers-in-arms. But he had no use for friends. Until . . . now.

"Don't care much what happens to me, boy, but I'd appreciate if you didn't slit Leis's throat. Or her boys's."

The door closed gently. Lying nearly naked in the dark burlap, one word rattled around in Chism's head: *friend*.

CHAPTER 13

Barrels

With the fire extinguished, the smokehouse cooled quickly. The damp burlap that had protected Chism from heat soon chilled him as he lay under the bench, waiting for the old man to return. He didn't have any leather to stroke, steps to count, or weapons to practice with, and it proved impossible to lay still. Half a dozen times, he went to the door only to be scolded by Cactus when he cracked it enough to peek out. Cactus eventually dragged his chair over to block the door.

It was nearly half a day later when Cactus finally permitted him to leave the smokehouse. Leis was shocked when her grandfather brought Chism, half naked and shivering, into the house, but it didn't take long for him to convince her to shelter what she saw as a wayward boy. Keeping one eye on Chism, Leis fetched him a blanket, heated water for a bath, and gave him bread with honey. The bread was warm and smooth, melting like a snowflake when it hit his tongue. The honey was clear and more flavorful than any he'd ever eaten. If he could only eat one thing for the rest of his life, that bread with honey would be it.

All four of Leis's sons were fascinated by Chism, but the oldest, an eleven-year-old boy with a conspicuous cowlick, goggled openly at Chism and Thirsty. The boy's bangs stuck up and out, reminding Chism of oversized buckteeth.

Buckhairs, thought Chism, allowing himself a small chuckle.

Steam rose from the bath Leis poured. No sooner was she out of the room than Chism dropped the blanket, stripped out of his unders and boots, and climbed in. The tub was the bottom half of a barrel large enough for a man to squeeze into, and easily big enough for Chism. The water burned, especially on his toes as they thawed. The arrow wounds didn't look infected—Ander had done a superb job tending it—but some blood and pus oozed into the water.

The bath was so peaceful that it made Chism uncomfortable. He tried to relax and enjoy it, but leisure was foreign to him. He stayed in just long enough to thaw his bones.

As he stood dripping, knee-deep in the water, Buckhairs entered with a cloth for drying. He handed it to Chism and said, "I know my numbers. That's a *13*. Why do you have a *13* on your back? And what are those stripes on your legs?"

The boy reached to touch the scars, but Chism lunged out of the tub, kicking water onto the straw-strewn floor of the small room. "Don't touch me. Ever."

Withdrawing obediently, the boy said, "Someday I'm going to have a sword like you. I'm going to be a soldier and maybe even have a *13*, too."

Even though the boy was about three years younger than him, Chism was self-conscious. Covering as much as he could with the small cloth, he tried to sound self-assured. "Have you practiced your sword today?"

"I don't have a sword," said Buckhairs.

"If you want to be a soldier, you need to address me as 'Sir'. Do you have a stick?"

"Yessir."

"Have you practiced with your stick today?"

Buckhairs shook his head then added, "Sir."

"Do you have a bow?"

"No, Sir."

"Spear?"

"No, Sir."

"Knife?"

"Yessir. My second grandfather gave it to me 'cause I'm the oldest in the family."

"Have you practiced with it today?"

Again the boy shook his head. "Ma says I can't even pretend fight with it." Chism waited, staring, until the boy added the title. "Sir."

"What about fighting trees?"

"Trees, Sir?"

"A tall stump is even better. Find someone who knows something about swords or knives and ask them to teach you what they can. Then practice every day. *Every* day. When that skill is perfect, find someone else and have them teach you. Then practice . . ." He let the words hang in the air.

"Every day, Sir," said the boy.

Chism nodded. The boy was no tweedle.

"Let me get dressed. I'll give you a lesson later."

Before he was even out of the room, Buckhairs announced that "the Soldier" was going to teach him to fight.

The clothes Leis provided fit snugly. They were Buckhairs's, after all, but no one else's would have fit any better. Even old, bent Cactus's clothes would hang off the ends of Chism's arms and legs. Buckhairs's outfit was made from the same sturdy wool Chism had grown up wearing, but it still chafed. For over a year and a half, Chism had worn nothing but a uniform, and he longed for the sturdy cotton.

"You have a name?" demanded Cactus when Chism entered the main room of the house.

He nodded. "Chism."

"Prism?" barked Cactus.

Leis leaned toward her grandfather. "Chism. *Ch*, like chicken."

"Like *challenge*," corrected Chism.

"Spit out why you're running," ordered Cactus. "And do it before I die, which could very well happen before dinner."

Chism eyed the youngsters, which was enough for Leis to send them outside with chores. Buckhairs began to argue until Chism gave him a steady stare and a shake of the head that sent him rushing out after the others.

He'd make a fine soldier, thought Chism. Only the youngest boy, who was too young to stand, remained behind.

After telling them he was a King's Elite, Chism told the story from seeing Duke Jaryn for the first time to creeping out of the creek bed earlier that day. He abbreviated the part about his speech to the Elites, dwelling on the Circle and Sword to make sure they understood the reasons for his actions. Cactus and Leis listened without interrupting.

"We've got to get you back to the interior then, so Cuora and Antion can decide what to do with you," said Cactus, scraping fingers through wispy hair. "Shouldn't be too hard."

"How do you figure?" asked Chism, wondering not for the first time how far the old man was into his dotage. "They've harried every step I've made so far."

"Quiet down, youngster, and let me talk." Under his breath he muttered, "Always in a hurry, no-patience kids . . ." He gathered his thoughts and said, "My grandson, Leis's brother, is a merchant. Travels to the interior every month or so. He was supposed to be here two days ago, but it's not uncommon for him to come late—in winter, anyway. He'll have some crate or another to stuff you into and get you out of Far West."

Leis nodded, and Chism didn't have any other suggestions. If he thought of a better plan before the merchant arrived, he could leave whenever he wanted.

Three days passed with no new ideas for Chism. He spent them indoors, away from the eyes of neighbors. The boys pestered Chism unendingly, which seemed to amuse their mother. He wasn't sure exactly what color the four boys' hair was, but all four had the same hair, which was much lighter than his own.

True to his word, Chism gave Buckhairs his first lesson after selecting two sticks from the pile the boy had gathered. He had learned the boy's real name, Eram, but preferred the nickname. They started lessons with five defensive sword positions. Chism instructed him to go through all of them a hundred times every morning. Once he mastered them, he could reduce the number of repetitions to fifty.

Watching from the small window, he felt a glimmer of pride when the boy passed through each stance exactly one hundred times before taking his first break. Buckhairs pleaded for more lessons, and Chism taught him as much about the basics of swordplay as he could. The other boys watched, but none wanted to devote their time to learning. Chism wouldn't have turned any of them away, but was especially glad that Baen, the six-year-old, took little interest in fighting. Baen was the same age Chism was when he started learning, and it was no life for a child.

The two middle boys spent most of their time watching the road for their father and Uncle Tonin. Both were expected any day, their father having taken a cartful of honey to Knobbes two weeks prior. Leis kept her sons close to home to prevent the boys from bragging about "the Soldier" to their friends, so they passed the days bundled on the front porch.

Tonin arrived first, riding in a slow-moving wagon pulled by four oxen. Three burly men with cudgels, whom he referred to as "the Boys," headed straight for the creek. Tonin was a portly man with a soft smile and hard candies for his nephews. But he was much less accepting of Chism than Leis and Cactus had been.

"Lowan leaves for two weeks and you open your home to a fugitive because Grandfather thinks it's a good idea? He's a hundred years old—"

"Hundred and four! Don't try and cheat me," snapped Cactus, rising an inch or two despite his crooked back.

"Yes, Grandfather, but do you have any idea how many soldiers are searching for him? I passed three roadblocks on my way into Far West. Everyone heading out is being searched top to bottom."

"You haven't even heard his story, Tonin," said Leis. "At least listen before you decide."

Tonin looked ready to call the Boys, but the pleading eyes of Cactus and Leis convinced him to listen. Chism told the same story the other two had heard.

When he finished, Tonin looked between his sister and Chism. "Leis, I know that's a story to wring anyone's heart, but look at this kid. He's barely bigger than Eram. I don't know who he is, but he can't be the Elite that the whole province is searching for. He's probably a runaway who heard about the manhunt and decided to play soldier for a while. Look at me—I'm fat, and I could whip him black and blue."

Chism told Buckhairs to run for two of his practice sticks.

"You want to fight me, boy?" His shock manifested as a one-syllable laugh from deep in his belly. "I'm three times your size. You don't stand a chance! You'll see, Leis, and after I bruise him, I'll drag him to the Provincials myself, and they can do what they want to him." He removed his traveling cloak.

Buckhairs returned with two sword-length sticks, and Chism motioned for Tonin to select one. The house was not large, and everyone in the room except the fighters pressed against the walls.

While still looking at Tonin, Chism spoke to Buckhairs.

"You'll see today that size is one of the least important factors in a fight. For many large men, it's a disadvantage because they rely on it too much. Always remember it's a sword fight, not a size fight." He motioned for Tonin to begin the duel.

Holding the stick like a club, Tonin came at him. Chism didn't budge from the spot where he stood. Using nothing more than the five defensive positions, he repelled Tonin's attack. The positions were so ingrained that Chism didn't even think. He just rotated his arms to block the offensive.

Time after time, Tonin left himself open for a blow, but Chism restrained himself. He hoped Buckhairs would see the openings he passed up. Attack after attack, Tonin threw himself at Chism but only scored a few glancing blows. The trader sweated and grunted as he swung the branch, missing badly with the majority of his strikes.

When the man was near exhaustion, Chism took advantage of an opening to place the tip of his stick at Tonin's chest.

"Yield."

The trader dropped his stick and collapsed into a nearby chair. "How . . . how did you . . . do that?" he asked between gasping breaths.

Ignoring Tonin, Chism looked to Buckhairs. "He's as big as three of me, but I could have stabbed him thirty-two times. Why?"

"Defensive position," Buckhairs said confidently.

"No," said Chism. "Because of discipline. I could have dominated just as easily using thrusts or swings or footwork. The key is disciplined practice. Do everything perfectly, and do it perfectly a thousand thousand times."

"Yessir," said Buckhairs.

Tonin looked baffled. The room was quiet except for his labored breathing.

Cactus broke the silence. "You remind me of myself when

I was younger, boy. Quick, agile. Handsome. I knew there was a reason I liked you."

Chism smiled. The expression had become surprisingly common over the three days he'd spent with the family.

Tonin stood loudly and approached Chism. He offered his hand, which Chism stepped away from, offering a small bow instead. With a quizzical expression, Tonin said, "My apologies, young man. You could have hurt me badly and done even worse to Leis and her family before the Boys and I arrived. I owe you an apology."

The apology didn't mean anything to Chism; he still didn't have a way out of the Provinces.

Cactus spoke up. "Quit yappin' and get him home."

Still catching his breath, Tonin regarded Chism. If the merchant refused, Chism would be back to sneaking through the wilderness and trying to avoid the militia. With a sigh, Tonin said, "I may regret it, but I'll help you get to the interior."

"Will your . . . Boys go along with it?" asked Chism.

"Oh sure. They've no love for soldiers who harass honest merchants." Tonin pulled the bench out from under the table in the kitchen and straddled it. With a playful grin he added, "Or soldiers who harass dishonest merchants for that matter."

A day later, Chism made short farewells. He had never spent any time inside a real home, and part of him regretted leaving. Aware of his aversion to touch, none of them embraced him or offered to clasp arms, which suited Chism perfectly.

Cactus was the last to speak. "I'm not saying you gotta give up your spunk, but you're a fool if you don't mix in some forethought. Better to be alive with some spunk than to be dead from too much it."

After thanking them one last time, Chism climbed into one of the water buckets secured to the side of Tonin's wagon. The trader swore they were the only items never inspected at the border. Thirsty was wrapped and stowed among Tonin's goods as if it were nothing more than a rusty practice sword. Chism's last sight of the family that had treated him like one of their own was a glimpse of Buckhairs going through his defensive stances.

Travel was cramped, dark, and worse than bumpy. He would be bruised more than he had been in Elite training by the time they stopped for the night. With nothing but a water skin, a small chamber pot, and a strip of leather from an old pair of Leis's shoes, Chism counted away the trip. For once his small stature was a blessing. It was allowing him to escape, but the barrel wasn't large enough for him to move or stretch.

The Boys' banter was much like that of soldiers on the road, and the bits he could make out were often crude but strangely comforting. After more than twenty-six thousand strokes of his leather, the wagon finally stopped for the night. Chism was as bent as Cactus when Tonin helped him out of the barrel.

He wondered how he would force himself into the barrel seven more times. But there was no other choice; he'd given his word to Lieutenant Fahrr.

Though the first two days passed uneventfully, Tonin insisted that Chism stay in the barrel as long as the sun was up. It was a big enough risk to be transporting a fugitive; Tonin didn't want the added risk of being surprised by a group of soldiers or a roadblock. Even when the oxen stopped to graze, or Tonin stopped to trade in towns along the way, Chism remained imprisoned. He stayed up every night practicing with Thirsty for hours and pacing until morning. The exhausting nights allowed him a few hours of restless sleep in his barrel cell during the following day's travel.

On the third day of confined travel, they reached the first roadblock. True to Tonin's prediction, Chism heard the soldiers search the entire wagon with the exception of the water barrels. When the wagon started moving again, it was on a much smoother road—still jarring, but not nearly as violent.

Finally, the Telavir Spoke.

Another roadblock two days later produced the same outcome as the first, and three more days of rough travel brought them to the Fringe Road, which separated the Provinces from the interior. As they pulled to a stop Chism heard Tonin greet one of the guards.

"Afternoon, Bly."

Someone too far away for Chism to hear offered a muffled response.

"Judging by the number of guards, you still haven't caught that Elite you were looking for," said Tonin.

"The boy won't escape," said a friendly-sounding voice. "Probably frozen in the mountains somewhere. His bones might turn up in the spring, but he won't get out of the Provinces on any roads."

"Do we really have to do the whole search, Bly? I've been through it twice already this trip, and we've known each other for over a decade."

"Sorry, Tonin. Orders trump friendship. If any of these soldiers let the captain know I skipped a search, it would mean my hide."

"Go ahead, Boys. Open it up again," grumbled Tonin.

The familiar noises of soldiers bustling through the wagon filtered into the barrel. Being blind to the outside always set

Chism on edge. He didn't even know how many soldiers manned the roadblock.

When Bly spoke next he was much closer. "Mind if I fill my skin? That water you carry from your sister's creek is the sweetest I've had."

Chism didn't hear Tonin move to stop the soldier. In a hurry to empty his own waterskin, Chism spilled some of the liquid from his chamber pot between his feet. Luckily, it didn't make any noise, but Chism squatted in the former contents of his water bag and chamber pot.

He cursed silently and thought, *Why did I let them stuff me in a barrel too small for Thirsty? Should I run or fight when they open the barrel?*

The tiny pinpricks of light from the barrel's lid were eclipsed by sunlight flooding up into the barrel as the cork was removed. A trickle of liquid escaped and Chism heard Bly much more clearly. "This one's almost drained." He kept the cork out for ages, collecting what was left before stoppering it again.

Chism didn't hear the soldier drink, but a loud spitting noise told him Bly had tasted the water.

"Tastes like vinegar! It's gone bad, Tonin. Looks like the Boys forgot to clean and fill this one."

"I'll have words with them about that," said Tonin, sounding sincere. "Come back here; the other barrels have plenty of that sweet water." His voice faded away as he went on.

Drops of nervous sweat added to the rank mixture in the barrel. Tonin and Bly were too far away for Chism to make out their words, but they sounded casual. Regardless, Chism crouched, ready to spring if the top of the barrel was opened. He wondered if he had made a mistake in trusting Tonin. There was still a chance he had brought him this far to hand Chism over to a soldier who was a friend. Or wait for the reward money to increase. Bly might grow suspicious of the water. Or . . .

The creak of the wheels and jostle of the wagon made Chism flinch, but he realized that they were moving again.

After sloshing through three thousand and ten strokes of his leather, he was finally released from the wooden prison. Tonin kept his composure, but the Boys couldn't contain their laughter over the surprise in Bly's drink. One of them caught Chism by surprise with a hearty slap on the back, but he ducked away before they could congratulate him further.

Another one said, "You got some nerve, making water for Lieutenant Bly to drink."

"I don't know how you kept from laughing, Tonin," another added. "What I wouldn't give to see Bly's face!"

Chism didn't bother to tell them that a spill, not spunk, had caused the incident. The three continued to laugh uproariously as they set up camp and cooked dinner.

For the remainder of the trip, Chism rode in or walked alongside the wagon. Tonin explained, "You may have been a dangerous fugitive in Far West, but here in the interior you're just a boy in too-small clothes who's coming along for the ride. Provincials don't hold much sway in the interior, if they even come here. But I still don't want you wearing that sword, just in case word of the reward's bled over the border."

The road led slowly downhill as they left the Wasteland Mountains behind, and it didn't take long for the air to grow dryer and warmer. The only snow was on faraway mountain peaks. But the grasses were also sparser, meaning more stops for longer periods to allow the oxen to graze. Eight days passed in relatively easy travel. When they stopped in towns, Chism just hid inside the wagon. Free from his barrel prison, Chism pulled out his stitches and did his share of chores—gathering wood, tending oxen, and cooking meals. His leg was stiff, but the worst of the pain was gone.

On the morning of the ninth day, Tonin announced, "The

next town is as far as I go. This is the northernmost part of my route."

"It's really dry. Does anything grow here?"

"Sure. Cotton, oranges, corn. Irrigation ditches bring water from the river. A few decent craftsmen, too. I can't spare any coin or food to help you get to Palassiren, but folks here will hire you on long enough to earn your way. Too bad the mirror maker got a new apprentice a couple months back, or he could have taught you a skill." Apparently Tonin had forgotten that Chism's skill was wrapped inside the wagon. He continued, "Still, winter means harvest time in Shey's Orchard; there should be plenty for you to do."

An hour later, the first farm came into view. Black cattle dotted the low hills. Chism darted into the wagon to retrieve Thirsty, then jumped down and climbed onto the cattle fence.

"Tonin, Boys, I thank you for what you've done. If there's ever anything I can do to repay you . . ." Not finishing the sentiment or giving the men a chance to speak, he vaulted over the fence and set off at a jilty jog for the farmhouse.

CHAPTER 14

Madness

*T*wo weeks after setting off on the Eastern Spoke, Hatta returned to the Hub. Still no Cheshire Cat, but the two weeks were a success overall. Tired of spending valuable traveling time foraging, he had stopped in the town of Yendlie to earn food. Not only did he come away with a sack of food, but also a variety of wonderful teas for which Yendlie was famous.

But he still didn't know which Spoke to take. Five he'd travelled, three he hadn't. In the time it would take to track down Tjaden and ask, he could try the three, so he decided to rely on his luck. It was a good day for luck. And even if good luck didn't happen, even bad luck kept him from dire luck or whatever kind of luck was worse than that.

Examining each Spoke, Hatta removed his traveling hat in order to think. None of the roads seemed any more likely to lead to a cattish creature than the others. On a whim, he tossed the hat into the air and admired the spinning turtle-shell pattern. Light and dark purples spun and hovered in the air, coming down slowly, too soon, drifting to land in the middle of the Spoke to the northwest. Purples weren't exactly trustworthy colors, but the hat itself had been a trustworthy companion. After dusting it off, Hatta started down the Northwest Spoke.

A day and a half later, Hatta entered a forest of oak, birch, silkwood, and pine. Most of the trees were bare, and the few that still held their color were needly and green and thick. The dead leaves underfoot had given up their gold, red, and orange. Brown had consumed the other colors and covered the forest in a dull carpet.

To Hatta's delight, a fork appeared in the road a couple hundred paces past the first trees. Tjaden had mentioned a fork in the road. Or it might have been a pitchfork and a toad. Hatta didn't see any pitchforks, so he hurried to the split in the road. Mostly trees. Nothing that resembled a cat.

Hatta said, "Good day?"

"Good day yourself," said a tenor voice low in the trees. A large-headed cat with an even larger smile emerged from behind a tree. It jumped into a pale tree and lounged along a branch. It had gray fur with black stripes that had blended into the mat of dead leaves but stood out vividly against the bark.

"Mr. Cat? I'm Mr., um . . ." Hatta hadn't thought far enough ahead. "Well, you see, I don't actually have a surname."

"Feel free to use mine if you like. And please, call me Cheshire." The animal's voice was high and mischievous like an eleven-year-old boy's. It gave Hatta the impression that fun was about to be had. And if not fun, at least a very enjoyable time.

Hatta tried the cat's surname, but he wasn't comfortable with it. "'Hatta Cat' doesn't seem to fit, but I thank you just the same. Would you be a cat, perchance? Or merely by name?"

"I'm no more a cat than a prairie dog is a dog or a titmouse is a mouse."

Hatta nodded, and Cheshire continued happily. "Guinea pig, mongoose, catfish."

"As I understand it, a catfish is a fish."

"Ah," said Cheshire, smiling as widely as ever, "but it is most definitely not a cat."

Sound logic. But the non-cat's name still puzzled Hatta. "Why, then, are you called 'Cheshire Cat' if you *are* a Cheshire Cat?"

"Why not?"

"They don't call me 'Man' or 'Human'."

"But if you were the only one, I wager they would."

That was as sensible a statement as Hatta had heard all day. He was surprised how easy it was to talk to the creature, even about things on which, at first, they didn't see eye to eye.

"You are entirely delightful," Hatta said. "How is it that you talk?"

Cheshire tilted his head and smiled wistfully. He trilled, "How is it that other animals don't?"

"Oh, but they do! Some of them helped me find food on my way to Palassiren, and a rath once spoke loudly at a wedding I went to."

The smiling creature nodded. "All animals talk in their own way. It's people that don't listen."

"I'm going to save the kingdom some day," blurted Hatta. He felt so comfortable with Cheshire that he didn't mind telling him.

"Of course you are," Cheshire said confidently.

"I am? Sometimes people act odd when I tell them."

"As you can see, I am not *people*. You are more important than even you know, Hatta."

The optimistic praise made Hatta nervous. He was reluctant to trust Cheshire. Believing too much in his destiny could very well get him in trouble. "How do you know it? Because sometimes I wonder if mad thoughts make me think it."

Cheshire considered for a moment then answered, "How do you know when an animal is comical or hungry or bored when most people have no idea?"

"Sometimes I can just tell things."

"Ah," said Cheshire, nonchalantly satisfying an itch on his neck against the bark of the tree. "So can I."

Hatta made himself comfortable on the colorless carpet of leaves. In a very short time, he and Cheshire had arrived at a level of friendship that usually required a much lengthier journey. The two friends spent hours chatting about likes and dislikes, words and ideas, theories and riddles. Cheshire proved to be expert at solving riddles, and he didn't seem to mind Hatta's inability to figure out the riddles he posed back.

As night began to fall, Hatta realized he hadn't eaten all day. "Would you know where I might find food?" He still had a little from Yendlie, but as long as there was an animal who would tell him straight out, rather than making him interpret, it made sense to just ask. He could keep the Yendlie food for the trip back to Palassiren.

"Of course, Hatta. There's a frostberry patch not far from here." Cheshire shifted, and suddenly all Hatta could see was his brilliant, toothy smile. When he closed his mouth, Cheshire disappeared entirely. The next Hatta saw of the curious animal was a smile reappearing near his feet. As he watched, Cheshire's body seemed to disengage from the background of dead leaves and walk past him up the trail. It was as though someone had lit a Cheshire lamp, though to Hatta's knowledge there was no such thing.

"Was that disappearing?" asked Hatta, unsure if his mind was trying to deceive him again.

"Not really, no. That's just a little trick I do."

"Would it be magic?" asked Hatta.

"If I could spin a web, would it be magic?"

Hatta shook his head. "If you were any type of spider, you could do that."

"What if I squirted ink at annoying predators? Or emitted

a noxious spray that could be smelled a mile away? Or excreted a shell so I could get out of the rain? Magic?"

Hatta shook his head again. "Many animals do those things."

"So maybe I'm just a species able to turn my colors on and off. Or maybe it is magic. Call it what you like." Cheshire grinned.

Following Cheshire along the trail, Hatta said, "I would think it convenient to blend away when one wanted to. That's a trick I'd like to learn."

"You could never manage in such vivid clothes."

"But I care for colors so."

"We all make choices, don't we?"

Cheshire turned off the path and into the trees where no path existed. Hatta followed, and soon they reached an area brimming with frostberry bushes. With cold weather on the way out, the berries were shriveled, but Hatta ate voraciously for some time. He only stopped when he noticed Cheshire materialize in the fork of a nearby tree.

A thrill ran through Hatta as he watched Cheshire seem to come into being. Even if it wasn't magic, it was close enough to stick in Hatta's memory forever.

"I thank you, Cheshire. The berries are most delicious." Unsure of the protocol for interacting with the talking animal, Hatta lightly patted Cheshire's head, leaving deep purple spots on the gray stripes in the fur. He stared in wonder at his stained fingers and the spots they had left. The purple was so pure and intense that he wiped the fingers of his other hand along the light stripes in Cheshire's coat.

Cheshire cleared his throat. "If you keep that up, it's going to make blending in very difficult. At the end of the season the berries' color is particularly concentrated. "

"Oh dear!" Hatta attempted to wipe away the juice with his tunic, but the color had set. What a remarkable dye!

Cheshire faded, more quickly than before, but the purple

smudge and stripe stayed behind, floating in the air. Hatta bent one way then the other to get a better view. He'd never known colors to float unattached.

As quickly as he had faded, Cheshire reappeared. He twisted his head and began to work the purple stripe with his tongue.

With a quick nod of his head, Hatta sent his hat tumbling to the ground. He picked the darkest berries within reach. Pure, thick purple ran between his fingers and coated his hand as he mashed the berries. When both hands were sopped, Hatta ran them through his own hair. It was much longer than he realized. If he stretched it out as long as straight as it would go, he could see the superbly dyed ends.

Under his breath, he mumbled, "If only one of my mirrors were here."

"Ah, yes. Your mirrors. Your magnificent, crucial mirrors."

"I think they have something to do with my destiny."

"You think correctly, but they're only cobbles in your path. The cement is your powerful kindness. I doubt even *you* can realize the monumental consequences of your kindness."

Hatta stared, eyes wide and smile crooked. "Would you be a figment of my imagination? Sometimes my thoughts seem so mad, and nobody ever approves of them."

"I am as real as the purple in your hat and hair. And besides, without madness all the world makes sense. Who would ever want to live in such a place?"

"Not me," muttered Hatta. He was torn. Though he never felt happier than during the times he was caught up in illogical creativity, it was a major source of conflict with other people. Why was it always necessary to choose between happiness and sanity?

Cheshire would be a dangerous friend.

"Insanity," said Hatta, still mesmerized by his royal purple hair. "That always seemed the strangest word. It actually means being *out* of sanity. Shouldn't someone who's *in*sane be very sane? *In* means *out*. Curious."

"And they think we're the mad ones," laughed the smiling Cheshire Cat.

It occurred to Hatta that Cheshire was one of the wisest creatures he'd ever encountered. "How old would you be?" wondered Hatta aloud.

"I," said Cheshire proudly, "am exactly as old as myself. Not a day older."

"As am I. Which is fifteen years plus the age I was when my brother was born."

"So you don't actually know," stated Cheshire. "That's odd. For a human."

Hatta nodded. "I can't remember being born, and my father never told me what day that was."

"So what day do you celebrate your birth?"

"I never have," said Hatta. "How could I?"

The smiling animal considered for a moment. "You could celebrate every day. An un-birthday of sorts. It's only fair, after all. You have years to make up for."

The animal's logic was indisputable. For almost two decades, Hatta had denied himself a yearly celebration simply because he didn't know when to do it. He continued to mash berries, eating the pulp and applying the tint to his hair. Though it was difficult at times to force himself into making new friends, it often turned out so wonderfully.

"I wonder if I might remain with you here for some time."

Cheshire's smile grew woeful. "You have a duty to perform, Hatta. As do I."

"What would that be?"

"To help people such as you on their journeys."

"And what duty would I be performing that you would be doing your duty by helping me perform it?"

"Why, saving the kingdom, of course."

Hatta no longer cared whether Cheshire was real or fake, misleading or reliable, sane or mad. No person in the kingdom made him feel as jubilant as Cheshire did.

After wiping his hands clean on the bark of a nearby tree, Hatta retrieved his hat from the ground. Tipping it, but not placing it on his newly dyed hair, he said, "I thank you for everything and everysuch. I do hope we meet again."

"Be assured of it, Hatta. Your journey is long."

With a pleased half smile, Hatta turned and hiked back to the road. In the dimming light, he walked proudly toward Palassiren, silently debating the merits of sanity versus happiness. The choice wasn't as obvious as it always had been in the past.

CHAPTER 15

Colors

The reception Chism received after walking the mile to the cattle ranch's farmhouse was nothing like the small town courtesy he expected. He passed a gaggle of boys of all ages spread out in varying tasks, but no one spoke to him. They all had scratches and bruises and scuffed knees that showed through torn pants and eyes that were hungry for another fight. He couldn't shake the feeling of being a slab of fresh meat walking down a corridor of hungry dogs. Under different circumstances, he would have enjoyed sparring a while.

The woman who came to the door—it took Chism a moment to realize she wasn't a burly man in a dress—quickly told him that she had more than enough boys for one cattle farm. She added that even her boys had boys, every one of them tougher than a scamp whose clothes didn't fit. And if he didn't let her get back to slinging hash for the horde, she'd let them prove it.

Once his back was turned, Burly became more helpful. "Try Mikel's orchard," she blurted. "It's the big one northa town. I sent my youngest there a few weeks ago, and he's had plenty of work. Mikel's got no boys of his own there anymore, and Steffen'll enjoy having a morsel like you around for a while."

Chism waved over his shoulder but didn't slow down or meet any of the boys' challenging stares; he had a purpose. Skirting the town, he walked nine thousand four hundred and four steps and arrived at a small red brick house surrounded by groves. Compared to the cattle ranch, it seemed deserted.

The woman of the house came to the door quickly; she couldn't have been more different than Burly, both in looks and demeanor. Even before Chism could finish asking if there was work to be had, she reached out to brush the hair out of his eyes. He stepped back and scraped his long bangs away from his forehead.

"You've been on the road alone?" she asked. When Chism nodded, she said, "Come inside and eat something. Rest." The concern on her face told Chism that if he let her start, she would never stop mothering him.

Chism never had a mother, had never had anyone dote on him in the slightest. This lady would do it gladly if he gave her a chance. Doty was a good name for her.

He wasn't there for charity. "If there's no work to be had, I'll look somewhere else, Ma'am."

"There's work," said Doty with a sigh. "Give me just a moment and I'll send you out to my husband with his lunch."

Chism left Thirsty with Doty and noticed puzzlement on her face. It was obvious she wanted to ask why a boy would carry such a sword.

But Chism wasn't a boy. He'd believed that for years and if there had been any doubt, he'd proven it in the creek bed in Far West Province.

Carrying a wicker basket with enough food for four men, he set off to find Grower Mikel by the orange trees at the north edge of the farm. The brawny farmer was glad to see Chism, at first for the lunch, but then for the extra pair of hands. He was not without reservations, however.

"I can't pay a man's wage to a boy."

"Let me work a day, and pay me what I'm worth," said Chism. Grower Mikel agreed.

Introductions were made to Steffen, the young man working alongside Mikel. The resemblance to the family with all the brawler boys was clear, and though he had scars, Steffen lacked the recent bruises and scuffs his brothers and nephews so proudly displayed.

Probably because there's no one to scrap with here.

"Today's easy enough," said Mikel once lunch was finished. "Just picking fruit. Tomorrow you'll prove your salt."

Mikel handed Chism a large sack with a wire-framed half circle at the top. When Chism placed it over his shoulder, the bottom of the bag almost dragged on the ground. The wire held the opening wide in front of him so he could use both hands to pick.

Mikel said, "Pick any oranges that are more orange than green. Twist them like this so you don't plug the fruit." He twisted a piece of fruit off the tree and held it up to show Chism that the top of it was intact. Chism held out his hand and took the ripe orange. Mikel and Steffen plunged into the trees, arms reaching and retracting rapidly.

Oranges. Of all the work to find, why did it have to be stupid colors? Chism looked at the orange Mikel had picked. He compared it to an orange on a nearby tree and saw no difference whatsoever.

What do I do?

Chism's legs were as stiff and unmovable as tree trunks. Sweat ran down his armpits. It was a sensation Chism barely recognized—he was terrified. What would it say about him and all his manliness if he failed at a task a three-year old could do?

The fruit in his hand didn't look any different than anything else around him except in shape and texture. Orange had always been a color Chism felt he could understand. Because of the fruit with the same name, he associated a certain tangy sweet taste to it. Other colors, such as purple and pink, had nothing concrete to anchor them to. But it wasn't like he could taste every piece of fruit.

Steffen looked over his shoulder at Chism and scowled. The permanent scowl on his face got deeper, anyway.

Figure something out, Chism ordered himself, and walked to an area the other two had already picked over. He held the ripe orange up to one that they had passed and squinted at both pieces of fruit. The ripe orange was lighter than the green, but he had to look closely and squint a little to see it.

Chism wanted to walk away and find someone else who would give him an easy job—digging ditches, mining coal, or hauling rocks.

An orange came flying at Chism and hit his leg near his injury. Steffen had thrown it.

"Gonna help us?"

Chism gripped the orange in his hand and drew back, ready to throw it as hard as he could at Steffen's face. The memory of pain in his leg hummed where the orange had hit. The memory of walking through the creek with major blood loss and no sleep also came to mind. If Chism could do that, he could do anything. Even sort stupid colors and keep himself from killing Steffen. Maybe without even fighting him.

Choosing a tree near Mikel's, Chism used the ripe orange to gauge the other oranges. In direct sunlight the difference was slightly more pronounced.

"Is this one ripe?" he asked Mikel and was answered with a quick nod. "But not this one?" He held an orange he thought was green.

Mikel leaned back out of the foliage.

"What part of 'orange' did you not understand? I can't supervise every piece of fruit." His tone wasn't cruel, but it was obvious Mikel wondered if was talking to an idiot.

From where he stood on a ladder, Steffen said, "You've hired yourself a genuine tweedle, Mikel."

"I'm not stupid," said Chism, picking a few bright oranges while they watched him. "I just never picked oranges before."

"Don't know your colors? I'd say that's the definition of stupid." Steffen was already after the tussle his mother had mentioned, but Chism didn't take the bait.

Mikel gave Chism a curious look, and the three went back to work. The sounds of rustling leaves and grunting men filled the orchard. Chism did his best to stay in the sunlight even though it meant working mostly on ladders—up and down then moving the heavy ladder over two arm lengths. When his sack was full, Chism struggled to lug it to the large bin, but tried not to let his limp show. The arrow wound complained about the hard work, but Chism wanted to keep up with Steffen, who worked as hard as anyone he'd ever seen.

As Chism finished each tree, Mikel followed up, reaching for one or two ripe oranges. "Did these ones insult you?" Mikel asked.

Chism just kept picking.

Straining his eyes and brain was exhausting work but Chism pushed through. After a couple hours, they switched from oranges to lemons. Steffen went right to work. Chism thought he saw a pattern in which fruit the bruiser picked and which he passed, but he wanted to be sure so he snuck up behind him.

In Steffen's midstride of dropping a lemon into his sack, Chism swiped it from his hand.

Steffen spun toward Chism and came toward him with fists clenched at his side. "S'that your plan? Take my lemons 'stead of picking your own?"

Chism had to back away to keep Steffen from bumping him with his chest or head. The temptation to throw a kick was even stronger than the urge to throw the orange had been, but Chism resisted. Chism could knock down a man like Steffen a hundred times and he'd just get back up for another.

They had gone six steps, Steffen forward and Chism backward, when Steffen realized what he was doing. He glanced at Mikel, who gave him a stern look.

"Stay away from me, tweedle," said Steffen.

Chism was happy to do exactly that. Yellow and green turned out to be a little easier to distinguish. It was more of an issue of brightness with the lemons, not color. Still, by the end of the day, Chism looked forward to whatever Mikel had planned for the next day. It had to be better than colors.

The sun had set by the time they got back to the house. Appetizing smells emanated from the kitchen. Doty smiled when Chism came in and reached for his shoulders. He ducked away.

"Sorry," he said. "I don't like people touching me."

The words were a mistake. Steffen reached out a hand to poke him, but Chism swiped his wrist out of the air with the back of his hand.

"Alright then," Steffen said. His sour face looked happy for the first time that day. He faced Chism with his hands raised, ready to try poking or slapping. "S'all it takes, is it?"

"No," said Doty, standing protectively in front of Chism. "You may not touch him as long as he's here."

"Where's the fun in that?" asked Steffen.

"I mean it, Steffen. Not one time. I won't have a bully in my house."

"Bully?" asked Steffen with an expression that said he didn't understand the concept. "Never heard of it. Unless you mean 'brother'."

Doty gave him an I-will-brook-no-nonsense glare, and

Steffen stalked to the table with a shrug and a scowl. Chism considered standing up for himself. What man wanted a housewife to protect him? But standing up meant starting a fight and that wouldn't get him to Palassiren any faster, so he let it go. Ander and Cactus would be proud.

The meal spread on the table made Chism think of the time he'd spent in Leis's house, and he was surprised by a pang of longing. After the situation he'd grown up in, Chism never expected to long for anything called home.

The three men ate stew and corn the same way they had worked—in silence. Doty spent as much time glancing around the table as she did eating. Eventually, looking at Steffen and Chism, she took Mikel's hand and said, "It's almost like having Tjaden and Ollie back home."

At the mention of his training partners' names, Chism choked on the turnip he was chewing and went into a coughing fit. Steffen's hand came off the table and Chism turned his head to see it ready to slap his back.

"Steffen," said Doty in a rising voice that brought the hand back down.

Steffen groaned and slid a cup of water toward Chism. "S'right," Steffen told Chism. "*The* Tjaden. The Vorpal Knight. You're sitting at the table of a hero."

There was bitterness in Steffen's voice, but Chism knew the words were true as well as anyone. Better than most, in fact.

Doty beamed, but Mikel went back to his meal as soon as Chism regained control.

"You're Sir Tjaden's parents?"

They both nodded. Even Mikel's chin rose with pride.

Steffen spoke again. "You can hear all about the heroes . . . after dinner?" He made a hopeful expression at Doty, who nodded.

Mikel explained, "Steffen's heard the story one or two times."

"Yeah," said Steffen. "Only one or two. Hundred."

Chism didn't want to embarrass himself the next time he ran into Tjaden or Ollie, so he called up the name he'd heard Mikel use for Doty—Lira.

When dinner was finished, Steffen excused himself and Lira started immediately into the account without being prompted. She began with Tjaden and Steffen's fight at the Swap and Spar, and Chism suddenly understood Steffen's attitude. Through fourteen months of Elite training with Tjaden, Chism had never found out that Tjaden wasn't a local champion. It was assumed that every Elite recruit was the best their towns or cities had to offer.

The rest of the story was as accurate as could be expected from the proud mother of a Knight. And she didn't leave out Ollie's role in slaying the Jabberwock.

For one short moment, Chism considered telling them he'd been through the Academy with Tjaden and Ollie, but he didn't want to explain the rest of the story about how he ended up in Shey's Orchard, so he stayed quiet. He now recognized Mikel from the Elites' induction ceremony, but the grower either didn't recognize Chism or had chosen to respect his secret. Either reason suited Chism. After Lira's hospitality, Chism felt guilty keeping a secret that would have delighted any mother, but it was for the best.

The next morning, Chism worked blisters into his palms using a hoe to weed for hours straight. Try as he might, he couldn't keep up with Steffen, even though he wasn't far behind. Steffen didn't give him any trouble. Apparently he'd gotten over whatever problem he'd had with Chism the first day.

At lunchtime, Steffen tossed Chism an orange to go with his lunch. After peeling it and biting into a large slice, Chism saw the smile on Steffen's face just as he tasted the bitterness of an unripe orange. Chism felt like as much of an idiot as Steffen already thought he was. It would feel so good to smear the orange in Steffen's face and force him to eat it. A fight would end the pranks with most people, but Chism knew in his gut that Steffen would just get worse after losing a fight.

"It's delicious," said Chism with juice dripping down his chin. He forced himself to eat the rest of the slice then set the orange on the ground and ignored it. Hopefully if Chism didn't react to the pranks, Steffen would get bored with them.

No such luck.

That night, as Chism climbed into bed, he found the body of a snake they'd killed earlier in the day. The next day, Chism got up from the dinner table to check a noise outside. When he came back and took a bite of black beans, he realized Steffen had slipped a spoonful of pepper into them. It burned his mouth like the sun itself, but Chism at the whole bowl.

Five more days passed working for Mikel, which was enough to earn what Chism needed to buy food for his trip to Palassiren. Mikel relented on the statement he'd made when Chism arrived, and paid him a thrippenny. A man's wages after all.

With a sack of food slung across his back, Thirsty at his hip, and a bag of oranges in his hand that Mikel assured him were all ripe, Chism set off. The days were cold and the nights close to freezing, but the coins he carried were enough to buy a room at an inn every night. Twice, travelers offered him a spot on the back of their wagons even though he tried to keep to himself.

Each step or turn of the wheel lengthened the road behind and shortened the road ahead. But the success of his escape from the Provinces and the progress of his journey only brought him closer to trial with Lady Cuora and the rest of the Council. Analyze it however he could, beheading seemed the only possible outcome.

At least he would arrive with empty pockets. As Ander often told him, *Only a father or a fool dies with money in his pocket.*

CHAPTER 16

Crowds

Palassiren was different when Hatta returned from visiting the Cheshire Cat. He wasn't even inside the city gates yet when he noticed it had changed colors. It was still a multihued cacophony, but the weave of colors had grown much tighter and darker around the city entrance. A large crowd was gathered just inside the gates, all facing inward and fiercely whispering. They stared at a gap in the middle of the crowd where a man in a magnificently green uniform, dark as a holly leaf, sat on a chestnut horse. He appeared to be waiting for something.

Nearly every face in the crowd was twisted in anger or at the least, irritation. Some people shouted at the man on the horse, harsh words that Hatta tried to not comprehend. He wanted none of whatever had brought such an edgy group together, so he put his head down and dodged through the crowd. The throng grew thicker. Hundreds of citizens were jostling their way into the courtyard. They pressed so hard that Hatta couldn't get through.

He stood at the far side of the courtyard from the city entrance when the crowd began tapping and clapping. Looking around, he saw a woman in a bright red dress arrive above the plaza along the inner walkway of the city walls. She had wonderfully wild black hair and was accompanied by red soldiers and blue Elites. Whoever she was, the people of the city loved her.

The green-garbed soldier on the horse didn't wait for the woman to speak. He unfurled a scroll and began reading. Despite the mutterings of the crowd, Hatta could hear the man's words, but the commotion made it hard to focus. Something about Provinces and borders and Elites.

With each sentence, the crowd grew louder and its anger glowed brighter. What started out as a simmering shade of rose blazed into the color of flame.

Hatta wanted out. But his attempts to excuse himself through were met by blind elbows and shoves. Standing as still as he could, Hatta huddled under his turtle-shell hat—at least he had his beloved hat—eyes brimming and too scared to move.

The man continued reading, but Hatta did his best to block out the words. Even after the soldier finished, the crowd murmured and ranted. There was the sound of horse hooves, shouting from multiple voices, and considerable jostling from the crowd.

Hatta chanted verses to distract himself from the hullabaloo:

> *Patience and merit and amity strive,*
> *Worry and cunning and bully connive.*
> *Old wizened targus keep dreams in a hive*
> *Unlucky are those who survive.*

Feeling slightly more relaxed, he continued with another of his favorite childhood verses:

> *Tripita tripe, the foxes like*
> *to scurry and swish and dash.*

*Perfida pratt, the shoehouse rat
nibbles the cobbler's moustache.*

    The relief was not total, but it was enough to allow Hatta to remain planted and wait for the horde to thin enough for him to escape. He didn't know what became of the green soldier or the woman of the walkway, but eventually the crowd shifted and cleared, allowing him to shuffle toward his alley.

CHAPTER 17

Collision

*W*hen Palassiren appeared on the eighth day, Chism stopped to enjoy a moment of accomplishment. He was about to fulfill his oath to Lieutenant Fahrr and prove that his word was worth more than his life. With a sigh, Chism took one step toward the city, then another.

Inside the gates, a ring of hundreds of people in the courtyard blocked his way. They were all staring at a man on horseback, but Chism was too short to see any more than that. He pulled himself up onto the wheel of a wagon at the back of the crowd.

The horseman in the center of the circle was reading from a scroll. His uniform was dark and bore the flame and stars insignia—a Provincial soldier. Chism didn't have to listen very long to confirm his suspicion.

"... the tyranny of kings and rule of a Council that spurns our interests. No longer will we bow to foreign leaders."

The crowd was a meshing of repetitive shapes and indistinguishable colors, but Chism could feel the tension as they listened to the soldier on horseback read in his formal tone.

"We, the Twelve Provinces, declare our separation from the kingdom of Maravilla. Your tax collectors are no longer welcome; your soldiers no longer required. The days of your Elites roaming our lands with impunity are over. Our borders are sealed to your soldiers and officials. Only under the banner of negotiation shall any be admitted.

"Friends have become enemies, and allies are now foes. Eventually, you will submit to your proper role as an Interior Province, or, like a snake with a rat in its clutches, we, the Provinces will squeeze the life out of the interior."

The man rolled the scroll then stared up at the walkway along the inner city wall. "A pox on Lady Cuora and Captain Markin and a pox on the kingdom of Maravilla!" He spat on the cobbles then stared defiantly up again.

Chism jumped down from the wagon wheel stepped a little further into the city to see the target of the soldier's gaze. Captain Markin, leader of the Elites, and Lady Cuora, head of the King's Council, looked down on the man. They were flanked on either side by soldiers in wide-brimmed helmets and square-cut tunics. Captain Markin watched Lady Cuora, ready to follow whatever orders she gave. Thick strands of dark hair circled Lady Cuora's face, and she appeared ready to jump down from the wall and strangle the Provincial with her own hands.

The Provincial didn't wait for her to find words and issue an order. He threw the scroll into the street and spurred his horse toward the gate.

"Seize him!" shouted Lady Cuora.

Captain Markin was only half a breath behind her. "Seize him!" he echoed.

The lax city guards were out of position to block his exit, and no one in the crowd wanted to be trampled. The militiaman would be out of the city within moments. Chism considered drawing Thirsty to cut the horse's legs out from under him, but it was never a good idea to kill a horse if it could be avoided. He had his knives, but the order was to seize, not kill. As much as he hated the idea, he was going to have to touch the soldier.

In two steps, he was scrambling back up the wagon. No sooner was he in position than the Provincial approached, spurring his horse wildly. Chism was one of the last people the soldier would pass before reaching the gatehouse.

Silently, Chism launched himself into the air straight at the oncoming soldier. The man's eyes widened in surprise. He must not have expected a citizen, especially a poorly dressed child, to get in the way. But there was no time to change course.

They collided head on.

Gasping, swearing, and leaning to one side, the soldier attempted to shove Chism away, but Chism had both arms entwined in the man's uniform. He lay across the soldier's lap. One shoulder felt like it had been stepped on by an ox. Ignoring the pain, Chism spun and leaned to the right, but his weight wasn't enough to dislodge the soldier from the saddle.

The pain in his shoulder was excruciating; it was hard to concentrate on anything else. With his arms still wrapped in the soldier's uniform, Chism placed both feet squarely on the running horse's ribs. After gathering everything he had left, Chism let out a bellow and pushed off with all his strength. As he and the soldier started to fall, Chism felt a wrenching pop in his right shoulder. He tried to hold on to consciousness through the pain, but blackness took him.

Men in wide-brimmed helmets loomed over Chism when he came to. Pain pulsed from his shoulder and radiated through the rest of his body. He turned his head, to see if his shoulder had been pierced with a sword. It didn't appear to be bleeding, despite flaring with pain that made him clench his teeth and groan. Nearby, the Provincial soldier lay face down under four Palassiren city guards.

Chism realized that guards around him were asking questions, but before he could make sense of the words, they separated to make room for two more people—Captain Markin and Lady Cuora.

Captain Markin stopped suddenly.

"Elite Chism?"

Lady Cuora was unfazed. Multiple snakes of black hair—only black could be *that* dark—hovered like thin waves around her head, but her face was a model of control.

"So you're the cause of all our trouble?" She looked at Chism like she would a hog in the market. Flippantly, she said, "I didn't think you'd come, but Fahrr and Marky swore you would. Typical soldier. Brave and loyal but not too smart."

Pain made responding impossible.

As Lady Cuora turned away, she said to Captain Markin, "The headsman will be happy, anyway. More work for him." Without looking back at the city guards, she yelled over her shoulders, "Bind him tight, boys. He's more of a man than two of you put together."

Chism recognized some of the soldiers' faces. They would not enjoy binding an Elite tightly, but they would follow orders. Chism knew that this time he couldn't count on being underestimated.

"Forgive me, Sir," said Mister, a soldier twice Chism's age. "Orders, you know?"

Chism had never learned the man's real name. That was the great thing about nicknames—they were nearly impossible to forget. Mister held shackles apologetically toward Chism.

Even the thought of moving his right arm caused his head to swim. The only position he could tolerate was crossing his arm over his chest. After placing a sling on the injured arm, another soldier placed Chism's left arm over the right and shackled both wrists. A swathe relieved some of the agony by holding both arms tightly in place against his chest. Gently, the soldiers helped Chism up and led him into the city.

A mountain of pressure suddenly lifted—at last, escape was an option. His oath was to turn himself in, and that promise was now fulfilled. He had accomplished his goal of making it back to the capital, and now he could finally work toward freedom.

I should have run when Ander suggested it.

But the done was done, as his brother used to say.

The injury would complicate his escape, but Chism hadn't come this far to walk peacefully to the headman's block. Sooner or later he would find a way out.

Nothing had stopped him yet and he didn't know anything that could.

CHAPTER 18

Schism

Hatta hurried through the nearly empty streets of Palassiren, only looking up long enough to find his way to his shop. The angry taint of the crowd that he had just left behind in the courtyard clung to him like a bad odor. He was tempted to find somewhere to wash his clothes and bathe, but the thought of his waiting mirrors pulled him forward.

His pace increased when he reached the alley. Sneaking past the tailor's shop, Hatta removed his key from an inside pocket of his coat. He tried it in the door but the door didn't seem to need it, so he ducked inside. His breaths came long and deep as he leaned against the solid wood of his door in the dim light.

It took an hour for his nerves to subside. If not for an urgent matter, he would have stayed hidden for the remainder of the day. Unfortunately, he had a delivery to make.

After selecting a specific mirror, Hatta sidled back into the city streets. The palaces were easy to find; the main road led straight to the inner gates. In the few hours he'd spent in Palassiren, Hatta hadn't gone close to the inner city, and he was surprised by the level of activity there. A long line of people made their way past the guards leading into the inner walls.

Hatta waited his turn, and when he finally reached the gate, he told the guard, "I have a delivery for Elora who's from Shey's Orchard where her husband named Tjaden is also from, who's an Elite." That seemed like a lot of words.

The gruff guard said, "You mean Lady Elora? The Vorpal Knight's woman? She's a maid to Lady Palida, but you can't get into the White palace unless you have business."

Digging through the pockets on his coat, Hatta said, "Then I have business in the form of a very important letter." He shoved one of the letters into the guard's face. "Very important indeed. You see, I promised I would deliver it."

The guard muttered under his breath as he inspected the letter. "On any other day we'd deliver it for you, but we can't spare anyone. Don't make any trouble; Lady Cuora will extend no mercy to troublemakers today." The name was familiar, but Hatta couldn't recall anything specific about her. He would definitely do anything possible to avoid her, in any case.

The letter went back into his pocket, and Hatta carried the lightweight mirror past the guard, thanking him profusely. The guard didn't notice; he was already interrogating the next person in line.

A string of palaces stretched out in a line on the other side of the courtyard, the one in the middle being the largest. Constructed of polished, pale blue stone, it rose like a peak above the other buildings inside the inner gate. The palace on the left was ornamented with candied-cherry red, including a grand staircase leading to the front entrance. The stairs began pale pink at the bottom but grew more intensely red with each step.

In contrast to the blushing palace, a noticeably colorless one spread out on the other side of the large central palace. It was as stark as the other was vivid. No paint adorned the structure, and the pale granite had been sanded until no color remained. Unfortunately, the unpleasant white palace was where he would find Lady Palida and her ladies-in-waiting. Swerving around the conflux of people that filled the courtyard, Hatta entered the drab palace.

A butler, dressed entirely in the same monotonous white, screened entrants. Hatta gathered his confidence and walked past with the mirror held prominently.

"Delivery for lady-in-waiting Elora." He didn't look to see the manservant's response, and when no sound followed him into the bleached interior of the palace, he kept walking and wiped the sweat from his forehead.

Contrary to his expectations, the inside buzzed with twice as much activity as the exterior. Servants carried boxes, chests, furniture, and decorations as if they had suddenly decided to redecorate the entire palace. The only colors in sight were the natural browns, blondes, and orange-reds of servants' hair. Hatta smiled, feeling strangely invisible as the only vivid item in a monochromatic environment.

It wasn't hard to locate the chamber of the ladies-in-waiting, but Elora was nowhere to be found. He asked a young, white-clad girl where Elora might be and was directed toward Lady Palida's quarters. In the disorder, he was able to enter without being challenged and found Elora in the Lady's antechamber, packing various hairbrushes, hats, shoes, and other items. Everything was white.

She looked much more mature than she had a mere four months before. The brown leather herbal belt he'd seen her wear across her chest in Shey's Orchard had been replaced with a white one. This one also had wonderful tiny pockets, pouches, and straps.

"Elora, it's me, Hatta," he said and offered his most friendly half smile.

HATTER

"Hatta!" She embraced him as an old friend, even though their time in Shey's Orchard only overlapped by a week. Her wide smile was not only infectious, but it was crooked. Scars shaped *her* smile, but Hatta didn't know why his was crooked. It just always had been. For a moment, he merely enjoyed her presence.

"If you were a man," Hatta said, "I'd say you were a hail fellow well met. Hail female well met doesn't have the same ring, but nothing is as luxurious as the embrace of an old friend. Even a young old friend."

Elora smiled her dazzling smile. "What brings you to Palassiren?"

"Delivering letters and gifts. Two letters and one gift, truth be told. I've not much experience or custom as a messenger." He held the letters and mirror toward her.

Elora's eyes went wide, and she grasped the papers first. While she read, Hatta inspected his mirror for the last time. It was a fine piece—the metal's sheen was like liquid. A clear reflection spanned a hand and a half across the center of the mirror. Around the bluish metal edges, the reflection was somewhat cloudy.

It was the fringes of his mirrors that fascinated him. The borders gave a somewhat gloomy yet colorful reflection, but looking into the center was like looking past a cloud of confusion and seeing a true image of himself. The edges weren't straight and defined like most mirrors; they curved like the edges of a splash of water. He still didn't know what role his mirrors would play in saving the kingdom, or what role he himself would play, for that matter.

"Your mother opined that you would love this one." He looked into the cobalt borders in different places, seeing varying reflections of himself looking back. "Since you care for the color blue."

Elora had finished reading and held a letter to her chest. Her eyes were moist, and it took her a moment to acknowledge his words.

"This is for me?" She took the precious mirror and inspected it. "It's very unique, and in a way, kind of beautiful." With a perplexed expression, she said, "My father didn't make this."

Hatta shook his head.

"Did you make it?" Surprise showed clearly on her face as he nodded. "You learned so quickly. I'll treasure it, Hatta. Thank you."

"That would be my first colored mirror. I'm glad you find it unique."

"Hatta, I wish you had come under better circumstances. I don't know if you've heard, but the kingdom has been torn apart. Lady Palida doesn't think it's safe to stay even one more night." She looked around the room at everything left to pack.

A familiar sick feeling filled Hatta's stomach, and he asked, "With harmony being so pleasant, why must people so often choose discord?"

Looking at him with pity, Elora opened her mouth to answer but caught herself. "You look so gaunt, Hatta. Have you been eating?"

"The money I should have in order to buy food was spent on rent, and I had to stretch the food from Yendlie. I plan to sell my mirrors, then buy some food."

"When was the last time you ate?" she demanded, coming forward to place a hand on his shoulders. Elora turned and called into the chamber, "Yuli! Come in here." She began searching through the piles of packing material and produced a large sack, not unlike the one her father had used to pack food for Hatta before he left Shey's Orchard.

A mousy girl appeared from deeper in Lady Palida's quarters, and Elora told her, "Run to the foodstores and pack this as full as you can. I want foods of all sorts."

"But m'lady, the Lady's things—"

"Can wait," Elora finished. "This is more important. After you fill it, find a servant to carry it here while you run to the kitchen for some bread and a plate of whatever meat they're serving. Hurry, we have work to do."

"Yes, Lady Elora." The girl left the room at a trot.

Servants who have servants? How deep does it go?

The thought of a sackfull of food made Hatta hungry, but how could he accept it? "Elora, I haven't a way to pay for the food. I thank you, but I'm sure I can manage."

"Is that right?" She looked up at him and smiled her innocent, scar-crooked smile. "You tell me exactly how you intend to manage, and I'll leave you alone."

Hatta was stuck. The only animals in a city this big would be scavengers like rats and pigeons. They could never lead him to more than a few crumbs. And what scavengers considered food was often uneatable.

After only a moment, Elora continued, "I didn't think so." Her face turned serious. "Hatta, the kingdom is in serious danger. Lady Palida and everyone else who has anything to do with the Provinces are leaving the city. Tonight. I'm bound to Lady Palida, but Tjaden and all of the Elites from the interior will remain loyal to Captain Markin, King Antion, and Lady Cuora. I'm sure it will work out eventually, but some people are saying the only way this can end is with war."

War. A dirty word. Worse by far than other curses men used. But there was something that he could do to prevent it. Only he still had no idea what it was.

"What do you call this?" He touched the strap of her herb belt where it hung on her shoulder.

"An herbal sash." She fingered some of the vials and pockets. It held healing powders and potions. Elora was somewhat of an apothecary.

"Have you considered *herbolier*? I've seen men wear such and call them bandoliers, but they usually carry knifes and darts and other ugly things."

"*Herbolier* sounds perfect." Elora smiled and adjusted the sash. On her right wrist was the faded red ribbon she'd always worn, and on a finger of that hand was a ring he hadn't noticed before.

"Have you had that ring long?"

She held it out for him to see. Leaves and vines of gold circled her finger. Two flowers, one rose-colored and one subtly green, seemed to grow from the vines. "Tjaden gave it to me when he saved me. There's a story behind it that I'd love to tell you when we have more time."

"I'm destined to save . . ." he began, but he paused, thinking of how to explain it. In his pause, a strange retinue stormed into the room.

A servant carrying a large, thin mirror led the group. He walked backward, facing the mirror toward a curious pair—a boy not even up to Hatta's chest and an apparition of a woman who was pure white from head to toe. Not only was she draped in white, but as Hatta inspected her, he saw that her skin, hair, eyelashes, lips, and fingernails were white too. Everything except her eyes, which were what truly captured Hatta's attention. They were dazzling blue. It seemed that all the color that should have been spread throughout the rest of her body was concentrated into two small rings.

He could only wrest his attention away from the woman to examine the boy in short bursts. Dressed in a thick robe the same color as Hatta's purple-dyed hair, he carried himself as if leading the group of servants behind him.

Next to Hatta, Elora made some sort of bowing movement, but Hatta was too intent on the Lady to notice much. Her eyes. Never in his life had he seen such an intense concentration of color.

The pair cut off their conversation when they reached Elora and Hatta. The white Lady looked at Hatta curiously.

"My Lady," said Elora, "this is Hatta, a friend from Shey's Orchard." The word 'friend' made Hatta smile, but at the same time he was intrigued that Elora spoke to the Lady's reflection in the mirror that the servant carried.

"To meet a friend of Elora's is a pleasure." As she spoke, the white-clad servant angled the mirror so Hatta and the Lady could see each other, and she addressed his reflection rather than his person. "Lady Palida am I."

Even in the reflection, her eyes engulfed him, and he couldn't respond. Her age was difficult to tell, but Hatta guessed she was a decade older than him. Perhaps as old as thirty? Hatta stared into the mirror and confirmed that she truly was white—not albino or blonde, but white.

"Your eyes," he managed, and she raised a white eyebrow. "My Lady, that is . . . I've never seen coloring to equal them. I could swear they are living sapphires. And yet your skin lacks color in the extreme."

"Your pardon, My Lady," Elora interjected. "Hatta was on his way out to allow us to continue to prepare your things." She made another bow toward Lady Palida's reflection.

"Would you be the king?" Hatta asked the boy, ignoring Elora's escape attempts. He'd heard Maravilla had a boy king.

The boy nodded and smiled, looking over Hatta's garish clothes. "I am," he said but didn't have a chance to say more before Elora tugged Hatta's sleeve and led him to the door. Hatta watched over his shoulder.

The king quickly forgot about Hatta and Elora and turned to Lady Palida's image in the mirror. "My place is here, Mother, and I think it would be best for you to stay and appeal to diplomacy."

"Too late is it. To stay here for me longer is not safe. Of your father and you is the land of Palassiren." Placing a tender hand on the boy's shoulder, she said, "Onion—"

"Mother, please." He looked around, embarrassed. "That is not a proper name for a king."

Smiling, she apologized.

King Antion continued. "I refuse to just give up the kingdom, and I don't see any way to avoid war with the Provinces. They completely surround us. I fear if you walk out now it will mean the end of Maravilla."

Though Hatta was almost out the door, he called out, "Don't worry, I'll soon save the kingdom with my mirrors and kindness!" The mirror bearer didn't have to shift the angle to allow Lady Palida to see Hatta; she just glanced over the shoulder of her own reflection. The last view Hatta had of the room before Elora dragged him out was the brilliant gaze of her piercing eyes.

With a look that showed more shock than anger, Elora asked, "You do realize that was the king and one of the members of his Council."

"I found them very gracious. Might you tell me about her colors?"

"That's not really something that's polite to ask about, Hatta." Elora touched her cheek. "No one asks about the scars on my face, and they don't talk openly about Lady Palida's color and mirrors."

"Among lions, the ones with scars are the most eminent."

"Lions?" asked Elora, but Yuli arrived just then. She placed a plate of food in Elora's hands, then disappeared into Lady Palida's quarters.

Elora said, "I don't have any more time, but I'm so grateful to you for bringing the letters—"

"And the mirror," cut in Hatta. "Please don't forget the mirror."

"Of course," said Elora. "I'm honored to have your first mirror."

A manservant, dressed in white, delivered a bulging sack. Thankfully, Elora only had time for a very short farewell. Hatta hadn't eaten a proper meal for a week, and the plate of bread and beef was almost too much for his shrunken stomach. After cleaning the plate, he picked up the rucksack and left the palace.

Activity around the palaces had increased. Now that Hatta understood the reason behind the bustle, he saw a bit of order in the chaos and realized he was witness to a momentous event in the fate of the kingdom. It was an occasion he had no desire to witness, but if he was going to learn his role in saving the kingdom, he should probably observe its peril.

Nearly every quarter of the plaza was full of people going one way or another. Far to his left, there was a clear pocket surrounding a large sculpture. He put a hand to the brim of his hat and made tipping motions in one direction and then the other as he crossed the courtyard. It required numerous stepping-around's and pardon-me's, but he arrived with plenty of action left to witness.

The sculpture itself made him regret the effort. From the side he'd seen only a curve of dark blue stone. From the front—or was it the back?—he saw a blue Circle and white Sword, twice as tall as a tall man or three times as tall as a short one. It seemed there was no escaping the Elites.

There was no other quiet corner of the courtyard and the curve of the Circle was an inviting curve that offered a view of nearly the entire plaza. Hatta climbed up and settled inside. An occasional passerby raised an eyebrow or lowered two, but nobody said anything.

A line of wagons, coaches, footmen, and horses took shape in front of Lady Palida's palace. Gaps in the line filled in, and it grew longer as more and more people joined the procession. Last to arrive were Lady Palida and her retinue, including two mirror bearers this time, through which she inspected her convoy. Even though she was over a hundred paces away and night was beginning to come to the city, Hatta was sure he saw her eyes giving off their own light.

She and her son, King Antion, bowed to each other's reflections. The king, encircled by blue-clothed Elites, walked north toward the largest palace. Elora emerged from Lady Palida's palace carrying a small travel case and, to Hatta's delight, her mirror! Before she and Lady Palida climbed into their carriage, the red-clothed Lady whom Hatta had seen on the walls of the city arrived with another contingent of soldiers.

Brief words were spoken through mirrors between the white and red Ladies before Lady Palida turned and entered her carriage. Elora moved to follow her, but the Red Lady stopped her, seized the mirror, and inspected it. Even from the distance, he could see Elora fidget. After exchanging a sentence or two, the Red Lady shoved the mirror into Elora's waiting hands, and Elora darted into the carriage.

As the procession lumbered toward the inner gates, a small rush of men moved to join it. They were clad in blue; half wore the Circle and Sword. The Elites and Fellows formed the rearguard as the people of the Provinces fled Palassiren.

The Elites who didn't leave looked on as their brothers-in-arms departed, and the gulf of pain in Hatta's chest deepened. Whatever event had caused the schism in the kingdom went deep enough to separate men who considered themselves brothers.

Husband and wife. Mother and son. Brothers. The conflict had just begun, and already too many people were separated from those they loved. Squinting through the night, Hatta saw the outline of the boy king on the large palace's center balcony. His hands went repeatedly to his eyes as he watched the procession thread through the inner gates. He was only a few years older than Hatta had been when he'd lost his own mother, and Hatta felt no shame in sharing a tear with the young monarch.

"I'll do my best, Boy King," said Hatta quietly into the distance. "Of course, I can't make any promises, because there's a chance I'm mad. On the contrary, there's also a chance I'm not mad."

Even after the refugees cleared the courtyard, Hatta remained at the statue, looking across at the king. The boy's father, King Barash, had been killed by the Jabberwock a year and a half before, and now his mother was being forced to flee. Hatta would stay and keep him company as long as the king watched the empty courtyard.

A quarter of an hour later, the king retreated, and Hatta followed his example. He walked back to his shop feeling torn and trodden on. He hoped that somehow the grief he carried away was grief that the boy wouldn't have to endure.

The morning after the schism, Hatta's first thoughts were of his mirrors and his shop. He rushed to open the doors of his business for the first time, sure that the departure of everyone associated with the Provinces would not prove a damper on his business. He didn't have nails, or a hammer for that matter, or any easels to display his mirrors, so he had to set them on the floor, leaning against the wall. It wasn't hard for him to go next door and greet the tailor in his confident mood, and the old man was happy to see him.

After initial greetings, Hatta produced the large rucksack and said proudly, "I can repay your kind food now. I have . . ." he paused, looking through the sack, "a gourd, a portion of a ham, plenty of bread . . ."

"That's not necessary, young man. I have sufficient; keep that for yourself."

The old tailor told Hatta that he would be happy to send his few customers to see the mirrors, and he even found two racks that could double as easels, which he cheerfully lent to Hatta.

Hatta's first customer walked through the door an hour later—a woman, followed by a servant who carried a tied package. She browsed for a few moments, then left without speaking. Over the course of the day, a few more people entered and left with only a word or two. A well-dressed couple offered his highest hope and deepest worry. The woman was intrigued and even used the word "distinctive," but her husband was quick to express his opinion.

"Why would you want a mirror that's half cloudy? Only half of the surface reflects clearly. Mirrors should be square. These hazy, wavy borders are a waste of material." He didn't even acknowledge Hatta, who was standing ready to assist or answer questions.

The lighting in the building was insufficient. That was it. Hatta hadn't considered the north-facing shop in late winter. Hopefully it would change as spring came, then summer.

An hour after dark, Hatta closed the door on his first day as a shopkeeper, hoping it wasn't a sign of things to come.

Pennies and pounds mattered little, but saving a kingdom would be difficult at this rate.

CHAPTER 19

Knight

*I*n Chism's hometown, T'lai, a man and woman who everyone called the Twins held the illustrious distinction of being undetainable. As a matter of pride, they had escaped every prison in the region. Chism doubted that even the Twins could find a way out his current quandary.

Security in the Palassiren prison was tighter than the barrel in which Chism had escaped Far West Province. The gate to his cell didn't open even one time after he was locked inside. Food arrived on a tray under the bars. They provided a special bucket for necessities that was shallow enough to slide back and forth as well. No visitors were allowed, even Ander. At all times, one guard was assigned to do nothing but watch Chism. When Chism attempted conversation, the guards acted as if he hadn't spoken.

Even without the injured shoulder and gimpy leg, Chism wouldn't stand a chance of escape. Lady Cuora had always been hard, but Chism could tell by the diligence of the guards that their fear of her had grown since he'd left on campaign months earlier. If Chism escaped, the guard responsible could very well take his place under the headman's axe.

Two days passed. Two infinites. Without Thirsty, Chism couldn't do proper morning routines. The healing shoulder wouldn't allow full motions anyway, so Chism was limited to mentally repeating sword forms thousands of times.

By the time guards came to escort him to trial, Chism was ready to accept anything rather than the tedium of another minute in the cell. The guards slid shackles into the cell and didn't open the door until he had secured them to his hands and feet. Nine guards escorted him. That had always been one of his least favorite numbers.

The throne room of the King's Council held three elegant chairs. The last time Chism was in the room, there had been four. Where one throne used to sit, Chism noticed the outline of four tiny squares on the floor that were cleaner than the tile around them. The other three seats were occupied, so the missing throne obviously belonged to Lady Palida. After being cut off from outside contact for days, Chism couldn't think of any reason why Lady Palida's throne would have been removed.

Any of the four council members could pronounce judgment on any particular day. Yet here sat three rulers of Maravilla to pass judgment on him. If everything else didn't underscore the seriousness of the charges, that did.

With the chair missing, the room was off-balance. Asymmetrical. They hadn't taken time to center the three remaining chairs. Another bad portent for the trial. To make matters worse, Chism hadn't caught the first rays of the sun in days.

Three people sat to judge him, but the verdict would depend on Lady Cuora. Chism had never known Captain Markin to defy her. If ever he did, Chism hoped it would be today. Captain Markin was the Captain of the Elites, and Chism's crime against Duke Jaryn had been committed when he was an Elite. The boy king, Antion, stood equal on the Council with Captain Markin and Lady Cuora. However, if those two sided together, Antion's decision would mean nothing.

If the boy king even supported Chism. A chicken would likely befriend a fox before a noble would forgive an assault on a duke.

Lady Palida had always been an enigma to Chism. He couldn't predict where she'd stand if she was present, but she wasn't so he didn't spare her any more thought.

He did have two supporters in the throne room—Lieutenant Fahrr and Ander. They stood behind Chism and to his right, forced by the guards to stand apart from the prisoner as if they would aid an escape after insisting he return to Palassiren for trial. Lieutenant Fahrr wore a new patch on his shoulder. A liquid metallic sword inside a fluid circle in the shape of a Q—the Quicksilver Squadron patch, which Chism would never wear. Lieutenant Fahrr kept a stolid expression when Chism glanced at him.

Ander, on the other hand, nodded supportively. Ander's gray hair was longer and more unkempt than Chism remembered, as though it had been tousled by strong winds on the way to the trial. It may have whitened in the short weeks since they'd seen each other. He didn't wear the Quicksilver patch.

Lady Cuora sat up on her throne and leaned ever so slightly forward. She studied Chism with dark eyes. Lady Cuora's hair was wild, and serpentine. Unlike Ander's hair, which looked as if it had never been brushed, Lady Cuora's had the look of being arranged, but in a manner Chism had never seen. It reminded him of a pile of thin, black driftwood. In her early twenties, very young for her position, she had a strong build and a plain face. No one would ever describe her as beautiful. In fact, *homely* was more accurate, but when Chism looked into her eyes, *volatile* seemed like a much better fit.

An unfamiliar young soldier loomed behind Lady Cuora, wearing the same shade as her. His prominent underbite gave him the look of a cruel bulldog. He obviously held a position of power, but he must have ascended in the few months Chism was away because Chism had never seen him before.

Lady Cuora motioned, and a page recited the charges. "Chism, an Elite, stands accused of assault on the body of Duke Jaryn of Far West Province. After disabling three guards, he placed his sword to the Duke's throat and threatened his life in order to plead the case of a commoner, whom he claims was mistreated by the Duke. By his own testimony and the witness of his lieutenant, the incident occurred thus. The matter now rests in the Council's hands."

Captain Markin fidgeted and glanced sideways at Lady Cuora, who continued studying Chism.

King Antion was the first to speak. "Do you admit to bodily assault on Duke Jaryn?" He was remarkably composed for a nine-year-old.

"Yes," answered Chism. "But not without cause."

"In defense of a commoner?" asked the king. "A pig farmer, if we were informed correctly."

Chism nodded, and King Antion considered.

Lady Cuora spoke, causing nearly everyone in the room to flinch.

"And you've succeeded in splitting the kingdom. Are you pleased with the results of your actions?"

Splitting the kigdom? That seemed like a major overstatement. "I don't—"

"Don't answer unless I tell you to! We find you guilty."

"Verdict before trial?" objected Chism. Lady Cuora's impulsiveness did not surprise him. He'd seen and heard enough of her rash judgments during his time in Elite training to know what to expect.

"In the court of royal opinion, trials are of little importance," she answered.

King Antion spoke up, "We have not ruled yet, Lady Cuora. I would like to hear the case before we decide."

Chism admired the boy. Very few people had the nerve to stand up to her.

Rolling her eyes, Lady Cuora asked, "Who assaulted the duke?"

Following her previous orders, Chism didn't reply.

"You may answer the question," said Lady Cuora with a contented look.

"I assaulted Duke Jaryn."

"And the long-term results?" She gave a small nod to prompt an answer.

Chism's eyes went back to the four small squares that marked the absence of Lady Palida's throne and he wondered how far the consequences of his actions had spread. He shrugged and said, "I've been traveling alone or locked up alone for weeks."

Lady Cuora looked at Captain Markin and said, "Marky?"

"Secession, my Lady."

Lady Cuora brought her gaze back to Chism. "You took actions that resulted in the division of my kingdom. Have I convinced you of your guilt, Elite?"

She appeared to be waiting for an answer, so Chism said, "If you insist on placing blame, look no farther than the Circle and the Sword." He avoided looking at the insignia on the uniforms of Elites in the room. It was painful enough just mentioning it.

Lady Cuora motioned with her scepter at the giant tapestry of the symbol that hung on the wall behind Chism. He felt it looming behind him but he refused to look back at it. Lady Cuora regarded Captain Markin. He squirmed under her gaze.

"He says it's the Circle and Sword's fault, Marky," said Lady Cuora. "Perhaps they should be on trial."

Captain Markin stilled himself but didn't answer. In command of a battlefield, there weren't many men better than Captain Markin, but in the political arena, he was pitifully inept.

Addressing Chism, she continued. "The Circle and Sword have held this kingdom together since before your first breath.

Which one has broken custom and caused our current predicament? Will it be the Circle or the Sword that I send to the headsman?"

Tapping her fingers on the curved wood of her dark throne, Lady Cuora considered her own question. After a few moments, she gave up and motioned for Chism to answer.

"My actions against Duke Jaryn were in defense of the Circle, my Lady. He had a duty to defend one of his citizens against a corrupt earl, but he turned his back as if she were a piece of dirt with no more connection to him than a raven has to a writing desk."

Lady Cuora interrupted, "You care more for one filthy woman in the street than for the integrity of the kingdom?"

The chains of Chism's shackles clinked as he gripped them tightly. The motion caused his shoulder to burn. Not waiting for permission to answer, Chism spoke. "*Jaryn* violated the Circle. As an Elite, it was my sworn duty to remind him of it using the Sword. I care no more for the woman than I do for the duke. What I care for is the Circle and the Sword that I took an oath to defend." He knew his voice was rising, but he didn't care. "I'll kill any bloated, self-important noble that—"

"Chism!" Ander stepped forward. "Toes and odors! Think about what you're saying and to whom. A young wolf doesn't growl when the alpha's teeth are at his throat!"

Lady Cuora raised an eyebrow, sending Ander sheepishly back into his place alongside Lieutenant Fahrr. Before returning her attention to Chism, she graced Ander with an amused grin.

"So you're a hero?" asked Lady Cuora. "A defender of the people?"

He'd never thought of himself as a hero and couldn't care less if other people saw him as one. It had been four years since Chism decided that he would never run and hide only to await a more severe beating when he finally returned home. Never again would his father or any man be able to torture a child over a trifle or on a whim. Not when Chism had the ability to stop it. No matter the consequences.

Lady Cuora studied him as if trying to listen in on his thoughts. Chism knew his fate was being determined at that very moment.

"Marky," said Lady Cuora, reminding Chism that two other judges sat in the chamber. "Do you want this Elite back?"

Captain Markin sat up straight. He glanced uncertainly around the room and his mouth moved. He didn't get any words out before Lady Cuora came to his aid. "Of course you don't. He's too volatile to be in any squadron." The man that Captain Markin had become since his association with the Council made Chism sick. Shifting her gaze to the young king, she asked, "Are you going to demand his head, King?"

The boy had a look of intelligence, and though Chism didn't know what Lady Cuora was thinking, he had a feeling the boy knew. "I've always said that the headsman is overworked, Lady. Do you have an alternate sentence in mind?"

"I *may* be able to extend a slight mercy in this case," Lady Cuora said in a tone of forced graciousness.

Chism's heart beat faster, panicked at the thought of years in confinement. That would be worse than death. It was better for his body to die now than for his mind to sink into insanity and worthlessness when he was finally released. Shackled as he was, he would never make it out of the building, but there was the possibility of death in an escape attempt.

Lady Cuora stood and walked a circle around Chism. "You returned to Palassiren to face trial solely on the strength of your word." Another circle. "You subdued a Provincial soldier at personal risk, even though you had no duty."

Maybe if Chism took Lady Cuora as a hostage, he could escape the city. Maybe die in the attempt or escalate his sentence to include execution.

Cactus's advice about forethought came to mind, and he resisted.

Back in front of her throne, Lady Cuora said, "I am in need of a hero, boy. You see, I have a rogue, and Brune is most roguishly delightful." A grin split the mouth of the young man behind Lady Cuora, his eyes dark and cruel. "It would do to have some balance. Blackguard," she motioned to the young man. "And white guard." She indicated Chism. "Rapscallion and champion. A Knave and a Knight." The fire in her eyes brightened with each word.

"Is the arrangement acceptable to all?" She looked around the room, collecting nods from Captain Markin, King Antion, Lieutenant Fahrr, and finally Chism, before announcing, "This Elite is hereby pardoned of all previous crimes so long as he remains in my service or until this Council decides to unpardon him. Release the prisoner and get him a Knight's pin. Make it red."

Guards rushed to unshackle him.

A Knight. Chism was too stunned to speak, but it certainly beat rotting in a cell.

CHAPTER 20

Angel

Hatta swept his small shop for the third time, hoping cleanliness would show his mirrors in a brighter, more inviting manner, but it made no difference. The north-facing door just didn't admit enough light to catch the shades and hues of his mirrors and show off their perfect mix of haze and clarity. The poor lighting was why he hadn't sold any in three weeks since opening the shop. It didn't help that nearly all of his customers were patrons of the old tailor next door. Almost to a person, they were middle aged or older with stuffy tastes. Other than the tailor's customers, only a handful of shoppers in a week found his out-of-the-way alley.

To make matters worse, the purple was fading from his hair, and he had no dyes or berries to repair it.

After his three chaotic trips, Hatta never wanted to leave his alley again. Reports of the effects of the division in the kingdom came in bits and pieces from his few customers and the tailor. Apparently the entire economy of Palassiren, and of Maravilla as a whole, was in jeopardy. Part of the problem was due to the mass exodus of people and part was due to speculation on the future of Palassiren and the new kingdom of the interior. Yet another reason to hole up in his alley.

Hatta sat down in front of his shop, waiting for customers to appear. The hard biscuit and dried apricot lunch spread in front of him represented the last of the food from Elora. More than two months of rent still remained, but that would do him no good without food. The city that should have provided him an audience to whom he could sell his mirrors would instead starve him. There was no way to forage within the walls, and if he went out to scavenge, he couldn't tend his shop.

Today had to be the day he finally sold one, even if it went for a pittance. Thursday seemed as good a day as any to finally start selling. Unless the day happened to be Friday. If so then Firday seemed like the perfect day.

Lifting the last bite of spongy apricot, Hatta toasted himself. A ray of sun caught the apricot and made it glow. He lowered it into shadow and the apricot went dull. Again, into the sunbeam and it lit up. An idea struck Hatta—a brilliant idea.

Leaving the elastic morsel behind, Hatta ran next door to the tailor's shop. "Would you, perchance, have a saw that I might borrow?" he blurted at the old man, who had his back turned.

The tailor dropped the bolt of cloth he held and turned, breathing rapidly and clutching his chest. "You should consider offering a greeting before startling one out of his shoes, young fellow."

Hatta shifted from foot to foot while the old man caught his breath. "A saw, you ask? I have a small one in the back." The tailor shuffled away and Hatta heard the slow movement of boxes and other items.

"Shall I lend a hand?" asked Hatta hopefully.

"Patience, young man. Patience."

Hours seemed to pass as Hatta paced a short path between

bolts of cloth and smocked mannequins. The jostling sound was replaced by that of shuffling feet, and the old man emerged from the back of the shop, proudly carrying a narrow saw with a long wooden handle. It looked like something a farmer would use to prune trees, but it would work.

After hurrying to retrieve the saw, Hatta thanked the tailor over his shoulder and added, "I'll most likely bring it back today."

After stacking two barrels, Hatta climbed onto the roof of his small shop. Eyeballing the center, he pried up a square of half a dozen wooden shingles. There was no purchase point in the boards under the shingles, but one of them had a knot along an edge. Using the wooden end of the saw, he pounded until the knot fell out of the board, leaving a perfect eye hole into his shop.

After descending to move his mirrors to the safety of the back room, he climbed to the roof again and commenced sawing. The sun was still above the horizon when the hole was complete, but just barely, so he clambered down, knocking over the barrels in the process. He ran into the back room of his shop to retrieve his mirrors and hastily leaned a few of them against the walls.

Hatta stepped back to view the improvements. The sight of the fading sunlight reflecting from all directions brought tears to his eyes, and he knew the morning and midday light would be even more spectacular. He spun in slow circles, letting his eyes drift from jade to rose to sky-blue to peach to violet until the light gave out. Morning couldn't come soon enough.

After returning the saw to the tailor, along with his thanks, Hatta picked up the last bite of apricot from where he had dropped it earlier and went inside to bed. Just like the first night crafting mirrors in Shey's Orchard, his excitement kept him awake for hours. Something good was coming soon.

By the time the sun rose in the morning, Hatta was in front

of his shop, waiting for his luck to change. One mirror would be enough to buy food for weeks.

Just one mirror.

After an hour, a servant from one of the palaces visited the tailor. He was dressed in a dull, red-trimmed vest. It had probably been bright at some point, but now it showed years of service. As soon as the man exited the tailor's shop, Hatta approached him.

"Would you spare a moment to look at my fine mirrors?" he asked, reaching to corral the servant toward his shop. He'd never been as forward with any potential customers, but he was in high spirits.

The man allowed Hatta to lead him into the shop, where new light poured in like life in springtime. To his amazement, the servant wasn't interested in mirrors, stating that his errand was for cloth. The servant left Hatta standing flabbergasted, staring around the room at his mirrors.

Sometime later, Hatta heard another voice coming from the tailor's shop, and his expectations rose again. After shaking his head to clear it, he went to gather another customer but was disappointed to see it was only the landlord.

"Hatta," said the large man in a booming voice. "How goes your business?"

"Greetings, landlord. Business goes well. I feel I'll sell my first mirror today. Would you be in need of a mirror perchance?"

"I've already got one, but I don't mind taking a look."

After bidding farewell to the old tailor, the two walked toward the shop.

"You'll see they're very unique," said Hatta as he followed the landlord into the shop. The man stopped suddenly, and Hatta walked into his back.

He must be shocked by my inimitable mirrors, thought Hatta, smiling. But the landlord wasn't even looking down at where they leaned against the walls. Mouth hanging open, he stared through the hole in the roof.

"My shop . . ." His mouth moved, but it took him a moment to form words. "What have you done to my shop?"

"It's for the light, you see? That's why I couldn't sell any mirrors. Light just couldn't get in."

The landlord's gaze shifted to Hatta, and his eyes narrowed. In a matter of moments, Hatta saw a red undertone spread through him, just like the bandersnatch before it ran.

Frumious landlord, thought Hatta. *I'd rather be back with the bandersnatch.*

"You cut a hole in my roof for *these*?" His mouth formed a frown around the last word and he picked up the lavender-tinged mirror and threw it at Hatta. Luckily, the landlord's anger blinded him, and he missed, but the mirror struck the doorframe with the tinny sound of a thin bell. None of Hatta's mirrors were made of glass, but the metal was badly dented. Hatta went to retrieve it, but the landlord grabbed him first.

"You'll pay for this, you tweedle-headed cretin!" Spittle flew from his mouth. Using the lapels of Hatta's coat, the landlord slammed him against the wall.

"But I haven't money." Hatta wanted to crawl into a ball in his back room until the landlord went away, but the large man's grip was much too strong.

In a quieter but much more threatening voice, the landlord said, "You'll pay if it has to be paid in blood."

Ducking and raising his arms above his head, Hatta wriggled out of the maroon coat. There had to be a way to make it right, to smooth things out with the landlord.

"I—I can fix it." Hatta thought of fleeing the city, but that would mean leaving his mirrors behind. The tailor was much too old to protect him; there was no relief there. Hatta hurried to where the barrels lay toppled in the street. As he started stacking them, the incensed landlord stormed after him, throwing Hatta's coat into the street with a yell.

"Don't fear! I'll just start right away." Legs shaking, Hatta started climbing, but he was no further than halfway up when his legs were pulled out from under him. He fell faster than he thought possible and struck his chest on the lower barrel.

Pain filled his upper body. All the air in his lungs was forced out and refused to come back in. Heavy fists and heavier feet pummeled him even as he struggled for a single breath.

Hatta hadn't considered that dying might be the exciting event he'd woken for that day.

Even worse, his killer was angry with him, and if Hatta died, he'd never have the chance to make things right. Coarse words singed his ears as blows bruised his body. Just when he needed distraction more than ever, Hatta couldn't think of a single rhyme.

The blows unexpectedly stopped. Were it not for the intense pain and his craving for air, Hatta would have thought himself dead. Cracking one teary eye, he peeked past his own protective arm.

The landlord lay face down alongside him in the dirt of the alleyway, struggling against two red-clad soldiers. He was ranting about the roof of his shop and blood payment. Hatta knew he should feel safe, but he couldn't bear to come out of his defensive ball. He gasped and choked on his tears, but he didn't dare surface. Silently, he longed for the safety of his town hat.

A woman's harsh voice cut in, making Hatta retreat further into the safety of his arms. "What is the meaning of this?"

The landlord finally spoke in coherent thoughts. "He cut a hole in my roof, Lady. He may be a tweedle, but he has no right to ruin my shop."

"A hole in a roof isn't justification for a hole in a man's head. That's why we have magistrates, you fool. Now it's you who'll be judged, not him."

Breath returned in racking sobs, but Hatta didn't dare uncurl from his fetal position. He felt a hand on his shoulder and cringed, but it was a soft, supportive hand.

"Let me see you," said the woman's voice in a commanding yet gentle tone. Her small kindness only caused renewed blubbering.

"Are you the mirror maker?" she asked.

She had his full interest. With a deep breath, Hatta finally gained control of his sobbing.

"He's a menace is what he is!" shouted the landlord, but the woman's touch was a shield.

Knowing she was there, Hatta found strength to open his eyes and slowly lower his arms. Through tear-blurred eyes, he looked into the face of an angel. Twisty black hair fell in thick strands around a simple face with fiery brown eyes. An unruffled countenance in a storm of poised curls. And her cloak was more vivid than a fresh strawberry.

She had asked a question, but somehow Hatta had forgotten it. Such vibrant colors often had that effect.

"I can't seem to find the question I've been asked," he said.

"Are you the mirror maker?" she repeated.

"Um, yes. I would be the mirror maker." Pain registered from somewhere, but it was a dull feeling coming from the background.

"How badly are you hurt?" she asked. "I haven't seen anyone smitten that soundly in some time."

"I'm definitely smitten, but I don't think I'm hurt."

If the startled grin on her face was any indication, she'd caught his dual meaning. "Well then," she cleared her throat and stood, "let's see to this situation."

She walked confidently into the shop, considering the hole in the roof and the damaged mirror in the doorway. Hatta sat up and watched her with wonder. She was the most beautiful woman he had ever seen.

In a matter of moments, she was satisfied with her assessment. Speaking to one of her attendants, she said, "Pay the landlord damages for the roof, minus the cost of the ruined mirror, or vice versa depending on the cost of each. Then take him to the magistrate and let the magistrate know that I won't be disconcerted if he spends a few days in a cell before trial."

The guards roughly pulled the landlord up and bound his arms. Hatta turned away from his hateful glare. It was a possibility that the man might never forgive him.

As the guards led him past the Lady, she stopped them with a small signal and addressed the landlord. "Count yourself lucky that my Knave is on errand with my Knight. He's nowhere as gentle as I am."

Just like after his conflict with the mule, part of the weight lifted off Hatta's shoulders as soon as the landlord turned the corner. When the Lady next spoke to him, he forgot the rest. "Do you have any idea how long I've sought you, mirror maker?"

"Hatta," he managed, finding it difficult to speak in her presence. She was red. Not in color, but in personality. As red as anyone he'd ever met. She turned slowly toward the shop. It was easier to speak to her back. "And what would your name be?"

"I am Lady Cuora." She was in the shop, but he couldn't muster the courage to follow. Rejection and scorn from other potential customers had bounced off of him like hail on a turtle's back, but Cuora had come specifically to see his mirrors. He had never felt so . . . he wasn't sure exactly what he was feeling. Vulnerable? Indebted? Adoring?

Hatta was more than smitten. He might actually be in love, and it was new territory. The darkest day of his life had suddenly become the most vibrant, and the price he'd paid to meet Cuora was worth ten times the beating.

But he still couldn't bear to watch as she inspected the mirrors. She had delivered him once today; hoping for more would be unreasonable.

I should run, he thought, and his feet turned away from his shop. *Better to carry the memory of her rescue than her rejection.* So slowly it was barely noticeable, his legs began to carry him away.

Half a dozen retainers and guards stood in the alley, waiting. They only gave Hatta infrequent glances. One of them was the servant who had been in his shop earlier that day.

That would be how she found my shop. But how did she know to look in the first place?

Then he remembered a black-haired Lady in red, brusquely inspecting Elora's mirror before she left. That *was* a convoluted route.

Though it hadn't been long, the distraction was enough to keep him from running away too fast until Cuora came out of the shop. Once he saw her, he was unable to flee.

Cuora considered him as if noticing his bright clothes for the first time. He had always been proud of his garish colors, but under her gaze, he wished the apricot of his shirt was as rich as the day he'd bought it and the blue of his pants a touch brighter. And there lay his maroon jacket in the dirt of the street. His hair had lost—

"How much are your mirrors?" she asked.

Hatta would have given them to her if she asked, but her tone let him know that wasn't an option. He only wanted enough to buy food for a while. "Half a penny, Cuora." Hers was one name he'd never struggle to recall. "For one mirror, that would be."

"Ten cuppies? Hogwash." She sniffed and looked back into the store.

She hates them, thought Hatta. *It's never too late to run.*

Turning back, she said, "I would never consider adorning my palace with something so cheap. They are worth a duodec apiece, and that is what I'll pay."

Twenty pennies! He hadn't saved that much in a year in Frenala.

"That would be too much," he insisted, "and one of them isn't for sale." Pulling away from her gaze, he went inside and picked up his last mirror.

Six colors infused the mirror's uneven edge: shades of blue, green, yellow, orange, red, and purple. They were subtly incorporated into the metal in the perfect blend. As with all of his mirrors, the outer part was hazy, but in his masterpiece, a slight haze continued toward the center, clearing up by degrees. The inner portion, just large enough to see a face, was as lucid as any mirror, but it appeared impossibly clear in contrast.

Cuora stood beside him. He angled the mirror to look into her face and almost dropped it when he saw her beauty. She was the image of perfection.

Gripping him with her gaze, she said, "But this is the most magnificent of them all. I look through the haze and see—"

"Madness?" offered Hatta. No, that wasn't right. "Sanity?"

Less bold than he'd seen her up to that point, she said quietly, "Most people are not the front they put on. We all have factions inside us, battling for control. In your mirrors, I can see all of myself, not just the face I have on at the moment. Both halves—Lady and woman." In an even quieter voice, she said, "I can see you more clearly as well. Not just this," she laid a hand on his cheek. "But this," her hand went to his heart.

"Beautiful," said Hatta, wishing her reflection would last for days.

"I'll pay you two duodecs."

Hatta didn't reply and Cuora said, "Four." She broke the stare, leaving Hatta reeling.

"Why would you do that?"

"For the mirror," she said.

"This mirror?"

"Yes."

"Why would you give me eighty pennies for a mirror I wouldn't sell?"

"A pound."

Her direct speech confused him. "Beg pardon?"

"I will pay you a pound of pennies for this mirror."

Running a shop was much different than he had imagined. For almost a month, no one buys anything. Then a heroine appears when he needs her most and insists on paying many times more than the asking price. But she can't seem to understand the simple fact that one mirror is without price?

Baffling. Dealing with animals was never so complicated. Hatta shook his head and said, "No."

"Do you realize who I am?" Through her frustration over the mirror, slight amusement showed.

Hatta nodded. "You're an angel. *My* angel. Even a king or queen could never outrank that." Confidence was an unfamiliar emotion, but as long as Hatta held it, he'd milk it dry.

Cuora was at a loss for words.

Glancing at his dull boots, Hatta asked, "Would you still be buying any other of my mirrors?"

"Yes. Twenty-two mirrors. One pound plus two hundred pennies. Minus the damages to the roof."

Hatta doffed his hat and gave a small bow. "Truly, you are my heroine."

"And you," replied Cuora, "are bleeding."

Hatta touched the back of his head, and his hand came away streaked with blood as bright as Cuora's skirt. It reminded him of the beating, but the pain was still very far behind him.

"You will be my guest today. My physician will tend to you, and then I will enjoy your company. You're quite different than anyone I've ever met, Hatta."

The compliment thrilled him. Different was wonderful! As long as it didn't turn into strange or mad.

Hatta picked up his jacket and dusted it off. He donned it, replaced his hat, and in another burst of boldness, offered Cuora his arm. She smiled her amused smirk and allowed him to lead her out of the alley.

CHAPTER 21

Winners

Hatta held his mallet in both hands, turned his back to the croquet ball, opened his stance, and swung like a woodchopper splitting a log. The ball shot through his legs, and he bent over to watch. It bounced off two wickets, neither of which was his intended target, and came back through his legs to rest in the exact spot from which it had started.

Cuora giggled momentarily, then blushed and covered her mouth. The sound was as splendid as the buzz of a bee.

"You should swing like that more often," she said. "I'll be guaranteed the win."

"Perfect," said Hatta, standing and spinning to face her. "If you continue to giggle, I've already won."

"I do *not* giggle." She tried to make her face straight, but traces of her smile still showed in all the corners—lips, eyes, jaw.

"Perhaps you don't giggle at present, but you did giggle just now, and if I have my way, you shall giggle in the future."

"Croquet is not about fun and laughing," said Cuora sternly.

She lined up and hit her tomato-colored ball through the center of another wicket.

Hatta leaned to rest an elbow on his mallet and his chin on his fist. The mallet was much shorter than he expected, and he ended up bent over awkwardly. He turned his head to look up at Cuora and asked, "If not funning, then what would croquet be about?"

Cuora took a moment to tuck away a few black tresses from in front of her face into the other thick wisps of hair. It did nothing to tame her striking, tousled flair. After another moment of gazing quizzically, she pointedly placed her mallet stick-down into the grass and leaned on it in the same graceless manner as Hatta.

With a twisted back, twisted head, and twisted smile, she said, "Croquet, my love, is no different than anything else—it is about winning."

My love. Less than a half day since they had met, and already Hatta was her love.

"Then we are in agreement," said Hatta. He unbent and walked to her, motioning for her to remain in the same position. He resculpted a few of the thickest strands of hair into a heart shape then stepped back.

"Perfect," he said. "Now you look like a . . . like an . . . hmm. You don't actually resemble anything I've ever seen. I congratulate you."

A snort found its way into Cuora's laugh as she stood. Her eyes went wide, and she said, "Listen to me chortling and giggling like a tweedle. What would the Council say?"

Hatta had never met the Council nor had any idea who they might be, so he shrugged.

"Now," said Cuora. "How are we in agreement if I say croquet is about winning and you say it should be about fun?"

"Why, it's simple. If one plays for fun, it's impossible to do anything but win. Fun is a personal choice."

Cuora looked at her ball, which wasn't far from the finishing stake. Then she looked at Hatta's ball, which wasn't far from the starting wicket. The heart Hatta had shaped in her hair still held above the other tresses. She bit her lip, took aim with the mallet, and threw it like a dart. It came to rest in the middle of the final wicket.

"If we've already won," she said, "there's no reason to finish the game."

Hatta bowed to her and clapped. "My compliments, my love and my life, on the winningest game of croquet I've ever played."

"Based on your performance, I'd wager the only game." She crooked her arm in his and began leading him toward the nearby tea table.

"In that wager you would be correct." He stopped and looked down at the lush grass. "Why don't we tea here?"

Cuora shrugged and motioned for the servants to bring the table.

"No, no," said Hatta. "The verdant verdure of the grass will be my chair, and the resplendent splendor of you shall be my tea."

Cuora's demure blush lasted only part of a moment. Hatta knew there was a point at which praise and adoration exceed what one can comfortably accept without being carried away in conceit. Hatta had obviously found Cuora's limit. There was a stark possibility that he might someday doubt it had happened, he would never forget what it had looked like.

It was Hatta's strong conviction that every woman should be forced to endure such admiration at some point. The fact that he'd achieved it on their first day together pleased him no end.

As Cuora sat, her dress spread like a large red poppy. Her crossed ankles protruded only slightly. Hatta crossed his own ankles and sat facing her. The setting sun illuminated one half of her face perfectly and left the other in shadow. She looked like two entirely different people—like the bright days and black days of Hatta's life.

Resting her hands on one of his knees, Cuora asked, "How did I live so long without you?"

Her touch made his heart bounce. Its lingering made his heart run in place as it bounced.

"You didn't," he finally managed to say.

The eyebrow on the bright side of her face angled upward.

"That was someone else," he explained. "The person who has spent the day with me is a different person than the lady she was when she woke up today."

"And how would you know that?"

"Because the man in front of you is not a man I've ever known before."

Hatta had never kissed a woman, but the smile on Cuora's face was entirely too kissable to resist.

CHAPTER 22

Friends

*F*or the three weeks following the departure of Lady Palida and the Whites, Chism spent half his time attending to Lady Cuora and the other half on various other tasks. As boring as escort duty for Lady Cuora proved, Chism preferred it to going on damage control assignments with Brune, the Knave.

Brune was the antithesis of an Elite—no honor, no skill at fighting, and no sense of justice. Chism despised him. He was cruel but not stupid. Chism watched every minute, waiting for him to step over the line, but Brune never went quite far enough. The Knave reported only to Lady Cuora, and her standards were much different than the Elites' or any other soldiers'. Her only concern was that her orders were carried out; how it happened mattered little. Now that she had Chism to temper Brune, she thought she didn't have to worry about him. Cuora obviously cared quite a bit for the Knave; it would take a severe transgression for Lady Cuora to intervene.

So much for Chism's blessed freedom and the prestigious

life of a Knight. Most days, babysitting the Knave was a fate worse than death.

The rising moon cast tall night shadows across the bricks of the inner city as Chism, Brune and six guards returned from a day's work. Anxious to be free of Brune for the day, Chism bid farewell to the guards and increased his pace across the courtyard. Seven palaces, all in a line, spread out before him. The perfect symmetry of the line of buildings was a welcome sight at the end of the day. The shades varied, but on either side of the king's huge manor were twin palaces, with more on the far side of those that matched perfectly. Instead of seven separate buildings, Chism saw them as equal halves of a whole.

From behind, Brune said, "See you tomorrow. Partner." The Knave was aware of Chism's hatred and taunted him at every opportunity.

As usual, Chism didn't respond.

He already knew it was three hundred and forty steps from the gates to the armory in the military district, but he counted anyway to distract himself. Mully, the armorer, had been in the armory after breakfast and was still there twelve hours later. He loved swords and saddles and armor and arrows like a mother loved her babies.

An attendant helped Chism remove his leather armor. Thirsty stayed at his waist.

"Anything exciting happen around here today, Mully?" Chism asked as a pair of guards entered.

"Just arming and disarming, Sir Chism. Quiet, just as I like it."

One of the recently arrived soldiers, whom Chism had nicknamed "Chug" after hearing about his tavern habits, spoke up. "We had some excitement. The Lady finally found that mirror maker she's been searching for. A bit of a tweedle, he is. His hair's purple, of all colors."

Brune entered along with the other guards in Chism's group. Chism cursed under his breath, anxious to be away from Brune's ugly face. And his loud mouth and cocky attitude.

Chug continued his narrative. "Anyway, when we got to the alley where the mirror maker sells his mirrors, the landlord was there, and none too happy. We heard him say, 'Then you'll pay in blood!' and set to beating the poor man. And it was a decent sort of beating. May have killed him if we hadn't stepped in."

Brune dropped his sword on the ground and ignored Mully, who had come forward to take it from him. "Things like that only happen when I'm gone! I would've shown that landlord what a real beating feels like." Brune was always brave when he had half a dozen men on his side.

"Not Lady Cuora," said Chug in answer to Brune. "She sent him to the magistrate with orders to let him stew for a couple of days."

"What was his problem with the mirror maker?" asked Chism.

"He cut a hole in the roof. To get more light for his mirrors, he said. Turns out he didn't need the light because the Lady bought every one of his mirrors. And not only that—she brought him back to the palace. Cancelled her whole afternoon to spend the day with him. Maravilla's on a path to civil war, and she spends half a day croqueting and sipping tea with a mirror maker! He's only leaving just now. Probably still crossing the courtyard."

Chism had no reason to rush out and catch a glimpse of the man. If Lady Cuora was as enamored as it sounded, the mirror maker would come again.

"Let's hope he comes back," said Brune. "A man's company is exactly what Lady Cuora needs." Some of the guards who'd entered with him chuckled.

Brune never opened his mouth without boasting, taunting, or being crude. And it rarely failed to garner an encouraging reaction from most guards. Chism had spent enough time around soldiers to know the direction the conversation would turn, so after a quick thanks for Mully, he left the armory.

The next morning, after morning routine with Thirsty then breakfast, Chism reported to Lady Cuora. The mirror maker had made an impression. For one thing, Lady Cuora was grinning. Lady Cuora was a ruler, first, last, and all—she didn't have personal emotions or interests and never took time for relationships. Nothing came before the kingdom, and Chism respected her immensely for it. Though their methods differed, deep down Lady Cuora and Chism were kindred souls. It was odd to see her invest anything of herself in personal interests.

"M'lady," said Chism with a slight bow.

He waited for her to demand an account of the previous day's activities. It never came, so he started. "We found four spies in the houses of the merchants you sent us to search."

She should be interjecting, wresting control of the conversation. But for the first time since he'd known her, Lady Cuora listened placidly.

The four spies had been dressed as servants, with mantles dyed to match the color of each house. But underlying the recent dye job, Chism had noticed the faint remnant of the Flame and Stars crest of Far West. None of the other guards in his group saw it until Chism pointed it out. They were too focused on the colors. Chism's inability to see colors had paid off.

Lady Cuora didn't ask for the details, though. "Off with their heads," she said in a mild voice, as if she didn't really mean it, not like her usual compelling orders.

Chism had to smile when he thought about how disappointed Brune would be when he arrived to find out he was too late to carry the instructions to the headsman. Brune always arrived an hour or two after Chism, and this time it would work against him.

"If you have more, let me hear it, Knight. I have an extremely busy day." She still spoke quickly, but without brusqueness.

Chism shook his head and took his place at the side of the room.

"I don't need you this morning, Knight. You're dismissed."

Chism didn't wait to be told twice. He'd never seen Lady Cuora in such a mood, and he wouldn't waste it. Whoever had audience with her today would be fortunate.

After instructing a guard to take the message to the headsman, Chism was free of responsibilities. How long had it been since he had nothing to do and the freedom to do it with? Not since that night in Knobbes that had changed everything. Chism felt years older than the boy who had held the sword to Duke Jaryn's throat, though less than two months had passed.

A pair of guards saluted as they passed Chism in the hallway, and he realized he was staring into the air like an idiot. They were gone before he had a chance to return the salute. He stopped in the hallway, considering his options, and noticed two new mirrors on the wall. They were odd-shaped and much too artistic, but they had obviously impressed Lady Cuora.

The mirrors didn't help Chism come up with any ideas. His daily practice with Thirsty was already done, and he had no family in the capital to visit. Taverns were out of the question; he still couldn't stand them. As tortuous as it was at times, standing honor guard for Lady Cuora was preferable to walking just so he could count steps or sitting around stroking a leather strip.

He considered returning to the training grounds to view the current class of Elite recruits and see for himself how drastically the numbers of the Elites had been cut by the departure of Lady Palida's followers. But Chism was no longer an Elite. He would never wear the Circle and Sword again, and he couldn't bear the thought of seeing the other soldiers proudly displaying the symbol.

And even among his former brothers he had no friends.

Curse you, Cactus! He resisted the urge to break something and gripped Thirsty's hilt instead. The old man's friendship had given Chism a taste, awakening something he'd always assumed he lacked the capacity for. That family had planted a seed that continued to grow no matter how much Chism despised the idea of friends.

Curse Mikel and Lira and their kindness too! It was the only treatment he couldn't defend against.

Chism had always been a loner, but he had never once felt lonely. Before spending time with the two families, he wanted a friend like he wanted a boil on his backside, as Ander would say.

Ander! Brotherhood did not equal friendship, but there was a possibility Ander was a friend. With conflicting pangs of guilt and relief, Chism realized Ander was no longer a Fellow and no longer connected to the Elites. Caught up in his duties as the Red Knight, Chism had given Ander very little thought.

Gripping Thirsty, his only sure friend, for confidence, he went in search of his former Fellow. It took an hour to locate Ander in his out-of-the-way quarters on the third floor of Lady Cuora's palace. The door was ajar, and sounds of tinkering came from inside.

Chism knocked and called, "Ander?"

Before Ander came into view, Chism heard his voice. "I'll eat two dozen turkey toes if that isn't a young Knight from T'lai." He sounded pleased, and it surprised Chism. Ander appeared in the doorway with a delighted smile and hair that hadn't been tended to for days.

"So you started wearing a borogove on your head, Ander?" With Ander, Chism didn't have to worry about being offered a handshake or a slap on the back.

"A dozen borogoves couldn't match this impressive shag," said Ander, preening his thick, white hair with his fingers. "Come in, come in."

Ander's quarters were cluttered with all manner of trinkets, small metal panels, paints, papers, sketches, and contraptions.

He cleared a box of nails and a pair of awls from a wooden chair to allow Chism to sit.

Picking up a small bowl full of springs, Chism asked, "So you're getting paid to tinker now?"

"No." Ander's snowy hair belied his youthful face. He couldn't be older than thirty five. "To be honest, I don't know if anyone even realizes I'm here. One of Lady Cuora's people gave me this chamber while we waited for you to return to Palassiren, and I never moved out. The servants get me what I need. I'm not paid, but my needs are more than met. And you, Chism. How is knighting?"

Chism gave a brief account of his three weeks as the Red Knight.

"Well, I have to thank you, boy," said Ander.

"What for? Splitting the kingdom or getting you kicked out of the Elites?"

Ander grunted. "I never belonged in the Elites. And I can't say that I miss soldiering. But thanks for not dragging me around on your duties. I'd do it if you asked, but my place is here. Take a look at this." He handed Chism a metal gauntlet.

Chism put his hand into the metal glove. It was much too large for him, but it had a different feel than most gauntlets. It covered his hand and wrist, but instead of overlapping hinged plates, it was a combination of plates and chain, reducing the weight considerably while increasing flexibility.

Gripping and releasing the fine gauntlet, Chism asked what he had come to find out. "Are we friends, Ander?"

"May your tongue fall out of your mouth and be eaten by a hundred cats! What kind of question is that?"

Chism usually understood Ander perfectly, but that answer could mean anything. He waited for more.

"Of course we're friends, you pig shaver!" spat Ander. "What did you think we were?"

Shrugging, Chism said, "Partners. Warriors. Brothers?"

"Those too," said Ander. "All of those."

Chism wondered how he could misinterpret their relationship for so long, and he began to question whether he had other friends he hadn't considered.

None came to mind.

"I admit sometimes I wish you'd be cursed with incurable eyelid spasms for all the trouble you cause me, but I'd do anything for you."

"Thanks, Ander. I . . ." *I what? I'm really bad at this friend stuff.* "Thanks."

After another hour with Ander and his inventions, Chism ate lunch in the kitchens and then returned to Lady Cuora's throne room. Brune arrived at the same time. He scowled as usual when he looked at Chism's Knight Pin, which was as red as a Sixteenery ribbon, with a gold rim. So he'd been told. Though Cuora had given him the title Red Knight before she knew he was as colorblind as a pocketwatch, she'd had plenty of laughs about it since.

When Lady Cuora returned, she still looked uncharacteristically content.

"Did your man friend visit today?" asked Brune, managing to imbue the question with impropriety.

"No. I forbade him," said Lady Cuora, sitting on her padded throne. "Today was entirely too busy. As if my man friend concerned you, Knave."

Somehow, Brune's manner resonated with the Lady. His rise to power from some obscure town had been pure luck of compatible personalities or something else Chism couldn't explain.

"Why Brune?" blurted Chism.

Lady Cuora looked at him and raised one eyebrow.

"You had your choice of thousands of soldiers," said Chism. "Why'd you pick a common bully?"

For a moment, Lady Cuora considered as if trying to think of the best way to explain it. Chism didn't look at Brune; he had no interest in the Knave's opinion of the question.

"Do you have a coin, Knight?"

Chism had a few in his pouch. He fished one out and dropped it in her hand.

"Perfect," said Lady Cuora. "A penny. What symbols are on either side of this coin?"

"Circle on one side, Sword on the other," said Chism.

"I have always believed in two sides of a coin and that if a thing is done, it should be done to the utmost." She turned the coin over a few times in her hand. "Brune is like you—"

"Brune is nothing like me," said Chism.

"If I were allowed to finish speaking, I would say Brune and you are the same in that you both fit perfectly into the slot I have placed you, which is to say you are opposites." Lady Cuora held up the coin. "He is knavish, not too ambitious, and has no morals." She flipped the coin. "You are knightly, not too ambitious, and have an inflated moral code. You both fit perfectly."

"What good is someone without any morals?" asked Chism.

"You judge him as worthless?" Lady Cuora looked at Brune, but Chism didn't follow her eyes. She looked back at Chism, tilted her head meaningfully and said, "A *thirteen*, would you say?"

Her smirk let Chism know that the word was hand-picked for him, even though they'd never discussed his scar and his past. Chism didn't even realize she knew anything about it. He wanted to change the topic of conversation.

Lady Cuora spoke before he could think of anything to say. "The fact that you can't see the value in him is more proof you are in the correct role. Now, Knave, weren't we talking about something more pleasant?"

"When will I have the pleasure of meeting the man who has so transfixed my liege Lady?" asked Brune.

"He'll be here tomorrow, Knave. But, unfortunately, you won't." She gave him a teasing smile, the kind that only encouraged his impudent behavior while causing his countenance to darken.

With a pouty look, Brune asked, "Where do you need us to go?"

"Not *us*. Just *you*. My Knight was off today, so he'll have the chance to attend audience tomorrow."

Boring duty is better than Brune duty, thought Chism. Brune looked offended to the core.

"Don't worry, Knave. You'll have your chance to meet him. If I have my way—which I always do—he'll be around for quite some time."

CHAPTER 23

Black

Hatta's lips could barely decide which tune to whistle as he made his way toward the inner city. If the streets were emptier, he would've skipped.

After months of faded clothes, he'd finally refreshed his wardrobe. His new pants, light- and dark-yellow striped, complemented his coat, which was the color of a clear summer sky. Even in the largest city in the kingdom, he'd been unable to find a cobbler with purple leather and had to settle for turquoise boots. The color was definitely growing on him. If Cuora liked his somewhat dim clothes two days before, these would surely impress. The purchase of the clothes and enough food for a few weeks hadn't noticeably lightened his new purse.

Cuora was entirely different than the woman he always imagined he'd fall in love with. New verses rolled through his mind as he wound through Palassiren toward the palaces.

I painted her a gushing thing,
With years perhaps a score;

A little thought to find they were
A half a dozen more;
My fancy gave her eyes of blue,
and hair like lemon drink;
I came to find the blue was brown,
the yellow black as ink.

As Hatta approached the gatehouse leading to the inner city, his step halted. It was in vain, however; the guards admitted him immediately, glancing at his new attire with what had to be admiration.

The meeting with Cuora was set for midday, but when men had arrived at his small, empty shop to repair the roof two hours before noon, he couldn't bear to stay for the repairs. The landlord had been forced to pay for the mirror he'd ruined, and Hatta only had to give a fraction of the coins back for roof repair. It was decided and done, and he had no desire to recall a conflict that could be disregarded through simple absence of the premises. He'd much rather spend the remainder of the morning observing discreetly as Cuora held court.

After climbing the colorful steps to Cuora's palace, Hatta paused to take in the large entry chamber. The ceilings were the highest he'd ever seen, supported by thick, scarlet marble columns. A wide staircase matched the exterior steps, pale pink at the bottom intensifying into crimson at the top. It led to the living quarters and was flanked by two hallways on the ground level. The one on the left led to the kitchens and laundry areas. Hatta followed the hallway on the right toward the throne room and noticed two of his mirrors, both red, on the walls of the corridor.

Stopping in front of one, he admired it in its new setting. The brilliant silvery crimson was a perfect adornment for Cuora's elegant home. Even though Cuora assured him she had plenty of uses for other colors, he found himself wishing he'd made more red mirrors. If he ever made more, they'd all be red.

Seeing his new clothing in his own mirror hanging on Cuora's wall brought a heartfelt, if crooked, smile to Hatta's face. Rich purple hair hung out from under his town hat like painted thatch hanging off the edge of a roof. The stain from the berries had been uneven and had started to fade, so Hatta had purchased high quality dye in the marketplace the day before. The green of his hat and purple of his hair perfectly matched the colors of the bruise around his left eye. But even bruises and pains couldn't dampen his exuberance.

Enthusiasm? he wondered, searching for the perfect description. *No, ebullience.*

Pleasing chills raced up his arms and down his spine when he heard Cuora's voice from the throne room, but he was too far to make out the words. By the time he reached the doors, she was done speaking and the only sound was a wailing woman. Hatta motioned for the guards at the doors to remain quiet and leaned against the wall just out of sight of the room. He listened to Cuora's audience without being seen.

A man with a cruel voice said, "On your feet, woman. Or I'll drag you to the stocks." The whimpering faded as the woman left the throne room by another exit. Hatta was puzzled at how the woman could be so unhappy in Cuora's presence and why Cuora didn't act to save the woman as she had rescued him.

The next voice was clear and loud. "The next case, my Lady: Harkonin, a merchant, was caught in the act of holding a meeting in which he denounced Lady Cuora and Captain Markin. He called for the heads of the aforementioned Council members and proclaimed support of Lady Palida and the Provinces. The gathering was witnessed by one of the city guards as well as a bird trader. Both have given sworn testimony to Harkonin's treason. The matter now rests in Your Ladyship's hands."

The silence from the throne room was so sudden, Hatta wondered if the doors had been closed. When he shook himself and looked, he realized that the wall he was leaning on was actually one of the doors.

A proud man's voice broke the calm. "Those reports are exag—"

"Silence!" The woman's voice had the finality of an axe.

Could that be Cuora? Though the word was not directed at Hatta, he felt it like a slice across his heart. He was glad she couldn't see him cringe.

She continued in a quieter, accusing tone. "Did you or did you not call for my head?"

The man did not answer at first. A shuffle of feet and slow jingle of chains told Hatta the man was fidgeting. "I . . . simply stated that the kingdom would be better off in Lady Palida's hands."

"Guard," said Cuora, "are the witnesses present?"

"Yes, my Lady."

"Have them speak."

Hatta heard people moving around the room and regretted his decision to visit Cuora at court.

Eventually, a man spoke. "Well, my Lady, you see, he said we needed to start an uprousing. An 'insuregency,' he called it. And he said your heads were the price of peace for Maravilla."

"It's true," said a woman. "Just as the guard said. And, asking m'Lady's pardon, Harkonin said your head was the first we needed, and Captain Markin's would come easy."

"What say you, Knight? You know Marky. Would his head pop off like a dandelion without me?"

If the Knight answered, it must have been with his shoulders or an expression of the face.

More silence pulled Hatta toward the room, but he was careful to stay hidden. In another jolting voice, Cuora demanded, "Do you swear to your testimony, under penalty of death?"

"I do," said the guard witness.

"Yes, m'Lady," said the woman witness.

"For the crime of treason, the sentence is death." Was Hatta imagining it, or did she sound indifferent? She continued in the same tone. "Off with his head."

Sounds of struggle came from the throne room, and the condemned man shouted as he was dragged from the chamber, "Down with Cuora! Down with Markin! Unite Maravilla and the Provinces under Palida and Antion!"

It took a moment for the proceedings to sink in, and when Hatta realized the full significance, it hit him like a spear through the gut. Cuora had just sentenced them to . . .

Hatta ran back down the corridor to find somewhere to throw up, but he only made it as far as his mirror before losing his breakfast.

No, he thought. *That didn't really happen. I imagined it, or this is a horrible dream, or . . . or . . . or . . .*

But he knew he couldn't doubt that he had witnessed Cuora's true nature, and just as surely, he knew he couldn't stay in Palassiren. Not with someone who could send a man, a real person, to his death. Without apology and without compunction.

The kindness from the alley by his shop was the anomaly. In the course of deciding punishment of the landlord and restitution for the damage to the roof, she'd made an exception when she'd treated him gently—a counterfeit benevolence. The cheerfulness of the croquet field had come from a half of her he hadn't known was merely a counterpart.

Loving a woman who was able to so easily condemn men to . . . he couldn't even think the word. But it would tear him apart every day.

Tears ran freely, mixing with the strings of vomit on his lips and chin. Hatta pleaded with the person in the mirror, trying to convince him that what he had heard was a figment of his madness. That he had misinterpreted the unseen events. But the argument was hopeless. It had to be sanity because it didn't make him happy; it gave him no hope. His mad thoughts always did.

The reflection that looked at him from the mirror was not the same man that greeted him on his way into the vibrant palace. That person had known hope and joy. This man's clothes were the same, but the colors had fled. The man who looked back knew nothing but sorrow and disappointment. *And pain*, the multicolored bruise reminded him. This man's mood had always been one color: drab, monochromatic black.

Wiping the fluids from his face with a coat sleeve, Hatta shambled from the black palace. No amount of winning was worth that much pain.

CHAPTER 24

Royalty

*C*hism and Thirsty were alone in the cold air on a balcony of Lady Cuora's palace. It was the highest and smallest balcony, and he'd never seen it used before sunrise. It had proven to be an even better location to catch the sun's first rays than the Circle and Sword statue.

Forty-five. Forty-six. Someone else was on the balcony. Chism didn't look to see who.

Forty-seven. Forty-eight. Lady Cuora stepped into view at his side.

Forty-nine. Fifty. He sheathed Thirsty and faced Lady Cuora. Something serious was afoot for her to call on him, especially so early in the morning. Bloodshot eyes undershadowed by dark folds told Chism that she hadn't slept well, if at all.

"What is it, my Lady?" The dress seemed to be the same one she'd worn the day before. He wondered if the puffy eyes might be from crying, but that was impossible for Lady Cuora.

When she spoke, the tentative voice did not seem to belong to her either. "I need you to find someone. A mirror maker.

Tardad knows where his shop is." A middle-aged servant stepped out from behind Lady Cuora and offered a small bow.

"Of course," said Chism. "Are you . . . hurt, my Lady?"

Lady Cuora looked over the low balcony wall toward the city and put her hands on the railing. Whether she would admit it or not, that was definitely hurt showing in her eyes. She shook her head.

"The mirror maker was expected at the palace yesterday. I should've sent someone last night. When he left the palace, his purse was so fat. I hope he hasn't done anything unwise." Her hands moved to her midsection as if to settle her stomach.

"I'll go immediately."

"Take my Knave and Tardad but no one else. I don't want to startle him with a crowd." She turned to walk out of the yard, but then she paused briefly. "Do not, under any circumstances, allow my Knave to treat him roughly."

Chism cursed his bad fortune, brooding his way to Brune's quarters with Tardad in tow.

"Wake up, Brune," yelled Chism, pounding the door. He couldn't make out the exact words of Brune's reply, but it included several vitriolic curses reserved for early mornings. The door was not bolted, so Chism pushed his way in.

The Knave's arms flew to cover his eyes from the lamplit hallway, and he muttered, "What do you want?" A ceramic mug crashed against the wall near Chism's head, the pieces breaking again as they hit the floor.

"Get dressed," said Chism, picking a crumpled tunic off the floor and tossing it to him. "Lady Cuora has business for us."

Brune continued to complain as he crawled from his cot, loudly relieved himself in a chamber pot, and dressed.

"Sometimes I wish I would've stayed in Shey's Orchard," he said, finally joining Chism in the corridor.

"Where?" asked Chism.

"Shey's Orchard. It's between here and Hannil Province." After wiping the sleep from his eyes, Brune shuffled along the tiled floors. "It's got a fine inn, and I was second only to the innkeep. I'd be giving the orders by now instead of waking in the middle of the night to run errands for someone else."

The same town I passed through to get here, thought Chism. *What are the chances of that?*

Though little of Chism's week in Shey's Orchard had been spent within the town itself, he knew the inn was barely big enough to require two stories. But Chism wasn't about to reveal anything about his time there, so he listened to Brune brag about how important he was in the "grand city of Shey's Orchard" as they meandered through the outer city toward the marketplace. Caught up in tales of his glorious past, Brune didn't bother to ask about their destination.

The little alley that Tardad led them to could not be more out of the way, making Chism wonder how the man ever sold anything. There was no answer the first time Chism knocked, so Brune stepped in, preparing to kick the door in.

"No," said Chism, blocking the door. "We do this my way."

"Says who?" Brune grabbed Chism's shoulder. "Get out of my way."

Chism swung his foot behind Brune's knee and used the Knave's momentum to take him straight back into the dirt. Chism left him floundering like a cockroach. With his back turned, he added, "Says Lady Cuora. And if you touch me again, even she won't be able to protect you."

"I owe you for that one," said Brune from the ground.

"Anytime you want to repay me," said Chism absently as he tried the door. The hinges creaked as he pushed it open. "Hello? Mirror maker?" He hadn't even thought to ask the man's name.

No answer. Enough light trickled in from the door to let him see the shop was empty except for a single mirror on a wooden framework. A door at the back of the shop opened into small, vacant sleeping quarters.

The mirror was the same style as Lady Cuora's new purchases, and inspecting it further, Chism found a note. During extra tutoring at the Elite Academy, he'd learned to read. Angling to allow light from the doorway to shine over his shoulder, he read the six words, written in careful script: *For the Queen of my Heart*.

"What's it say?" asked Brune from the doorway.

"It's for the Lady. You can ask her." Chism suspected she would tell Brune eventually, but he would enjoy seeing the Knave writhe in ignorance until then. He lifted the mirror off the stand.

They walked in silence back to the inner city and found Lady Cuora pacing in the entry of her palace. When the pair entered alone, with Chism carrying the mirror, her eyes filled with tears.

"No," she uttered as they approached. Chism passed her the note, wondering if he imagined the tremble in her fingers, then held the mirror so she could look into it. There was no way to know how a woman who routinely ordered a dozen executions before lunch would react. Her two guards sensed the tension as well and shifted uncomfortably.

The note and mirror only increased the flow of tears. With a shaky voice, she managed to say, "I knew it. That's why I couldn't go myself." She attempted to blink her tears away as her hand traced the wavy border of the mirror. Each bat of her eyelids sent water dripping down her face.

"What does the note say?" asked Brune. His underbite and clenched eyebrows made him look ready to rip someone's throat out. "I'll find him and make him pay. Just say the word."

Her eyes sharpened as they swept to Brune, changing instantly to tempest. "Summon Marky, Knave. Tell him to meet me in my throne room. Knight, escort me back to the shop." She stormed from the palace, and down the ornate stairs. Chism motioned the bewildered guards to follow and rushed to keep up with her.

No one spoke as they wound swiftly through the city streets. Once back in the small alley, Cuora entered the shop with reverence. The guards stood on either side of the door while Chism tried the only other shop in the alley, where an old tailor was bent over a table.

"Excuse me," said Chism. "Do you know where the mirror maker went?"

Looking up through spectacles, the old man said, "No, but he departed in a hurry. I don't know what occurred, but he looked as though someone ripped his heart out and took his soul for good measure."

Lady Cuora pushed past him. "Do you recognize this script, tailor?" She held the note out.

"I should," he answered. "It's mine."

Stressing every word, Lady Cuora asked, "Where is he?"

The old tailor's eyes widened when he looked up at her face. "Lady Cuora. A pleasure to have you in my shop."

Lady Cuora stared down at him, waiting for an answer.

"Oh, the mirror maker. You see, I just finished telling your man that I don't know. I'm awfully sorry."

"What did he say before he left?"

The old man scratched his bald head. "He wanted me to show him what I knew about making hats, M'lady."

"His exact words?" Her words were as sharp as her stare.

"He said, 'Would you consider teaching me to make a hat I might hide in?' As close as I can recall, anyway."

"And you did?" asked Lady Cuora.

The tailor shrugged and looked nervously around the shop. "We only had one evening. He already knew a bit. I can't say I agree with his views on style, but he's got skill, sure enough. He'll manage."

"Tell me every word he said to you last night."

"Begging your pardon, Lady, but my mind doesn't work

like that anymore. You know how he was prone to babble. Well, last night it was about going to mine cinnamon or synonyms. It didn't make any sense to me. I always thought cinnamon grew in sticks."

"Cinnabar," said Lady Cuora.

"That might have been it," said the tailor with a small chuckle and a shrug. "Still means nothing to me."

"It's a red ore from which mercury is extracted. What else did he say?"

"Not in so many words, Lady . . ." The tailor paused as if considering whether to speak the words he was thinking. He looked down at the cloth in his hands and said, "But I could see he cared for you something fierce."

The emotions on Lady Cuora's face were impossible to read. Rage? Loss? Confusion? She breathed deeply. "Send word to the palace if you recall anything else. I would be most appreciative."

She fled the shop and the tailor let out a long sigh of relief. Chism tailed Lady Cuora as she hurried through the outer city.

Summoning one of the guards with a finger, Lady Cuora ordered, "Muster the Elites in the courtyard in front of my palace." She dismissed him and ordered the second to gather her personal guard and have them assemble with the Elites, fully armed and armored. He hurried off as quickly as the first.

Alone with Lady Cuora, Chism asked, "My Lady, what does any of this have to do with the mirror maker?"

She stopped abruptly, and Chism had to backtrack two steps. "It's time for a change, Knight. It's long overdue." At a faster pace, Lady Cuora started toward the palace. "I thought I could be two people: a ruler first and foremost, and a woman on occasion. As if it was possible for a body to have a heart while not having one! I believe impossible things on a regular basis, but that pushed the limit."

That was exactly why it was best for Chism to be who he was and no one else. Lady Cuora didn't offer any other explanation and Chism didn't ask. Apparently the issue had to do with love—a concept he understood even less than friendship.

Captain Markin was pacing the throne room when Chism and Lady Cuora entered. Brune glared at Chism, but his former Captain didn't even notice him. His attention was on Lady Cuora.

"You look ghastly, Cuora. What is it?"

"This nonsense of rule by council is over. We should have exiled the young king along with his traitorous mother."

Captain Markin's mouth hung open. "But, he's the son of King Barash, who was the rightful ruler of Maravilla—"

"And is now dead," finished Lady Cuora. It was obvious by the tilt of her head that she didn't appreciate Captain Markin questioning her. "The Provinces defy us. Why should we allow the son of their queen to rule alongside us, even as a figurehead?" Markin waited for Lady Cuora to continue, which she did only after closing her eyes and drawing a slow breath. "You and I will be married. I will rule as queen with you by my side as king." As an afterthought she added, "And Antion can run crying to mommy."

Captain Markin froze, his face like the unbelieving visage of a man rescued from the headsman's block.

But Lady Cuora took no notice and spoke lowly to herself as if working out her feelings by stating them out loud. "Cuora the woman is gone. I am a ruler. A queen." Without looking at the note in her hand, she tapped it against her open palm. "Yes," she continued with a wry smile. "I am the Queen of Hearts."

The great room plunged into weighted silence. The Queen of Hearts was an obvious reference to the note from the mirror maker—*For the Queen of my Heart* it said on the envelope. Still, Chism could make no sense of it. It seemed the opposite of what she was trying to accomplish, but that was standard practice for her. It obviously amused Cuora.

Eventually, Captain Markin approached her from behind and settled his hand on her forearm. "Do you mean it, Cuora?"

"Of course, Marky." Linking arms, she led him from the room with Chism, Brune, and two Elite guards sharing shocked looks before following them into the corridor.

Her voice regained its directness. "We should have formed a partnership when you suggested it years ago. Maybe I could have avoided this whole mess." Chism knew more about the current mess than any of them, but still didn't know everything.

Moving his hand to encircle her waist, Captain Markin said, "If this situation is what it took for you to accept my hand, then blessed be it."

Spotting the new mirrors on the walls ahead of them, Lady Cuora patted Captain Markin's chest and said, "You go ahead. The Elites are assembling in the courtyard. Wait for me in the entry."

Obediently, Captain Markin and his two Elites went on. With an unreadable expression, Lady Cuora stared into the odd mirror. Her back straightened, and her eyes grew more focused until Brune's voice shattered the moment.

"He couldn't have been *that* special, could he, Lady?"

"You have as much couth as a suitor at a funeral, Knave."

With a determined step, Lady Cuora walked to the grand entry of her palace. Captain Markin waited there, looking more severe and confident than he had since taking his place on the Council.

"The Elites are the key to a smooth transition," said Lady Cuora. "Is there any doubt of their loyalty to you?"

Chism knew the answer.

"None," said Captain Markin. "An Elite's loyalty is to the corps of the Elites. They swear allegiance to the Elites and to the Captain of the Elites in defense of the king. If the king happens to be the same man as the Captain of the Elites, it only simplifies the issue."

"Well, my dear king," said Lady Cuora, formally linking arms, "it's time we became even more royal."

Ten hours later, Chism stood on the main balcony of the queen's palace with the newly proclaimed queen and king, Brune, and a half squadron of Elites standing guard as Antion's retinue formed a train out of the inner city. It was a bloodless coup, or "modification," as Lady Cuora referred to it.

Not "Lady Cuora," thought Chism. *Cuora, the Queen of Hearts.*

The Elites in the courtyard were in the same situation as Chism. He had seen on their faces when the new queen and king explained the *modification,* that most of them felt uncomfortable with the change in rulers. However, with no affront to the Circle and Sword, they simply followed orders, which came from the pair that now ruled the interior kingdom of Maravilla. *Usurpers*, some would call them. But at least they were peaceful usurpers.

No one spoke on the balcony as they watched the fleeing faction until the Queen excused Markin, Brune, and the rest of the guards. Chism felt their curious gazes as they filed into the palace. Along with them, he wondered why he'd been the only one retained.

As soon as they were out of earshot, the Queen confided, "I'm worried, Knight." The timorous tone had returned to her voice.

"I can see that, My Queen. Your eyes keep wandering to something far away, and there's fear on your face."

"He's too young and decent to survive in this world. I'm sending you to find and protect him. Please."

Chism had never heard the word *please* pass between her lips. She felt more strongly about the mirror maker than he'd realized. Strongly enough to send away her Knight.

"When you find him, send me word that he's safe."

"As you say, Highness." It couldn't be worse than palace life.

"I've chosen a different path, and there is no part for him in it. But I need to know he's not left to his own resources." Bringing the full force of her gaze to Chism, she said, "Swear to me you won't abandon him until I command you to."

"I swear it," he said without hesitation. A nagging feeling told him his life was about to become much more interesting. "But how will I know him? We never met."

The grin from two days before returned to her lips. "He'll be easy to find. You've never seen anyone so colorful. I take that back—*you've* never seen *anyone* colorful. He wears a purple, turtle-shell hat, dresses finely in garish colors, is the most ingratiating person you'll ever meet—"

"And his name is Hatta," finished Chism. He looked away from the queen as his own strong emotions rose suddenly. Of course. After everything Chism had been through, of course it would be Hatta. He took a moment to compose himself, chiding himself for not realizing it sooner.

"Yes," said Queen Cuora. "Didn't I mention that?"

Chism shook his head, still not trusting himself to speak.

"Then how did you know?"

Chism turned to look out over the courtyard, debating how much to tell her. Keeping secrets had always served him well.

"Knight, how did you find out his name if I never spoke it to you?" she demanded.

"You didn't need to, my Queen. The description is unmistakable." Only two years had passed since they had seen each other. It felt like half a lifetime.

Hatta would not be happy to have Chism on his trail. Chism himself still wasn't sure how he felt about the whole thing.

Chism faced the Queen, hoping his mask of impassivity hid the emotions swirling inside.

"Hatta is my brother."

CHAPTER 25

Complements

Traveling the Northern Spoke in late springtime turned out to be even more difficult than doing it in winter. Snow and frozen roads could be sheltered against, but soggy roads and incessant rain proved more insidious than a blizzard. Chism and Ander took advantage of inns along the way, usually staying two or three days at a time to wait out rainstorms.

Chism's constant pacing during their stays had driven Ander to teach him chess, and Chism took to the game like some men take to drink.

When Chism had asked Ander to accompany him, Ander's only condition was having as much time as he wanted to pursue his tinkering and creating. One of the projects that took Ander away from the chess table was a set of playing cards he was designing. Featuring the players of the current political environment, four castes were represented: hearts, diamonds, spades, and swords. The former Lady Cuora was depicted by the Queen of Hearts. Fair Palida graced the Queen of Diamonds. Markin's formidable likeness fit the King of Swords, and Antion held a spade. According to Ander, a spade was the perfect implement for the boy. Not only was it small enough for him to heft, but a true weapon would be inappropriate for a child.

The explanation amused Chism, who had been proficient with a sword by the age of nine. The whole project was a grand waste of time, but Ander wasn't happy unless he was tinkering or sketching, and with all the time they spent waiting, it didn't do Chism any harm to keep his end of the bargain.

Somehow Hatta had crossed the kingdom, learned new trades and, most surprisingly, stayed alive for two years. As long as Chism could remember, things turned out for Hatta, no matter how unwise his decisions were. It was a happy, accidental luck. Serendipity, Hatta called it. Even though Chism had seen it as they were growing up, he still didn't believe in it. Something so insubstantial could only last so long.

Chism hoped it held out at least until they were reunited.

The path he and Ander followed kept close to the Northern Spoke, but as Chism predicted, it meandered haphazardly. They couldn't merely press northward on the road because Hatta was likely to veer off the path without explanation. So they tracked him through every village along the way.

At least they didn't have to bother with taverns. One of the few traits Chism shared with his brother was hatred of drink. Shopkeepers and traders were the best informants, and it appeared that Hatta had acquired an interesting collection of dyes, tools, cloth, and crafting materials. The amount of money he spent was mindboggling. Chism couldn't imagine how his brother had come by so much.

Many farmers reported seeing him pass with his small cart and paired horses, sometimes doubling back a half day's travel to revisit a town. Other times, Chism and Ander passed through three or four villages without any reports of him. It was exactly what Chism expected.

After three weeks, they reached the intersection of the Northern Spoke and the Fringe Road. Previously, the Fringe Road had been an insignificant border between the Provinces and the interior of Maravilla. Since the split in the kingdom, it was now the official boundary between two hostile nations. The assault on Duke Jaryn had occurred on the other side of the kingdom, but the Provinces were unified against the interior, and Chism wasn't anxious to find out how far his infamy had spread. Nothing but the search for his brother could make him cross back into the Provinces.

That or an Elite mission, he thought with nostalgia. He just hoped the current journey wasn't in vain. There was a chance that Hatta would run off again without even speaking to Chism.

Chism waited while Ander entered Selvage, the town just north of the Fringe Road, to find out if there was a reward for Chism's head. When he returned with supplies, Ander reported that word of the split in the kingdom had reached Selvage, but thankfully no one knew anything about a fugitive Elite or a boy with a high price on his head.

The weather improved over the next two weeks as the pair approached the northern reaches of the Provinces. Within days they would be out of the Provinces and in the mountains that led north to places too cold to live.

A shopkeeper in a town called Marrit claimed Hatta had bought some mining supplies there two days before. They'd catch him soon. Traveling fast with such heavy tools would be impossible. They *had* to catch him; they were running out of kingdom.

As they left Marrit, Ander mentioned Hatta for the eighteenth time. "How can it take so long to find a man with purple hair and apricot pants?"

As long as talk didn't turn to possible outcomes of the reunion, Chism would go along. "The thing about Hatta is that he's always in exactly the right place or exactly the wrong place, but sometimes you don't know which until days later."

"Are you nervous? Excited?"

Chism still didn't know exactly what he felt. They hadn't parted under good circumstances, and it was far too much to hope that they could ever be as close as before.

"I don't know," said Chism. He dismounted and went to the side of the road to scoop up a few stones and stay out of conversation range.

Every hundred steps, Chism placed a small stone into his right pocket. When he collected ten in that pocket, he dumped it and added one stone to his left pocket.

Twenty-eight stones later—twenty-two in his left pocket and six in his right—he spotted a small stone hut a mile or so off the road. From his current distance, he couldn't make out any people or animals, but it was worth investigating. A path led eastward toward the hut, but once they were on it, scrubby trees blocked their view.

Just as he had every day of the trip, Chism wondered how Hatta would react.

Hatta, at sixteen years old, had been the one to flee—and without a word of farewell. Chism was destined for the Elites; it was all he ever wanted to do. Yet his older brother hadn't sent Chism so much as a single letter. And who could blame him after witnessing his younger brother, only thirteen, run their father through with a sword even as Hatta pled for their father's life?

The apprehension surprised Chism, but over the course of five weeks, he'd realized there was no one in the world he cared about as much as Hatta. If Hatta didn't accept him, it would be like losing a hard-won friend.

There's that word again.

The clearing and hut appeared suddenly after a curve, and Chism saw a man with a fine coat and checkered hat from behind. After more than two years apart, he'd found his brother.

Hearing them approach, Hatta turned. No surprise showed on his face, and Hatta smiled his customary half-grin. The worn town hat on his head told Chism he intended to stay at the ramshackle hut.

Hatta seemed to have aged more than the two years of their separation, but his crooked smile was as welcome a sight as Chism had ever seen. Leaving his horse to Ander, Chism walked anxiously forward, coming to stand face to face with his only living family member.

"I'm pleased that you've found me, brother," said Hatta, refraining from physical contact. The gesture, or lack thereof, told Chism they weren't as far apart as he feared.

A joy that Chism had never found in his time with the Elites filled him. "Me too, brother. You've had some interesting adventures."

"That day I fled was the worst of my life. My mood was black; everything was black when I left."

Chism couldn't tell if he was talking about fleeing Palassiren or T'lai. Hatta thought every bad experience was the worst day of his life. But at least he could forget and move on. Chism had a habit of dwelling on negativity until it festered.

Hatta's eyes lit up, and he said, "But I've learned all manner of truths about colors."

From the inner pocket of his coat, he produced and unfolded a circle of cloth with varying shades in a circle. To Chism's eyes, each gray tone faded into another very similar one. He shook his head, but Hatta persisted.

"Colors fit into a circle, Chism. This is yellow, and next to it is green because yellow and blue are green. So blue would be on the other side of green. Then purple.

"I know you can't see it," continued Hatta, "but this is red. It would be the color of you. And Cuora. Though her red makes yours look muted. And across the circle from red is green, which would be my color. But they're not opposites. No, they're not, though I always assumed they were. Even though they seem opposing, they're actually complements."

Chism had no interest in a lesson on colors he couldn't distinguish. "Hatta, we need to talk."

"Yes, talk." With a crooked smile and fingers that danced on his wheel of colors, Hatta continued. "See purple here? It would be the pure color of wildflowers. And across from it is yellow, the sun's color. Complements. Not opposites. And here, orange, which is sunsets. Its complement is blue, the color of water. And there's white and black, which aren't in the color circle, but it still works. Like Cuora's Knight and Knave. I haven't met them, but she told me they're white and black. Not opposites. Complements. "

Chism wanted to argue; he wanted no comparison to Brune. In an insistent voice with no harshness he said, "Hatta." In his entire life there had never been a reason to be harsh with his brother. Angry, frustrated, but never harsh. "Let's talk inside while Ander tends the horses."

"Horses, aren't they wonderful? What a relief you didn't have to come all this way with mules for companions. Ornery animals, those."

Chism walked toward the roofless stone hovel with his brother chattering nervously about mules in his ear. Before crossing the threshold, Hatta reached for Chism's shoulder but brought his hand up short.

"Please leave Thirsty outside. Please?"

Things were not going well, but Chism still held out hope, so he unbuckled his belt and sheath, leaving them at the threshold. An argument over Thirsty could very well make Hatta run again. In addition to causing another estrangement, that would make it hard to keep his oath to the queen.

"Did you come here to make more mirrors?" asked Chism, wanting to talk about anything except colors.

"No, I've made the mirrors I wanted to," said Hatta matter-of-factly. "I'm after cinnabar. It would be where mercury comes from."

"Mercury, huh?" said Chism with a pained grin. "When I was an Elite, I was in Quicksilver Squadron."

A look of confusion and worry settled on Hatta's face. "*Was* an Elite? Have ten years passed already?"

Chism saw his brother struggling with the mental math and helped him out. "No. I . . . didn't last that long."

Hatta was clearly relieved, but Chism didn't know if it was because the timeline made sense or because Chism was no longer a soldier.

"Where have you spent the last two years, Hatta?"

"Palassiren. And before that Shey's Orchard and Frenala. And I was in T'lai before I ran." His eyes darted around the run-down room, looking for something to distract himself. If Chism didn't keep the conversation on track, Hatta would start picking flowers or naming the color of the grout.

"I know. I was there with you." There was no more putting it off; he had to address it. "Why did you run, Hatta?" Tears made their way into his voice. "I finally solved our problem, and you ran off."

The restlessness of Hatta's eyes spread to the rest of his body. He fidgeted, refusing to make eye contact. "I . . . I recall telling you not to . . . do it. To kill him." He forced the last out in a rush. "I definitely told you not to."

"And I explained why I had to." Chism fought to control the volume and tone of his voice. "Why didn't you stay? With Father gone, neither of us needed protecting. I told you he would never hurt us again."

"But I was afraid, Chism," Hatta said, tears brimming. He acted three years younger than Chism, not three years older.

"I would never hurt you, brother. I did it to protect us. It was just a matter of time until one of us ended up dead instead of him."

"I know. I know. That wasn't the cause of my dread."

Worried he wouldn't be able to control his temper, Chism waited in silence.

"I never wanted much. Just peace—no conflict. We couldn't do anything about . . . him, but we could do anything about ourselves. So I found the colors. No matter what time of year, I found any color I wanted, even the colors of the other seasons." Talking about his memories of colors calmed him noticeably. "In summer, I found wintery blue algae hidden behind rocks. In winter there were autumn-brown crawfish that turned summer-red when they boiled. And the spring wildflowers gave me whatever color I needed at the time I needed it."

Chism couldn't take any more talk about colors. The remedy for Hatta's anxiety was poison to Chism at that moment. He shouted, "You found your colors, and what did I find? A sword!"

He reached reflexively for Thirsty. His friend wasn't there. Chism felt alone and abandoned. Again.

"You're older than me! You should have protected me!" The tears formed in *his* eyes now. He knew he sounded like a pouting child, but he didn't care. "But you just wanted to *appease* and *mollify*, and your little brother had no choice but to pick up a sword! Your fantasies were perfect for your escape, but I didn't have the colors. Or anything else. You failed me, Hatta! And I was just trying to protect us!" He stopped yelling and waited for Hatta to run from the shack, wondering how far he'd have to chase him.

But Hatta didn't run. Chism saw his own pain reflected in his brother's face like a mirror. Without speaking Hatta stepped closer, reached out his arms, and brought Chism into a careful embrace. It was his only defense against Chism's abuse. Kindness had always been his only defense and his only weapon. Chism wanted to shrug away. Push back. Fight. But he was caught in a thick web of kindness, under the spell of a master. His brother's voice gave him the strength to abide the embrace.

"Do you care to know what I feared?"

Chism's muffled sobs were his only answer.

"I was scared I couldn't stay with you because perchance we were too different. That if I didn't run, we might stop loving each other. I could abide Father, but I couldn't abide falling apart from you." After a pause, he added, "But that was when I thought we were opposites, not complements."

Chism couldn't bring himself to return the embrace, but he forced himself to accept it and stood, darkening the shoulder of Hatta's coat with tears.

As if suddenly realizing something, Hatta added, "Just like I ran from Cuora and from Shey's Orchard and from Frenala. It seemed impossible that everything could turn out as I hoped, so I ran. Even though it meant traveling with that cantankerous mule."

A blubbery chuckle escaped Chism. He withdrew slightly, and his gentle brother retracted his arms. For a moment, Chism wondered if his brother's touch was magic. The pain he felt had abated along with the grudge. And the same absence of pain was clear in Hatta, his emotional mirror.

Chism wiped his eyes and said, "I'm glad you don't have to be here alone any more, Hatta."

"Alone isn't what I've been. Twice the Cheshire Cat visited."

"Who?" asked Chism. It wasn't the first time Hatta had invented imaginary companions or fantastic creatures.

"Cheshire. He's a Cheshire Cat. You should see how he turns on and off his colors. Though I wonder if you wouldn't be able to see him at all; he relies so much on color." Hatta's fingers bridged and touched his lips. "You two just have to meet."

"Speaking of that, let me introduce you to Ander."

Chism led Hatta outside to where Ander stood with a staff-length stick, poking it into a shallow vat.

"What kind of potion are you brewing?" asked Ander.

"Oh, it's not a potion, but beaver pelts that fell into some dilute mercury. It wasn't until this morning that I noticed them."

Ander was captivated by the sodden hides. "Do you mind if I experiment with it?"

"Feel free. If you didn't have a use for them, the mercury *and* the pelts would both be ruined! I'm Hatta."

"Ander." He looked over Hatta, who smiled nervously. "You're as colorful as a chromagrove, lad."

Some of Hatta's anxiety faded, and he offered a small bow.

Ander slapped him on the back. "I think you and I will get along wonderfully."

CHAPTER 26

Glue

*H*atta stared at the wall where his turquoise boot hung. The solution he'd found had caused a whole new problem. The original problem was finding a way to build hats without sewing. The seams were unsightly to him of late and he searched for a new way to attach the different hat parts. He attempted various solutions, and apparently, if the shoe in front of his face could be believed, the one that worked was tree gum mixed with iron ochre. As a final test of the new glue he had ground a small batch under his heel the evening before and pressed his boot against the cement wall.

And there it was when he came out in the morning. He attempted to force it off the wall by pulling, but the stitching began to complain before the leather budged.

Hatta scratched his head. Usually a solution was a solution, not a problem. This one was both until he came up with yet another solution.

Out of the corner of his eye, Hatta saw Chism coming back from his morning sword practice routines. Chism pulled his tunic on, and walked casually to where Ander was breaking cinnabar ore with a sledge hammer. Hatta tagged along at a distance and went into the small hut he used for hat making. It was near enough to Ander's work area that he could overlisten to their conversations and since it had only three walls, he could observe them as well.

Chism settled onto a log not far from where Ander was breaking the ore. Ander stopped swinging the sledge hammer and wiped his brow. He held out the tool and breathed heavily.

"Feel like being useful, or do you plan on being like all the rest of the bumps on that log?"

"You're so good at it, though," said Chism with exaggerated praise. Hatta had seen them banter over the month since they had arrived and was almost positive that they joked around most of the time.

"So practice," said Ander. "Maybe someday you'll be as good at smashing rocks as me."

"Tempting," said Chism. "But I wouldn't want to make Thirsty jealous."

Ander's breath was apparently caught so he picked up the sledge hammer and went back to work. Then the amazing thing happened. Chism stayed where he sat and watched him work. A smile came to Hatta's face. Some days Chism spent hours with Ander, even after the day's duties were done. They sometimes played chess, sometimes sparred and sometimes just sat in silence while Ander tinkered or sketched and Chism polished Thirsty or read a book.

To Hatta's knowledge, his brother had never had a friend. What a wonderful thing to see a first friendship develop! The fact that his little brother was involved made it all the more wonderful.

Hatta was careful to never use the *friend* word around Chism. If he knew what was happening between him and Ander, he might resist.

Things had been perfect since they showed up. The shack was a comfortable home. Ander built a kiln that turned out to be necessary to extract mercury. He used the mercury and beaver pelts to make a new kind of felt that was the perfect material for hats. Every day Hatta's skill improved and his hats became more creative and higher quality.

He ignored the stiff constraints most hatters followed and let his designs flow. Instead of straight cylindrical hats, he allowed the curves of his hats to extend beyond the circle of their brims. Ander's felt gave him the versatility his creativity demanded.

Yet with all that, an itch to run prickled Hatta right between his shoulder blades every time he thought about how wonderful his life was.

Hatta shrugged off the itch by going out to where Ander and Chism were shoveling the crushed ore into the furnace. Maybe one of them would have an idea for his boot.

"I have a small problem one of you might help with."

"Good morning," said Ander.

Chism asked, "Where's your other boot?"

"That would be the solution," answered Hatta. "Or better said, the problem. Both actually. If you'll follow me, I'm sure you'll see quickly enough."

They put down their shovels and followed Hatta to the door of the house.

Ander laughed when he saw the boot. "You finally got the glue right?"

Hatta nodded. "The gum sap wasn't strong enough by itself so I added some iron ochre since metal is strong and I love the color of the ochre."

"Interesting way to test it," said Chism.

"Problematic way to test it," said Hatta.

Chism pulled on the boot until the stitching stretched.

Hatta said, "If the boot was made with my new glue instead

of stitching we could most likely pull until it came loose, but unfortunately my glue wasn't yet invented when the boot was made."

"Do we have butter?" asked Ander.

"Good idea," said Hatta. "Perchance a good breakfast will help us think. But we don't have butter."

"I wasn't going to eat it," said Ander.

"Who was then?" asked Hatta.

"You can remove sap with it," said Ander. "You'd be amazed how many things butter can fix."

"Butter," said Hatta. He'd never considered using it on anything but food. "Hm."

"What about oil?"

"Olive oil?"

"Should work," said Ander.

Hatta retrieved the oil from the house and Ander poured a few drops between the toe of the boot and the wall. "Give that a few minutes. If the top edge comes free, pour on a few more drops."

"I thank you."

Ander and Chism went back to the kiln and Hatta stared at the boot. It reminded him of himself. Not only in the striking color of it, but being stuck. He had the same urge to run as he had to tear the boot off the wall.

There was no explanation, but he knew running would ease the prickle, let him relax. At the same time, he'd had too much of running; it was time to stay put for a while.

But there was the kingdom to save, and sequestering himself with mercury and hatting was not going to do it.

The battle between madness and sanity raged inside him nearly every day lately. On one hand, his ambitions to mend the rift in the kingdom seemed completely illogical. Not only was he nobody, but saving kingdoms sounded like the kind of thing that required conflict and the inserting of himself into conflict. On the other hand, when he thought of what would make him happy, it was staying away from fighting and conflict.

Usually sanity and happiness were at odds, but in this case, the conditions that should make him happy—staying far away from any, all, and every conflict—also seemed the sane thing to do. So why wasn't he happy? The disparity had never existed before and it set Hatta's head spinning in very suspicious directions.

And frankly, made him unhappy.

The only way he felt he could ease the unhappiness was by pursuing the unlikely chance that he might be able to mend the kingdoms, but that was sure to lead him into conflict, indubitably producing unhappiness. Sometimes he thought about it in circles for hours.

Hatta pulled lightly and the glue at the toe of the boot gave way a fraction of an inch. He added a few more drops. And waited. Eventually something would come along that would be the olive oil to the glue that held Hatta. When he left, hopefully Chism would go along.

During their trip into Marrit the following day—which Hatta took with both boots on his feet and none on the wall of the home—they heard about increased hostility between the Provinces and Maravilla. No progress, or even effort, had occurred toward reunification. Lady Palida led the Provinces and the Whites as their queen, but no word had reached them regarding Antion and how he would fit into the new government. Skirmishes between Maravilla and the Provinces were common and, according to rumor, escalating daily.

One talkative shopkeeper claimed both kingdoms were drafting able-bodied men into their armies. "Gobbling 'em up like a hungry sow," he said. Motioning to Chism, he continued, "The boy'll probably be exempt, even though he's got a sword.

They haven't said anything about making boys fight. But you two look healthy enough, purple and white hair aside."

Chism smirked but said nothing. As repulsed as Hatta was by war—even thinking the word made him want to spit—he had to admit the idea of being conscripted while Chism sat out was enough to send anyone into a stupor.

The secluded mining camp and home should have provided Hatta with a sense of security from the storms that raged across kingdoms, but the thorn in his back kept prodding him toward the road. Only his devotion to Chism gave him the strength to resist. It was unclear what kept Chism and Ander close, but keeping them out of the trouble was just another reason to stay.

Halfway through a sleepless spring night, Hatta lay awake on his cot naming the shades of shifting silver cast by the full moon. "Winter Ash. Slate. Snow in Shadow. Moon spot. Moon surface. Moon eclipse. Lakedusk. Minnowbelly."

Cheshire sauntered into the room. The creature was as easy to see in the shadows as in daylight. It wasn't that he emitted light but that light wasn't needed for him to be visible.

"Good morning, my boy," said Cheshire in his casual tenor voice.

"Yes, and to you," said Hatta, sitting up on his low cot. "I've given it much thought, and I'm still of the opinion that you're real."

Cheshire's grin remained the same width, but his eyes brightened. "I can't tell you how relieved I am to hear that, but I must ask how you've come to that conclusion." He settled into a comfortable position at the foot of the mattress. His confident grin made Hatta want to smile forever.

"Well, Tjaden said he met you. And many people know Tjaden because of, you know, Jabberwocky issues and such. Chism even said he knows Tjaden from being Elites together. And Chism's as real as I am."

"That's proof enough for me." The Cheshire Cat stretched languorously. "How wonderful it feels to be real."

"I thank you. No, actually you're welcome. Yes, that's it."

The pair sat in silence for a few moments, Hatta reveling in Cheshire's presence.

Eyes closed, but still smiling, Cheshire said, "You've stayed here longer than I expected."

"Me too. But we're leaving soon. Tonight, methinks."

"A wise choice. Soldiers are about in the region to conscript more recruits, who presumably will be sent to yet other towns to conscript more soldiers, who . . . you get the point. I just couldn't bear to see one such as you forced to endure that."

Hatta felt as if whatever held his stomach up had suddenly been removed, and he grasped his belly to stabilize it. After a few deep breaths, he said, "I should tell Chism. And Ander."

Rising quickly to walk into the front room, Hatta turned to thank Cheshire, but just caught the faintest glimmer of the oversized smile fading away. "I thank you," he said into the air, then hurried out.

"Chism," he said, nudging the foot of his brother's mattress.

Chism sprang from the bed, fists raised, making Hatta glad he hadn't tried to shake him awake. Even after months of not being a soldier, his brother was always ready to defend himself.

"It's nothing," said Hatta. "Except that we ought to go."

"Go where?" Chism started to calm and rubbed his eyes.

"It's not the *where* that's important. It's the going."

"What are you talking about, Hatta? More bizarre dreams?"

"How could I dream if I haven't yet slept?"

Chism sighed and pressed his temples with fingertips. "It sounds like you're running again, Hatta."

Hatta's insecurity returned. "I . . . think I'm not, but even so, at least I've told you this time." Chism, who still hadn't met Cheshire, wouldn't understand the forewarning.

"Tomorrow," said Chism, climbing back onto his cot.

Hatta shook his head, but he wasn't sure if Chism saw. "No. Tomorrow is only good for tomorrow. It should be tonight." He only knew one way to convince his brother. "I'll most likely leave in an hour, and I don't relish the idea of separating from you again."

He stepped over to Ander's cot. "Ander," he whispered.

Amidst some unintelligible words, Hatta heard, "breath that could infest a chicken with maggots . . ."

Scrubbing the crawling sensation off his arms, Hatta spoke louder. "Ander. It's time we left."

The shaggy-haired man sat up and stretched. The feral silhouette was frightening, so Hatta backed up to the doorway and said, "You'll want to pack. For the journey."

Hurrying away without turning his back, he heard Ander ask Chism, "Why'd he have to wake me from such an enjoyable dream?"

Hatta dressed in his accustomed traveling suit: maroon jacket with apricot pants. And, of course, the purple turtle hat. He packed his other suits of clothes, his hats, and all the felt that was cured enough. After tucking away the bulging coin purse and heavy vials of mercury, he was ready to go.

Chism and Ander went about their preparations in silence. Hatta was just glad to see them going along with the journey. Within the hour, the three men started on the path that led to the Northern Spoke with the two horses Hatta had brought and the two of Chism and Ander.

The scrub oak was just tall enough to obstruct their moonlit view of the landscape, even astride the horses. Except for insects and the hooves scraping on gravel, the night was quiet and the horses easily managed the slow pace along the familiar trail. Hatta had to remind himself to not talk out loud to the horses. Chism and Ander would be bad-tempered enough about the hasty departure; any other odd behavior might cause contention. So he satisfied himself with pats, touches, and quiet praise. At one point, he leaned close and whispered, "I can't say how glad I am that you're not a mule."

The animal nickered in agreement.

Two hours later, light the same color as the gravel leaked from under the eastern horizon as they approached the outskirts of Marrit

"Shame we didn't think to bring vittles," said Hatta. "If we care to wait in Marrit for a shop to open, we might buy some."

Chism chuckled—a sound that made Hatta want to whoop with joy—and said, "Ander and I packed plenty of food, Hatta. Enough for weeks, maybe more."

"Wonderful! It looks as if this journey's destined for success." Hatta looked at the light on the horizon. He was wrong; it didn't look like gravel, it was more of a bluish mercury. A whistle appeared on his lips and Hatta didn't stifle it.

They skirted Marrit and other small towns, traveling at night for two weeks to avoid towns and large groups of people. When Chism or Ander asked about their destination, Hatta simply told them, "South." They seemed glad just to be leaving the Provinces.

Half a day away from the Fringe Road, the outskirts of another small town appeared at sunrise. As Chism started to lead them into the woods, Hatta heard a gruff voice from shadows say, "Halt. Name yourselves."

The sound of steel sliced through the morning as Chism whipped Thirsty free and ordered, "Name yourself first or die a bandit's death."

Bustling surrounded them, and Hatta knew it would end in violence if he didn't intervene. "It's just Hatta and Chism and Ander. And four horses. Who would you be?"

The gruff speaker answered, "On Queen Palida's authority, stay where you are and lay your weapons ahead of you on the road and you won't be harmed."

"I'll lay my weapon into your gut first, then your companions'," said Chism.

From behind, a man said, "That sword won't do much good against arrows." The silhouettes of two archers with drawn bows blocked the road.

Feeling sick to his stomach, Hatta risked an arm on Chism's shoulder. "Their bows, Chism," he said in a pleading tone. "And from the rustlings, there must be more hidden."

With a grunt, Chism pulled away and turned his horse to face the opposite direction. "I'm sorry you don't understand," he whispered. "Ander can explain later. Never think I don't care about you, brother."

Chism spurred his horse and lunged northward. Arrows flew all around. Hatta screamed and leaned forward, hugging his horse's neck tightly. Turning his head to look behind him, he saw Chism race past the two men in the road. In a zigzag pattern he faded into the early morning.

Armed soldiers surrounded Hatta and Ander, pulling them roughly from their saddles. Hatta hardly noticed the violent impact with the road. Dirt mixed with blood from a split lip, filling his mouth with a brown metallic taste, but it was overshadowed by the taste of abandonment.

After all they had been through, Hatta never expected Chism would be the one to run away.

CHAPTER 27

Distraction

"They might have let me keep my hat," complained Hatta, feeling very exposed.

"It's a shame, Hatta, but I think you'll wear a soldier's helmet before that turtle hat again," said Ander.

The morning sun, as yellow as it would be all day, warmed them where they sat, back to back, in the middle of the Northern Spoke. Two uninterested guards slouched fifteen paces away on either side.

Hatta refused to believe what was trying to become very clear. On occasion, he was able to disbelieve things if they weren't directly in front of his face—one small benefit of instability.

Digging for more reasons to doubt the situation, he asked, "What do you suppose the soldier might have meant when he said, 'Welcome to the White Queen's Army'?"

"It's as clear as melted ice, Hatta—we've been conscripted. Like it or not, you and I are soldiers in Palida's army."

Distracting Hatta from bone-deep anguish, a rabbit emerged from the bush in front of him. And what a rabbit it was! Unlike any creature Hatta had ever seen, it shimmered from one color to another, lingering on each just long enough for Hatta to truly appreciate the rich hue before it blended into another. June-bug green changed to lilac, which in turn became pale blue that reminded Hatta of the tiny flames that appeared at the edges of a campfire.

As quiet as a morning glory opening for the day, the hare hopped forward and rested between Hatta's feet.

"Do you have the time?" it asked in a small voice.

Did it really speak? Or had Hatta's skill at interpreting animals improved considerably? He'd never been asked the time before, not by an animal, but new adventures were the norm of late.

"I would think it's still morning," said Hatta. "I do apologize, but I've never been very much concerned with time."

Ander responded, startling Hatta. "Me neither. When I'm hungry I eat, when I'm tired I sleep, and when nature calls, well, you know."

The rabbit, now the color of leaves at the peak of their fall transformation, shrugged. "I didn't have anywhere to be anyway." It spoke just loud enough for Hatta to hear, causing him to wonder if Ander could make out anything. Their heads were less than a hand apart, but they faced opposite directions.

The urge to converse with the hare overcame Hatta's concern about Ander overhearing. "I hadn't planned on being *here* today. I can think of many places I'd rather be, but I can't think of many places I'd rather be less."

"You're as logical as a fish is wet," said Ander. "I thought I was done with soldiering. Even when Chism asked me to accompany him to find you, I never expected this."

Waiting until Ander finished speaking, the golden rabbit said, "Don't worry, Hatta. You'll find a way out of this. There's still saving the kingdom to consider."

That was the second unusual creature that referred to Hatta's marvelous destiny. For some reason, it made him nervous to discuss it openly, though every so often he still believed it to be true. But with Ander listening, he didn't want to discuss it.

With a glance at the lounging guards, Hatta asked, "Do you think you'll be noticed? Would it matter?"

"With this remarkable mane?" asked Ander, with a shake of his head that caused his hair to brush Hatta's. "I stand out like a new cuppy. It's only a matter of time until someone recognizes me. My only chance is if they don't link me to Chism."

The odd rabbit grinned a toothy smile, apparently enjoying Hatta's double conversation. "They won't see me. I'm much too quick. Besides, I'll be going soon."

"Why?" asked Hatta, disappointed. When the rabbit left, so would the only distraction from his contemptible fate.

Ander spoke. "He didn't tell you, but Chism made serious problems with a duke in Far West Province. I'd be surprised if there wasn't a high price on his head throughout all the Provinces."

With no warning, the lime-colored rabbit dashed into the

brush and disappeared. The crunch of approaching footfalls followed immediately.

An angry man with white stripes on the shoulders of his uniform ordered, "On your feet." A handful of guards followed silently.

Using each other's backs to push off, Hatta and Ander shimmied to a standing position and turned sideways so they could both face the officer. Ander was as relaxed as a cat in a tree, but Hatta felt more like a bird in a cat's mouth.

"Would obtaining my hat be a possibility?"

The request drew much more of the man's attention than Hatta wanted. The strong-jawed officer glared into Hatta's eyes, forcing Hatta to drop his head and look away. He regretted not pressing Cheshire to teach him the disappearing trick. He tried to scoot behind Ander's shoulder.

In a growl, the officer said, "You've got bigger problems than your hat. The boy who fled this morning—who was he?"

Hatta squeaked, "He would be my—" but Ander's voice rode right over him.

"He said his name was Chism. From T'lai, if I'm not mistaken. Said he was looking for adventure."

The officer's attention whipped to Ander. "And who is he to you?"

"A helper, that's all. I make fabrics, and my friend here mines mercury. The lad worked for us."

"How long have you known him?"

"A month, maybe two. Just since he showed up at our hut."

How did Ander lie to the man's face without any outward sign? Even listening to the lie made Hatta fidget, but no more than when the officer had been staring at him.

"Describe him," ordered the officer.

Ander jostled Hatta as he tried to pull an arm loose, but the ropes prevented it. "Up to my shoulders in height, hair as black as burnt charcoal, with eyes even darker. Thin jaw line that's never seen a razor. If I'm being honest, the lad was troubled, Sir. Never talked about his past, but I could tell it was murky."

"Is this him?" He signaled to a soldier who held up a parchment with Chism's face. The rough drawing disturbed Hatta. The artist had drawn his brother with unforgiving eyes and a frightening scowl. Words and numbers were written in fancy letters above and below the sketch, but they meant nothing to Hatta.

"That's him, or I'm cousin to a clownfish," said Ander. "Is there really a reward for him?"

The officer grunted. "Before lamenting the missed reward, you should consider your luck that you didn't end up dead."

"But he's just a boy," said Ander with genuine shock. It looked genuine anyway, but Hatta had seen him lie once already.

"That boy is a rogue Elite. He nearly assassinated a duke in Far West Province."

"Dimples and dandruff! It appears we owe you our gratitude for scaring the scamp off."

I thought Ander loved Chism, thought Hatta. *More lies?*

"Say nothing of it." A meaningful grin showed on the officer's face. "That's what brothers-in-arms do for one another. You're members of the White Queen's Army now, after all."

Hatta felt his face pale and he pulled against his bonds, looking for something to lean on. "No, we can't be. I . . . I . . ." Everything was turning black again; he had no defense against such plainly spoken truth.

What a shame that the dirt in the road was so uniform in color. Even the gray gravel on the road outside of Palassiren contained shades of gray, as well as the occasional bluish pebble.

Umber. That's not distracting in the slightest. The thought of life as a soldier wilted his spirit.

Offering a shoulder for support, Ander came to his rescue

once again. "Pardon my sensitive friend, Captain. What he's trying to say is that we are already in the service of Lady Queen Palida."

The captain looked amused. "Is that so? In what capacity?"

"Craftsmen. As I mentioned, I work in textiles and he makes mirrors."

"Yes, Palida cares for mirrors a great deal," said Hatta. Now that was a decent topic of conversation. "Did you know she never looks directly at anyone?"

"Of course I know that," said the captain. "Anyone who's ever seen her knows that. But I thought you were a mercury miner."

"Mercury is a key ingredient in his mirrors," said Ander. "We've mined enough and now we're traveling back to her," said Ander.

"Surely you carry a writ from the queen or some other proof?" With an innocent expression, the officer waited for Ander to shake his head. "No? Forgive me for not being entirely convinced. I feel our current need for soldiers outweighs her need for a tailor."

"With due respect, Captain," said Ander, "we are not unknown laborers whose presence will go unnoticed. We both know the queen can be, how should I say this . . . quirky at times? Look at this hair, Man. Even if I was the worst tailor in the Twelve Provinces, she wouldn't turn me away."

It was true. Lady Palida was obsessed with all things white, and Ander's hair was nearly as white as Chism's was black. *Hmm, complements.* Hatta managed a minuscule smile at the discovery, but it only lasted until he looked back at the sneering officer.

"White hair may be rare, but it's hardly proof." He looked at Hatta. "You say you're a mirror maker?"

Hatta started, "I . . ." but couldn't bear the man's gaze so he nodded.

"We didn't find any mirrors among your belongings. Tell me, how exactly does one make a mirror?"

Careful not to look at the captain's face, Hatta hesitantly explained the most common metals used to make mirrors: tin, mercury, silver. Gaining confidence, he delved into the mixtures of each and what would happen if concentrations were incorrect. Halfway through the explanation of building frames, the captain cut in.

"So you are a mirror maker." Hatta felt the man's gaze leave him. Addressing Ander, he said, "But what is a clothier doing with a soldier's spear?"

"A man must have a way to protect himself," said Ander with a shrug. "Lady Palida herself gave that to me. It once belonged to an Elite Fellow! She said even if I couldn't use it well, it might scare off would-be bandits."

"And why are you here in the northern Provinces instead of serving at her side?"

"Cinnabar, Sir," said Ander. "We mine it for mercury—me for my fabric, and him for his mirrors."

With a quick glimpse, Hatta saw the captain was still wary. Deep in thought, the man paced slowly in front of them. "Every draftee has one excuse or another. I want to believe you. I *almost* believe you. But you haven't produced any proof that you've more than glimpsed the queen in a hallway. And your association with that rogue Elite is too much coincidence." His considering countenance snapped back to the stern gaze, and Hatta knew he'd decided. "We'll meet up with her forces eventually. You will stay with us until then. And please don't desert, because I'd hate to hang you before we can verify your story." He looked over at an underling. "Assign them to Worick's Squadron." He spun and marched away.

Hanged if he didn't stay to fight? Hatta didn't know if he would faint first or vomit then collapse into it.

Ander swore. "Lizards and onions!" That didn't sound appetizing at all, especially with Hatta's current nausea. But there was something about onions.

What is it about Onions? Onion, onion, onion. And it hit him.

"Onion! That's it," shouted Hatta, moving toward the officer. The guards stepped in front of him. "The queen's king son, I mean the king, the queen's son. Antion. She calls him Onion, but not when people can hear. He doesn't care for it, but she only says it because she loves him very much."

The captain froze, and it took him a long time to turn. With a pensive look, he finally said, "Onion. That's some proof I can work with." In a voice barely loud enough to be heard, the captain said slowly to a soldier, "Make them messengers. Give them a copy of my letter to Queen Palida and have them depart immediately." To Hatta and Ander, he said, "I'm sure loyal servants of the queen won't mind carrying a missive. Since you're already on your way to find her."

They didn't argue. "I'm not releasing you from conscription," said the captain, "but we can't have too many messengers." Without further comment, he spun and strode away.

Hatta sank to his knees in relief. His two hours as a soldier had been the worst of his life.

CHAPTER 28

Selvage

*C*hism stroked felt-gloved thumbs against fingers as he scanned the encampment that infested the town. His flight originally took him north, but he'd circled around, eventually reaching a low hill to the south that gave him the best view. Though the terrain was much different, he had flashbacks of Quicksilver Squadron entering Serpent Gap while he looked on. However, back at the Gap, he looked forward to the outcome, confident that his brothers-in-arms could deal with whatever circumstances came up. He was just as confident that his brother could *not* deal with the current situation.

Staying and becoming a prisoner wouldn't have done either of us any good, he told himself for the sixteenth time. *I haven't abandoned you, brother.*

The camp came to life as he looked on, but he was much too far away to make out individual activities, and he had no idea where Hatta was being held. Or Ander. Hatta would stick out if Chism could see colors, but that was worthless wishing. Hopefully they were still together. Ander's experience as a Fellow gave them a small chance of escaping or at least being treated humanely. If they got separated, Hatta was capable of getting himself into any situation.

"Move, curse you," he told the camp at large. If tents didn't come down soon, then the army—he called it an army, but the group was no larger than three hundred fifty men—would stay for at least another day, giving Chism no chance of making a rescue until the following day. Once the soldiers marched, Chism would have many more options. Sneaking into camp under disguise and leading Hatta and Ander to safety would be the easiest, especially in the chaos of making or breaking camp. He also considered an ambush if Hatta ever appeared close enough to the borders of camp that Chism only had to fight four soldiers. Maybe even six.

Every minute his brother spent as a conscript would be agony for both of them.

Chism's patience was rewarded. Tent poles lowered and men bustled, preparing to march. He wouldn't have to wait until the next day to act after all.

A half hour later, the regiment lined up facing south, nearly the direction in which Chism waited. He watched hopefully until the soldiers started moving. He had been lucky enough to flee in the right direction, and now had a considerable head start on the soldiers.

After retrieving his horse from where he had tethered it near the road, Chism started south on the road at a trot. As a lone rider, he could cover distance twice as fast as the battalion, which gave him plenty of time to analyze possible locations for ambushes and escapes. But the land he passed was flat, adorned with nothing more than the same scrubby trees that surrounded the mining homestead. Chism wasn't entirely sure what he was looking for, but he didn't see any way to use the current terrain.

An hour passed without any change in landscape until a

few small farms came into view on either side of the Northern Spoke. In early summer, the fields should have been full of farmers, but nearly everyone Chism saw was a woman or young boy. The people who noticed him watched closely, and some even stopped their chores and withdrew to locations out of Chism's view. It didn't even seem like the same town he and Ander had passed through two months before.

Located just north of the crossroads of the Northern Spoke and the Fringe Road, Selvage was almost big enough to call a city. As one of nine towns in the kingdom that allowed travel along major routes in any direction, Selvage was an important center of commerce. Technically it was in the Provinces, but it was close enough to the interior that loyalties might be divided.

Two months previous, Ander had reported no signs of any kind of search for Chism. Chism hoped that still held true.

When he entered the town, he noticed the same lack of activity he'd seen in the fields. Most people hurried inside as he approached, and the ones that didn't flee eyed Thirsty with mistrust. The shops all appeared to be closed—odd for a town whose lifeblood was trade. A cloud of caginess hung over the village. He couldn't even talk to anyone because they fled every time he approached.

Townsfolk shouldn't be so scared of a lone boy.

Watching for a dead-end alley or someone out in the open who couldn't duck inside, he spotted a woman scurrying out of a shop and saw a much better opportunity. A shopkeeper would have no choice but to attend to him.

Chism tethered his horse to a post outside the shop and casually gripped Thirsty as he approached the door. Leaving Thirsty outside would set a shopkeeper at ease, but any advantage would be greatly overshadowed by the risks of not having it handy in a bind. *Besides,* Chism thought, *abandoning friends should be avoided when possible.*

The shopkeeper's eyes darted to the back of the store when Chism entered, but the man held his ground uneasily, not sure if he should stay or run. Chism had never seen such a prominent nose. It was like a parrot's beak, and the man's flowing hair was brushed back like plumage.

"What do you want?" he asked tersely.

The shop was empty of people and nearly empty of supplies. Some baskets were vacant. Others held a few potatoes or some flour or dried corn. More shelves were bare than stocked.

"What happened here?"

"Who are you with?" asked Parrot. "White or Red?"

"Neither. I'm trying to stay out of it." Then he added, "Just like you."

"What's a boy doing with a sword like that?"

"Like I said," answered Chism, "I'm trying to stay clear any way I can."

Parrot looked Chism up and down, considering. With an exasperated sigh, he said, "The Reds came through first. They *appropriated* the supplies they needed. Only those of us with cold cellars or hidden stocks were left with more than a couple of days' provisions." He wore a look of disgust. "Not two days later, the Whites came. There wasn't much in the way of goods for them to seize, but in the end they took much more than the Reds."

That explains why there are no men left in town, Chism thought.

"They took volunteers first," Parrot's face flushed, and he couldn't hold Chism's gaze. "But that wasn't enough to fill the quota, so they held a lottery. Four out of five men were conscripted." His voice was low, as if embarrassed, and Chism realized the man was feeling guilty because he avoided the draft.

Chism didn't know what to say to ease Parrot's feelings of cowardice or culpability.

"Folk had some coin, but with all the men gone, it didn't last long. We're traders, and without goods, we have nothing."

Motioning to his shop, he continued, "I was lucky enough to have this stored away under the shop, but nearly everyone's buying on credit. A few still barter, but not many have anything of value left to trade, and I just can't bring myself to turn away hungry folk."

Still Chism had nothing to say. The shopkeeper continued. "It's the blessing and the curse of living in a merchant town. Under normal circumstances, coin flows freely, but when the goods are gone, you're left with no way to provide. There are only a few farms around the town, and the farmers have been glad to take on the men who are left. But unless something drastic happens, we'll never be able to put away enough before winter."

The armies should be supporting the Circle, Chism thought. *Instead they've become its worst violators. I have to do something.*

No, he corrected himself. *That's not my concern anymore. My concern is watching out for Hatta.*

With the armies "gobbling up conscripts," as the store owner in Marrit described it, Hatta had certainly been drafted, if not imprisoned. More than ever, Chism had to find a way to rescue his brother, even if it meant drastic measures.

"Where are the armies now?"

Parrot shrugged. "They had a battle outside of town on the day between their visits here. I don't know where they went off to, but wherever it is, isn't far enough."

"Battle?"

"The Whites called it a skirmish. When they took the conscripts, they claimed they needed to replenish their ranks."

"Where was the battle?"

"South of town, at the crossroads."

"Thanks," said Chism, and he turned to leave. Then he stopped. Reaching into a pocket, he pulled out six silvers and four cuppies. Half of his coins. "Can I trust you to get these to people who need them?" He knew they would be worth little in Selvage, but eventually trade with other cities would resume.

Looking at the coins like a starving father at a loaf of bread, Parrot nodded. Chism dropped them into Parrot's palm. He wanted to do more, try to mend the broken Circle, but he wasn't like Hatta—he couldn't save the world. The thought amused Chism, and he shook his head and smirked in spite of himself.

The ride out of town was as disheartening as the ride in. Like the northern outskirts, very few farmers specked the landscape south of town. Approximately a quarter mile out of town, where the Northern Spoke and the Fringe Road met, he found the battle site. What was once a flourishing wheat field north of the Fringe Road and west of the Northern Spoke was now completely desolate. Leaving his horse to graze on the ruined wheat, Chism wandered through the field, startling crows and vultures. Here and there lay broken pieces of shields and splintered arrows. Swarms of flies pointed him to body parts—some fingers, a hand, remnants of entrails, and some fleshy chucks he couldn't identify. All of them had been picked over by animals. In many areas the ground was crusted with blood—he didn't have to see colors to recognize it. More indications of the shattered Circle.

Along the western edge of the field, he saw a mound of fresh dirt, four paces wide and twenty-four across. A mass grave. He estimated more than fifty but less than a hundred were buried there.

Meaningless loss of life. Abuse of the people they should be protecting. Chism pictured Hatta's body, hacked and rotting under the berm, and knew he not only had to keep Hatta alive but also had to prevent him from even seeing this. That didn't give him much choice as to where to stage his rescue.

Without another glance at the tragic scene, Chism returned to his horse and set off to the north without a plan. An hour north of town, Chism left the road to find a vantage point. The legion still ambled south. It was amazing they ever arrived anywhere at that pace.

One boy against three hundred and fifty soldiers. It wasn't the worst odds he'd faced, but his luck could only last so long. No matter what Hatta said, there was no such thing as perpetual serendipity.

"Indefatigable," said Hatta, adjusting his superb traveling hat.

Pondering, Ander said, "Fatigue means tired. Fatigable is able to tire. *De*fatigable would be unable to tire, *In*defatigable means not unable to tire, or able to tire."

"Yes! But it doesn't mean that at all," said Hatta.

With a nod Ander said, "Indefatigable."

"Another one, then," said Hatta. "Prison and jail are the same, right?"

Ander nodded.

"So a prison*er* and a jail*er* are the same, right?"

"I suppose they should be, but they're actually opposites," said Ander.

"Yes! And what about inflammable? It means that something burns easily and quickly."

"That's what flammable means, too," said Ander. "*In*flammable should be the opposite of flammable. Very good, Hatta. You've given this some thought."

"It's just that perfidy does not agree with me, and words that mean what they don't say, they bother me. But I noticed that you can lie like a grey cat can meow."

Ander barked a laugh. "And you spew the truth like a man with the scour purges."

"I thank you," Hatta said. He wasn't sure exactly how, but Ander's statement felt like a compliment.

They were a few hours south of the Whites on the Northern Spoke. Hatta wanted to travel north, in the direction Chism had fled, but Ander said that would be too suspicious. They needed to take the message for Queen Palida and find the main body of the White Army, or at least act like that was their intent. So they plodded southward, nowhere near the path that Chism had fled on.

Scraping came from the slight curve ahead. Ander heard it too and they both pulled their horses to a stop. The sound was familiar but out of place on the vacant road. Hatta stayed put and Ander took the lead, holding his spear ready.

The noise continued steadily. *Thwish, thwish, thwish.* Like the scrape of claws on wood.

Ahead of Hatta on the path, Ander lowered his spear and said, "Well, if it isn't the fish that swam away with the hook. How'd you find us?"

Chism, whittling unproductively on a stick, stepped onto the road. "I was on that rise over there working on a rescue scheme that most likely would have gotten us all killed. And then I saw the two of you walking a mile ahead of the army."

"Welcome," said Hatta.

"I don't know how you do it, brother," said Chism.

"Mostly I try to do something else and it just happens." Greetings were so much more pleasant than farewells, no matter how brief.

Chism mounted and the three resumed their travel southward as Hatta and Ander told about being conscripted then being charged with a new duty. Before they reached Selvage, Chism explained the plight of the town and made it clear that he wanted to avoid it. But when Hatta heard about the people in trouble, he knew he could do something. Even if it seemed insignificant, there was some way he could ease their suffering.

Sometimes I wish I had a plan before stepping in blindly, thought Hatta. *Sometimes.*

Surprisingly, Chism and Ander didn't disagree. With an

exasperated sigh, Ander said, "It's hard to argue when I've nowhere else to be."

Hatta urged his horse forward, and Chism and Ander followed.

I never thought I'd be a leader, Hatta thought.

As they approached Selvage, they wandered through a verdant landscape, but the animal life seemed subdued. Very few birds flew, and Hatta didn't spot any critters scurrying. A tension hung in the air, and Hatta did his best to ignore it, focusing on his freedom and the clear road ahead.

There were fewer people going about town than when Hatta passed through two months before. When they reached the wabe in the center of town, he realized why. A procession was preparing to depart, and many of the townsfolk were loading wagons with all manner of crafts: brass candlesticks, multi-colored rugs, fabrics and clothes—mostly brown and other earthy colors—and even some uninspired mirrors. None of the items were abundant. It was as if everyone in town brought whatever random items of value they could find.

Chism and Ander pulled up short to observe the convoy, and Chism asked, "Notice anything odd?"

Hatta looked more closely. The wagons were well-matched, light-brown oak, but the horses varied considerably. The contents of the wagons had been loaded unsystematically, not grouped by type of wares, and late-arriving citizens piled objects in wherever they fit. Still nothing too unusual.

"They're almost all women," said Ander.

Distracted by the wagons and items they contained, Hatta hadn't noticed. There were more than twenty women. Maybe as many as forty. He wasn't quick with numbers like Chism. Among them he could see less than five men.

As was their custom when they encountered groups of people, Chism took the lead. He approached the first wagon where a stocky woman who resembled a pig in shape and coloring was shouting orders to the rest of the convoy from where she stood on the seat.

"What's all this?" asked Chism in his straightforward tone.

The woman looked over the three—Hatta pulled his hat lower when her gaze scraped across him—and said, "Just because they took our men, we aren't about to shrivel and die. We're off to trade for provisions."

"We can help!" said Hatta, raising his arm to be noticed from behind Chism and Ander. He heard Chism groan, but from what Chism had told him, these people needed assistance.

Looking inconvenienced, the woman answered, "It's a kind sentiment, but a boy and a madman will just eat what little food we have without scaring off a lone, crippled bandit." Pausing to consider Ander for a moment, she added, "The soldier's welcome. If the hair's any indication, he's got a fair amount of experience. But you'll not be wanting to separate, I assume." Without waiting for an answer, she scolded a boy for dragging a finely carved rocking chair through the dirt.

If he and Chism weren't welcome, Hatta would still do what he could. After dismounting, he retrieved a rucksack of food from the supply horse and laid it in Ander's lap. Then Hatta untied his heavy coin purse and held it up to the woman as an offering.

Like a pig on a perch, she looked down and demanded, "What's this?"

"Coins," said Hatta. "At least a pound of them. And Ander has food of his own for the journey; he won't need to drain your rations."

Before the woman could reach down for Hatta's purse, Chism snatched it out of his hand, and Ander exclaimed, "Don't give up the barn and farm with the bull, lad! Especially a bull that's not yours to barter over."

Sometimes Ander made the strangest statements. It made no sense, but he seemed to be saying he didn't want to accompany the group.

"But Chism and I aren't welcome, Ander."

"I haven't said I won't go," said Ander. "But if I'm the feastday goose, I'll at least have a say as to how I'm trussed and when I'm cooked."

Chism removed some coins, then tossed the purse back to Hatta. "Do what you want with those. I've kept enough to provide for your needs for a while." Hatta didn't see the point. He'd always provided for himself in the past, fat purse or skinny.

How could Ander not see that they needed him? Unsure how to convince him, Hatta waited on Ander, who looked at Chism. A raised eyebrow, a nod, a slight shrug. Something passed between the pair, but not out loud.

"I may be a sheepdog abandoning the flock to tag after a lamb, but I'll accompany you," he told the woman, and Hatta rushed to grasp his hand in congratulations. Ander scooped up Hatta's coin purse and said, "I'll see that this is used properly."

"Yes, of course," he told Ander. "And I'll see to saving the kingdom finally. Perchance I might do something about this war." It was more goodbye than Hatta was comfortable with, and unfortunately they still had to reload packs, dividing possessions and such. It was agonizing after already bidding farewell.

When he and Chism walked out of the town on their own feet, Hatta felt as free as a rabbit in a field. Somehow he had convinced Chism to allow Ander to keep all three horses to help with the caravan. The armies had left far too few for such overloaded wagons. He'd thought that Chism would resist, but he only said, "If it takes us longer to get wherever you're leading us, then we'll stay out of trouble longer. That suits me fine."

With nothing more than what they could carry on their backs, Hatta and his brother continued their journey.

No sooner were they past the town limits than Chism detoured from the road and picked his way through the silent forest. He gave no explanation, and Hatta didn't ask for one. Chism had followed him blindly enough; Hatta could return the favor for a while. A mile or two later, Chism led them onto a road heading east.

When darkness began to fall, Hatta still felt as proud as a puffed-up bullfrog. He was with his brother again, and they'd accomplished something.

The next morning when Hatta awoke, Chism wasn't in his bedroll. Hatta found him nearby on a small outcropping of rock, staring across a prairie.

"I still don't know how you do it, Hatta, but it's always something big." Whatever Chism was referring to, *he* had led them east the previous night, not Hatta. "I came for my lucky rays, and I found this."

Joining him on the boulders, Hatta looked to the southwest. A shallow valley spread out for miles, the morning light painting a fresh picture. Then he saw what Chism was looking at. Surrounding the empty basin were soldiers. Red-uniformed on one side, white-striped on the other. Hundreds? Thousands? More?

"How many are there?" he asked Chism.

After a moment of consideration, Chism answered flatly, "All of them."

CHAPTER 29

Final

The Kirohz Valley pressed into the landscape like the imprint of a giant, oblong bowl, stretching miles from brim to brim. Uniform prairie grass covered the floor, green and bending in the breeze. The meadow seemed to flow as if molten. Bristly trees lined the rims of the valley like bursts of green fire.

The natural beauty was marred by the revolting sight of two armies camped just inside the tree lines to the north and south. The Red army of Maravilla camped on the left, led by Cuora and Markin. To the right, on the north side of the bowl, was the combined army of the Twelve Provinces. Their uniforms varied in color, but all featured a wide streak of white paint across the chest or shoulders.

The scene in front of Hatta eclipsed the sum total of every confrontation of his life, and he wanted nothing to do with it. But the nauseating feeling in his stomach would stay with him forever if he left now.

On any other occasion, thousands of men assembled together had the potential to be momentous. Hatta imagined the cities that could be built, the art that could be produced, and the love and brotherhood that could be nurtured. The possibilities were limitless. However, these men hadn't come together to build or create. They had come to destroy. They had come to fill the bowl with blood and bodies.

Fighting a wave of nausea, Hatta leaned on his brother's shoulder. Surprisingly, Chism didn't pull away, though Hatta felt him tense up. There was no outstretched hand or offer of encouraging words, but at least Chism didn't let him fall.

"What are we doing here?" asked Chism, and his tone said he, too, would rather be anywhere else.

After such a long journey, there was no reason to avoid it. Forcing a smile, Hatta said, "If I were to wager a guess, I'd predict saving the kingdoms."

Closing his eyes, Chism drew a deep breath. Hatta had no idea what emotions Chism was struggling with, but the inner tempest was obvious.

"You're a hatter. What could you possibly do?"

"That I haven't figured out. My mirrors helped me get to a place where I met some of the people who people think are powerful. People who would make decisions, I suppose." Glancing between the two armies arrayed to do violence, it was difficult to make up his mind. "I suppose I might start by delivering this message to the White Queen." Struggling to rally enough courage, he told himself, "I am the White Messenger, after all."

The first step toward the Whites took effort, but each succeeding one came easier. Before long, it was all downhill.

With a string of curses under his breath, Chism rushed past and stood in his path. "Hatta, I don't know what goes on inside your head, but it's clear you don't always know what's real. You have your reasons for what you do, but nothing good can come from walking into that valley. Not for you and not for me."

Chism had never mentioned Hatta's instability. Of course he'd seen it over the years, but it was comforting that they never had to talk about it. With it finally out in the open, there was no reason to explain or excuse.

"You're right, brother. I have no idea if it's fact or fancy, but I've waited this long to find out, and I know only one way to do it." He considered freeing Chism from the obligation to accompany him, but what was the point? Either he would come or he wouldn't.

Stepping around his brother, Hatta threw himself to the wolves, walking into the valley and toward his glorious, uncertain, terrifying fate.

From behind, Chism muttered something else about madness. Hatta heard Thirsty's blade seesaw against its scabbard and knew his brother followed, ready for whatever lay ahead.

War. Killing. Violence. Foul, incomprehensible concepts. He might as well attempt to fathom the stars in the sky. But there weren't any stars there—just blueness and a sun too yellow to look at.

※

With everything to lose, Chism followed his brother's meandering steps. Hatta had to know that Chism's head carried a high price; they had talked about it over and over again on the road. As usual, Hatta didn't consider the consequences of what he was about to do. Duke Jaryn and the Provincial forces would not show any mercy, and Chism didn't plan on holding back if he had a chance to sway the outcome of the day. Hatta might go like a sheep to the butcher, but Chism was going like a bear.

Though the message Hatta bore was intended for Queen Palida, he angled left, toward the camp of Queen Cuora. Predictably unpredictable, Hatta took the most indirect route possible.

Sentries challenged them as they approached the eastern edge of the encampment. At the sight of weapons, Hatta shied away and stopped, but Chism continued, striding confidently past the drawn swords.

He said, "I'm personal bodyguard to the Queen of Hearts."

Hatta sparked up at that. Keeping Chism between him and the armed men, he said, "Yes! He's the Red Knight."

Red Knight, thought Chism. *How does Hatta even know about that?* He had purposefully avoided mentioning it to Hatta. But either because of Chism's confidence or the ridiculous title, the sentries lowered their weapons and allowed the pair to pass.

Once past the outer guards, they walked freely through the camp. The first men they saw were career soldiers in matching uniforms—cooking, mending tents, sparring, and tending to all sorts of camp duties. Though he'd never been part of a large war campaign, Chism knew the layout was by design. Conscripted soldiers from across the kingdom would make up the interior of the camp. The career soldiers would be stationed around the exterior, each with the duty to keep watch for deserters, which were not uncommon in such an army despite the threat of hanging.

The next group of soldiers wore mismatched clothes, their shoulders stained with paint. On this side of the battlefield it had to be red. A few young men tussled as a dozen others of varying ages looked on. Some of the faces looked vaguely familiar, but he couldn't place them until Hatta, deep in concentration, pointed out a face he knew.

"Cull," said Hatta to himself. "Something cull."

"Grower Mikel," said Chism and realized the tough young men wrestling were Steffen and his family. He'd bet his horse on it, if Ander hadn't led it off. The young man Chism worked with in Grower Mikel's orchard looked at ease with his rough relatives. True to form, out of the thousands of soldier's in

Queen Cuora's army, Hatta had wandered upon the men from Shey's Orchard.

"Hello, Mikel!" said Hatta. "Imagine meeting you here of all places." In the pleasure of seeing a familiar face, Hatta seemed to forget exactly where "here" was.

"Hatta, Chism," acknowledged Grower Mikel, glancing back and forth. "You two are acquaintances?"

"No," said Hatta before Chism had a chance to speak. "We would be brothers. Ever since Chism was born, anyway."

"Is that so? I'd sooner expect a bird and a fish to be kin than you two."

A burly man with a round belly and a staff approached. Speaking to himself again, Hatta said, "Shelf, shellef, Tellef! How would you be this fine day?"

"As well as any conscript could be, I suppose." He looked at the exuberant Hatta with skepticism.

Realization dawned on Hatta's face. "Oh. You two are, that is to say, you're here involuntarily."

Grower Mikel laughed sardonically. "That's painting it in bright colors, lad. If it weren't for penalty of death, not one of us would stay. Except maybe Titus's sons." He motioned to Steffen's group, who had taken up sparring with staffs.

"But you're not soldiers," said Hatta.

"That matters little to the nobility," said Innkeep Tellef.

"If you've no desire to fight, why are you here?"

Chism decided to speak up. "It's not that simple, Hatta. Those sentinels we passed when we entered the camp aren't just watching for the enemy. They're also guarding the draftees. If anyone tries to leave, they'll catch and hang them."

Appalled, Hatta said, "But they're all on the same side."

With a pained look, Innkeep Tellef said, "As far as I'm concerned, there are no sides. I'd be tending my inn if I had my druthers, open to Whites and Reds alike. But what the boy says is true. We could try resisting, but there'd be blood, and not a little bit. Our best hope is to go along with the army and hope it never comes to fighting."

Nodding, Grower Mikel said, "That looks less likely every day. I don't know what's gotten into the nobles' heads. I was always of the opinion that Lady Cuora was fair and competent, but now there's too many queens of this or that, and such-a-color kings."

"But you're so many," pleaded Hatta. "If you were to put down the weapons and walk out of camp," he trailed off.

Both men shook their heads, and Innkeep Tellef spoke. "A group of men from Arrula tried exactly that. A dozen ended up hanged, with the rest spread out so no two of them could conspire. Now, not only are they forced to fight, but they have to do it without any friends or family around."

Mikel nodded past Chism at a lifeless-looking man sitting limply in the shade of a shrub. "Darnel there is from Arrula. Watched his brother hang."

Predictably, Hatta's face paled, and he clutched his gut. The innkeep offered an arm of support, which Hatta leaned on as he wiped his eyes. He looked at Chism, obviously considering the loss of a brother, and Chism felt a sliver of hope that Hatta would abandon his mad quest.

"It's not too late to leave, Hatta. I can find a way past the guards."

Hatta shook his head. "Not until we've done what we came to have done."

It would do no good to ask what that was. If Hatta ever had a plan to begin with, he never had the same plan by the end.

A man Chism had seen once or twice in Shey's Orchard approached, and without speaking, he and Hatta warmly embraced.

"Master Aker," said Hatta, sounding much less cheerful.

He must know him well to recall the name so quickly, thought Chism.

"So you're caught up in this too?" said Aker.

"Oh, no. I'm just the White Messenger."

All three townsmen looked around, but Hatta's words hadn't drawn any interest.

"You should keep talk of the Whites quiet in this camp," warned Aker.

"Yes, I suppose I best." Continuing with trademark innocence, Hatta announced, "I saw Elora in the palaces. Lady to a Lady she was, and I delivered the letters along with a mirror. Little did I know I'd be in the messenger business again so soon."

"Thank you, Hatta," said Aker. "She sent a letter after leaving Palassiren. As far as I know, she's still attending the White Queen." He looked in the direction of the White army.

"Speaking of, my next message is for that very woman. Best of luck, and I hope you find the means to quit soldiering soon." With his trademark crooked smile, he left the trio watching his back.

Chism nodded his farewell and hurried to catch up.

After fourteen steps, Hatta suddenly turned and ran back to Aker. Digging in his coin purse, Hatta produced a few coins and pressed them into Aker's hands. "For the foodstuffs you gave me before some of my travels. It turns out I didn't need them, but a man and his woman were in dire need. Roof or Riff or Ralf was his name. Since they can't repay you, I will."

Hatta hurried back to Chism and led him deeper into the camp. They walked through scores of small camps where men from villages across the kingdom milled in supportive clusters, interspersed with bands of career soldiers. One of the groups was comprised of men from Frenala, and Hatta had a similar reunion with them while Chism watched.

As they talked about the travesty of the situation, a horn sounded from the center of the front ranks and spread like a wave to trumpeters along the outlying parts of the camp. It was a single blast, not signaling battle or attack, merely calling for readiness. It was enough to get men armed and moving forward.

Hatta took the opportunity to separate nonchalantly from the Frenala men, and the pair allowed themselves to be caught in the flow moving northward toward the eventual battlefield. The press grew thick as Chism followed his brother through the throng of conscripts and soldiers, and Chism was jostled repeatedly by the larger men.

Though he twisted and turned to fit through gaps without making contact, the soldiers closed in on him. In a battle he could cut himself free, use Thirsty to create some room to breathe. These men weren't intent on hurting him, but he was caught in a mass migration that he couldn't take much longer.

Hatta always chanted nonsense words when he couldn't deal with a situation, but that never worked for Chism. Every brush against a shoulder, each jostle from behind, every touch, whether purposeful or accidental, fueled his anxiety, causing his hand to reach involuntarily for Thirsty's hilt. He focused on staying close behind Hatta.

Just as he was about to scream and start punching, a dull-looking fellow with a pair of cudgels gave him a shove from the side, saying something about "boy soldiers" and sending him reeling to the ground. Incensed, Chism rose to his feet to teach the man a lesson when he was distracted by a strange shape dodging in and out of the feet of the swarming men. It had the appearance of a large cat, but it appeared camouflaged somehow.

Bracing against the shoving crowd, Chism observed the nimble creature for a moment. With implausible agility, it avoided every footfall by a hair's width and did so with an enormous grin. Somehow, the soldiers flowed past without even noticing it.

It made no sense. A few of them should at least glance down at it.

The contrast of cat against the background reminded him of camouflage training as an Elite. Even the most skilled recruits had been unable to construct concealment to fool Chism. He felt the same twinge of pride the Elite training had elicited. Even colorblindness had advantages, sometimes significant ones. Everyone else put too much stock in color, relied on it to distinguish everything in life. But Chism grew up noticing shapes and contrast, even among items of the same shade.

Is this what Hatta goes through when he sees things other people don't? The mixture of pride and confusion made it hard to focus on the events that surrounded him. For a moment, Chism felt a pang of sympathy for his brother and looked up to see where he'd gone. With a shock, he realized he'd lost Hatta in the crowd when he fell.

"Hatta!" he shouted, but the ruckus of the army covered his voice. He tried jumping up, scanning for the turtle shell hat, but he only caught small glimpses over the nearby men, and he was knocked to the ground again.

There was no sense in walking in the direction Hatta had been headed; he never traveled a straight line.

Curse this color blindness!

Hatta's garish clothes would stick out, if only he could see them.

Through the clamor of the army, Chism heard a calm tenor voice. "It appears you've misplaced your brother." The noise came from the direction of the camouflaged cat.

"What?" demanded Chism, watching more closely.

Dancing between legs and under feet, the cheerful cat said, "I can help you find him." Chism was in a mood to strangle the obnoxious cat, for the grin if nothing else, when he remembered something his brother said about a magical cat.

"Do you know my brother?" he asked, standing in front of the cat. Men poured around Chism like a stream around a branch, giving the cat enough of a respite to stop dodging.

"That would depend on who your brother is."

"Hatta. You just mentioned him." He continued to scan the camp, but without success.

"You could have other brothers." Somehow, amidst all the chaos, the cat was calm.

"I don't have time for this," said Chism. "Do you know Hatta or not?"

"As a matter of fact, I do," said the cat. His face was flat and round, with cat features such as whiskers and pointed ears. His smile was endearing and unsettling at the same time. "Cheshire's my name. Shall we go, then?"

Chism peered around one more time for his brother but saw no sign of the turtle shell hat. It was probably best to ignore the cat. Cavorting with fantastic creatures was Hatta's way.

But what chance did he have of finding Hatta among thousands of men? And what chance did Hatta have if Chism didn't find him? Madness or no, his brother needed him.

"It appears I have no choice, Cheshire," said Chism grudgingly.

"There's always a choice." When Chism didn't answer, the cat said, "Right this way, then." With a nod of his head, Cheshire began picking his way at a slight angle to the flow of the men of Maravilla.

The cat dodged effortlessly around ankles and feet, but Chism had to work to excuse himself through. The crowd slowed but thickened, yet Cheshire always kept just within Chism's view. The route they traveled was different than the one Hatta had been on, but that was to be expected. As they approached the front lines, the pace of the soldiers slowed, then stopped, and with eyes fixed on the cat, Chism continued pushing in pursuit. Touching so many strangers was one of the most difficult things he'd ever done, but if he lost the cat, he'd lose his only hope of finding Hatta.

Of a sudden, after squeezing through two uniformed soldiers, Chism found himself in the open meadow. On his side of the valley, a hundred paces to the west, a delegation was forming. On the opposite lip of the bowl, some Whites gathered in a similar group. Though Chism lacked the skills for it, negotiating was a good step. At the very least, it might delay fighting until he and Hatta could escape this madness, figuratively speaking. Chism had little hope that his brother could ever escape the madness inside his head.

Like a lone bannerman assaulting an enemy force, the cat's tail protruded from the meadow grass, leading a straight line toward the Whites. Chism's faith in the unusual cat was fading, but what option did he have? If nothing else, Hatta could work his kindness on this side of the battlefield while Chism worked Thirsty on the other. The thought of wielding his friend after so long thrilled him, and he plunged forward with renewed resolve.

The sea of men grew thicker by the step, forcing Hatta to hunker beneath his hat and weave between them, changing direction frequently. The camp had no end. Of course, it was possible that he was going around in circles. Without paying attention to people or landmarks, there was no way of knowing.

Soldiers jostled him increasingly, and his attempts to dodge between them became more difficult as he penetrated deeper into the camp. With each bump, brush, and nudge, their terrible violence rubbed off on him, dirtying his coat and sinking into his person. He wanted to sweep it off himself after each contact, but in such a crowd it was pointless. If he continued to think about it, he'd be frozen.

"Methinks we may never get there," he told Chism.

Chism didn't answer.

Still upset that I won't give up yet, he thought. But whatever Chism's reason for staying, Hatta was glad to have his company and his support.

After another minute through the maze of bodies, Hatta said, "I thank you for staying, Chism."

Still no answer. Perhaps he hadn't heard. Hatta peered over his shoulder and realized with horror that he was alone. Had Chism abandoned him again? They were doing that to each other much too often. In desperation, he scanned the crowd, paying particular attention to the direction from which he had come. But even rising on tiptoes, Hatta was unable to see over the heads of the soldiers. Between Chism's short stature and his bland clothes, which matched most of the conscripts', it was pointless. Another reason people should dress as individuals.

Struggling to slow his breathing, Hatta muttered a nonsense poem. Deep down, he knew it was only a distraction, that whatever he was trying to hide from was still every bit as present, but the verse soothed him nonetheless.

The tension faded somewhat, but he had to repeat the rhyme and recite another one before he felt strong enough to go on by himself. The Red soldiers continued their congregating, moving toward the edge of camp facing the White Army.

With head lowered, Hatta wedged through a wall of soldiers and found himself facing a new color of uniforms—a circle of dark blue, surrounded a pace or two away by the grays and browns of townsmen. It was like a close-up view of a single royal wildflower against a background of dead leaves and dirt, and he paused to take it in.

"Hatta?" One of the blue petals detached from the circle and approached him. "Hatta, how did you end up here?"

It was the Jabberslayer's Fellow, about a hand shorter than Hatta. *Small. Small, smallie* . . .

"Ollie!"

His Elite, Tjaden, followed, and Hatta greeted him as well. That name was easy since it started the same as Jabberwock.

"So they drafted you, huh?" asked Ollie.

"Yes, but it was the White Army, and I was only a soldier for two hours, which was more than plenty. Now I'm messenger to the White Queen. The White Messenger, that is."

At mention of the Whites, Ollie and Tjaden glanced toward the other army. As they turned back, Ollie's focus snapped back toward the meadow and the Whites. "Jay," said Ollie, pointing to the dead man's land between the armies, "doesn't that look like Chism?"

The black-haired young man walking toward the White front lines was indubitably Chism, and Hatta breathed a sigh in relief. Until he realized that they were hundreds of paces apart.

Why would Chism wander off to the Whites?

"Of course it looks like Chism; who else would Chism look like?" asked Hatta. "I was wondering where he runoffed to."

With a quizzical look, Ollie asked, "You know Chism?"

"Yes, since I was three years old. Or four."

"I thought you were from Frenala," said Ollie.

"When I was in Shey's Orchard I was from Frenala, but when I was in Frenala I was from T'lai. Just like my brother," he added with a smile.

"Brothers?" exclaimed Tjaden. "I don't know if I've met two people more different than the pair of you."

"Bizarre brothers both, but brothers besides," added Ollie with a grin.

"And not only brothers, but friends," said Hatta. "It would be fair to say that we care for nothing in the world more than we care for each other."

"I know you're peace-loving, Hatta," said Tjaden, "but Chism instigated the avalanche that led to this disaster."

Hatta refused to acknowledge that. True or not, no good

could come from believing harsh remarks about a friend or a brother. Forcing a smile, he said, "Speaking of Frenala, did you find Fletcher the fletcher?"

"Yes!" said Ollie, reaching over his shoulder to withdraw an arrow. "I was skeptical, but you were right. He makes the truest arrows I've ever shot." He thrust the thick-shafted weapon at Hatta, who accepted it as he would a hissing snake.

It was Hatta's first time holding an arrow, and it was much sturdier than he expected, as thick around as his pinky. For a weapon of war, it had a bit of beauty, if he ignored the gleaming metal point. Two of the feathers were dusty red, like a hazy sunset, and the other was the same dark blue as the Elite uniforms. The shaft was polished and smooth, a dark, grainy wood.

"What a difference good arrows make," said Ollie, and Hatta eagerly handed the arrow back. "I owe you one for the recommendation."

Tjaden said, "You wouldn't know it to hear him talk, but Ollie is quite possibly the best archer within fifty paces."

Ollie rolled his eyes and said, "Fifty paces? Wow."

"Maybe sixty," said Tjaden, holding back a smile. "Actually, there are only a handful of archers in the valley who are better than Ollie. I never thought I'd see it, but he reached a point where his skill surpassed his mouth. After that he had no choice but to be humble."

"For soldiers such as yourselves, this would most likely be great fun," said Hatta.

Their smiles faded quickly, and Tjaden said, "This is the worst possible scenario. I think Elora's on the other side somewhere."

Ollie's face mirrored some of the pain on Tjaden's. "If the nobles can't work something out, we'll end up fighting against other Elites. They're like brothers to us."

Hatta understood not wanting to fight one's brother, yet at the same time he was more confused than ever. Everyone he talked to opposed fighting. Nobody wanted to kill and surely no one wanted to die. Did they? So why were thousands gathered to kill and be killed? Everyone blamed the selfish nobles, and he thought of Cuora. But even she, with her two stark personalities, couldn't desire something like this.

"Isn't there something you might be able to do, Tjaden?" Hatta pleaded. "It was you who killed the Jabberwock when other soldiers couldn't do it for decades." Someone had to do something, and Tjaden was as likely a hero as anyone Hatta had ever met.

The Elite grunted. "I wish I could, but I'm just a soldier."

The royal blue that Tjaden and Ollie wore started to fade, and looking around, Hatta saw the reds on uniforms and green of the grass dampening quickly. He was sinking again. It was time to move on. "Well, I'll have a look into it, then."

They said some goodbye words as Hatta walked on, unsure of his options and unsure of his destiny.

As Chism broke through the mass of soldiers, he heard one ask another if they should stop him.

"Nah," said the second voice. "The boy's anxious for battle. Let him find out how much fun it is."

He mentally dared them to try to stop him. It had been a long while since he'd resorted to violence, and the thought was appealing.

The Provincial forces were gathered a half mile north of Queen Cuora's army. Chism knew he was infamous in the Provinces and most likely hated by thousands. So what purpose would the cat have in leading him to his death? Other than abject madness, of course. Yet Chism had no other hope of finding his brother before Hatta did anything extreme.

Only a fraction of the meadow lay behind him. The walk would take a while, so Chism counted to calm himself. Before long, the numbers were high enough to demand his attention, and he purposefully avoided shorthand methods of tracking his march. Hundreds and hundreds of steps ate the meadow, and when he reached nine hundred, he could make out the faces of individuals on the White side.

The enemy soldiers studied him as he approached, so Chism did the best he could to keep his face down while still watching the Cheshire Cat. It was best to avoid recognition for as long as possible.

Ten paces short of the front lines, Chism heard an order to halt, and he did so. Even without looking up, he felt dozens of arrows pointed his direction. Thirsty begged to be drawn, but Chism resisted and stood still as soldiers approached. It was not time to die yet.

Chism glanced at the cat. The creature sat bathing himself, unconcerned.

"What have you brought me to, Cat?" spat Chism. But the cat didn't answer, and violent hands were on Chism, dragging him into the hostile camp.

From behind, the cat trilled in his boyish voice, "I'll wait here, then. You won't be long." A few of the soldiers looked around for the source of the voice, but none settled on the camouflaged cat. Chism wished he could strangle it.

In desperation, he told the soldiers, "I'm looking for my brother; he's the messenger to the . . . White Queen."

Cats and colors! he swore. If he survived, he'd have to remember that one for Ander.

"Tell it to the sergeant," said one of the men.

Another added, "And you'll keep quiet until then."

"I'm a sergeant. He can tell it to me," said a familiar voice at his right.

Turning his head, Chism saw Butcher Lopin from his hometown of T'lai. Backing him up were fifteen other faces he knew. Ison, the innkeep, Jubal, a wheat farmer, and Jubal's brother, Jakel, stood foremost.

Hope and panic rose simultaneously. Chism hadn't seen any of them for years and he had no idea how a reunion would turn out.

With a sneer, one of the soldiers who held Chism said, "We're taking him to a real sergeant. You're just a conscript."

"A conscript who outranks you, Soldier. And I said we'll take him from here."

Chism wasn't surprised to see Lopin as a squadron leader. People listened to Lopin like children obey a stern father. Even this haughty soldier would have no choice.

The soldier reluctantly thrust Chism toward Lopin and stomped away without speaking. The men from T'lai circled Chism, two deep. The inner circle closed so tight they almost touched him, and Chism's hand went automatically to hover over Thirsty's hilt. His departure from T'lai had been hasty, and as a prisoner. There were probably some people in town who thought he got off without sufficient punishment after the incident with his father.

As if personal grudges weren't bad enough, there was the huge price hanging over his head. Blood pounded in Chism's ears. His Elite training fought to take over.

Lopin stood in front of him in the inner circle. Growing up, Chism always saw him as fair. But what was his idea of justice in this case? It was Lopin who first gave Chism lessons in swordplay, so in a way he had played a role in what happened.

"We've all heard about your adventures, Chism," said Lopin in a detached tone. "Elite Academy, some successful campaigns, and then the incident with Duke Jaryn."

Chism forced himself to wait silently. Out of their sight, he frantically stroked his thumbs over his forefingers on both hands. He truly did not want to kill anyone else from his own town. Outsiders attempted to peer into the circle, but the men from T'lai stood too closely. They wouldn't let anyone know what they intended until they were good and ready.

Lopin continued. "And we've seen enough of Duke Jaryn to know he's a pompous snake who needs to be brought down a notch or two. You've been wronged most of your life, lad." A few of the others grunted in agreement. "But what possessed you to march right into our camp like you were invincible? You can't expect the Provinces to accept you like a prodigal son."

He was far from in the clear, but at least he had an ally. Maybe some of Hatta's serendipity was rubbing off.

"It's Hatta. And . . ." he glanced in the direction of the cat in the meadow. Mentioning the cat wouldn't help. "And he has a letter for Queen Palida. You know him, Lopin. He can't handle a situation like this."

Lopin cursed. "If Hatta's here, he won't find the queen. She's not even in the camp. That horn was for the parlay with Lady Cuora, or the 'Queen of Hearts,' as she calls herself now."

Chism wanted out of the camp. It was insanity to have come in the first place.

"That's where Hatta will be," said Chism. There was no doubt. "Get me back to the clearing."

"I'll do more than that," said Lopin. "I'll escort you to the parlay myself. It's the least I can do for a friend."

Friend? There was that word again. He had never considered Lopin a friend; the man was three times his age. Expecting glares and curses, he glanced around the circle. Every man nodded when he made eye contact, and a few reached out and slapped his back, causing Chism to shy away involuntarily.

Taylin, one of the undetainable *'twins'*, said, "I'll go along,

Sarge. I'd like to do what I can for Chism." The rest of the group voiced their agreement, stunning him.

"Where's Jeruca?" Chism was surprised Taylin's wife wasn't with the group. He'd never seen one without the other. Innkeep Ison stepped to the side, revealing a soldier with bulky clothes and a helm that hid all of her hair and most of her face. Jeruca. She smiled sheepishly, and the men from T'lai laughed.

In the middle of a potential war, with Chism's life at stake, they were as relaxed as a group of friends sitting in a tavern.

Friends, he thought. He had grown so accustomed to solitude that it felt awkward. The urge to get away from the Whites grew even stronger.

"No one goes with us," said Lopin, ending any argument. "A whole squadron approaching the council could be the spark this tinder pile is waiting for. Taylin, just escort us to the clearing."

The men of T'lai—and Jeruca—turned to face south. With Taylin as spearhead, they sliced the ranks of soldiers. They only had to cover fifteen paces, but the curiosity over the strange newcomer made it a slow maneuver.

Like a bubble escaping the surface of a lake in slow motion, the squadron opened into the clearing. The cat waited indolently.

"Done so soon?" he asked, smiling his infuriating smile.

I should skin you and keep your teeth for a prize, thought Chism, but Lopin was too close to say it aloud. He started toward the center of the meadow with Lopin at his side.

"Can I talk you out of this, Chism?" asked Lopin as they walked. "You really should get away from here."

Chism shook his head. "I have to see to Hatta."

"I can look out for him. Showing your face in that council will be a death sentence."

"It won't be the first time," muttered Chism.

But Lopin was right. If Chism didn't get out now, he never would. And if he went to the parlay it would be the end for him.

What did it matter though? He'd accomplished nothing significant in his life, and seriously doubted he had much left to accomplish. His whole life felt like a waste of effort. Conflict followed wherever he went, and his attempts to protect almost always ended in strife or death. If there was value to him, to his life, today would be the chance to find out. If he could end the conflict, he would do it, no matter the consequences. Anything short of endangering Hatta. Though Chism was no longer an Elite, he still cared more for the Circle and Sword than he did for his own life.

Prancing at Chism's other side, the cat said quietly, "I see you already know where you're going. But if it's all the same to you, I'll come along. This could turn out to be quite a spectacle." He still smiled like an idiot. Lopin looked around, but if he heard the voice, he must have assumed it came from the ranks of soldiers.

Come a little closer, Kitty, and my boot will show you a spectacle. But the cat kept his distance as Chism paced toward the gathering of leaders with his two unlikely companions.

As Hatta broke away from the blue-clad Red Elites, a group separated from the body of the Red army. Cuora and Markin rode a pair of matching copper-colored horses. She was every bit as handsome as he remembered, and a tense thrill rushed through him along with a streak of nervousness.

According to Chism, Cuora felt nothing but concern for Hatta. But would she be as gracious once she learned he was hale and happy? Or at least hale. Her callous judgments were the reason he'd fled, and a small part of Hatta worried about the possibility of being the target of her heartlessness. But regardless of how she felt toward him, she was still his angel.

A few nobles and various scribes and attendants accompanied Cuora and Markin on foot, flanked by Tjaden and Ollie on one side and a pair of Elites with patches that looked like mercury on the other. The hitch in Ollie's gait made him seem slightly merry, like a child who was too excited to walk naturally.

Heeling Cuora on a slightly less impressive horse rode some sort of knight covered in red armor. His bulldog face was familiar, but Hatta couldn't remember if he should feel pleased or uneasy. The appropriate feelings usually came with first impressions, but for some reason, this man confused him. Involuntarily, Hatta's eyes went to his feet. The boots appeared to be fine, but nothing out of the ordinary except for the red greaves which covered the front.

They should be purple. Yes, the boots should be purple. And the face? He struggled to remember. The man resembled a much less confident, shamed young man fleeing Tellef's inn back in Shey's Orchard. Hatta couldn't remember the name—a sure sign there were no hard feelings—but the queen's attendant was definitely the man who had played the cruel joke with the adulterated tea and possibly tried to burn down the inn. Yet instead of apprehension, Hatta felt unperturbed. Peace had been made with the bully by using the boots in the road, and everything was right between them. It had to be, because the discomfort would be overwhelming otherwise.

However, he had misjudged in the past, and this time might be no different.

As if a mirror image, a group detached itself from the White Army and converged on a pavilion in the bottom of the bowl.

Cuora will stop this madness, and we'll all return to our peace-loving lives.

Hatta wanted to be there to witness it, so he ventured into the meadow, walking at an angle after Cuora's troupe. The delegation had almost arrived at the pavilion when she noticed

Hatta and pulled her horse to a stop, looking at him with hard eyes. Hatta's stride faltered, and he stopped as uncertainty about his role swept over him.

Insecurity, admiration, contentment, and worry swirled in Hatta's heart in the few moments their gaze lasted. Then Lady Cuora's face relaxed. She smiled as softly as butter, and the world around him shone in bright, buoyant hues again.

Cuora nudged her horse toward him, and Hatta took a step forward.

Markin, the new king, cleared his throat and said, "My Queen, the Whites await."

After looking between Hatta, Markin, and the pavilion, Cuora stilled her animal. With a tender nod and smile toward Hatta, she straightened her back. The stern composure showed on her face again, and she turned to lead her small group toward the parlay.

She was the perfect woman, but so much more. Too much more. As Hatta trailed the party to the parlay, he spared some thought for more verses about Cuora.

> *My fancy gave her eyes of blue,*
> *With hair like lemon drink.*
> *I came to find the blue was brown,*
> *The hair as black as ink.*
> *She has the bear's ethereal grace,*
> *The bland hyena's laugh,*
> *The footstep of the elephant,*
> *The neck of the giraffe.*
> *And if you were to ask me how*
> *Her charms might be improved,*
> *I would not have them added to,*
> *But just a few removed!*
> *I love her still, believe me,*

Though my heart its passion hides,
She's all my fancy painted her,
But oh! how much besides!

The queen of his heart was the most capable person he'd ever met. If anyone had the ability to save the kingdoms, it was her.

From across the battleground, Chism wasn't surprised to see his brother approaching the parlay. The meandering stroll was unmistakable and the hat only confirmed it. Addressing Cheshire, he said, "It was a circuitous route, but you've kept your word." He still wanted to strangle the cat.

"What?" asked Lopin.

"Nothing. Talking to myself."

The fool cat just kept grinning.

A hundred paces ahead of Chism, the two delegations met under the shade of a large, open tent, both wary of each other. Twenty-three people in each party. Adding Chism, Hatta, and Lopin, the total was forty-nine. Uneasy, Chism scanned again. He never miscounted, but it was worth the effort to double check. Forty-nine. He knew he should be formulating a plan, but he couldn't focus. Sweat beaded on his brow, and Chism lost what little confidence he felt.

What's the cat leading me to now?

The cat! Adding the cat, the total number at, or approaching, the pavilion was fifty. Chism breathed a deep sigh of relief.

Elites on both sides watched everything, especially each other, but the nobles kept their attention on their counterparts. Thirsty began to hum, and Chism's pulse pounded when he saw lumpy Jaryn in the group, jowls shaking frenetically as he argued with one of the Queen of Hearts' nobles. Chism slipped in behind Lopin, easily blocked by the full-bodied butcher. A plan to end the conflict began forming in his head.

Thirsty would be thrilled.

Cuora, Markin, Palida, Antion, Tjaden, Ollie. The young man from Tellef's inn. Hatta recognized so many of the people under the pavilion. Chism had arrived, of course. Even Elora was there, doing whatever it is that ladies-in-waiting do for the ladies they wait on. Her eyes were locked on Tjaden, who spared as many glances as he could for her in between his vigilance of the scene. The longing in the lovers' eyes stung Hatta. Another reminder of the calamities of such conflicts. Other familiar faces just blended together.

Palida, the White Queen, spoke to the opposing nobles via a large mirror, saying something about the rights of kingdoms. Her white skin, hair, and dreadful, colorless dress made her stand out. But even in daylight, her eyes shone like living sapphires. It took effort, but he dragged himself away from her brilliant eyes. A man in fine robes the color of a blue jay interrupted her with an argument that was just as hard to follow.

At any time Cuora would step in and solve it.

Hatta didn't know how long he could stand and wait. He thought about the colors of the robes and the way the wind made the grass flicker between shades of green. But angry, rising voices made his scalp prickle and the soles of his feet feel like they'd been through itch oak.

And Cuora still did nothing but argue.

I have to do something, else why am I here? Why have I been promised that I would save the kingdoms if I can't do it now?

An idea struck Hatta, and he reached inside his coat for Palida's message.

Taking the final steps up to the pavilion, Chism's hand tightened on Thirsty. If he ever released it, he expected to see imprints of his fingers in the hilt. The sword sang silently to him, and Chism knew he had to be the one to end the war he'd started, no matter the cost. All the times he could have died had brought him to this point. Death here was not only a very real possibility, it might turn out to be a considerable asset to two kingdoms.

Lopin came to a stop near the northeast corner of the pavilion. Peering around him, Chism saw and heard the nobles quarrelling. Palida's Elites watched Lopin and him warily but didn't bother them.

As long as you come no closer, their gazes said.

Ruddy Jaryn was wedged into a chair on the west end of the tent. Chism recognized many other faces, but none of them changed his plan.

"Move along the outside to the west edge," he whispered to Lopin.

Trying not to be conspicuous in his cover, Chism shadowed the large man around the council. But even after arriving at the closest possible point, he was still ten paces away from the fat noble, with an Elite and Fellow blocking him.

They wore wolf patches on their shoulders. Chism knew of Grey Wolf Squadron but didn't know the men. There was no way to know exactly how quick or vigilant the Elite and Fellow were, but by virtue of the Circle and Sword on the Elite's chest, they would be ready for a rushed assault. The only consolation was that the soldiers had no reason to challenge Chism as long as he stayed shielded by Lopin.

Time raced as Chism considered his options.

I have to get close to Jaryn and put a stop to this conflict before Hatta does something foolish.

No sooner was the thought in his head than Hatta did exactly that.

Oblivious to the consequences, Hatta strode toward the middle of the council with a folded paper held high.

"Urgent message for Palida!" he managed before one of Queen Cuora's Elites brought him up short with the point of a sword. It was Lieutenant Fahrr.

The nobles were merely annoyed by the interruption, but all the Elites drifted to place themselves between the intruder and their respective rulers. It was exactly the distraction Chism needed.

With a vengeful smile, Chism broke from his cover and ran at Jaryn's back, the only sound coming from his friend escaping its sheath. It had been such a long time since he'd smiled so sincerely. Before anyone realized what was happening, Chism stood in a familiar position, looking down at the top of Jaryn's head, sword forcing jowls out from under his chin.

"Remember me?"

The duke only trembled and croaked in answer.

The sword at Hatta's chest disappeared as far as Hatta was concerned when he saw Chism dart around the butcher and draw Thirsty. It was happening all over again. The sword that killed their father would kill again. And Chism would surely die.

All eyes were still on Hatta, and he froze.

I was supposed to save the kingdom, not lead Chism here to plunge it into . . . war. For once profanity was appropriate. *I never should have come. I truly am mad to think someone like me could save kingdoms.*

It was time to run or hide, and he reached slowly for the brim of his hat.

"It's time, Hatta," said a welcomed voice. He looked around for Cheshire, unable to see him. Yet there was no mistaking the pleasant voice. "This is what you've come for. Your travels, your mirrors, your kindness, your love for your brother. It was all for this. You have the power to save the kingdoms."

It didn't matter whether it was sanity or madness; Hatta had to at least try, even though dozens of eyes were on him. With tears of dread, he said in the loudest voice he could muster, "Don't do it, Chism. Please. Don't do it, for me."

Gradually, eyes shifted to the fat, red man and Chism, and within moments Hatta was forgotten. The structure of the council changed immediately. Everyone had forgotten their allegiances—nobles intermingling as far from the hostage as possible, while soldiers edged slowly closer. Servants huddled around nobles or hid behind them, except for Elora, who ran to Tjaden.

Hatta seized Chism's gaze. "Don't kill him, Chism. Not again."

Every Elite had a weapon in hand but didn't dare approach the pair. The red-armored bulldog by Cuora also held a sword and paced, anxious to use it. Tjaden held his sword ready, maintaining a defensive posture with Elora behind him. Ollie stood between Tjaden and Hatta, one of his tragically beautiful arrows nocked and aimed. Hatta had seen Ollie shoot near perfectly at three times the distance, and that was before the new arrows.

"I'm sorry, Hatta," said Chism. "This is how it has to end. He dies, I die, and everyone can forget the schism happened."

The center of the meadow was deafening with caustic color but empty of sound. To Hatta's relief, Palida still used her mirrors to observe the scene. He admired her consistent quirkiness. Frequent nervous looks passed between the rival queens.

From where she sat, Cuora placed one hand on the red armor of her guard to still him. As if pleading him to stay out of it, she shook her head at Hatta. But there was no other way—no one else could intervene.

Looking back to Chism, Hatta shook his head. He could say nothing.

"You were right, brother," Chism insisted. "We are here for a reason. This is the only way."

Hatta knew his brother was wrong. He would not be party to violence of any kind. "No," he said, still shaking his head and walking toward Chism.

In a low voice, Ollie said, "I've got him, Jay." Hatta couldn't believe how calm Ollie was, staring down an arrow at a man he intended to kill.

"Wait," Elora told him, clinging to her husband. "Let Hatta try."

Torn between blocking Ollie and going to his brother, Hatta chose Chism. He could only do what he could do.

With every step, Hatta expected Ollie to release the arrow. There was no way he could stay wound that tight for long.

"Don't try to stop me, Hatta," said Chism. "If I don't do this now, there *will* be war. Do you want *war*?"

"No," said Hatta. He repeated himself in hushed tones. "No, no, no, no, no." In a matter of moments, he would be close enough to touch Chism. The sword was unmoving, but Chism's feet shifted, and he was breathing rapidly through clenched teeth.

His brother had always been the confident, steady one.

Maybe I'm getting through to him!

Without thinking, Hatta reached out and slowly wrapped his hand around Thirsty's tip. The sword seemed to pulsate with darkness. Knowledge of the blood shed by the blade almost made Hatta release it, but that would mean death to the duke, death to Chism, and most likely a bitter . . . continuation of violence.

Eyes locked with his brother's, Hatta pulled with slight resistance. The sword was sharp, and it dug into Hatta's hand, but Chism held firm. Tensing against the pain, Hatta pulled harder, wondering how much force was required to cut through four fingers.

"No," begged Chism, his eyes gleaming like black flames. Hatta just returned the word. "No."

Even though he was much smaller, Chism's strength was considerable. Hatta increased the force of the pull, and the blade cut into his fingers. His face twitched in response to the pain. In the corner of his vision, bright blood oozed between his fingers and around the blade. It was the color of life, the color of his heart. But he kept his eyes fixed on the black recesses of Chism's eyes.

"You've shed my blood, brother." Tears ran down Hatta's face and showed in Chism's as well. "Mad or not, I still love you enough to stay right here."

Chism finally broke the gaze and gasped when he saw Hatta's blood on Thirsty.

Hatta knew he had won.

Chism felt as if he no longer had control of Thirsty.

The blade did not come away instantly, but almost imperceptibly the duke's blanched jowls fell into their natural droopy position. Then a hair's breadth of space appeared. Then a finger's width, and a hand. Hatta gradually relaxed the tension on the blade, but Chism had no desire to put it back to Jaryn's throat or through his heart.

With a loud sigh, Chism let Thirsty fall to his side. The duke checked his throat for blood and looked around, ready to run.

"I'm sorry I hurt you, brother," said Chism. *But I'm afraid you've just killed me. A fine reward for loyalty and trust.* Hatta took a step to the side and pulled the brim of his hat down to his eyebrows.

Elites began closing in. Ollie still had an arrow ready, and Chism knew how well he could shoot. Without a hostage, Chism would surely be overpowered and killed. But the pain of drawing Hatta's blood hurt worse than the knowledge of his own death. He tossed Thirsty to the ground, where it landed on the carpet with a dull thud. For the first time ever, it didn't beg to be held.

Jaryn scrambled from his chair, shrieking, "Elites! Seize him! Kill him! What are you waiting for?" He hid behind Queen Palida's large mirror, peeking around like a fat baby terrified of a monster.

Tjaden and Ollie looked at each other uncertainly, but the point of the arrow continued to stare at Chism. From behind them, Elora placed a hand on each of their shoulders and shook her head when they turned. They both wordlessly let their weapons fall to their sides.

Lieutenant Fahrr was next to speak. "Enough," he said, shaking his head. "This is what started the division in the kingdom. I was there. I saw it." He kept his sword but lowered it.

The other Elites followed his example.

"This is ridiculous," said Queen Cuora. Addressing Chism, she proclaimed, "Knight, I revoke your pardon. Now someone off with him so we can get back to what we came for. Knave, deal with him." She motioned expectantly, and Brune slinked forward like a hungry dog.

Chism considered diving forward to retrieve Thirsty; Brune was no match for Thirsty. But he quickly dismissed the idea. He had drawn Hatta's blood already and would not add another drop. Brune would finally have the payback he longed for.

The Knave was only a few paces away, moving toward Chism with a sadistic look. He raised his sword.

"Time to get even."

"Yes!" said Hatta, moving to stand between Brune and Chism. "Get even. Yes."

Why now? thought Chism. *Of all times to completely lose touch with reality, Hatta, why now?* Brune didn't need any extra encouragement.

Brune halted, looking confused and eager. He also looked like he was wondering if Hatta was insane. Hatta did look the part, standing unarmed with his hat pulled low in front of the fully armored Knave.

"I intend to," said Brune. "Out of my way, tweedle."

"Get even right now," continued Hatta. He folded his arms tightly across his chest and looked down at his boots. "Get even with *me*, for the tarts and for pleading with Innkeep Tellf for you and leaving boots in the road, and coins, when you left Shey's Orchard. I know you appreciated them. I know because I believe you said 'thank you,' and now you owe me. So kindly repay me by not killing my brother. It would be the decent thing to do." He looked as confident as a kitten facing a bulldog.

At first Brune smirked, and Chism wondered if the Knave would stab Hatta for his audacity. Or at least thump him with his hilt. Part of him hoped Brune would make a move against Hatta, giving Chism a reason to renege on his personal ceasefire.

"You owed me before you owed him," Hatta said without looking up. "And you owed me more."

The sound of clinking metal rasped under the pavilion as Brune adjusted the grip on his sword with his gauntleted hand. His eyebrows lowered, nearly obscuring his eyes.

"I didn't ask for your favor!"

Hatta flinched but held his ground.

There was no way someone like Brune would give in; he was a knave by profession and personality. With every important person in two kingdoms watching, he couldn't possibly back down to something as feeble as kindness.

But Chism remembered the power Hatta had wielded the day of their reunion. He'd never faced anything like it.

Brune tilted his head down and to the side to peer back

at Queen Cuora. She must not have been worried about harm coming to Hatta because she just sat there, grinning amusedly, as relaxed as a lady at the theater.

"I didn't ask for anything!" Digging some coins from a pocket, Brune hurled them at Hatta.

An invisible wall separated the Knave from Chism. All of Brune's scowling and pacing and shouting couldn't find a way past.

Brune tossed his sword onto the carpet to join Thirsty. "I fight men, not imbeciles." He stormed away from the pavilion.

"Will wonders never cease?" The Queen of Hearts chuckled audibly. "Who would've thought the Knave of Hearts actually *had* a heart?" Growing more somber she said, "Somebody follow orders and finish this. Or I won't have time for croquet before dark."

From Chism's left, a noble's dueling sword flew forward and landed where Thirsty lay with Brune's sword. It was Duke Enniel, and he had added his epee to the peace pile. Chism hadn't seen the duke since rescuing him and his family from bandits nine months before.

"I'll spill no blood today," said the duke. "My family lives because of Sir Chism."

Another of Queen Palida's nobles, a tall young man with flowing golden hair, stepped forward and removed a small knife from his belt; he wore no sword.

Before the man could speak, Hatta looked at him and said, "I already know you. You're a traveler, not a noble. You were dirty, starving, and worried that your woman might die."

The man blushed, and a few nobles snickered. "My name is Marquess Raouf," said the man. "Certain individuals objected to my choice of a wife, and we were forced to elope." More tittering from behind raised hands. "Regardless, the rations you proffered surely kept us from begging and possibly from starving.

I pledged that if ever I was in a position to aid you, I would return the favor." He added his small blade to the growing pile.

Lopin came forward and wordlessly pitched his sword in, as did a few other nobles that Chism didn't recognize. The Elites and Fellows retained their weapons but sheathed them, or in Ollie's case, shouldered.

With a sneer, Cuora looked at Markin. "Wonder of wonders. Soldiers with soft sides. What are you waiting for, Marky? Aren't you going to join the peace party?"

When King Markin stood, she exhaled and rolled her eyes. Chism expected his former Captain to vacillate, but with a defiant glare for his queen, he placed his sword at the top of the mound.

Jaryn stepped out from behind the mirror. "You can't just let him go. He tried to kill me! Again!"

Some nobles looked away; others shook their heads at him. When he realized he had no support, his eyes narrowed, and he stared at Chism. There was nothing he could do but take a seat.

With the entire assembly unarmed, King Antion rose and walked to the center of the tent, showing more poise than a ten-year-old should possess. "This truly is a day of wonders, Cuora. And now that the swords are out of the way, I have a proposal."

As King Antion laid out his plan, Chism whispered to his brother, "You've done it. You've saved the kingdoms."

Hatta turned to face him, wearing a concerned look. "What? I . . ." Hatta looked around and saw the pile of blades on the carpet. Recoiling, he asked, "I've done what?"

"You've ended the war. Those swords are on the ground because everyone has refused to fight. Because of you."

From what Chism could see under the hat, Hatta looked perplexed. "What could I do? I'm just a hatter."

"You did what you always do, and somehow, you've done this. And saved my life as well."

Chism watched as Hatta's eyebrows unfurrowed and the rest of his face relaxed.

"I did it," he repeated. "It's impossible, and I did it!" The delight finally reached his face and the corner of one side of his mouth rose in his typical smile. "Impractical. Unbelievable. Not possible. But I did it."

Then something happened that Chism had never seen. A tug started high in Hatta's cheek, and slowly the other corner of his mouth turned up, producing a full smile on his brother's face. His eyes had always held a hint of instability, but now there was no mistaking the full-blown madness.

Chism knew his brother was completely mad because for the first time in his life, Hatta's smile wasn't hiding anything or forcing emotions he didn't feel. His brother was truly happy.

Somehow Hatta had done it. It was impossible. Of course, he hadn't really done it; only a madman would believe that. Perchance. But he didn't care. For the first time in his life, he didn't even attempt to discern truth from madness because he was happy. Not a happiness that he had to coerce onto his face, but joy that came from within. Unforced and undoubtable.

And it felt wonderful.

How had he ever believed it was better to be a sane nobody who was prone to uncomfortable situations than a madman who honestly believed he had saved two kingdoms and thousands of lives?

Why did I wait so long? he wondered as he chortled to himself.

"Don't worry, brother. I've done it. I've saved the kingdoms like the Cheshire Cat said I would." So Chism wouldn't have to mention it, he added, "And, yes, I realize I'm completely mad!" This time he guffawed.

It was so easy not having to feign sanity. No more would

two sides of himself battle for dominance! No more putting on a false front like the haze in his mirrors! Hatta was complete. It took going mad to save the kingdoms—*I truly have done it*, he assured himself—and he counted it a bargain. Or was it saving the kingdoms to go mad? Either way, as far as he was concerned, his work was done.

Hatta turned and entered the sea of grass, leaving the nobles to settle the details. He chanted merrily as he walked.

*Tripita tripe, does Chism like
to scurry and swish and dash.
Perfida pratt, the shoehouse rat
nibbles on Ander's moustache.*

He hooted at his cleverness. Ander didn't even wear a moustache!

Cheshire sidled up to him, as did the color-changing rabbit, only appearing at the peak of each hop then sinking into the shin-high grass. Hop. Bronze. Hop. Emerald. Hop. Ash. The colors were impressive, but the whole affair seemed just a touch too ideal. Even in a perfect world, there was such thing as too much perfection.

"Pardon, Mr. Rabbit. Or Ms. Rabbit if it so fits."

On its next leap the hare shouted, "Haigha!" It was tangerine-colored.

"Excuse me?" said Hatta.

"Haigha." Hatta waited until the hare surfaced again, this time azure. "It's my name."

"Ah, I see. Well would you mind toning it down?"

"You mean the hopping?" asked the pearly hare.

"Of course not the hopping. You're a rabbit after all."

"Fish swim . . ." Auburn.

". . . birds fly . . ." Navy.

". . . and hares hop." Cardinal.

"I never imagined myself asking this," said Hatta, "but it would actually be the *colors* I'd like you to moderate."

"The colors?" The crimson currently on the hare almost made Hatta rethink his request. It was the exact shade of Chism's persona. But if Hatta could find the strength to leave his true love, he could go through with his request.

"Yes, the colors. I'd prefer if you didn't display them so."

After the next hop, the indigo rabbit didn't resurface. "What color would you prefer?" it asked from below grass level.

"Prefer?" said Hatta. "Oh, my, how kind of you to ask. I'm tempted to say white, but I think that would be taking it too far. Perhaps a grainy brown? Like the color of a rabbit?"

A moment later, Haigha appeared, looking every bit like a brown hare.

"Thank you, Haigha. I do hope it wasn't much of a bother."

"None at all, my friend. But I am perplexed by the request."

Resuming the trek, with Cheshire loping at one side and Haigha hopping on the other, Hatta explained. "I do realize I'm mad as a hatter, but a world that's too perfect is a façade that's difficult to believe. Any world I imagined would never have a plain brown hare. It would more likely contain a multi-hued or color-changing hare. And I intend to continue to be the man who saved the kingdom. It just feels so safe."

"If there's a sounder argument . . ." replied the hare between hops, ". . . I've never heard it."

"I thank you." Turning his attention to the left he said, "And I thank you, Cheshire."

"For nothing, Hatta. I merely told you it would happen. You were the one with the courage and skills to accomplish it."

"Yes. I do have a fair number of skills, don't I? Naming colors, mirror-making, hattering, talking to animals, saving the kingdoms, friending . . ."

With a smile as wide as the Cheshire Cat's, Hatta continued to enumerate his vast array of talents as he left rulers and soldiers, kingdoms and Provinces, and everything else behind.

Epilogue

*C*hism whittled as he rode under a canopy of half-naked trees. Leaves crunching beneath hooves provided percussion for Ander's upbeat whistling. People often talked about colors of fall, but Chism always enjoyed the crisp sounds and textures.

The color of their uniforms was significant, even to Chism. Dark blue once again, complete with the Sword and Circle embroidered on the chest.

Squirrels, deer, foxes, toves, and hares scampered away as the pair wound through the forest. This part of Maravilla contained more animals than any other Chism had seen. The Queen of Hearts—Chism still avoided thinking of her as the *Red* Queen—had selected the land for that very reason. She knew the animals pleased Hatta and that he had a way with them. Located only fifteen miles from Palassiren, she set the land aside as a safe haven where Hatta could live undisturbed.

The two kingdoms were still independent, the Provinces ruled by the White Queen Palida and Maravilla ruled by the Queen and King of Hearts, the Reds. In the Kirohz Valley, the factions had created a league of kingdoms. In mockery of the wondrous display of peace at the parlay, the Red Queen had suggested the name Wonderland, and surprisingly, the other nobles agreed. Chism suspected that most had done so in order to turn the farce back on Queen Cuora.

The clearing with Hatta's home finally came into view. Asymmetry usually annoyed Chism, but the house Hatta built was so wonky it couldn't even be described as uneven. The roof looked like it had been taken off and put back on crooked. There were at least two balconies with no doors leading onto them. Most of the home was brick, installed in a diagonal pattern, but one of the front corners was plaster with some sort of stitching from ground to roof. None of the windows were square, and the front door had five sides and no square angles.

As with previous visits, Chism saw Hatta at tea at the long table in front of his house. He appeared to be alone. While Hatta was within view, but out of earshot, Ander said under his breath, "I didn't think it was possible, but his colors are even more outrageous than before."

Hatta had always arrayed himself in a variety of shades that Chism couldn't distinguish, but Ander's words were confirmed by the sight of fewer solid colors and more checkers, stripes, and patterns.

Hatta's new hat was checkered, like his old town hat, but there were intricate underlying patterns as well. A small card with the price of the hat was tucked inside a band just above the brim. Ten pennies and six cuppies. A ridiculously high price for a hat, yet they sold faster than Hatta could make them. Of course he couldn't charge a nice round number.

After Chism and Ander dismounted, Hatta came to stand very close and said, "Greetings, brother."

"You're more colorful than ever, Hatta," said Ander. "I swear, if a rainbow could mate with a wildflower, the offspring could pass for your twin."

"I thank you, Ander," said Hatta, still wearing his full smile. "I call this new hat color farcical. Introductions, then." Signaling a particular chair pulled back from the table, he said, "Ander, this is Cheshire. Cheshire, this would be Ander."

Ander looked at the empty chair and said uncertainly, "It's wonderful to meet you."

"Don't play make believe, Ander," said Chism. "Cheshire's real, so don't talk to him if he's not there."

"Open your black eyes and look," said Ander. "He's right... now where did he get to?"

Ander scanned the area where Cheshire had faded into Chism's view, seated in the chair he had thought empty. The cat's smile was as vexing as ever.

"Hello, Cheshire," said Chism.

"Hello to you," the cat said. Then he faded out. Chism heard, "And it's wonderful to meet you, Ander. Unfortunately, I can only turn my color *off*," he reappeared to Chism's view, "or *on*." He disappeared again. "But not both at the same time."

So that's how I saw the cat in the Kirohz Valley when no one else could, thought Chism. *The fool cat turned his colors off.*

"We should be glad none of us is color *deaf*, or we wouldn't be able to hear you at the same time," said Hatta. It made no sense, but half of what Hatta said now was just as confusing or more so. "Enough of standing around; let's sit and have some tea."

The table, capable of seating a full squadron of Elites, was cluttered with teapots, cups, saucers, sugar dishes, and platters. Before selecting a chair, Chism removed a bulging purse from his pack and tossed it onto the table. He was glad to be free of the heavy burden.

"Targus said the last shipment of hats sold before he even received them. He's sending a man tomorrow for the next batch, even though you'll probably only have half of the hats done."

HATTER

Chism never learned the old man's real name, but he resembled the wrinkled Targus from the late Lord Captain Darieus's museum.

Ignoring the purse, Hatta asked, "I hope the old tailor is well? I'm lucky to have such a reliable friend selling my hats."

"Indeed," said Ander. Signaling his uniform, he said, "As you can see, we're officially Elite and Fellow once again."

"I'm sure that's very wonderful for you," said Hatta, neither meeting their gaze nor looking at the uniforms.

"He's promised to warn me before he threatens the life of any nobles," Ander assured him.

But it wasn't jest; Ander had insisted on the pledge before resuming his post as Fellow. Chism still planned to defend the Circle and the Sword, but now he had to advise Ander before doing anything rash. "I've actually been promoted to sub-lieu," Chism told his brother. "That's short for sublieutenant. We've been assigned to Scaled Tiger Squadron. They're near the border with the Western Domain."

Hatta peered into his teacup. "But aren't you the Red Knight? Don't you need to be close to Cuora?"

"We convinced her that some experience with a squadron would be helpful," said Chism. He hadn't thought Cuora would agree even though it was what he wanted more than anything. The life he'd always wanted, and once had, was back.

The teacup couldn't hold Hatta's attention. He began fidgeting with his coat, obviously uncomfortable with talk of soldiering.

From the empty chair, the Cheshire Cat said, "What about the new emblem you designed, Hatta?"

"Ah, yes," said Hatta, unpleasantness forgotten. He unbuttoned his checkered coat. Sewn into the multicolored tunic was a circle to match Chism's, but instead of a sword in the center, it featured a toothy, oversized grin.

Cheshire appeared and smiled, as if Chism couldn't recognize the resemblance between the smiles on his own.

Hatta said, "It's the Circle and the Smile." He looked quite proud.

"We each have our weapons, brother," said Chism.

After a short lull, Hatta said, "First a platter in the sky, then a rock half-concealed. A thin fingernail am I, then no part revealed."

Seeing the confused look on Ander's face, Chism said, "It's a riddle. He uses them to change the subject when he's uncomfortable."

"A riddle, huh?" Ander sat up in his chair and began mumbling to himself.

"Be careful, Ander," Chism warned. "Sometimes there's no solution."

Grinning, as always, Cheshire said, "With enough madness, there's always a solution." He was much easier to tolerate with his colors on.

"The waning moon!" exclaimed Ander. "A platter, a half rock, a crescent fingernail, then gone."

"Yes! Wonderful, wonderful," said Hatta.

Before his brother could pose any more riddles, Chism asked, "Do you ever get bored without any human company, Hatta?"

"Switch chairs!" announced Hatta as he stood and moved halfway around the table. Chism knew the routine, so he stood and moved one chair closer to Hatta.

Following his example, Ander scooted, as did Cheshire, who announced, "For the benefit of those who can't see me with my colors off, I am now switching chairs."

"You see, Chism? It's an entirely new party. Tea?" He picked up a teapot but glanced at it, confused, and gave it a gentle shake. Removing the lid, he tsked and said, "You know that's not appropriate when we have guests." With two fingers, Hatta reached into the teapot and removed a small, sleeping mouse. Cheshire licked his sharp teeth as he watched Hatta place a tiny dormouse into the front pocket of his coat.

"Terribly sorry," said Hatta. "There's never a shortage of animals. I do enjoy them so." After a short pause, he added, "Except mules. I've never been able to make friends with a mule. I had a bandersnatch friend once, but never a mule."

"Speaking of pack animals," said Ander, "the horses I took along when I accompanied the Selvage women made all the difference. They were foolish to attempt the trip with so many wagons."

"I thank you for helping me save them, Ander. It's a talent of mine, you know—saving towns and kingdoms."

"And nobody does it better," said Ander. "Together we saved a town from starving. Dozens of people. Maybe more."

"I'm glad you're well, Hatta," said Chism, "but we should be back on the road. With our new assignment, it will be some time until I visit again." They were brothers and even friends, but Chism always kept his visits short. He could only handle the thick madness for short periods.

"Sometime, long time, time after time. Anytime but never."

"You should know," said Chism, "that the kingdoms are secure as ever. I know you're not interested in the details of politics, but there hasn't been any more talk of war."

Hatta looked as if he had tasted something unpleasant. "Please don't use such language, Chism."

Unwilling to leave Hatta with the negative sentiment, Chism said, "Your hats are a symbol of peace. People wear them to show the nobles how they'd feel about ever reverting to . . . a peace-less state."

"Targus is even sending them out to the Provinces," added Ander. "He could make a lot more coin selling only in Palassiren, but cares more about spreading the message through the kingdoms."

Hatta was positively beamish.

"Also," said Chism, "Lady Elora is back in Palassiren. She's attending the Red royalty now because Tjaden's base is Palassiren."

"Best to keep people who are on the same side on the same side, I suppose."

As they stood, Ander said, "I've attended some unusual tea parties, but none to match this one."

Hatta smiled even more proudly. Without embraces or further goodbyes, Chism and Ander left Hatta with his animals, his hatting, and his blissful madness.

Their assignment to hunt down Scaled Tiger Squadron somewhere along the western border would take weeks. They could afford a couple of days for a detour to the south. If Chism didn't visit the first person to ever call him friend, he might not have another chance.

Friend. The word still tasted wrong in Chism's mouth, like cream on the verge of spoiling. Cactus had planted a seed that Chism couldn't smother. He wasn't even sure he wanted to smother it. The infiltration mission into the Western Domain wouldn't teach him anything about friendship. For one thing, he'd be surrounded by enemies, and what could he learn about friendship in a setting like that? Even his new squad, Scaled Tiger would be antagonistic toward him as soon as they saw him and the orders he carried from the queen. They already knew they were embarking on the riskiest mission in the current ranks of the Elites, but they wouldn't know about Chism until he showed up.

Yes, a couple of days trying to learn an impossible lesson from a cranky old *friend* was exactly what Chism needed, even if he couldn't say why.

"Impossible lessons and risky missions," Chism said. "How can a man living on fate-granted time ask for more?"

Ander mumbled a few words, then looked up. "For a Knight, you aren't very intelligent."

Looking down at his Knight Pin, Chism answered, "You think they give these out for intelligence?"

"Flies and floggings, no. Someday I'll teach you that when impossible tasks arise, a smart leader sends other people to do them."

"Leader," said Chism, trying to make it sound like one of Ander's curses. "You trying to pick a fight?"

"Leader. Show off. Friend. When they bury you, those are the three words I'll have them inscribe on your monument."

Chism groaned and they rode to the sound of the horses' *clip-clop* for some time. "Impossible lessons, risky missions, and intolerable companions. Why does fate hate me?"

"Fate hates everyone, Chism. The good news is it loves everyone just a tad more."

"Why is that hard for me to believe right now?"

"Because it could be worse," said Ander offhandedly.

"Really? How?"

"One word." Ander smugly stared forward. "Cheshire."

Chism looked around, worried the animal would appear at the mention of its name. "Now you're just being cruel."

Ander smiled. "This is going to be fun!"

Chism heeled his horse, ready to be done with the trip already. As he pulled away he muttered, "And people wonder why I don't want friends."

The End

If you enjoyed Hatter, please share with friends
and post a review online.

Coming Soon from Daniel Coleman
Red Knight

Chism the Elite prepares for invasion and explores firsthand the benefits and dangers of the thing people call friendship.

Author's Note

The character Hatta appears as a messenger in Lewis Carroll's *Through the Looking Glass and What Alice Found There*. Though he is never referred to as a hatter, his speech and mannerisms strongly resemble the character known only as "the hatter" from *Alice's Adventures in Wonderland*. Even the name, using standard British pronunciation, is identical.

Haigha appears alongside Hatta in *Through the Looking Glass*. While he isn't referred to as Hare, the text states that his name is pronounced to rhyme with 'mayor', lending more credibility to the widely accepted theory that Hatta and Haigha are the same Hatter and Hare from *Alice's Adventures in Wonderland*.

In naming the other inhabitants of Wonderland—Chism, Cuora, Markin, Palida, Antion, etc.—the author has taken license.

The poem "My Fancy" originally appears in Lewis Carroll's *The Hunting of the Snark: and Other Poems and Verses*. In *Hatter*, it is attributed to Hatta with changes made to the poem to reflect Hatta's evolving view of Cuora.

Finally, regarding the Hatter. The term "mad hatter" does

not appear anywhere in Lewis Carroll's writing. The phrase "mad as a hatter" predates Carroll and is most likely the basis of the character. It is commonly believed that the Hatter was mad due to mercury used in hat making, but Carroll never clarifies the basis of the Hatter's madness.

Acknowledgments

*T*he cast involved in creating a book is as vast and varied as the characters of the book itself. The members of the best writing group ever, for example: Eric Bishop, an Ander who always has my back and helps me understand myself. Nancy Felt, who like Lieutenant Fahrr is wise and not afraid to set me straight. And E. A. Younker, a Tellef who always offers a smile or some needed advice, not just to me, but to anyone.

Then there's my beta readers. First, my sister, friend, and Cheshire Cat, Veronica Beynon who is always there at just the right time with a touch of humor, a touch of advice, and precisely the right amount of wonderful nonsense. My other beta reader and fellow author, Elizabeth Dorathy is Hatta's Elora—a friend from a long ago home and a kindred spirit. April Coleman (Hi, Mom!) is as caring and supportive as Lira and Leis and probably the source I drew on for these characters.

The interior artist E.K. Stewart-Cook, my Mirrorer Aker who put intangible ideas onto paper. My cover artist, Antonio José Manzanedo who like Haigha is bursting with colors, yet nobody I know has ever seen him in real life. And Daniel Friend, who has been seen by people I know, and therefore is a verified real person and editor, not my imaginary companion despite his unlikely name.

I can't leave out my creative mentors: John Berry, who I am tempted to call the mule, but would more accurately describe as Cactus—a teacher and friend even when I don't know I need either. And Timothy Barrett who like Tjaden knows there is no jabberwock that can't be slain.

Most difficultly, the love of my life, Jodie. Saying she is the Queen of my Heart does not tell the whole story. When I'm Chism, she is Thirsty—if she isn't by my side I feel incomplete. When I'm Hatta, she is colors—the source of my greatest hopes and often a distracting maelstrom to my emotional spectrum.

Lastly there is you, Reader. You are Hatta's hats and mirrors; Chism's Circle and Sword. Without you, my writing life is bleak. In the words of Hatta, I thank you.

About the Author

Daniel Coleman juggles writing, firefighting, family life, and large animals (figuratively speaking) in small-town northern Utah. He shares Hatta's dislike of confrontation and Chism's love of numbers.

Daniel Coleman also writes award-winning Contemporary Fiction (Gifts and Consequences). You can find him at all these places and more:

www.dcolemanbooks.com
www.facebook.com/authordanielcoleman
Twitter @dnlcoleman

Jabberwocky is the surprising story behind Lewis Carroll's classic poem.

Find out how Tjaden, Elora, and Ollie defeat the invincible Jabberwock. You might know how it ends, but you won't believe how it happens!

PRAISE FOR *JABBERWOCKY*

"Daniel Coleman has a brilliant take on Lewis Carroll's poem. This story is filled with magical creatures, bravery, danger, love and betrayal. Kids and adults alike will fall in love with this story."

—M.R. Ferguson, *ThePraefortis*

"Truly irresistible. This is definitely an author to watch!"

—Grace from MotherLode Review Blog

"Those greatly endeared with Lewis Carroll's whimsical tales would do well to pick up Jabberwocky by Daniel Coleman—a straightforward tale with a manxome twist."

—Amber Argyle, *Witch Song* Trilogy

"Daniel Coleman takes Lewis Carroll's poem and gives it a life of its own while remaining true to the initial writings. This novel kept me entertained from the first page to the last."

—E.A. Younker, *Future of Lies*

"Coleman vividly and magically makes the poem come alive and makes it easy to understand. If you are looking for a story with adventure, nail-biting suspense and romance, *JABBERWOCKY* is for you! I love this little gem of a book."

—Screenplay Diva from "That's Swell!"

"Daniel Coleman doesn't write stories, he crafts them. His characters are an equal balance of action and emotion, very memorable. He is an author worth collecting."

—Christine Haggerty, *The Plague Legacy*

"The world that Coleman created was extremely fleshed out and felt like a real place. The characters were relatable and the writing was excellent. One of those hidden gems that should get more attention. I totally recommend this."

—Michelle from In Libras Veritas

"Coleman has a captivating way with words. His characterization of the Jabberwocky is beautifully rendered. Readers young and old, those familiar with Carroll's Wonderland and those who have yet to discover it, will be enthralled. Coleman has made splendid sense of Carroll's spectacular nonsense, and I loved every moment of it. *Jabberwocky* is a MUST read!"

—Aeicha from Word Spelunking

Printed in Great Britain
by Amazon